Promises to Keep is "th[...]
and danger . . . Kat[...]
grabbed me on page o[...]
me until the very last word. A definite keeper!"

"A brilliant [...] iv-
ity that is beautiful [...]ur

"M[...]lly
pow[...]is
rive[...] your heart and don't let go. Bravo, Ms. Shay."

—*Romantic Times* (4½ stars)

"An unforgettable, touching love story."

—*Old Book Barn Gazette*

"Super . . . The lead protagonists are a charming duo and
the support characters add depth . . . Kathryn Shay's tale
is a beautiful Christmas story." —*Painted Rock Reviews*

PROMISES TO KEEP

KATHRYN SHAY

BERKLEY BOOKS, NEW YORK

PROMISES TO KEEP

A Berkley Book / published by arrangement with
the author

PRINTING HISTORY
Berkley edition / August 2002

Visit our website at
www.penguinputnam.com

ISBN: 0-425-18574-5

BERKLEY®
Berkley Books are published by The Berkley Publishing Group,
a division of Penguin Putnam Inc.,
375 Hudson Street, New York, New York 10014.
BERKLEY and the "B" design
are trademarks belonging to Penguin Putnam Inc.

PRINTED IN THE UNITED STATES OF AMERICA

10 9 8 7 6 5 4 3 2 1

To Jerry, my real life hero. None of this would have happened without your support and encouragement. Thank you for that and a million other things! I love you.

AUTHOR'S NOTE

Promises to Keep, my first mainstream contemporary romance for Berkley, deals with a subject very close to my heart. As a long-time English teacher, I've experienced all facets of life in a contemporary high school. The two heroines in my book reflect my philosophy on teaching and, believe me, I've shared their joys in working with teenagers today. Unfortunately, I've also felt their despair. Some of the events in the story are offshoots of things that have actually happened to me over the years; much of what I know about kids today is reflected in the characters I've portrayed. Teaching is one of the most rewarding professions a person can have. It is also one of the scariest, not only because of the violence in today's schools. Influencing young minds and hearts and souls —as good teachers do, and as the teachers in my story do—is a grave responsibility. I hope the book shows the agony and ecstasy of being involved in education today.

Within this school environment, two love stories evolve; both reflect my views on the relationship between a man and woman. As so often happens at work, when people are thrown together, especially if it involves danger, they grow close. But, like most normal people, my characters must work their way through many obstacles before they can be together. They do it, but the road is long and rocky.

• • •

I hope you enjoy this glimpse into the world of today's teenagers and how the adults in their lives are trying to keep them safe, as well as find happiness for themselves.

The Secret Service information included in the book is based on research. In October of 2000, that organization published the Safe School Initiative, which analyzes the nature of school violence and how to cope with it. All the information from that document is accurately reflected in the book. There really is a National School Threat Assessment Center in Washington. The reports from the Department of Education and the FBI, as well as the interviews with actual school shooters and the data on acts of violence, are also accurate. After a point, however, I veered off from reality to further the plot of the book. In truth, what I've written is what I think the government *should* be doing today. I created STAT, the School Threat Assessment Team, a task force to help schools deal with violence. The undercover operations conducted are also fictional.

I love to hear from readers. You can visit my website at www.kathrynshay.com, email me at kshayweb@rochester. rr.com, or write me at P.O. Box 24288, Rochester, NY 14624–0288. Please let me know what you think.

Kathryn Shay

PROLOGUE

———

THE sun shone in a crystal-clear blue sky, beating down on the heads of the mourners. *Mocking us,* Joe Stonehouse thought bitterly, as he wiped the sweat from his forehead. He closed his eyes because he didn't know where to focus them. He couldn't look anywhere without almost losing it. Beside him, his sister Ruth gripped his hand like a lifeline, though she leaned heavily on her husband's arm, too. Joe just held on to her. His gaze traveled to his niece and his nephew, both on their father's left. Both openly sobbing, as were Ruth and Al.

After all, they were standing before the coffin of their older daughter. Josephine "Josie" Callahan. Named after Joe. But when push came to shove, her beloved uncle—hotshot United States Secret Service agent that he was—couldn't save her. How ironic; he'd spent his entire adult life protecting others and he couldn't keep his own family safe. Of course, he'd been hundreds of miles away when a sixteen-year-old kid pulled out a Glock and gunned down Josie and four other students, then turned the weapon on himself. God, would his sister have to attend the other funerals, too?

While birds chirped in the quaint cemetery's trees, teenagers wept around the grave site. Preppy types cried alongside goths and rabble-rousers. Grief knew no boundaries, and Josie's friends had come together today to show respect for their popular classmate. He could still hear the excited lilt in his niece's voice, still see her green eyes, so like his own, sparkle with news. *Uncle Joe, I made cheerleading . . . Uncle Joe, I was voted homecoming queen . . . Uncle Joe, I got into Stanford, just like you.*

He sucked in a breath, struggling to contain the grief that ticked inside him like a bomb, ready to explode. Though he'd spent his life squelching his feelings, a necessity in his job, today he was losing the battle. His hands shook with the effort.

Concentrate on the mechanics. Say prayers. Hold on to your sister. Place a yellow rose on the casket. Josie loved them, and he sent her one for each year of her age on the birthday they shared. *Do not let the emotion out.*

Finally, the burial service ended. A tapestry of voices broke the quiet. As they walked to the cars—he and Al had to drag Ruth along—Joe prayed to a God he didn't believe in that he could do something to ease his family's grief and his own. As a certified clinical psychologist, who happened to work for the Secret Service, he should be able to do *something.* Maybe he could use Josie's death to help others. His niece would have liked that.

He had a plan, part of which he'd been tossing around inside his head for a while, even before Josie was shot. On the short walk to the cars, that plan crystallized. He glanced at his watch.

"You're not going anywhere, are you, Joey?" Ruth asked. The tree cast her grayish face in shadows, and she swayed like one of the branches.

He remembered so many times in their childhood and adolescence when she'd begged him, *Please, don't leave me alone.* Then, it was to protect her from their parents.

"No, Ruthie. I'm not going anywhere."

"You . . . you were on assignment when . . ." She couldn't finish the statement.

He tugged her closer and kissed her hair, emotionally ambushed by the smell—Josie must have shared Ruth's shampoo. "I'm here for as long as you need me, honey."

A bleary-eyed Al, still holding on tight to what was left of his family, threw him a grateful look.

Joe would stay here in this sleepy Connecticut town for as long as they needed him. But when he was done, he and his boss at the United States Secret Service were going to have a talk.

He slid into the car after his sister. As he slammed the door, he vowed he'd do *something* in Josie's name.

It was a promise he intended to keep.

ONE

Three years later

"MRS. Quinn, look at this." Heather Haywood thrust a flyer in front of high school principal Suzanna Quinn's face, while students rushed around them in the hall to get to class on time. "Everybody wants it. Can we do it? Will you participate?"

After she scanned the paper, Suzanna smiled down at her son's girlfriend. "Yes, Heather, we *can* do it if the after-prom Senior Bash Committee writes it up formally, gives it to your adviser, Ms. Cunningham, she approves it, and brings it to me."

The young girl pushed dark bangs off her forehead. "I *know* that, Mrs. Q. What I really wanna know is if the idea's okayed, will you sit in the dunking booth?"

And let four hundred members of the senior class take literal potshots at me? Oh, God.

At her hesitation, Heather added, "You want kids to come to the Bash, right? You want them off the streets after the Senior Ball, right? If the principal goes in the dunking booth, *everybody'll* come."

Suzanna chuckled. That was true.

Suddenly Heather looked away, staring blindly at the

rows of lockers facing her. "Zach would have loved this idea."

Suzanna's laughter disappeared at the mention of one of the most popular boys in Fairholm High School, who'd spearheaded this year's Bash. No one, including her, had had any idea he'd been carrying around a heart full of sadness until he'd downed a whole tumblerful of pills and died alone in his basement just weeks ago.

Faculty and students alike had been stunned by his death and poleaxed by the sensitive, witty suicide note he left, which included messages to many of his teachers. And to her. Suzanna suffered with the knowledge that she'd failed him; they all had.

Briefly squeezing Heather's slender arm, Suzanna whispered, "Yes, Zach would want it."

Heather shook off her sadness. Mischief replaced the gloom on her face. "Maybe even Max Duchamp would come to the Bash."

"Now that's a stretch, Heather." But Suzanna wished it was true. Though he was one of her hard-core cases, she sensed a little boy in him that was still salvageable. Unlike his friend Rush Webster, whom counselors, administrators, and teachers alike thought was a lost cause. She glanced at her watch, shoving Webster's sneering face out of her mind. She also banished Zach's choirboy look, which was hard to think about these days. "I've got a meeting at the Administration Building."

Heather's big blue eyes pleaded with her. Suzanna could see why her son Josh was so besotted, which was just something else to worry about.

"All right. If it goes through the channels, I'll sit in the booth."

Heather threw her arms around Suzanna and hugged her. "You are mad-cool, Mrs. Quinn."

It was at moments like these that Suzanna knew she'd made the right decision to take the principal's job at Fairholm five years ago. Even if she *had* questioned every single thing she'd done after Zach died. She hugged Heather, and said good-bye.

Hurrying down the hall and out the door, she tugged her

butter-soft leather coat closed over her suit, and tucked in the wool scarf her husband, Lawrence, had bought her in Paris just before he died. The biting late-February wind was arctic cold; midwinter in upstate New York always was. As she walked the short distance to the district offices, she reaffirmed the good she'd done, and thought about what she'd yet to accomplish.

She needed to reach some of the outsider groups like Duchamp and his friends. Max was interested in the military and often wore camouflage to school; his father had been a Vietnam vet. She wondered if she could capitalize on that. And Ben Franzi and his friends were into the Wiccan religion, so other kids tended to ostracize them. She made a note to get some information on that group. Then there were the dyed-in-the-wool geeks, the kids everybody picked on. She'd been hearing some rumors about bullying—especially in gym classes—and had given her assistant principal a directive to investigate them. Since Zach's death, she'd promised herself she wouldn't give up on anybody.

She was thinking about how to proceed with these on-the-fringe kids as she signed in at the Ad Building, greeted the receptionist, and made her way to the superintendent's office.

Dr. Maloney met her at the door. "Hello, Suzanna. Thanks for coming on such short notice."

She smiled. "This summons is unlike you, Ross. What's up?"

"Let me take your coat," he said as she entered his spacious office overlooking the track. Scanning the airy room with its oak furniture, rows of bookcases, and Syracuse University poster on the wall, she caught sight of the other occupants.

Two men. One was slouched over in the chair, his chin buried in a leather bomber jacket, his hands stuck in his pockets. She revised her assessment. This was a student. Ah, probably a new student, despite the fact that it was a month into the semester. A *difficult* new student, if she'd been called over here to deal with him. Across the room was most likely his father. The boy had dirty blond hair and the dad's was dark brown, but both had the same square-cut jaw and big build. Though the older man was clearly Wall Street in his Brooks Brothers suit—and his kid would blend right into the Village—they looked related. There must be fireworks at *their* house.

For a moment, she remembered the quiet harmony of her husband and son, playing chess in front of the fire, laughing over an A&E special, and Lawrence cheering loudly at all of Josh's basketball games. They'd been so lucky as a family.

"Suzanna. Sit down." Ross had hung her coat and returned to his desk. His kind brown eyes were troubled and his face wearier, more lined, than usual.

She sat in a comfortable leather chair across from the boy.

"Dr. Stonehouse?" Ross said.

The man at the window had been watching her. "Hello. I'm Joe Stonehouse." Crossing the short space, towering over her, he held out his hand. Moss-green eyes stared down at her. Up close, she could see some gray in his hair, though not as much as in Ross's. "Nice to meet you," he said in a neutral tone. Cold, really.

Grasping his hand, she smiled. "Suzanna Quinn. Nice to meet you, too." She nodded to the boy in the chair. "Is this your son?"

Something flickered in his eyes. "Ah, no. My nephew." He glanced across the room. "Stand up and greet your principal."

The boy shuffled to his feet, obviously against his will. He wasn't as tall as Stonehouse, about five-ten, but was stocky for a teenager, with weight-lifter muscles. Maybe she could get him into spring sports. His hair was shaggy and in his eyes, so she couldn't make out their color. "Hey. I'm Luke Ludzecky."

Everyone sat, Stonehouse a good distance from Luke.

Ross turned to Suzanna. "Dr. Stonehouse and Luke just moved into the district. We asked you to meet with them before Luke starts at the high school for a couple of reasons. One is that he's had some trouble adjusting in school in the past, and we want to do everything we can to help him be successful this time."

Like a man accustomed to being in charge, Stonehouse straightened. "Actually, his mother sent him to live with me because he's been kicked out of every other school he's attended. She thinks *I* might be able to help him."

Luke snorted. Stonehouse glared at him.

Interesting dynamics here, ones Suzanna had seen numerous times. "We'll look after Luke." She gave the boy a warm smile, to which he responded with an insolent stare. "I'm sure we can help you be successful this time around. What are your interests?"

"I dunno. Guitar, I guess."

His uncle put in, "The subjects he does like are history and government."

"We have great Social Studies electives. And a terrific music program. We might be able to get you some individual lessons on your guitar."

Stonehouse closed his eyes briefly and sighed. Suzanna hid a smile. The kid probably played an electric guitar that split his uncle's eardrums and scraped his nerves raw.

Luke stood. "Fine. Thanks." He turned to his uncle, his demeanor still surly. "I'm goin'."

Stonehouse gave Luke the look of a drill sergeant assessing his recruits. "All right. Just be careful driving. One more incident and—"

"I know!" Luke snapped. He nodded to Suzanna. "Ciao."

"See you Monday, Luke," she called out to his retreating back.

When the boy was gone, Ross shifted in his seat. "Suzanna, I have something else to tell you." His tone was strained. "Joe Stonehouse has been hired by the district as a temporary crisis counselor for the next few months."

"*Our* district?" Usually principals were consulted on the implementation of new programs. They were at least asked for their needs. "Is he assigned to one of the elementary schools?"

"No, he'll be working in your building, though he won't be under your supervision. I'll evaluate him, but his main responsibilities will be at the high school."

Her spine arched. "I . . . then why wasn't I consulted on the position?" She nodded to the man. "No offense, Dr. Stonehouse, but I'm always part of the decision-making process on whom we hire. This is highly unusual, Ross."

And the antithesis of what Suzanna believed in and how she ran her school.

Ross seemed uneasy. "Normally we operate that way. But the school board has been tossing around the idea of a position like this since September 11th, and recently, since the Riley boy's suicide."

"Understandable. Still, I can't remember the last time you hired someone to work in my building without discussing it with me, at the very least."

"I'm sorry. We decided to act fast."

"That's obvious." *It doesn't quite fit, though.* And why wouldn't she supervise this man, as she did the two other school psychologists and the social worker?

Steepling his hands, the superintendent nodded to Stonehouse. "Dr. Stonehouse agrees with us on the need for expediency."

"Don't get me wrong," she said. "I want all the help I can get. I just wish I'd had some say in whom we chose."

Stonehouse interrupted. "You've had a great deal of loss in your school, Mrs. Quinn. Zachary Riley's recent suicide, for example. I understand many students were close to him, that he blurred the clique lines. Then there are the hundreds of kids who've suffered from the death of a parent, divorce, or broken boy/girl relationships. I agree with the school board that you need more help ASAP."

"Of course we have those problems. But I don't understand the rush to get someone without input." *Mine, especially.*

Stonehouse glanced at Ross. It was one of those *Can't you control your troops?* looks.

Alarm prickled inside her. Years of listening to her educator's intuition kicked in. "Is something going on here I don't know about?" Suzanna asked bluntly.

"No, of course not. In any case," Ross said dismissively, "it's a fait accompli. Dr. Stonehouse starts on Monday."

Irked, Suzanna stood. "Well, then." Calling on every ounce of professionalism she had, she extended her hand. "Welcome aboard."

As Stonehouse stood and shook hands, she tossed Ross a meaningful look. It said, *We'll deal with this sometime.*

Then she turned and left the office.

TWO

THE National Threat Assessment Center, or NTAC, was located right around the corner from Ford's Theatre in D.C. Joe Stonehouse passed the famous landmark, remembering when he'd taken Josie there. Because the memory pricked, he shoved it away. He reached the Secret Service building and headed inside. Though it was Sunday night, they had business to take care of.

The route to the conference room was familiar, and the smell of lemon wax, cleaning fluid, and leather accompanied him. He'd worked at NTAC, a division of the Secret Service that analyzed potential assassins in order to preclude their attacks, for five years before Josie's death. Afterward, he became part of the Safe School Initiative, which addressed school shooters. Then, at his instigation, and with him at the helm, the School Threat Assessment Team, or STAT, was formed. They collected information about past school shootings and the shooters themselves for the purpose of preventing targeted school violence; they also monitored developing situations in high schools across the country. Then, too, since the World Trade Center attacks, school kids were even more messed up and needed help from adults.

And, in the event of a serious potential risk, they went

undercover in the buildings. Which was why he was here tonight. He pushed open the conference room door.

"You're late," a voice from the other side of the room said.

The remark came from his sulking colleague, who still looked like one of America's Most Wanted in his torn jeans, flannel shirt, and unkempt hair. Joe refrained from snarling. Once again, he cursed his luck that Ludzecky was the only agent available to go into Fairholm High School with him on such short notice.

"Traffic on Dupont Circle," Joe said tightly. Shrugging out of the jacket of his pinstripe suit, he sat down on a table and picked up the remote to view a Power Point presentation the government had prepared for them over the weekend. "All right, Suzie Q, let's see what makes you tick."

"How come we didn't have all this information before we went up to New York on Friday?" Ludzecky wanted to know.

"We had to move in fast, given what we found last week." Joe clicked on the appropriate icon to get into the program. "The data wasn't ready."

They'd been collecting information on Fairholm High School for months as part of STAT's program to keep tabs on high-risk situations in the nation's secondary schools. But two recent developments had propelled them to target Fairholm for immediate intervention.

Mrs. Suzanna Quinn's picture appeared on the big screen. He studied the blond hair, pulled back in a knot like she'd worn it two days ago, revealing gold hoops at her ears. Her light brown eyes were smiling. "This is Suzanna Quinn's professional photo." He noted she wore the same kind of suit she had on when they'd met. Tailored. Professional.

"Buttoned up like a four-star general," Ludzecky commented.

"At least she sets a good example for her troops."

He clicked on *background information*; the screen split, and statistics came up next to her picture.

"She doesn't look forty-three."

Joe thought she did. A good forty-three, though. Smooth skin. Only a few laugh lines around her eyes. Sculpted chin.

Married. Widowed. She'd been climbing the academic ladder, on her way to a college administration position, when her husband had died from a heart attack. She'd shied away from working at the local college where he'd taught the ethics of law. Instead, when she'd finished her doctorate in education, she called on her initial experience as a high school social studies teacher, then school counselor, and finally assistant principal; she'd applied for and received the principalship at Fairholm High five years ago. She had one son, Josh, a senior at the school. He scanned the rest of the general information. "This isn't what I need to know about her."

Ludzecky sighed dramatically. The kid should be on stage. "I don't understand why we didn't just tell her we were comin' in undercover. She's the principal, for Christ's sake."

That got Joe's back up. Superintendent Maloney had had doubts about Quinn accepting the undercover work without a fuss, and after Joe had read her files, he'd made the decision to keep her in the dark. Maloney hadn't been comfortable with that, and Joe himself had had second thoughts about it. But his instinct had told him to wait, and on more than one occasion, those instincts had saved his life.

"You read her mission statement for the school and her own personal essay on management style; she'd balk at covert actions. She's preached democracy and openness and flexibility with evangelistic zeal." He glanced at the screen. "What I want to know is why."

"Afraid she'll interfere with your commando tactics?"

"No, I was afraid her objections would make it harder for us to get into the school. You know time is of the essence, after the latest developments. I decided to go under covertly; when everything's set up, I'll let her in on the plan. By then, it'll be too late for her to do too much damage."

Ludzecky scowled. "Don't you get tired of playin' God all the time?"

Joe ignored the sarcasm which came in a steady stream from the young agent's mouth. He continued to flick through the files. Pictures came up of her son—he resembled his mother, with blonder hair but those same eyes. Her husband

was next. Joe clicked on an icon labeled *Lawrence Quinn.*
Fifteen years her senior. Second marriage. First wife de-
ceased. Professor at NYU in legal ethics. Ah, maybe this was
the source of her rabid belief in honesty at all costs. They
moved to Fairholm when their son was born; her husband
taught at a local college, and she took a teaching job at the
high school. Assessment by team: good marriage, low-key,
no known separations, seemed to love their kid.

"Geez, look at that," Ludzecky said.

"What?"

"The guy died on their fifteenth wedding anniversary."

"Yeah?"

The younger man snorted. "Not surprised *you* didn't notice," he grumbled.

Joe knew Luke's, and others', attitude toward him. They
called him Iron Man, Stone Man, the Ice King. Not that he
cared. His restrained personality was a hell of a lot better
than mimicking his parents. Besides, he hadn't always been
like this.

Joe nodded to the section on Quinn's husband. "It could
be just her husband's views that's got her so jagged on honesty. Your typical liberal couple." He tried to hide the disdain
in his voice, caused by the memory of the liberal couple who
raised *him.* Clicking the remote, he brought up the section labeled *parents.*

Her family grew up right here in D.C. Mother, Joanna
Carson. Schoolteacher. Raised four children on her own after
father died in 1960—two months before Suzanna was born.
Father's career path . . . bingo!

Even Ludzecky leaned forward and read with interest.
"Holy shit."

"Nathan Carson was brought down by good old Senator
McCarthy," Joe said, finding the last piece of the puzzle.

They read the report together. Nathan W. Carson was a
captain in the army when McCarthy's Communist-seeking
bullets had hit him. He'd been one of the several U.S. Army
officers brutally questioned in the infamous thirty-six hours
of televised hearings.

"I wonder if the superintendent knew about Carson and
that's why he thought she'd balk," Joe commented, almost to

himself. "Those investigations included undercover work, phone tapping, infiltrations."

"Not to mention that he was found innocent." Ludzecky's tone was grave.

"There was almost no proof against anybody McCarthy accused. Didn't matter, though, the damage had been done."

"Click again, see what happened to Carson." Ludzecky straightened and peered intently at the screen.

Joe brought up the next slide. "Damn."

Luke sighed again, this time sympathetically. He had yet to develop a hard veneer, which was one of the things that got him in so much trouble. That and his lack of plain common sense.

Suzanna Quinn's father had committed suicide two months before she was born. He'd "involuntarily resigned" from the army and never bounced back.

"Well, I'm sure she can be managed effectively," Joe commented.

"Goddamn it, Stonehouse, don't you feel any sympathy for the poor woman?"

Sick of the kid's needling, he snapped back. "Sympathy gets in the way, Agent Ludzecky. It's what keeps getting *you* in all that hot water." He fiddled with the computer. "Let's look at the other school personnel."

LUKE stared ahead blankly, but inside he was seething. He tried to hide it, tried to pretend interest in the parade of teachers that came across the screen, but Stonehouse's words hit a hot button. He could still see the big boss's face, hear his irate words. . . .

"You're on thin ice after the last operation, Ludzecky. If it hadn't come out all right, you would've been booted out on your ass."

Luke's hands had fisted with the effort to keep from responding. He hadn't botched it. Jesus Christ, he couldn't stand by and watch a girl get raped. The perps weren't from the targeted school, but they had a gun. Luke had jumped one of them; Stonehouse had been nearby and had gotten into the fray. The gun went off, and Joe had been superficially wounded. It took a while to regain their low profile at the school, crucial to fitting in and gaining kids' trust. Luke's interference had set the entire project back weeks, but it was a side effect that couldn't be avoided. Stonehouse hadn't agreed with him, though, that the girl was in real danger.

Instead of arguing with the brass, Luke had resorted to the inbred insolence that made him such a good undercover agent. "Yeah, I'm still here because it turned out all right, *and* because it's hard to find twenty-six-year-old agents who look nineteen. . . ."

Still, he wondered about his future. Because he was getting older, this would probably be his last assignment as a teenager. Given his rebel roots and unorthodox views—truthfully, he sympathized with Suzanna Quinn—would there be a place for him in the Service after this job? Did he even want there to be? He'd joined for complicated reasons, which he questioned every day.

His attention was snagged by a photo on screen. He whistled. "Wow, a fox. She a teacher?"

"Ms. Kelsey Cunningham," Joe said dryly. Man, the guy *was* made of stone if this chick didn't rock his jocks.

"Damn it to hell. Not one of *my* high school teachers ever looked like a harem girl." Those dark eyes and hair were something else.

"Control your hormones, Ludzecky. She's your home-room teacher, your U.S. Government teacher, and you're going to sign up for her Psychology elective."

"I'm gonna take two classes from her a day?"

"Yes."

"Hey, it's a tough job, but somebody's gotta do it."

"A variety of kids you need to zero in on are in those classes this semester."

"All the boys are takin' her course, right?"

"No, as a matter of fact, she has a reputation for getting along with the girls, too. She coaches the women's track team."

"Put up her bio."

Hmm. Thirty-one. Been teaching for eleven years—some kind of gifted child. Ah, Suzanna Quinn's protegée, brought to Fairholm by her former teacher. On the fast track to administration. "Too bad," he said aloud. "Too many good teachers leave the classroom."

Stonehouse didn't respond. He scanned her information. "Father, professor at Yale. Mother died when she was five. Look at that Research Team assessment."

Geez, Luke hated this section of the bios, hated these boxes they put everybody in. The beautiful Ms. Cunningham was categorized as a perfectionist, bordering on overly involved in school activities. Close to father. Shared many interests.

Luke refrained from commenting. He wondered if Stonehouse knew how he'd let his own father down. Shit!

He pushed back his chair. "I need a cigarette," he said, and headed for the door, his Doc Martens scraping the wood floor.

"We're not done here."

"I'll be back."

Feeling smothered, Luke escaped the conference room and strode out of the building. He found a pack of Marlboros in his pocket and lit one. Hell, he'd gotten hooked again, working undercover with so many kids who smoked. As he took a drag, he tried not to think of his father, but the images ambushed him in the shadows of Tenth Street. . . .

"You will not drink or smoke in my house, Lukasz."

"Okay, Pop."

"And you will go to school. Be successful. Take advantage of the gifts God has given you."

Luke had rolled his eyes.

"You will be the man of the family someday, *syn*. The only boy to carry on. . . ."

Luke hadn't listened then, and cut off the remembered words now. But his query slipped out into the night. "Would you be proud of me, Papa? I'm in the Secret Service."

Stash Ludzecky had been dead by the time Luke was done with his teen rebellion. As the only son, he had indeed been left to watch over his mother and seven younger sisters. Damn it. He didn't want to think about why he joined the Secret Service and the fact that most of the time he felt he didn't belong there.

Something he was afraid Stonehouse sensed. Clearly, the older man disapproved of Luke—they were as different as fire and ice. Though Stonehouse's seniority in the Service, and the fact that STAT was his pet project, made him the boss, Luke resented being ordered around and avoided working directly with him. They paired up this time only because of the urgency of this particular job. Well, it was supposed to last for a few months at the most, he thought, stubbing out his cigarette. He could handle it that long.

When he returned to the conference room, the computer was off and the lights glared from above. Stonehouse was gathering a pile of papers from the printer. "Here. Do your homework on the plane. Read the rest of the bios."

"What time do we leave?"

Stonehouse glanced at his watch. "Sixteen hundred hours." He looked at Luke. "I assume you have your stuff."

"I got what I need."

"We have to discuss something." If possible, Mr. Stick-up-His-Ass's posture got even more rigid.

"What?"

"Your living accommodations are different this time."

Often Luke went under as an emancipated minor. That way he could live alone and not endanger anybody else. "No shit."

Stonehouse sat on the edge of the table and folded his arms over his chest. Briefly Luke wondered if he slept in those suits of armor. "Since we're going under as uncle and nephew, you'll live with me."

"I guessed as much. It didn't take Einstein to figure out the arrangements." He added, "Doesn't mean I have to like it."

A sigh. "Look, we think this will work better. You hate your uncle. You can use that to get in with the kids and gain teacher sympathy. Maybe even the beautiful Ms. Cunningham will help you deal with that bastard you have to live with." Stonehouse stood and gave him a long-suffering look. "We shouldn't have any problem convincing people we can't stand the sight of each other."

Luke glared at him but summoned his professionalism. Grabbing his battered bomber jacket, he turned and stalked out the door. He waited until he was down the hall, out of sight and earshot, to kick a wastebasket across the corridor and let out a curse.

He was wrong. This was going to be a *long* few months.

THREE

——

"Is he in, Carol?" Suzanna asked the new crisis counselor's secretary when she stepped into the guidance suite, which buzzed with activity at eleven o'clock in the morning.

One of the first renovations Suzanna had pursued when she became principal was to enlarge this area. She'd created bigger, individual offices with soothing blue and green walls and new furniture. She'd also insisted on conference rooms and comfortable waiting and secretarial areas, as well as carpeting for the whole space. To her, counseling could make or break a school, and the facilities should encourage kids to come down; there should also be room to deal with them privately.

The always harried secretary nodded. "Yes, he's just finishing up with a student."

"I'll wait, then."

Sitting in a chair, trying to relax, Suzanna thought about the other things she'd done at Fairholm: implementing a mentor program for new teachers; setting up peer mediation and a Student Court for kids; in-servicing the hell out of the staff on flexibility, openness, and honesty in their dealings with students. Then, she'd hammered into them the need for a healthy respect in their interactions with each other.

Suzanna staunchly believed both were the backbone of a good, safe school.

And now she had Joe Stonehouse, the enigma, to help her. In the two weeks he'd been at Fairholm, he'd hit the ground running and hadn't stopped once. She admired his diligence and how well he worked with kids. Still, there was something about the man that didn't set right with her. Maybe it was just the way he'd been forced on her.

Don't let your pride get in the way, love, Lawrence would say. She'd remembered her husband's advice in her show-down with Ross, which had been tense and unpleasant. Ulti-mately the superintendent's explanations made no further sense, so she'd dropped the issue.

She pasted on a smile when the door to Joe's office opened. Ben Franzi stepped out. Tall and thin, with dark hair and eyes like onyx, he smiled at Suzanna. "Hi, Mrs. Q."

"Hi, Ben." She pointed to his armful of guitar. "How's the music going?"

"It's awesome. My mom bought me this Gibson for Christmas. I'm heading to the music rooms now to play."

"Good for you."

Stonehouse appeared behind the boy, towered over him, really, even with Ben's height. He was dressed meticulously as always—this time in a navy suit with a light blue shirt. His expression was friendly, yet somehow affected. Watch-ful, maybe. On guard.

"Mrs. Quinn? I was coming to your office, but Ben here got to telling me about his music and I. . . ." He offered a look that was supposed to say he was sorry, but didn't.

"No problem. I was out and around, and decided to stop by for our meeting." She said good-bye to Ben, noting the Wiccan pentacle around his neck and his sweatshirt, which read, *Freedom of religion means any religion.* "Don't be a stranger," she called after him, thinking about Zach Riley.

Inside, Stonehouse's office was . . . spartan. No knick-knacks. No pictures, not even one of the sister he'd cared enough about to take on her troubled son. There were a cou-ple of psychology degrees on the wall from Stanford and UCLA, but that was about it. Though she was grateful to get his help after Zach's suicide—it was so recent the wounds were still raw—she wished she knew more about Joe, but hadn't been able to unearth much in the way of a personal side to the guy.

Smoothing down her slate gray suit, she took a chair next to his desk while he sat behind it. She fingered the gold bangle at her wrist. "I'd like to discuss the group you're starting Monday and the others you have in the works."

"I—" There was a knock at the door. Frowning, he got up and opened it.

Lester Wells, Suzanna's assistant principal, was huffing and puffing at the entrance. "Look, I know you're busy . . . oh, I didn't realize you were with Suzanna."

She cocked her head. "Go ahead, Lester."

Small brown eyes, which sometimes matched his small mind, narrowed on Joe. "Your nephew's in the office again."

Joe's frown upgraded to a scowl.

Suzanna bit her lip. For some reason, it was reassuring to see Stonehouse brought down by one of the world's greatest levelers—a teenager. It made him more human.

"What's he done this time?" the counselor asked tightly.

"A fight. He says he was *stopping* a fight, but other kids say he started it. In any case, he threw a punch."

"Who broke it up?" Suzanna asked.

"Kelsey Cunningham."

Suzanna frowned. Not only was Kelsey her best teacher, she was also like a daughter to Suzanna, had been since Suzanna had taught her U.S. History and the girl had lived with them her senior year, when her father once again pulled the rug from under her and moved to New Haven. "Is she all right?"

"Yes. But mad as hell." He mumbled, "Probably broke a fingernail."

"Not funny, Lester."

"I'll be down as soon as I'm done here," Joe said. "Let the kid cool his heels until then."

"I'm suspending him. School policy for fighting."

"What else is new?" Stonehouse closed the door and sank despairingly into his chair. "I rue the day I told my sister I'd take that boy for the rest of the year."

"Raising kids is never easy."

"How would you know? You've got the angel child of Fairholm." He gave her a half-smile, making her realize how seldom she saw the gesture from him. And the nice things it did to his high cheekbones and square-cut jaw.

"He *is* a sweetie. I'm lucky."

Joe's face darkened. "It's never luck when kids turn out well. It's because they were raised right."

"Why, thank you." The compliment surprised her. This man had been miserly with his opinions for days, let alone any personal comments. His words also made her flush.

He straightened abruptly. "Monday's group is Kids of Single Parents." He picked up a neatly typed list. She'd noticed his attention to detail before. "You have a lot of them."

You, not *we.*

"Yes, we do. Most schools do, Joe."

"I'm hoping to mix up the cliques this way."

"May I see the list?"

He handed it to her. She was shocked to see Max Duchamp's name halfway down. Along with Ben's.

"Max is coming? That's a surprise. I know his mother's been dead since he was little. I guess you never get over it."

"Old or new, parental wounds cut deep. Franzi's father died just last year, didn't he?"

"Yes." She looked back down at the list and stopped cold. Oh, Lord, Josh's name. She drew in a breath.

"Your son's name is on there. Is that what you really wanted to know?" he asked, cutting to the chase.

She raised her chin. "Of course not. I'd never check up on him that way. I detest any kind of spying. He didn't mention his plans to join this group, but I'll tell him I found out—accidentally, of course—and we'll discuss it if he wants to."

Joe's eyebrows arched, making her feel as if she had to defend herself. The clock on the wall ticked loudly in the strained silence.

"It's tough having a mother as a principal," she said. "We have ground rules. Honesty is one. Noninterference is another."

"Both seem to be your mantra, Suzanna."

"Yes, they are." She didn't like the erratic beat of her

heart at his use of her first name. "Now, show me the rest of your plans."

He drew out a neatly typed sheet. "I'm considering a group for kids who are being bullied. It's a little-addressed problem these days." He handed her the outline. "Another is a Boys' Concerns group I'm hoping to start."

"Only for boys? What about the girls?"

Stonehouse hesitated, just enough to make her think he was weighing his words. "Your staff already runs a couple of groups for girls. Anyway, there's a lot of research about boys these days that says we don't listen to them enough. That we should provide more opportunities to let them talk."

"I wonder if we had more things like this, if Zach Riley. . . ." She let the words trail off.

"Suicide's a complicated issue." His face softened. "And what if's are normal. We should concentrate on the present, though."

"I know. I'd like to see that research on boys."

He studied her for a moment. It made her uncomfortable. Then he fished in the folder and drew out some papers downloaded from the Internet. "Here it is."

Ignoring the unsettled feeling inside her, Suzanna leaned over and concentrated on the counselor's articles.

READY to spit nails, Joe drew in a deep breath and made his way to Wells's office. The kid was *supposed* to keep a low profile. Before this was over, Joe was going to kill Ludzecky.

He'd reached the hall intersection when a woman coming around the corner bumped into him. "Oh, sorry," he said.

"Joe." It was Kelsey Cunningham.

He remembered Ludzecky's comment when they first saw the pretty teacher's profile, complete with picture. She *was* a beauty, though young. She didn't yet have Suzanna's inner poise—something that radiated from the principal's face and in the way she moved. Classic, understated and . . . appealing.

He cleared his throat, vaguely disturbed by his rumination. "Ms. Cunningham."

She tossed back the bangs of her short, dark hair. "I was on my way to see your nephew."

"I heard you broke up the fight." His jaw hardened. "He didn't hurt you, did he?"

They walked together, her long legs keeping stride easily, despite the slim skirt and heels she seemed to favor. "No, and you misunderstand what happened. Luke stepped in, trying to keep Smurf—Jimmy Smurfella—from getting beat up."

Not again. The kid had a regular Sir Galahad complex.

"I thought he started the fight." Joe scowled again. "It wouldn't be the first time."

Kelsey smiled her Miss America smile. "He's never any trouble for me in Government class or in Psychology."

Surprise, surprise. "He likes history."

"He knows more than I do about the setup of the government."

No doubt about it, Joe was going to kill the kid for showing off.

They reached the office together; Luke glanced up from his studied slouch. His beard had grown just enough to be scruffy, and his hair grazed his collar. Today he was dressed in threadbare denims and a flannel shirt over a red T-shirt.

Gracefully, Kelsey sat down beside him and placed her hand on his shoulder. Not a good idea, in this day and age of sexual misconduct charges. But Joe had noticed that many of the teachers here were habitually demonstrative. Even Suzanna was always patting a student on the back or squeezing his arm.

"You okay, buddy?" Kelsey asked.

Massaging his jaw, Luke looked cow-eyed at the young teacher. "He got in a jab before I took him down."

That surprised Joe. Secret Service agents were highly trained. He hoped Luke wasn't losing his edge.

"Need to go to the nurse?" she asked.

"Nah. I'm suspended anyway." He shot Joe a surly look. "Gonna send me home, Unc?"

"Yes. After we talk in my office." He spoke to the secretary. "May I take him?"

"Sure. Lester says he's out until the Student Court is held."

"Freakin' Nazi," Luke grumbled under his breath.

Kelsey said, "I'll straighten everything out, Luke. You shouldn't be punished for helping."

Luke stood. "Don't bother, Teach. It's dope. I got me a vacation." Grinning, he followed Joe out of the assistant principal's office.

IN the confines of his "uncle's" office, Luke sat on the desk while Joe paced. "I need a cigarette," Luke said.

"There's no smoking anywhere on school grounds." A glare accompanied Joe's glacial tone. "And you can ditch the James Dean act. Nobody's here to see you."

"Hey, you know the first rule of our operation. Never break cover. It's why we had to live together." Luke jerked Stone Man's chain a bit more. "A rulemonger like you should remember that."

"What the hell happened? You're supposed to be an angry kid, but keep a low profile."

"Hey, I tried to ignore it. They were raggin' on Smurfy boy, and then it got physical. The other kids say he's picked on all the time, especially in gym class."

"Who did it?"

Luke ducked his head. "Duchamp's buddy, Rush Webster. And his sidekick Morton."

Stonehouse snarled, "Oh, that's fucking wonderful." Maybe the guy didn't have ice in his veins after all. "You're supposed to be getting *tight* with the on-the-fringe kids, not alienating them."

"I know. But I couldn't stand by and let them take Smurf apart. Especially when Kelsey Cunningham was gonna jump in the fray. Geez, three-inch heels, tight skirt, and all."

"Protecting females is what got you into trouble the last time, Agent Ludzecky."

"That girl could have gotten raped."

"You overreacted. She wasn't in that much danger."

Though it rankled, Luke didn't let Stonehouse see he was affected. "Maybe I can use this fight."

"How?"

"To get in better with Franzi's group. He and Smurf are friends of a sort. They aren't exactly best buddies with Duchamp's gang."

Stonehouse conceded that point with a nod of his head.

"I'm gonna ask Ben to come over to jam with the guitars."

"Good idea," Stonehouse said begrudgingly.

"Don't strain yourself with the compliments, Unc."

Stonehouse's jaw hardened, "You've got to find a way to connect with Webster and Duchamp, too. And this Morton kid."

"I will. Am I *excused*?" Luke asked belligerently.

"Get out of here." He tossed Luke his keys and opened the door so others could hear. "Don't bang up my car on the way home."

"If you'd let me drive my own wheels. . . ."

"You lost your car for the last infraction, Luke. No telling what I'll have to do this time."

Luke smirked for the counseling staff. "Break my legs?"

"Get out of here," Stonehouse repeated, this time for show.

"My pleasure. Have a nice day, Unc."

AS the kids finished up the personality profiles, Kelsey Cunningham eased back onto her desk and tugged down her suede skirt. She was ever mindful of the suicide note Zach Riley had written—which still brought tears to her eyes.

And Ms. Cunningham, Zach had playfully penned. *Please, watch those skirts. We're only seventeen. Every red-blooded American male has trouble concentrating in your classroom as it is. . . .*

Such a waste, one she wouldn't let happen again. All the students needed more attention and Kelsey promised herself daily to give it to each of them.

Starting with Luke Ludzecky.

The boy had become a major player at Fairholm High in the few weeks he'd been here. Several teachers remarked that he had charisma, underneath the adolescent bravado.

"Done!" Heather Haywood announced when she finished her work.

Kelsey shook her head, and Heather clapped a hand over her lips. "Sorry," she mouthed.

From behind, Josh Quinn squeezed her shoulder. Suzanna had her hands full with that couple. Kelsey was putting her money on the mom in this case. Not only was Suzanna Quinn a top-notch principal, she was a first-rate mother—something Kelsey knew from personal experience.

The door flew open with a bang. Kelsey turned to see Max Duchamp stomping in. His poet's face—long and thin and nearly delicate—was scowling. His dark hair brushed his collar, and was pulled back, revealing tumultuous brown eyes. Crossing the room, he headed for his seat.

"You forgot to sign in, Max."

This was standard procedure for tardiness, so it wouldn't interrupt instruction, and Kelsey could deal with the kid at the end of class. Max glared at her. She glared back. Students tended to think she was an airhead because of her looks.

Then, his whole demeanor changed. She called it his *like me* act. There was a softer side to Max, and once when she'd expressed her concern to Suzanna, the principal said he'd written in his English journal about his need to please his father. Something Kelsey knew intimately. "Sorry, Ms. C. They got my man."

"I know. I was there."

Max's fist curled for a minute. The feral look in his eye chilled her. He was a kid who wasn't always soft.

"There's a Student Court tomorrow night to discuss it, Max."

"As if it'll go in our favor."

She handed him the classwork. He took it and trudged to his seat, his army boots—which complemented his camouflage shirt—scuffing along the carpet.

After a few more minutes, she spoke to the group. "All right, let's talk about personality disorders."

Twenty Psychology elective kids looked up at her. She was warmed by their interested faces, their desire to learn.

"Any general comments first?"

"All the disorders seem to deal with *over* something."

This from Morgan Kane, a pretty blonde who wrote blisteringly cutting essays for the school newspaper.

Kelsey laughed. "They do indeed." She pointed to the board. "Overachievers." Like Kelsey herself. "Overcompensators." Like Mike Wolfe, the baseball coach, who fed his insecure ego by getting women into bed. "Overprotectors." Like Luke Ludzecky. "Why do you think so many people go overboard, so to speak?"

The kids chuckled at her pun.

"Society expects it." This from Ben Franzi. "Look at TV shows like *Charmed* and *Buffy the Vampire Slayer.* You have to be *more* than human."

Ben's reference to the occult programs reminded Kelsey that a lot of teachers were worried about his and some of his friends' interest in Wicca. He'd done his freshman project on it—a thoughtful, thorough portrayal of his views of the pagan religion—and Kelsey had read more about it after that. Though non-Judeo/Christian, the religion seemed solidly based in ethical principles and was *not* devil worship. Still, she worried about him.

"I think Ben's right," Morgan said. The two had been friends since they were eight years old and lived next door to each other.

"Gonna cast a spell on us like Phoebe or Willow?" Max asked snidely, referring to two of the characters on the shows Ben had mentioned. Kelsey had watched both programs a couple of times, just to keep up with the kids.

"Screw you, Duchamp."

"Guys, that's enough. Max, not an appropriate comment. Ben, watch your language." She addressed the class. "Turn to the third page of the handout. It mentions Ben's point about impossible standards and frames the concept in a different way."

She was still thinking about impossible standards as she headed to the staff lounge to get some coffee. Glancing at her watch, a snazzy gold Gucci her father had given her for her thirtieth birthday, she sighed. Her father. Impossible standards. Ones she kept trying to live up to, despite all the things he'd done to manipulate her life.

"Hey, gorgeous, what's the sigh for?"

Not slowing down, she glanced over into the smiling face of Mike Wolfe. The kids had a field day with his name, especially since they were aware of his rep with women. "Hi, Mike. I'm dying for some coffee, and I have to make a call at three."

He sidled in close. "Not a guy, I hope." Blue-as-the-Caribbean eyes, fringed with thick black lashes, smiled out from a face to die for. Talk about gorgeous. Too bad he knew it.

"Yep, as a matter of fact, it is." She was phoning her father, but he didn't have to know that.

He clapped a hand over his heart, clad in a designer sweatsuit. "You wound me, Sophia." An old movie buff, he'd once told her she reminded him of Sophia Loren. It was hard not to be flattered. "Go out with me tomorrow night," he wheedled, as he opened the door to the teachers' lounge for her.

"Can't. I have Student Court."

"Is there any committee you're not on? Any club you don't head?"

"The chess team," she joked. "Though I play."

"Why am I not surprised?" They made their way to the front of the room. Drawing coffee for her—it smelled deliciously strong—he gave her a killer smile. "How about this weekend? I got tickets to something you'll like Sunday night."

"Really, what?" She sipped her coffee.

"The Wild Strawberries concert."

Kelsey favored alternative music, an interest her father would disapprove of. Was that why she gravitated toward it? At thirty-one, was she still balking at him the way she had when she refused to move to New Haven with him, then insisted on becoming a high school teacher, which had caused World War III in their relationship?

"How'd you get tickets? They're impossible to scrounge up."

"I charmed—"

"Whoops. Sorry." Tom Gannon bumped into Kelsey, spilling her coffee on her hand.

"Watch out, Gannon," Mike barked.

Pushing his glasses up his nose, the older teacher blushed right to the roots of his receding hairline. "I apologize. Are you all right, Ms. Cunningham?" He addressed everybody—both teachers and students—formally.

"Yes, I'm fine, Tom," Kelsey told him.

The man nodded, then circled around them.

"Creep," Mike said when Tom was a few feet away.

"Shh, he'll hear you."

"Well, he *is* creepy. Everybody thinks so."

Not everybody. Again, Zach Riley's note came to mind. *Mr. G.—lighten up. You're so smart. You have so much to teach us. But you drive us too hard.* Though he never talked to anyone about it, Tom must have suffered over that message after Zach died. All the teachers had regrets. Had they missed signs? If they'd taken more time with him, could they have prevented Zach's suicide?

"Kel, what about this weekend?"

Quickly she glanced at the clock. "Maybe. I'll catch up with you later." Turning, she strode away. She liked Mike okay, but his junior high mentality irritated her sometimes.

Back in her room, she dialed her father, feeling like a little girl again, obeying Daddy's edict. *Exactly three, Kelsey. I have a staff meeting at four.* Never mind it was a pain in the ass to get a long-distance line out of school. Or that she might be busy at *exactly* three. No one kept the illustrious Dr. Reynolds Cunningham waiting. Not even his beloved daughter.

As the phone call went through, she studied her room. On the back wall, framed photos of important historical figures smiled out at her. Around them were sayings about history. Posters with motivational quips and pictures decorated the rest of the space. She loved her room, with its thick carpeting, new desks, and huge windows with mini blinds.

Her father answered on the sixth ring. "Dr. Cunningham."

"Hi, Dad."

"Kelsey, how are you?"

"Busy as hell. You?"

"Same." She heard computer keys in the background. Her annoyance grew to pique. "I'm finishing up a chapter of my new book."

"How *is* the world of political intrigue?" Her father taught poli-sci at Yale and published nonfiction about the workings of the government.

"Hmm. Good," he said absently. She pictured the crow's-feet around his eyes and mouth, though he was still handsome at sixty, with a full head of steel-gray hair and the dark eyes she'd inherited. "How are you, dear?" *Click. Click. Click.*

Just tell him. Say what you'd say to anyone else. "It bothers me that you do other things while talking to me."

But she couldn't. They'd fought bitterly in her younger days, and by tacit agreement now, they both tried to keep the peace. It was only with Suzanna that Kelsey could be completely honest.

"I'm fine. Psychology's going particularly well."

"Did you get the article on schizophrenia I sent you?"

She rummaged around her desk. "Ah, yeah. It was insightful." She winced at the lie. *Please don't ask me about it.*

"Kelsey, is something wrong?"

"No, it's just been an upsetting day. We had a fight—" The words were out before she realized she shouldn't have said them.

"You weren't involved, of course."

"Um. . . ."

"Kelsey Lynne Cunningham, what were you thinking?"

"You don't think about a fight when it breaks out. You just act."

A sigh. *Here it comes.* "High schools are dangerous places."

"Actually, they're safer than anywhere else for kids."

"What about Columbine? Idaho? Arizona? Tell those grieving parents how safe secondary schools are."

"School shootings are rare, Dad, compared to the danger outside of the buildings. It's just the media hype that calls attention to them."

"That and the fact that teachers and students die."

"Less than one percent of the deaths of school-age children happen at school. The odds of someone dying here are one in a million. Literally."

"You seem to be well versed in the subject."

"A student of mine did her report on it."

Absolute silence. His favorite tactic when she backed him in a corner. One of the things Suzanna had given Kelsey was an openness and honesty that Kelsey had needed from an adult in her life.

"Why did you want me to call, Dad?"

In a moment, the computer keys clicked. Well, at least he'd stopped typing for a while. "I wish you'd take a position up here at Yale. You're wasting that brilliant mind in a public school."

"I like my job." Her tone was cool. This was off-limits, and her father knew it. He was breaking their unspoken pact.

"All right. I'll lay off. What time are you coming Friday?"

"I can't come Friday. I. . . ." What would he accept without sulking? "I have a date."

"Really, with whom?"

For some reason, big hazel eyes, shaggy hair, and an adolescent slouch came to mind. Geez, Suzanna was right. She needed a man in her life if a new boy in class was the only phantom date she could summon. "Mike Wolfe, a PE teacher."

"A jock?"

"He's nice." *Even if he does have an ego the size of Texas.* "Look, Dad, a student's at my door. I've got to go."

"Fine." Clipped, cold, condescending. Like her whole adolescence had been whenever she crossed him. *Cheerleading, Kelsey? Really. . . . A B+ in Math. That's unacceptable . . . I don't like the boy; he's unsuitable.*

Just once, she was going to do something shocking to totally freak out the illustrious Dr. Cunningham. "I'll see you about nine on Saturday, though. Take care."

He hesitated. "I love you, Kelsey."

Her heart leaped to her throat. "I love you, too, Daddy." And she hung up.

Kelsey sighed, feeling like one of the kids who sat before her all day. Embarrassed, she scrubbed her hands across her face and picked up the schizophrenia article.

• • • •

"HMM, it smells delicious." From the table where she sat in Kelsey's kitchen, Suzanna smiled and sipped a Pinot Grigio they both enjoyed, while Kelsey fixed fettucine Alfredo. "Thanks for cooking for me, sweetie."

Kelsey stirred the sauce and smiled back at her friend. "I love to cook for you."

Suzanna cocked her head, ever the mother, surrogate or real. "You look tired. Having a rough week?"

"Nah, just the fight. Poor Luke Ludzecky. He got caught in the crossfire."

"He's a character, isn't he?"

Kelsey thought of the troubled young boy and his uncle. What a mismatch. "Honestly, I like him."

"So do I. He's rough around the edges, but salvageable."

"Everybody's salvageable to you, Ms. Principal." Leaving the stove to drain noodles, which had been boiling, Kelsey crossed to the sink. "So what do you think of his uncle?"

"I think he's good at his job." Suzanna frowned. "But cold."

"He's got a nice butt."

Suzanna chuckled. Though she'd been a surrogate parent to Kelsey, and helped her through some rough times as a teen, they enjoyed an equal, woman-to-woman relationship now, as a mother might with her grown daughter. Kelsey valued it more than anything else in her life. "You going for an older man, like I did?" Suzanna asked.

Kelsey shook her head as she finished pouring sharp, cheesy sauce over noodles on two plates. "Nah. He's not that much older, anyway, is he?"

"He's forty-six."

"I'm thirty-one."

"Thirty-one? How did that happen?" Suzanna got a wistful look in her eyes.

Again Kelsey gave her a warm smile as she served the food. "Dad's going to be sixty soon."

Suzanna dished out the salad. "How is Reynolds?" she asked, trying for nonchalance. Kelsey's father was a difficult topic for them to discuss. Ironically, these days Suzanna seemed to resent him more than Kelsey did.

"Demanding as ever."

"He never changes, does he?"

"Nope. I'm going down there Saturday."

"Do you want to?"

Shaking her head, Kelsey put fork to food.

"Kel?"

Kelsey shrugged. "I have a lot going on here."

Suzanna took a bite of her dinner. "You could say no to him once in a while."

"Yeah, and when has that ever gotten me anywhere?"

"When you refused to move to New Haven with him."

The memory made Kelsey seethe. Not only had her father uprooted her in eighth grade to move to Fairholm, where she'd met Suzanna, but he tried to do it again three years later. She could still see him blithely amble into their house at the end of the summer before her senior year in high school and announce he'd gotten an associate professorship at Yale. He and Kelsey were moving immediately.

"I'd never been so blindsided in my life. It was worse than the first time, when he'd promised he wouldn't do it again." She sipped her wine and shook her head. "He really expected me not to protest again."

"Up until then, you were a dutiful daughter."

"Not that time. I lost it completely and made threats. He didn't know what to do."

Of course, Suzanna had come to the rescue. She and Kelsey had become close in ninth grade when, as her Global History teacher, Suzanna had seen Kelsey's misery and taken her under her wing. They'd gotten closer each year, so when Reynolds wanted to move again, Suzanna had offered to have Kelsey stay with her and Lawrence to finish out her senior year at Fairholm. Kelsey's father had been livid, but gave in eventually. "His loss was my gain. We all loved having you with us those months."

Kelsey shook her head, remembering. "Then he pulled that crap when I wanted to go into high school teaching instead of 'doing something more productive.' "

Suzanna covered Kelsey's hand but said nothing.

"I don't know what I would have done if you hadn't paid my tuition those last two years when he refused to give me any money. Remember what a fit he had then?"

"He got over it. Both times."

"And you lived up to your promise, lady."

He keeps pulling the rug out from under me, Kelsey had told Suzanna in complete adolescent outrage. *I'll never be able to trust him. What is this with adults? Can't you trust any of them?*

You can trust me, sweetie. I promise, I'll always tell you the truth. Tell you what's going on. I won't ever manipulate you like he's done.

"I tried to give you a sense of security, Kelsey."

"Well, you did." Because of those two huge betrayals by her father when she was a teenager, having a person in her life Kelsey could trust had become overly important to her. Her psychology background told her she was somewhat over-the-top about it, but thank God Suzanna would never let her down.

"I just feel bad he still has so much power over you," Suzanna said in between bites.

"Yeah, well, maybe when I'm old and gray, he won't. Meanwhile, I have you to keep me sane."

"That's one of the nicest things anyone's ever said to me. Josh tells me I drive him crazy."

"He won't know how lucky he was until he grows up."

"You, young lady, are a doll."

Kelsey smiled. "I had a good teacher."

FOUR

———

"BREATHE in. Now exhale," the yoga guru on the video-cassette advised Suzanna. On-screen, the soothing desert background was supposed to calm her.

Taking in a long, hefty gulp of air, then slo-ow-ly letting it out, she tried to center herself, strove for the serenity and receptivity of mind and body that the young man promised.

But it was almost impossible to achieve a peaceful state these days. So many things infiltrated her brain like tiny undercover spies, without her even knowing about it. Being a high school principal, she was constantly battered with details to weigh and decisions to make. But something was different lately.

As she tried to *listen to the wisdom of her breath and body,* Suzanna admitted to herself what was causing this lack of concentration.

Joe Stonehouse.

Tonight he seemed stuck in her brain. She could still see his green eyes turn steely when he was told Luke had gotten in trouble.

Ah, and then there was Luke. What was Suzanna going to do for that troubled boy who seemed more like a full-grown man most of the time?

Per the instructor, she dutifully stood, put her legs together and lifted her chest. Exhaled. Raised her arms. All the while, instead of reaching inner tranquillity, she wondered why Joe had taken Luke to live with him. They didn't seem to get along at all . . . maybe Joe was close to his sister . . . what was his family like . . . did his sister have the same mink-colored hair? What was the texture of his hair? Soft . . . no, it looked a little coarse.

"Damn it! What the hell are you *doing*, Suzanna?" she said aloud.

"Hey, language like that is inappropriate. You could get detention."

Suzanna looked up into the face of her son.

How would you know?. You've got the angel child of Fairholm.

She smiled at the boy of her heart and knelt on the rug to continue her routine. "How are you tonight, buddy?"

Loose-limbed in that unique teenage way, he dropped down and sat cross-legged so he was at eye level with her. These days he towered over her, but she could remember when she carried him on her hip and held his hand crossing the street. A wave of nostalgia threatened to choke her; to diminish it, she went into a lunge position and stretched her calf muscles.

He'd brought with him a bowl of fresh popcorn; the buttery smell permeated the house. Tossing a couple of kernels up in the air, he caught them in his mouth. "Who's got ya goin', Ma?"

She laughed at his phrasing. In addition to being smart, Josh was one of the most articulate students in the high school.

"This new counselor. I can't figure him out."

Josh nodded toward the TV. "Must be a big deal if the great Omar can't even distract you." He continually teased her about her yoga tapes and the class she took with Kelsey and her newspaper reporter friend, Brenda Way.

Suzanna smiled and lunged more deeply. "What do you think of Joe Stonehouse?" Maybe Josh would tell her about the Kids of Single Parents group.

"He's okay." Josh's light brown eyes darkened. "All the

girls are gaga over his nephew. Heather thinks he's hot. And Morgan Kane drools over him."

"*I* think Luke's a handful."

Josh stared blindly at the screen, as if his mind had wandered off elsewhere.

"Everything okay?" she asked as she stood to elongate her spine. Kids talked more if it looked like you weren't prying.

"Heather's acting funny."

"Yeah?" *Breathe. Exhale. Go down to a pushup position.* "How?"

"I think the word is *skittish*. Around me."

"Things been going well between you two?"

His face reddened right to his ears. Her mother *uh-oh* alarm went off. Forsaking the exercises, she grabbed the remote and put the video on pause. She knelt and brushed her son's cheek with her palm. "Honey, you can tell me anything. Even if it's personal."

"I know."

"Even if it's about sex. I *was* young once."

His eyes narrowed, and he angled his head. He had Lawrence's chiseled features, and sometimes his mannerisms were so like his dad's it brought tears to her eyes. "I . . ." His Adam's apple bobbed. "It's hard to talk about that stuff with you, Mom."

"I wish you'd try." Suzanna sat back on her heels.

No answer. More popcorn. Josh stared at the frozen screen.

"But if you can't talk to me, what about somebody else? Your school counselor?"

"Geez, Mom, I'd rather die than confide in No Neck."

She laughed at the nickname. It was singularly appropriate for the stocky counselor/coach who'd been at Fairholm forever. Joe had mentioned the guy seemed to take more interest in his wrestlers than in the kids he counseled.

Josh munched on his snack, but didn't get up and leave.

"You know, Joe Stonehouse is starting a Boys' Concerns group in a few days." She hesitated, wondering if she should steer her kid to somebody she didn't completely trust. Though she didn't think Joe was showing all his cards, she had an intuitive feeling about his ability to help teenagers.

Again Josh reddened.

"Honey, I know you signed up for the Kids of Single Parents group. I found out by accident, but it's okay."

He sighed. "I didn't tell you about it because I didn't want to hurt your feelings."

"It doesn't make me feel bad that you need to talk about your father being dead."

His look was forlorn, a lot like it had been when Lawrence died. In her mother's heart, she sensed he needed a guy to hash things out with.

Staring into his eyes, she grasped his shoulders. "Josh, kids can't tell parents everything. But you have to talk about things before you make big decisions about them. If not with me, then with someone else."

"Maybe."

"As I said, I think Joe Stonehouse is great with teenagers. You might want to go in and just shoot the breeze with him. I could set it up."

He shook his head. "No, if I want to do it, I'll arrange it myself." He stood, then leaned over and kissed her on the nose, bringing tears to her eyes again. "Love ya, Ma," he said, and walked toward the doorway; he stopped there and turned. "Thanks."

"For?"

"Letting me have some privacy."

"It's killing me, kid. Get out of here before I tie you up and make you talk."

He laughed and left.

Plopping back down on the floor, Suzanna hoped she'd done the right thing. Joe Stonehouse was a puzzle she was still trying to piece together, but if he could help Josh, she'd trust the guy.

Snapping green eyes flashed through her mind. And mile-wide shoulders. Very quickly, she banished the image and picked up the remote to restart the tape.

· · ·

"TWELVE." Joe counted out loud as he curled a fifty-pound weight up to his shoulder; he grunted as he let it down.

One more, he thought. *Best to push yourself a little further.*

He'd been in the workout room for almost an hour. One of the reasons he'd picked the sprawling two-story house—besides its being only four blocks from Suzanna Quinn's—was because of this finished area in the basement with its high ceilings and rows of windows. Joe wanted a place to exercise that wasn't claustrophobic; he'd insisted on state-of-the-art workout equipment to keep in shape, even though they'd be here only a few months. Secret Service agents couldn't afford to go to flab.

Besides, you're almost forty-six.

Over-the-hill, Josie had said on the last birthday she spent with him. She'd been fifteen, and he'd turned forty-two.

Still, he was in good shape. He noticed that women routinely checked him out. But many of them were attracted to the supposed glamour of his position. He *had* seen the high school teachers take a second look, though, and they didn't know he was a Secret Service agent.

"And what do *you* think, Suzie Q?" he asked aloud.

Shit!

He had no business wondering if she found him attractive. It didn't matter if she saw him as Quasimodo or Mel Gibson. The situation was too urgent for him to be distracted by frivolous things, and Suzanna Quinn had the potential to be a huge distraction. He did another curl just for good measure, then hit the treadmill. He was puffing hard, wiping the sweat from his face despite the lightweight T-shirt and gym shorts he wore, when he heard clomping on the stairs.

Ludzecky appeared all too soon. Joe glanced at his watch.

"You know what time it is?" Luke asked.

"Don't you have some homework to do?"

"What's got your jocks in a twist?"

"Your suspension," Joe lied.

"It shouldn't." The kid plunked down on a step. "Ben

Franzi called tonight and thanked me for helpin' out his buddy Smurf. He asked if we could jam this weekend."

"You're getting TLC from everybody. Including the lovely Ms. Cunningham."

"What does that mean?"

"Nothing."

"You seem to keep forgettin' I'm not a kid," Ludzecky said. "You got a problem, spill it."

Joe kept running and held his tongue. He knew he had to do something about this tension between the two of them. It wasn't caused only by Ludzecky getting Joe shot last time. The kid was the exact opposite of him in personality, and they grated each other like sandpaper on skin most of the time. But they had to work together.

"I got a problem with you alienating Duchamp and his gang. But you're on the right track with Franzi. Good job."

Ludzecky took a deep breath, as if the friction between them wore on him, too. "Thanks." He studied the floor. "Suzanna say anything about my suspension?"

"She was sympathetic to both of us."

"Really? She like me?"

Joe pictured pretty brown eyes smiling when she discussed the young agent. Her teeth were perfectly even, and she had full lips that she often painted peach. "She likes all kids."

"Her son's lucky."

So was her husband. Truth be told, Joe wondered about Lawrence Quinn. Fifteen years her senior. Rhodes Scholar. Was the guy good. . . .

Ruthlessly he cut off the thought. He had no business thinking about her husband. Or her. Or any woman. Though most FBI agents could lead fairly ordinary lives, the Secret Service lifestyle was nomadic; agents were always traveling—some were out of town forty weeks in the calendar year. Not to mention the danger they faced; most women couldn't tolerate the thought of their men intentionally jumping in front of bullets meant for others. Or going undercover, which could hold equal jeopardy. The Secret Service had a higher divorce rate than police, firefighters, or any other dangerous profession.

Clearly, Joe shouldn't make Suzanna, or her life with her husband, his business. In the long run, any feelings for her could go nowhere. That he'd even think about all this was an anomaly in his disciplined personality. To completely banish the thoughts, he ran faster.

"JIMMY, tell us what happened after you asked Rush Webster to leave you alone." Josh Quinn's voice rang out steadily in the conference room of his mother's office. The space, like others in the school, was homey with its paneled walls, upholstered chairs, and thick carpet. There were even pink carnations on a sideboard. Joe had seen vases of flowers in Suzanna's office a few times. Did a man send them to her?

Josh sat at an oval table with his friend Morgan Kane and three other students, constituting Fairholm's Student Court. A few witnesses and the defendants, the court's supervisor, the principal, and the assistant principal completed the circle. Slowly Joe was learning who were the movers and shakers of the school.

Red hair sticking up in all different directions, freckles popping out all over his face, Jimmy pressed his glasses up his nose. Not only did his surname lend itself to the epithet Smurf, so did his looks. "Webster pushed me into the bench. My tray fell and spilled tomato soup all down my leg." The boy glanced worriedly to the end of the table, where Webster stared down and drummed his fingers on the wood surface. His hair had fallen over his eyes, so Joe couldn't see their expression. But his mouth was a grim slash in his too-slim face. His body always seemed to be in motion.

"Then what happened?" Josh asked.

Jimmy fidgeted. The kid was nervous. Joe didn't blame him. Webster was a powder keg, and Jimmy's plump stature and general geek status made him a prime target for bullying. Joe made a mental note to look into Smurf's background.

In his two weeks here, Joe and Luke had begun to home in on which kids should be watched. Webster was at the top of the list, and Joe had studied his folder. He had a history of angry outbursts at school and he consistently used foul language. He was also as antsy as a three-year-old; he should have been tested for ADD. But he lived in a group home, and his parents had done little for him.

"Somebody got Webster off me," Jimmy was saying.

"Who?"

Smurfella's eyes lit up. Joe shook his head. Though he didn't get along with Ludzecky, the guy had a way with people, especially kids. "Luke. Um, Luke Ludzecky. Holy cow, Josh, he tore Webster right off me."

Josh turned away to hide a grin. It reminded Joe of the way Suzanna tried to conceal a smile. Josh had her blond hair, too; Joe wondered what Suzanna's hair looked like out of its knot.

"What happened next?" Josh asked.

"As soon as Luke let go of him, Webster swung around and threw a punch."

Slouched next to his *uncle,* dressed in his habitual uniform of tattered jeans and a shirt hanging out of his pants, Luke rubbed his chin.

Joe leaned over. "Timing off, son?"

Luke grunted.

"Did Luke punch Webster back?"

"Yeah, sure. When Webster came out swinging, Luke clocked him. Webster went sprawlin' halfway across the floor. His buddy Morton had to help him up."

Ludzecky cleared his throat, more than likely to hide smug male triumph. Testosterone ran heavy in his veins.

After a few more questions, Josh turned to Kelsey Cunningham, who sat with Suzanna at the midpoint of the table. "Ms. Cunningham, do you confirm or deny Jimmy's description of the fight?"

"I confirm it. Rush Webster hit Luke first."

"But Luke hit him back." Josh was trying to be fair. He'd make a good lawyer someday.

Kelsey's dark eyebrows rose. Tonight she wore a maroon high school sweatshirt, jeans, and boots—attire far too casual for faculty. Joe's gaze drifted to Suzanna's dark suit, which she'd accented with a pretty pink blouse and pearls.

"Well, of course Luke hit him back," Kelsey said haughtily. "Out of self-protection."

Which was for the court to decide.

Joe had wondered about this court since he first heard of it. Made up completely of students, and overseen by Kelsey, the panel dealt with the gray areas of policy. All school rules were sacrosanct. But in a case like this, where the punishment was suspension if the student threw a punch, yet the punch was thrown in self-defense, the court decided on a course of action. Suzanna would be present and give her input, but she'd abide by their decision. Joe thought the administration should make the determination, with the court's recommendation considered.

Kelsey answered a few more questions. Her gaze kept straying to Luke. She'd smile at him or nod reassuringly. Joe darted a glance at Luke. The kid's eyes were glued to the woman. Joe filed away that look, along with Ludzecky's whole demeanor around the young teacher, to think about later.

Then Luke gave his version of the incident. He told much the same story as the others. Damned if he didn't sound like a teenager with his slang and surly tone. He was good at his job, Joe would give him that.

Finally, it was Rush Webster's turn to speak. Once, in his early days with the Service, Joe had come face-to-face with a world-renowned counterfeiter who'd been hung up on child porn. Webster was a younger version of the man and had some of his mannerisms—the fidgetiness, the sneer, the barely suppressed anger. When Webster began to talk, he pushed his hair back. His eyes were cold slivers of brown in his face. "I didn't do nothing to Smurf. I was teasing him, only gave him a friendly shake of the shoulder, and he fell. Ask Morton." Webster's head whipped to Luke, who faced him down without blinking. "Then this jerkoff attacks me."

"Watch your mouth, Rush." Suzanna spoke for the first time.

He glared at her.

"Others said you struck first," Morgan Kane put in pointedly.

A gaze that could rip through steel leveled on Kelsey. Beside Joe, Luke tensed. "She got her favorites," Rush spit out.

"Witnesses besides Ms. C. confirmed it." Josh's voice was cool, but his eyes were troubled.

Rush's stare burrowed into Josh. "They didn't see right."

"Anything you want to add, Rush?" another court member asked.

A quick shake of his head. He fingered the chains hanging from the loops of his belt.

"All right." Josh stood. "That's it for the testimony. Time for the court to meet alone. We'll go to the office. Anybody can wait to find out our decision or you can hear about it tomorrow."

After the court members filed into the office, Webster threw back his chair, upending it, and strode out the door. Joe caught sight of a young girl in the hall waiting for him. She handed him a leather jacket, and they hurried out of sight.

Mulling over what to do about Webster, Joe meandered to the sideboard and poured a cup of coffee. Next to the pot, the carnations gave out a sweet scent.

Luke approached him. "What do you think?"

Joe put a hand on his shoulder. "I—"

"Luke." Kelsey Cunningham's voice cut into Joe's response.

Luke pivoted. "Uh, Ms. C. Thanks for the support."

She grasped Luke's arm. "*I* should thank *you*. Webster would have made mincemeat out of me." Subtly she drew him to the side, to talk to him alone. As they spoke, the kid grinned down at her; her smile was thousand-watt in return.

Jesus, Joe thought. *What the hell—*

Suzanna came up to him with another woman in tow. "Joe, while we're waiting, someone wants to meet you."

Joe looked over Suzanna's shoulder. A tall, thin woman, dressed in chic New York style, stared at him out of Hummel doll eyes. Her hair was short and cut around her face.

He recognized her.

•   •   •

SUZANNA smiled up at Joe. "This is Brenda Way; she's a reporter for the *Fairholm Gazette*."

Though Joe's expression remained unchanged, his eyes flashed with surprise.

"Brenda," Suzanna continued, "this is Dr. Joe Stonehouse. Our new crisis counselor."

"Crisis counselor, huh?" Brenda's tough-cookie veneer was in high gear tonight, though her usually pale complexion showed color. "Nice to meet you, *Dr.* Stonehouse."

"Ms. Way. Nice to meet you, too."

"Brenda's got her finger on the pulse of the school," Suzanna said. "Warts and all. She usually covers the Student Court, but she had another meeting tonight, so she just stopped by."

"How interesting." Joe's tone was neutral.

Suzanna gave her friend a one-armed hug. "Not compared to where she came from. But we love her."

"Where she came from?"

"Big city. Bright lights." Brenda's tone was almost taunting. Honestly, sometimes Suzanna didn't understand her former college roommate's behavior around handsome men.

"She was a hotshot reporter for the *Times,* got tired of New York, and came to Fairholm for a change of pace."

"Were you raised here?" Joe asked.

"No. Suzanna and I were roommates at Vassar. We parted ways after she married Prince Charming. When I left the city, I thought Fairholm would be a good place to settle, with the added benefit of being near my best friend."

Stiffly, Joe nodded.

"I'd like to do an article on you for the paper, Dr. Stonehouse."

"That's not a good idea. I'd rather keep a low profile."

Suzanna thought Brenda muttered, "I'll bet," but her attention was distracted by someone tugging on her arm.

Kelsey had come up behind her. "I have to go, Suzanna. I'm expecting a call from my father. Phone me later? I'd like to know what happens."

"Sure. Thanks for everything," Suzanna said.

Luke, who still leaned against the wall, straightened. "Thanks again for tryin' to help, Ms. C."

"You're welcome. I hope I see you tomorrow. We're going to start studying special areas in the U.S. government."

Luke's face brightened. "Special areas?"

"Yeah, the FBI, CIA, and Secret Service."

The coffee Joe had been drinking sloshed over his hand.

"Geez, I'd hate to miss that," Luke said enthusiastically.

For some reason, Joe glared at his nephew. The vibes between them were crazier tonight than usual.

Kelsey left, and Suzanna was distracted by her assistant principal. When she finished with Lester, she noticed that Brenda was gone. So was Joe. She approached Luke. "Luke, did your uncle leave?"

"I don't know, Mrs. Quinn."

She squeezed his arm in support. "You worried?"

He shrugged.

"No matter what the court decides, Luke, if you did stop those guys from picking on Smurf, thanks for doing it. We all need to take care of each other. I plan to speak to Morton and Webster myself about this bullying that seems to have cropped up."

She smiled, turned away, and saw the conference room door was open. Slipping out, she glanced down the hall. It was empty. She started to go back in, but heard voices. Following them, she got close enough to make out what they were saying.

"You don't understand what's at stake here." Joe's voice was cut-glass cold.

"Then tell me, hotshot. I might be washed up in New York, but I still got what it takes. And I care about Suzanna. What's this crap about you being a psychologist?"

Suzanna strode up to them.

Brenda whirled around. Her dark eyes were troubled. Stonehouse looked at Suzanna with a furrowed brow and angry scowl.

"What's going on here?" Suzanna asked.

FIVE

ONCE again, Suzanna faced Joe Stonehouse, Luke Ludzecky, and her superintendent in the top administrator's office. Only this time, it was ten o'clock at night, and Brenda Way was also there. Suzanna sensed something was *really* wrong.

They'd had to wait for Joe's explanation; he'd asked her to be patient, and said he'd tell her everything as soon as the Student Court was over. She'd been shocked to see him whip out his cell phone and call Ross Maloney to set up this meeting as if they were the best of friends or long-term colleagues.

Brenda said absolutely nothing and, after his call, Joe held a hushed conversation with his nephew. The atmosphere in the conference room was tense until the verdict came about a half-hour later. Based on testimony, Luke got a day's suspension, and Webster got five; the one they'd served today counted. Now, however, the whole incident seemed insignificant compared to what was going on with Joe and Brenda.

Ross began the meeting much as he'd done the last time. "Suzanna, I'd like you to listen with an open mind to what we're going to tell you."

Because she liked and respected Ross Maloney, she nodded.

Joe faced Brenda, looking bigger and more intimidating in his navy power suit than he had earlier. "And Ms. Way, I expect this information will remain confidential. I've included you because of our prior acquaintance. If you won't cooperate, I have to ask you to leave."

Brenda's dark brown eyes flashed with pique. "I would never do anything to hurt Suzanna or her school."

Then Ross said bluntly, "Suzanna, Luke and Joe are government agents."

"Agents?" She glanced at Brenda, who obviously knew this. Then she looked back at Ross.

"From the Secret Service."

"The Secret Service?" She sounded like an idiot, parroting Ross, but this had the earmarks of a TV special, not real life in Suburbia, USA. "I don't—" She stopped abruptly when his words sank in. "*Luke* is a Secret Service agent?"

The boy, who'd abandoned his adolescent slouch, gave her a self-effacing grin. "Others have a tough time believin' it, too, Suzanna."

It was odd to hear him use her first name. For weeks she'd thought this man was a kid, though there had been something oddly adult about him.

Stonehouse continued. "We're both from a new division of the Secret Service. Do you know what the National Threat Assessment Center is?"

Suzanna shook her head, but Brenda nodded. "*I've* read about it. It's a center that was established in the nineties to analyze threats made on public figures."

"Yes. NTAC's origin was investigating assassins. We call it targeted violence."

Suzanna remembered the term from reading she'd done. About school shootings.

Joe confirmed the connection she made in her mind. "A while ago, the Secret Service, in conjunction with the Department of Education, came out with a Threat Assessment document about school shooters. It was called the Safe School Initiative." She watched him. A muscle twitched in his rigid jaw, betraying emotion she hadn't seen from him before. Obviously, this was important to him.

"I read about the government's work in that area," she finally said.

Joe shoved his hands in his pockets. He was leaning against the wall, his shoulders stiff inside the navy wool. Occasionally, he raked a hand through his short hair. "Agent Ludzecky and I are part of a task force formed a few years ago as a result of that study. Its purpose is to prevent school shootings." Stonehouse straightened, the action heralding an important announcement.

Suzanna tensed, feeling as if she was about to receive a blow.

"Specifically, my team collects information on schools across the country and zeros in on those which have characteristics that could lead to an eruption of planned violence."

"Has my school been identified as one?" The thought made her stomach roil, and she clasped her hands together across her middle.

"Yes."

Brenda let out a low whistle.

Luke looked over at Suzanna and smiled sympathetically.

Suzanna shook her head. "I know we have fights, and racial conflicts sometimes, but all schools do." She thought a minute. "And of course kids were really affected by 9/11."

"We don't concern ourselves with ordinary juvenile aggression. You're right; your school is no different from any other institution of a similar size with similar demographics. And the kids *were* traumatized by 9/11. But other things have brought us to Fairholm."

"What?"

"Several risk factors."

"What are they?" Brenda asked impatiently. Suzanna remembered that tone from college when she strung out a story or explanation.

Joe addressed Suzanna. "We told you some of the truth at our first meeting. The suicide of Zach Riley last month started the whole thing. Do you remember the note he left?"

"Yes." How could she forget? The poignant, often funny

missive had made her cry at night for weeks. "It had messages for some of the faculty and students."

"There was a threat against you mentioned in it."

"Oh, that. Lots of the kids would like to see me . . . what did it say, *go down*."

Moving to Ross's desk, Joe drew a paper out of a briefcase he'd set there. He put on glasses from his pocket. "Specifically, it reads, 'Mrs. Quinn, some people in this school want to see you go down and they say they're going to make it happen. Watch out.'"

She cocked her head.

"The note warns you of a threat made against your life."

"Really? I thought it. . . ." She glanced at her boss. "We talked about this, didn't we, Ross? That maybe there was a sexual innuendo in the message."

Steepling his hands, the superintendent nodded to Stonehouse. "*They* don't see it that way."

"How did they get the note, anyway?" Brenda asked.

Stonehouse assumed control of the meeting, like a commander taking charge of a mission. "A while ago, our School Threat Assessment Team, which we call STAT, contacted superintendents across the country, explaining some of the risk factors that might indicate a threshold of concern."

At Suzanna's questioning look, he explained, "A threshold of concern is evidence that an individual or group of individuals might be on a path to violent action."

Still stunned, Suzanna stared blankly at him.

"Initially, we advised administrators to be cognizant of several factors. When we got in full swing, we asked the school districts to fill out forms, and notify us with updates, so we could keep a data bank on what was happening in each institution." His faced turned even more sober. "We've come up with a list of red flags for all schools to watch for."

Suzanna frowned. "I've seen this kind of list in publications on school violence. The indicators were things like students who are picked on or bullied; students who feel isolated; students who've shown an unusual interest in violent TV and video games."

Ever the reporter, Brenda straightened. "Profiling isn't reliable. The report on assassinations wasn't beneficial because there wasn't any one profile common to potential assassins."

Stonehouse began to pace. "You're right. STAT isn't based on profiling, or predicting, behavior in kids. Instead, it focuses on precluding violence, preventing it. We computer-analyze high schools that send us information." He shot a glance at Ross. "Several indicators sent to us by Dr. Maloney brought us to your school. Two recently. They were what caused our . . . urgency."

The knowledge that all this activity had been going on behind her back, that Ross had put two agents in her school without telling her, angered Suzanna, but she struggled not to overreact. After Zach's suicide, they couldn't afford any more catastrophes. "All right, tell me the rest. But let me say that this whole undercover thing doesn't sit right with me, and being kept in the dark about it is completely unacceptable."

A spark of admiration lit Stonehouse's eyes. "Well, maybe I can change how you feel. First, as we said earlier, Riley's note to you indicates a student or group of students has threatened you. Not overtly. But threats from violent offenders are rarely made directly. Shooters usually just tell other kids."

"You think someone told Zach?"

"Yes. Or he overheard a student brag about it."

She frowned, truly pained by this revelation. "I wish he'd told me. I had a good relationship with him."

"Kids don't tell the target. They don't tell adults at all." Joe glanced meaningfully at Luke. "But they do tell other kids."

"Ah, so we have the cute Agent Ludzecky in place to win their confidences," Brenda put in.

Luke smiled and Stonehouse frowned.

Suzanna was confused. "Are you sure about all this? My professional experience indicates that kids would tell their teachers, at least the ones they're close to."

"That's an erroneous assumption. I'll give you a case in point. Evan Ramsey, a shooter in Alaska who killed his principal and a student, and wounded two others, told some of his classmates about his plans. The kids gathered on the library balcony to watch. When those who knew were asked why they didn't tell an adult, they said it seemed like a betrayal. It didn't seem right."

Horrified at the anecdote, Suzanna was silent.

Her reaction seemed to unnerve him. "Look, Suzanna, our plan is based on research. The team collected information about past school shootings and the shooters themselves. Our study involved forty-one attackers who were current or recent students at the school targeted. We reviewed primary sources from law enforcement officials, mental health people, and school personnel. Each incident and each shooter were then reviewed by investigators from the Secret Service, social workers, independent psychologists, and educational experts. We compiled a file for each case. In addition, we conducted supplemental interviews with ten of the attackers to get their perspective on their decisions to engage in a school-based attack. Our findings are supported by that research."

Suzanna had had no idea of the report's scope. "I'm impressed."

"As I said, your school has enough indicators to bring us here." He returned to Ross's desk and drew another paper out of his briefcase.

"What are they?"

"Well, as I said, number one is that Zach's note indicates a threat made against you."

All right, she'd concede that if the Secret Service said so.

"You have the typical problems with teenage depressions and loss, but we came for other reasons. Though I expect to help there, too." He scowled. "And with bullying. Some of the most recent eruptions of violence in schools have been due to bullying. And it's a little-known fact that twelve students per year commit suicide because they're bullied."

"But can't we do that aboveboard—bring in regular counselors to help? Do we need the Secret Service to help these kids?"

"You wouldn't, if that's all we found. But Riley's note indicates a threat." He held up the paper. "And then we found this."

Her heart began a slow gallop in her chest. "What is it?"

He said quietly, "It's a hit list. Or at least part of one."

Stunned, Suzanna gripped the arms of the chair. "There's a hit list for my school?"

"Goddamn!" Brenda breathed.

Ross nodded. "It was turned over to us before we brought in the Secret Service. It's the reason we acted quickly. The owner of Pickles"—the local kids' hangout—"discovered it. It appears to target the high school."

Briefly, Suzanna buried her head in her hands. *Oh, my God.* She allowed herself to feel bad for only a few moments, then she gathered every ounce of strength she had and faced Stonehouse. "Appears to?"

Joe crossed to her and handed her the note. Brenda sidled in, and they read it carefully. It was a photocopy of a ragged piece of paper. At the top was the word *Kill.* Underneath were *uinn, ranzi, ingham,* as well as several other partial names.

"Are you sure this is a hit list?"

"Our experts in Washington analyzed it. We were sure enough to move in."

Only an idiot would ignore something like this. Collecting herself, Suzanna sat up straighter. "All right, I can see why we'd be singled out by your task force." She breathed deeply. "We need help. But do you have the right to just bulldoze your way into my building and do it with all this cloak-and-dagger?"

Stonehouse bristled. "The government of the United States has the right to plan and execute covert operations for the safety of its population. Members of our team always go into the schools undercover and alert as few people as possible." He added pointedly, "Besides, your top administration approved it."

She frowned. "Always? You've done this before?"

"Yes, in pairs, at five other schools, so far. All I can tell you is we've been successful in stopping the violence and that our operations were well-planned and well-executed maneuvers."

"You've been busy little beavers," Brenda said.

Suzanna ignored her. "I always thought kids just snapped

when they committed violence like this. Is it always so planned?"

"They don't just snap," Joe said, passion infusing his voice. "That's a dangerous misconception. Shooters *plan* their actions. They *pick* their targets." He paused, then went on just as heatedly. "Suzanna, if we're in there with you, if we see the kids are on a route to violence, we can roadblock it and get them help. Hopefully, before anybody is hurt."

Suzanna's insides grew cold. A hit list, even scraps of one, was heavy stuff. Yet this kind of subversive activity in her building was anathema to her. "I hate this kind of thing," she said, the conflict stirring inside her like a fight brewing. "But I can see that we need help." Her eyes narrowed on the superintendent. "Not that I agree it's ethically right. And, for God's sake, Ross, this is my building. If I'm in danger, if kids are in danger, I should have known about it."

Joe and Ross exchanged another look. Ross said, "Because of your philosophy of openness with the staff, of total honesty with the kids, we thought you might balk. And after the hit list, the agents had to get in here fast. We were afraid you'd delay it."

That didn't convince her. Stonehouse watched her, then said, almost gently, "The Secret Service also knows about your background, Suzanna. About your father."

Her eyes widened. "*What?* I've never told anyone about that."

"What's he talking about, Suzanna?" Ross asked.

She could feel the color leech from her face. She simply stared at Stonehouse. He stared back.

"Suzanna, are you all right?" Brenda gripped her arm.

Finally, she nodded, thinking about her strict but hardworking father who'd been a victim of the government's watchdog mentality. "I'm fine." Shakily, she stood and moved behind the chair. "I don't want to discuss this."

Stonehouse said nothing.

Luke spoke. "I'm sorry, Suzanna. I know this is a horrible invasion of privacy."

She ignored him, kept her back to all of them for a moment.

"Why hasn't the media covered your work after you leave each school?" Brenda, bless her heart, changed the subject.

Stonehouse was silent a while longer. Then he answered Brenda. "Because it's completely covert and must remain that way. To keep this hushed up, after we leave a town where we went undercover, we have no contact whatsoever with the people in the school." His voice became steely. "As I said earlier, secrecy is a requirement, Ms. Way. The whole situation *cannot* leak out. It *cannot* be revealed, or our operation will be shut down."

"Are you trying to quell freedom of the press, Stonehouse?"

"No, I'm telling you that you will *not* reveal this information to anyone unless you want to be responsible for endangering hundreds of students in Fairholm High School."

Brenda said, "Pretty heavy artillery."

"I've got bigger guns." He said the words almost apologetically. "Josh Quinn is a student in that school. Often it's the popular kids and teachers who are the targets. Especially ones involved in things like Student Court, ones who make *un*popular decisions."

Suzanna spun around. "Oh, my God!"

"We can't protect kids like Josh, or teachers like Kelsey Cunningham, unless we can get into their schools. If our operation becomes public, we're shut down." Joe cleared his throat. "It's vital that this be completely secret. Only selected personnel from each school know about the undercover work. So Suzanna, no one else, including your assistant principals and your teachers, can be let in on this." He faced Brenda. "And you, Ms. Way, may *not* write about it."

Again, Suzanna was stunned into silence.

He raised his chin. "As far as everyone's concerned, I'm the district's new crisis counselor, employed by Fairholm Central Schools, housed at the secondary building." He glanced at Luke. "And this is my incorrigible nephew."

"You're here to nail the kids," Brenda said.

"I am a trained psychologist. The degrees are real. I like to think I can do some good for the kids and students, as well as preclude the violence."

Ross put in quickly, "And he's a law enforcement official.

Besides being here to ferret out information from parents and kids, Suzanna, he can protect you. Your life has been threatened. You need somebody to stay close."

Her gaze whipped to Stonehouse. "You're going to play Big Brother with my kids and teachers, *and* be my watchdog?"

He didn't take the Orwellian reference well. His jaw hardened. "We'd hoped you'd go along willingly. This is important."

She stood, straightened her suit jacket, and faced the superintendent. "Ross, I disapprove of this spying on my staff and students. But"—she held up the papers—"I can see that we need help. Even from the government. I'll cooperate with what you want to do, but I'll also go on record that I think this is a violation of personal rights *and* the First Amendment. And it's against everything I've preached to my kids and staff about openness and honesty and democracy for five years." She glanced at Joe, remembering his words. *It's the popular kids, and teachers.* . . . She thought of her son, and of Kelsey Cunningham. "I just wish there were some other way to do it as effectively as undercover work."

Joe said, "There's no other way, Suzanna. You're going to have to let go of your principles to protect your kids, your staff." He waited a moment, then added, "And your son."

SIX

SHIVERING, Brenda drew her cashmere sweater close around her shoulders, blew smoke from her cigarette into Suzanna's backyard and counted her blessings. Could anything be more fitting than this? It was as if some journalistic deity had bestowed a second chance on the prodigal son. Or, in this case, the prodigal daughter.

"Brend, come back in. I need to *talk* about this." Sounding like she used to when she'd nag Brenda to come off the roof at college, where Brenda snuck cigarettes, Suzanna stood in the doorway of the kitchen and beckoned her inside. The woman still looked exquisitely groomed and attired at ten o'clock at night. Sometimes, it was hard to be best friends with Ms. Perfect.

"Hold your horses, I got an addiction."

"One you've conquered many times."

Taking a last drag and stubbing the cigarette out in Suzanna's geranium box, she headed back into the Quinn domain.

"I made minestrone for dinner earlier." Suzanna leaned against the granite counter. Up close, her friend's face revealed mauve smudges beneath her eyes. Brenda regretted her earlier unkind thought about being perfect. If anyone knew how Suzanna took things to heart, it was Brenda. "Want some?"

"No. I need some coffee. High-test, if you have it." Sitting down at the butcher block table, Brenda drew in a deep breath. A potpourri of homey smells—coffee, Italian spices, and bread dough—filled the air. "Fine kettle of fish, isn't it?"

Suzanna shook her head, dislodging the knot that she usually wore at the back of her neck. Frustrated, she pulled out the tie, and let her hair fall to her shoulders. "I can't believe it."

Brenda reached up and fingered her own short, auburn locks. Suzanna had shampoo commercial hair. It was thick and heavy, but the color was what snagged the eye. The unusual shade reminded Brenda of the wheat fields where she grew up in Idaho—a steely blond that sparkled in the track lighting over the counter.

Suzanna sighed as she poured coffee. "It sounds like a B movie, doesn't it?"

Which Brenda could turn into a number-one bestseller, given enough information and the balls to go public. She just nodded to her friend.

Suzanna carried the mugs of coffee to the table and sank onto the chair. "Not only am I furious, but I'm scared, Brend. My school, in danger?" Her brown eyes widened, and the moisture glistening in them turned them liquid with whiskey brightness. "And a hit list? It's incredible."

Loving the woman like a sister, even though she did play Pollyanna too often, Brenda reached out and grasped Suzanna's hand. "Hey, Suz, you know all schools are in danger these days, given what's happened at places like Columbine and Arkansas." She cocked her head. "I've seen this thing about hit lists, too, in the media. Kids do it as a prank. Or to let off steam. Even when they're serious, the lists aren't necessarily acted on."

"It's serious enough to make my school targeted by the Secret Service."

"I know. That's tough to digest."

Delicately, Suzanna sipped her coffee. Lawrence had told Brenda once that it was Suzanna's china-doll mannerisms that had first attracted him to his wife. "Thanks for cooperating."

Brenda arched a brow.

"By agreeing to keep this under wraps."

Well, she hadn't exactly *agreed*. What she'd said was she would never do anything to jeopardize Suzanna or her school. Which she wouldn't. But afterward . . . screw the secrecy that the government spies thought was so important.

"Especially since I know you feel as strongly about this kind of deception as I do."

Brenda didn't respond.

Absently, Suzanna ran her fingertip around the rim of the steaming mug. "Did you meet Joe in New York?"

Brenda's shoulders straightened. It was crucial that she not reveal too much tonight—even to Suzanna—before she had time to figure things out. "I met him during that famous counterfeiting case with Spike Romano. Since the Secret Service is a division of the Treasury Department, they were in charge. When they found out about Romano's kiddie porn operation in New York, some of the agents flew up to join the FBI and take him down. Romano was arrested, and there was a press conference."

"I'm surprised Joe was so visible. Don't Secret Service agents usually stay in the background?"

"He wasn't in charge of the case, the FBI was. But the Secret Service had been after this guy for a long time, so he worked in tandem with them." Brenda shrugged. "It was before Stonehouse got into covert operations, I guess. And it was years ago." When they were both younger and less cautious. The incident was right after Conrad Schenk had died. Brenda had missed her mentor so much, she'd acted . . . indiscreetly for months afterward.

"I see." Suzanna shook her head. "I can't get a bead on Joe. Even after working with him for a couple of weeks."

"What do you mean?"

"Well, he's great with kids. Thank God, he's a real counselor, or I'd have to put a halt to this. And he's good. He's asked some of the students down to his office on get-to-know-you pretenses and unearthed a lot of their problems by just talking to them. He's already started some significant groups. Hell, I even encouraged Josh to see him." She frowned. "But Joe seems so cold most of the time."

Brenda smiled. "The women teachers don't think he's hot?"

Suzanna shrugged. "Kelsey said she thought he had a nice butt." She closed her eyes. "I'll have to keep this from Kelsey. That's a problem."

"Why?"

"It's just that she has such a thing about trust. I've been the only adult in her life not to betray her trust, and if she finds out about this—that I kept this from her—it will hurt her more than I can say."

"She's an adult, Suzanna. Not the kid you took in. She should be able to handle it if she finds out."

"No, it'll be a problem. Especially since she's taken a special interest in Luke. And she's getting to know Joe, too. She won't take being deceived by them, and me, well."

Brenda ran her thumbnail around the lettering on her mug, which read *World's Greatest Mom*. "Do you think Joe's attractive?"

"He works for me, Brenda."

"Ah, no, he doesn't."

"Well, I thought he did."

"No chemistry?"

"Nope, not an iota. Not a spark. Not a millimeter."

They'd had this kind of conversation before, at three in the morning in the dorm room, while they sipped beer and discussed the male species. The memory brought a smile to Brenda's lips. "The party line when you're attracted to a guy, Suz."

"What?"

"The lady doth protest too much, methinks."

"Okay, I like his eyes. They're the warmest thing about him."

Not necessarily, Brenda thought.

"How did we get on this, anyway? I'm in the middle of the biggest crisis of my career and we're talking about how hot this guy is."

"Sorry. What are you going to do?"

"Do?"

"Yeah, you gonna go along when it violates every one of your principles?" She hesitated. "Ones I happen to agree with." Their belief in openness, their distaste for underhanded tactics, especially by the government, were the things they had in common. They'd met because of those beliefs.

"Of course I'm going along with it. What choice do I have?"

"There are always choices."

Suzanna smiled. "That's what you said at the first rally you spearheaded at Vassar. I remember how vehement you were, how much I admired you for speaking your mind." She smiled. "And Conrad was so proud of you. He left for the *Times* job in the city right after that, didn't he?"

"Yes." Where she'd followed him once she'd graduated. "You were just as vehement as I was, Suz. Then, anyway."

Suzanna scraped back the chair, stood, and crossed to the triple glass doors looking out over the cedar deck.

Brenda turned around and faced her friend's back. "I'm sorry if I've offended you."

"It's okay. I'm tired, is all."

Deftly changing the subject, Brenda asked, "Want to tell me what all that was about your father? You never said much about him, except that he died before you were born."

"I don't want to talk about it. I never could."

Brenda stood and crossed to Suzanna. Though she wasn't a toucher, she squeezed her friend's shoulders. "You should get some sleep. You're tired. It'll all look better in the morning. I promise."

Her hands clamping her elbows, Suzanna stared out into the starless sky.

"Come on, walk me to the door," Brenda said.

Suzanna turned. Arm-in-arm, they made their way to the foyer.

"It'll be okay, Suz, I know it will. You'll pull this off with finesse, like everything else you've done in your life." Suzanna had never bungled anything.

"Thanks for your confidence. You've always been so good for me." She smiled at Brenda, then studied her. "You all right? You seem a little distracted."

Shrugging into her calf-length red leather coat, Brenda shook her head. "I'm fine." She gave her friend a peck on the cheek. She was fine. But she needed a drink. Just one. Bad. "See you soon."

Outside, in the cold night air, Brenda took in a deep breath and whispered, "Oh, I'm fine, all right. And I'm gonna be a hell of a lot better."

Brenda might be a fuckup in a lot of areas, but she stuck to her principles, to her beliefs. Conrad had taught her to do that. This time, it was going to get her back on top where she belonged.

JOE waited until Brenda Way's little Miata pulled out of Suzanna's driveway, then exited his nondescript sedan and hurried up the slate walkway to the porch of the brick house. Cold night air prickled his face, and he stuck his hands in his coat pockets.

The sprawling contemporary was too big for Suzanna and her son. With thoughts of not alerting that son to his visit, Joe tapped the brass knocker lightly, hoping Suzanna was in the vicinity.

The door swung open. "Did you forget some— Oh, Joe."

For the first time in recent memory, Joe Stonehouse was speechless. Suzanna stood before him in such delicious dishabille that he'd truly have to be Iron Man not to react. He drew his beige raincoat closed over his trousers and took in a very deep breath. "Hi. Sorry to disturb you."

Her hand flew to the delicate pink blouse she'd obviously started to remove. Four buttons were undone, revealing a lacy pink bra underneath. Creamy white pearls nestled against even creamier skin, and all that glorious hair was unbound.

Turning, she fumbled with her buttons. "Um, come on in."

He stepped into the foyer.

She faced him again, the blouse closed, but that hair still wild around her now rosy cheeks. "What are you doing here?"

Good question. "I don't exactly know." He raked a hand through his own hair. "I . . . felt like we should talk after what you found out tonight." *And I was worried about you.*

Crossing her arms over her chest, she said, "I don't think there's much to say."

He glanced up the oak staircase behind her. "Is Josh asleep?"

"He's not home. He's staying overnight at a friend's. They had to work on a project after Student Court, and he called to say he was going to sleep there."

"Are you sure that's where he is?"

"Why wouldn't he be?"

"Kids get into all kinds of trouble when their parents think they're overnight somewhere."

She shook back her hair. "I trust my son. And I resent that accusation about his honesty."

"I'm sorry. I guess I'm just naturally suspicious." When she said no more, he did. "Look, Suzanna, I didn't come here to discuss your parenting skills. I came to answer any questions you might have, and to explain a few things." His gaze darted to the big modern grandfather clock behind her. "I know it's late. But may I come in for a minute?" He indicated the living room.

"I guess. It might clear the air."

After she hung up his coat, he followed her to the left, trying to keep his eyes off her bare feet. And shapely legs. Hell, what had gotten in to him tonight?

She indicated that he should sit on a tapestry sofa, and she took the matching love seat. He scanned the huge room with the skylights and floor-to-ceiling windows. An Aubusson carpet covered the hardwood floors. On an inlaid oak table sat flowers—daffodils. "Nice place."

Her eyes sparked with fire. "Haven't you seen it before?"

"Excuse me?"

"You don't have pictures of my house? Know how much I owe on my car? Checked out the catalog where I buy my underwear?"

He winced inwardly, but kept the stoic mask in place. "No, Suzanna, I don't know any of those things."

"I don't believe you. If you know about my father, then you know all that."

Joe realized he needed to proceed carefully—maybe it *had* been a mistake to keep her in the dark. "I'm sorry about your father. Sorry it happened. Sorry I know, when you've gone to great lengths to keep his story private."

Her eyes moistened, socking him in the gut.

"Did you ever tell *anybody*?"

Biting her lip, she looked away. "Lawrence knew. Brenda and I attended a seminar he gave at Vassar on government ethics—which, by the way, all the participants thought was an oxymoron. It's how I met him." Her gaze hardened. "But you probably know that."

He said as gently as he could, "I know about Lawrence."

"He was a good man. Integrity was crucial to him." Her look said, *Unlike you.* The unfair assessment stung, but he held his tongue.

"Is Josh like him?"

"Exactly. He got the best of Lawrence—his moral code, his belief in fairness, and his work ethic."

"And yours." Sitting forward, Joe linked his hands and dangled them between his knees. "Suzanna, what bothers you the most about all this?" He didn't need to clarify the *all this.*

Thoughtful, she stared over her shoulder a minute. "That it's unethical."

"In your view. Not in everybody's." When she said no more, he asked, "What else?"

She waited to answer. "Maybe that you know everything about me, have known it from the beginning. And you're a complete stranger to me. It's like taking my clothes off in front of someone who's still dressed."

He wished she'd drawn a different analogy; the images her words conjured made him uncomfortable.

Her color rose. He'd noticed that blush, in conversations and faculty meetings, when she was impassioned by something. "I know nothing about you, Joe. And you know everything about me. I hate that." She stood and began to pace. The full skirt she wore swirled around her knees.

"I'm sorry," he said again.

"Are you?" She rounded on him, her arms crossed defensively over her chest. "Then even the playing field. Tell me something nobody knows about you."

His heartbeat escalated, but he'd become an expert at

steadying it. "A Secret Service agent's life is not an open book."

"Tell me *one* thing," she challenged. "One big thing that might make me be able to tolerate your intimate knowledge of my life. Your infiltration of my school."

He'd lie. He'd been backed into corners like this before and prevaricated his way out. Anything for the good of the job.

But at that moment, he was tired of the job. Of being Agent Stonehouse. Stone Man. He hadn't seen his sister Ruthie in a while, and she was the only person with whom he let down. So he said, "My niece—" When was the last time he'd spoken her name? The words caught in his throat. He studied the carpet under his shiny black wingtips. "She was killed in a school shooting a few years ago." He coughed again, cursing himself for spilling his guts. "It's why I pushed for STAT."

He heard the furnace turn on. Noticed the lights were dim. And before him, Josie's smiling face materialized. He didn't let himself think about her too much. It hurt when he remembered, and Secret Service agents couldn't afford to be distracted by pain. Damn it, why had he gotten into this?

Still staring at the floor, he felt a hand on his arm. He glanced at it. Her fingers were long and slender, soft and very feminine, with polished nails. "Joe, I'm sorry."

His throat felt like it was full of the cotton candy Josie had loved. "It's okay." He looked up into sympathetic eyes, panicked at what his must reveal. "It was a long time ago."

"Do you want to talk about it?"

He shook his head. He couldn't, not only because it *was* too painful, but because agents weren't supposed to reveal their personal lives—what personal lives they had. And the shooting had hit the papers, so Suzanna would be able to identify his family if she knew the circumstances. Besides his job, Joe had nothing else in his life but Ruthie, Al, and the kids, and he treasured them more than he could say.

Turning away, Suzanna crossed to the other side of the room. He watched her pour something out of a decanter, heard the clink of glass in the now too-silent house. She returned with two snifters of amber liquid.

"What is it?" he asked.

"Brandy." Like the color of her eyes. "We both can use it." She sank onto the couch with him. Not too far away. For some reason, her proximity calmed him.

"I'm sorry," she said again.

"So am I." They smiled at the repetition of their apology. He sipped the liquor. It was smooth and rich and went down fine. "Don't blame Maloney. It was my decision. He wanted to tell you. So did Ludzecky."

Despite the gravity of the situation, she smiled. "Ah, now, there's a topic."

Joe closed his eyes briefly and shook his head. "You don't know the half of it. The kid isn't my nephew, but believe me, he does see me as a reincarnation of Simon Legree."

"For a specific reason?"

"Yeah, we have some history."

When he didn't elaborate, she asked, "Why are you working together?"

"We needed to come in fast after the hit list was found."

Her face, which had relaxed, tightened again. "I'd like to see the documentation the task force has on my school and take a look at the Safe School Initiative."

"I'll provide you with what I can. Some of it's classified."

She didn't want that answer. But she sipped the brandy and it seemed to soothe her. "I can't believe this. It's a nightmare."

"Maybe one I can prevent."

He liked putting that hope in her eyes. "Can you?"

"I have before."

"Will you tell me about that? It might ease my fears."

"In general terms. We've been in five other schools. I've gone into three, outside of this one. They had similar problems. In one, we didn't find anybody who was truly violent, and so far the school's been safe. In the others, we did. In one of those, some violence erupted, but it wasn't widespread. Only an agent was hurt." *And that thanks to Ludzecky.*

"You?"

He rubbed his arm. "How did you know?"

"Good guess."

"In the other two, we got help for the kids we thought might erupt, and for the parents. We also instituted some staff training in the school. I believe we helped a lot of kids. Our follow-ups say they're still on track." He leaned forward, warming to the subject. For some reason, she resurrected a passion in him that he normally buried. "Suzanna, in some ways, our study is good news. It says we can *do* something about school violence. It puts the onus on adults to listen to kids, to recognize and ferret out their problems."

"We try to do that already, Joe. We always have."

"Yes, you do. But it's not enough. No school does enough. We have to look at the pieces more carefully, not just watch for black clothes and trench coats."

"What do you mean?"

"We need to read their writings with more attention, listen to the despair in their songs. We need to develop deeper bonds with them."

"By tricking them?"

He stiffened almost imperceptibly. "I'm a trained psychologist. I'm here to help kids. They'll never know they've been tricked. When I'm done, I'll just leave, hopefully having helped them over some emotional humps."

"I wish I could be sure we can avert this kind of thing."

"Earlier I mentioned Evan Ramsey. I was one of the interviewers who spoke with him in jail. When we asked him what he would have done if a principal or counselor had called him in and talked to him about what the kids had been hearing—that he was going to shoot people in school—he said he would have told the truth."

Her delicate eyebrows arched. "Really?"

Joe nodded.

"Well, that makes me feel better. Now if I can just get past deceiving my staff." She shook her head, sending disheveled waves around her face. "I've spent my whole career fighting against deceit. I've forced teachers to stop bitching in the staff lounge and be open about their gripes. I've encouraged kids to talk to teachers, and to me, instead of seething and holding grudges."

"Right now, deception's a necessary evil. Things aren't all black-and-white, Suzanna."

"Joe McCarthy's sentiments exactly."

He resented the comparison. "Still, they aren't." When she didn't respond, Joe asked about something else he needed to know tonight, before he ran the background check tomorrow. "Will Brenda Way keep this quiet, do you think?"

"Of course. We both will. I'll lie to Kelsey Cunningham, who I love like a daughter; to Josh, who would never forgive me if he knew what I'd allowed in school; to everybody else whose trust I've earned."

"Isn't saving their lives, and the lives of all your students, worth compromising your principles for a little while?"

She stared at him with eyes more potent than the liquor he drank. "Yes."

"Then we have a truce?"

She nodded.

"Can I mention something else?"

"Of course."

"We have to discuss security for you. I'll explain more tomorrow, when you've had a chance to internalize all this. But another fact we unearthed was that revenge was the motive of over half of the shooters we studied."

"Revenge on?"

"The school. The other kids. The staff members who discipline them, suspend them. The principal is a favorite target."

The fear on her face made something inside Joe shift. For one crazy minute, he wanted to comfort her. Take her in his arms and tell her it would be all right. Maybe even take *her*, and make her forget everything but the feel and taste and smell of him.

Jesus Christ, this is all I need. He downed the brandy in one more gulp and stood abruptly. "I'm going to leave."

She rose, too. "All right."

Following him to the foyer, she retrieved his coat. He shrugged into it, and with his hand on the door, faced her. "Do you have a security alarm?"

"Yes. But I don't always use it."

"From now on, you do. Especially when you're alone at night." He was surprised at how disconcerted that thought made him. "Put it on as soon as I leave." He hesitated, as if he might say more. "I'll see you tomorrow."

When he opened the door, she called out, "Joe?"

His hands fisted. He needed to get out of here. "Hmm?" He didn't turn to face her.

"I'm sorry about your niece."

Nodding, he walked into the night. But he waited on the porch until she closed the door and he heard the *snick* of the lock.

She was safe, at least for now.

SEVEN

"ALL right, I'll go with you to the Wild Strawberries concert Sunday night." Kelsey smiled at Mike Wolfe as she hurried down the hall, not wanting to be late for class.

"Yes!" Mike punched the air with his fist, like one of the kids, then slid his arm around her shoulders for a brief squeeze.

She sidled away. "What time do you—"

In the crowded hall, someone jostled them from behind, knocking Mike into her. "Hey, watch out!" Mike said.

"Oh, sorry. I was just tryin' to get to Ms. Cunningham's class on time."

Mike studied Luke Ludzecky. "You new here?"

Luke ducked his head and gave Kelsey a half-smile. "Yeah, just moved to Fairholm with my uncle."

"This is Luke Ludzecky, Joe Stonehouse's nephew." She smiled. "Luke, this is Mr. Wolfe. He teaches PE."

The boy went to hold out his hand, then retracted it. Odd behavior for a kid.

Without self-consciousness, Mike continued to study him—checking out Luke's bulging biceps and well-defined pecs, visible through the black T-shirt he wore with jeans. "You do any sports?"

"Nah, I'm not much of a team player."

Mike tested Luke's biceps. Some kids shrank from a teacher's touch, but Luke didn't. It was a sign of maturity, but Kelsey expected no less from Luke. He was mature. Almost too mature. "Think about going out for baseball, Luke. I need strong men."

Luke beamed. Though Mike was a jock, and conceited, he knew how to relate to kids. "All right, Mr. Wolfe. I will."

Throwing Kelsey a conspiratorial wink, Mike moved closer to her. "Now, I'll try to distract Ms. C. a little longer so you can beat her to class."

Something flashed in Luke's hazel eyes, but Kelsey couldn't decipher what it was. "Yeah. Fine." He scuffed down the hall in his battered boots.

"What kind of kid is he?" Mike asked as they followed at a distance.

"Hard to read. Supposedly, he's in trouble all the time. But I haven't seen any sign of it."

"No boys give you trouble, Kel."

"Rush Webster does. And his buddy Morton, though I don't have him in class."

"Webster would give the Devil himself trouble. Morton picks on kids littler than him. I'm on him all the time about it in gym class. I'll take both of them out, if you want. I like to play hero."

She was distracted from Mike's flirting by two kids making out behind a pole, a few doors down from her room. They were in a big-time lip lock.

"Ah, young love," Mike said, tracking her gaze.

Kelsey stopped, not amused. Crossing to the kids, she shook the boy's shoulder. "Josh."

He jumped back, red-faced and a little dazed. Geez, no wonder these kids couldn't think straight when they came to class. Arousal did that to you.

Though it had been a long time since a man had truly aroused her. Disturbed by the thought, she scowled at the boy who was like her brother. He'd been only five when she'd lived with the Quinns, but they had gotten close and remained so.

"Kelsey," Josh said.

Josh's partner, Heather Haywood, turned scarlet. "Oh, Ms. C."

"Guys, you know better." Her look communicated that Josh especially needed to watch it.

"Sorry," they said sheepishly, and took off down the hall.

"Will you snitch to Suzanna?" Mike asked.

"No. I told Josh what went on between him and me would stay that way, unless it was something serious. But she'd kill him if she saw him necking like that in the hall."

"Suzanna should get a man in her life." His voice dropped to a sexy drawl. "A little necking would do a lot of people I know some good."

She reached her door. "I need to go."

Gently he grasped her arm. "You need *me,* babe," he said sexily. His Abercrombie & Fitch sweatshirt made his shoulders look broad and his chest massive. "Give me a chance to show you."

She shook her head. "Good-bye, Don Juan," she said dryly.

Kelsey was thinking about Mike, and how she wasn't attracted to him, as she entered the room. Kids were milling around. Luke stood at Smurf's desk, looking down at something. Though he wasn't all *that* tall, he loomed over the pudgy boy with a strong masculine presence. Luke playfully socked Smurf in the arm, and chuckled. Smurf gazed up at Luke as if he were a rock star. The kid had a bad case of hero worship since Luke had thwarted Webster. Kelsey was glad to see their friendship; Smurf needed a champion, as his valedictorian sister wouldn't even talk to him in the hall.

Kelsey said to the class, "Okay, everybody, take your seats."

Luke glanced up. He gave her a smile that eclipsed the lights. Then he sauntered to his desk, sank down in the chair, and draped himself over it.

Vaguely disturbed by his smile—it was a little too sexy—she turned to write on the board. "Today, we're going to talk about the special agencies in the government. Make these columns across the top of your notebook: CIA, FBI, Secret Service. For each, write what you know about them. You can brainstorm in pairs."

As the kids got to work, Kelsey wandered up and down the aisles. Rush Webster was out, suspended four more days. Kelsey was glad. Not only was he clearly the perpetrator in the cafeteria the other day, he was rumored to be into a lot of dicey things. And as she told Mike, he was one of the few kids who gave her grief. Dark places lurked behind those dark eyes. She could sense it as a teacher, as a woman. And it scared her.

Kelsey checked to see how much each student knew about the government agencies as she walked around. She stopped to comment on something to a young girl who needed to open up more, and she smiled at a pair of very slow learners. This particular Government class consisted of students with a wide range of abilities. Remembering Zach's suicide, she wished she could do more for all these kids. At Luke's desk, she peered down at him and Morgan, who'd pulled a chair over to work with the boy. Kelsey noted she sat close to Luke. "How's it going, you two?"

"Ms. Cunningham, Luke knows everything about these guys."

Kelsey glanced at Luke's paper, then bent over for a better view. A musky smell stopped her for a minute. Not only did Luke look like a man, he smelled like one. Forcing her attention to his work, she saw that all three columns were filled. The Secret Service was especially detailed. "How do you know all this, Luke?"

His face reddened. "I, um, surf the Net a lot. These places have web sites."

"Are you interested in one as a career?"

The boy next to Luke guffawed. "Fat chance. Those guys'll come gunning for him, not wanting to hire him."

"Prob-ly," Luke said good-naturedly. He gave Kelsey a half-smile, accenting a small dent in his chin she'd never noticed.

"Well, if you ever want to talk about a career in one of these areas, I'm available. My father did extensive research in Washington when he was writing a book that had some government officials in it. He learned a lot about these agencies."

Luke shifted in his seat, obviously uncomfortable with the attention. "Thanks."

Making her way to the front of the class, Kelsey faced the

kids. "All right, let's see what we know about these mysterious men and women of the special agencies. We'll brainstorm the facts on the board." She smiled. "Who would like to start?"

Morgan raised her hand. "Everybody knows this." She shrugged, the action making her pretty blond hair skim her shoulders. "The Secret Service guards the president and other VIPs."

"Yes, of course." Kelsey wrote the information on the board.

"They wear suits." Smurf always tried to be funny; his need to be class clown worried her.

"Well, Jimmy, we see them that way because of how they're portrayed in TV and movies. I imagine they wear all kinds of clothes."

"Sometimes none, when they're in bed humping hot chicks, like in that Clint Eastwood movie," a boy behind Luke declared.

Kelsey was about to defuse the comment, when Luke turned and said softly, "Not in front of the ladies, buddy."

The boy mumbled something back—a razz, probably—and Luke returned a comment Kelsey couldn't hear.

"What kind of training do they have to have?" one boy asked.

"Hmm. What do you think?"

A smart girl, whom Kelsey suspected was on drugs, said from her seat, "I know the FBI only takes college graduates, unless they have military or some other kind of useful background."

"Not the Secret Service, though," Smurf said. "All those guys gotta do is stand around like The Hulk and protect people."

"Actually, they do a lot more than that." The note of authority in Luke's voice claimed everybody's attention.

"Why don't you tell us, Luke?" Kelsey sat on the desk and watched him.

"There are two branches of the Secret Service. One is what you know, their uniformed officers. It's like a police force. The other is the Special Agent division. To be a uniform, you don't need college, though a lot of them have it.

To be a Special Agent, you gotta have a B.A. from an accredited college or three years of work in criminal investigation or law enforcement. Or a combination of both."

"Very good, Luke." Trying to hide how impressed she was—it wasn't good to favor one student too much—she directed her question to the whole class. "Does anyone know what division of the government the Service belongs to?"

No answer. Luke held his tongue.

Morgan glanced at his paper. "Luke knows."

"The Treasury Department." Again, a shy duck of his head.

"Why, what do they have to do with money?" Smurf asked, pushing up his glasses.

"The Secret Service was started to break up counterfeiting rings. It got into protection after that. The FBI is an offshoot of the Secret Service." Luke said the last proudly.

Surreptitiously, Kelsey watched him during the rest of the class. He seemed to be trying not to participate or share his knowledge. Maybe she'd embarrassed him by too much attention. Kids shouldn't be afraid to live up to their potential—she thought that was one of Luke's problems.

She wondered at that, enough to say, when the bell rang, "Luke, could you stay a minute after class?"

His eyes darted to the clock. "I can't, Ms. C. My Math teacher said if I was late one more time, he was writin' me up. Sto—I mean my Uncle Joe will kill me."

"Could you stop by after school, then?"

He hesitated. "Yeah, I guess. See you then."

And he was gone. Leaving Kelsey to wonder—a lot more—about her new student.

ONE of the real drawbacks of undercover work was the lack of a sex life. It was even more pronounced if you went under as a teenager. Luke was twenty-six years old and couldn't very well bed teenage girls; and of course, dating adult women was off limits. Sometimes, the enforced celibacy drove him crazy.

This was one of those times. As he walked into Kelsey Cunningham's classroom, he could smell her perfume. It permeated the air, subtle and sexy, whenever she was around. It was torture to a young boy's body. Or a man's.

"Oh, Luke, come on in." She was seated at the computer. "I was just e-mailing my father." The navy blue skirt she wore today rode up more than she let it do in class, reminding him of Zach's suicide note.

"Take your time. I got nowhere to go."

The keys clicked, and he looked away from her. *Forget your hormones, Ludzecky. Think about how to get information from her that you can use in the investigation.* She probably knew stuff about Smurf or Max that would help him understand them better. Feigning teenage restlessness—it wasn't such an act—he wandered around the room, checking out the posters on the wall. Those across the back had quotes about history. He read a few, then heard her say, "Luke?"

He turned to find her seated at a student desk, waiting for him. Sauntering over, he sat down. The beige tailored silk blouse she wore molded to her, and a faint line of lacy bra could be seen when she moved a certain way. He was a sucker for Victoria's Secret underwear, and he could just picture one of those little underwires on her. "So what's up, Teach?"

She smiled at the epithet. "Are you always such a tough guy, Luke Ludzecky?"

"Damn right." He stretched out in his insolent teenage boy slouch. "What about you? You always such a bleedin' heart?"

Delicate eyebrows made a vee on her forehead. "What makes you think that?"

"Lemme guess. You called me down here because you see *potential in me.* And you think I'm interested in government agencies. You decided you could maybe steer me to the right side of the law, instead of the wrong one."

Her half-smile was confirmation. Even her eyes twinkled. Their rich brown color deepened to how chestnuts looked after they were cooked. "Am I that obvious?"

"Just to me."

"Why is that?"

Uh-oh. Geez, Stonehouse was right. He had to stop showing off. "Must be it comes from havin' an uncle who's a shrink. He's always talkin' about how to read people."

She seemed satisfied with the answer.

"So, I'm right?" he asked.

Crossing her legs—blood pressure goes from eighty to three hundred in seconds—she cocked her head. "Luke, you do have potential. I hate to see you waste it."

"Am I? Wastin' it?"

"Are you trying to tell me I'm stereotyping you?"

He shrugged. "Everybody stereotypes everybody else. Take Smurfy boy, for example."

"He's a nice kid."

"He got an okay home life?"

"He lives with his mother and father and a sister. They're fairly well off, I think."

"The kids say his mother's really whacked."

"She's had some trouble with depression."

"She on drugs?"

"Why?"

"Some jerks tease him about bein' on Prozac, like his ma."

She smiled. "You worried about him?"

"I guess."

"I like that." Leaning back in the desk, she studied him. "What are you going to do after you graduate, Luke?"

"*If* I graduate."

"Don't you think you will?"

"Not if I don't pass Math. Well, Science, too, but I think I'm on top of that."

"You've been here how long?"

"Almost three weeks."

"I'd like to help you adjust, if I can."

Now, there's a thought.

"I could tutor you."

"I'm doin' okay in Government and Psychology."

"No, I meant in the other subjects."

He rolled his eyes, trying to remember to be Tommy Teenager. "Don't tell me. You were an A student in all subjects."

"Guilty."

"How come you teach kids like us, then? How come you're not at Yale, like your daddy?"

"How do you know where my father works?"

Oh, hell. "You mentioned it, I guess."

"Anyway, the answer to your question is because I like teaching kids like you."

"I'm all right, Ms. C. You don't have to make me a pet project."

"Can I ask you something personal?"

Oh, lady, you're really making this hard. "Sure."

"Why did you come to live with your uncle?"

He shook his head. "You gotta know this."

She said nothing.

"I was *incorrigible,* I think they called me. My mother couldn't handle me. And Superman came to the rescue."

"You don't like him, do you?"

In undercover work, it was important to stick as close to the truth as possible. "He's Mr. Perfect, for one thing. He's so straight, it makes my shoulders hurt just watchin' him."

She rolled her eyes this time.

"No, seriously. Sometimes I'm afraid he'll crack, keepin' up that rigid front."

"What's your mother like?"

He thought of Donuta Ludzecky—her round bosom, her hearty laugh, and the way she messed up his hair and took his cheeks in her hands. He missed her big-time. He didn't have to fake the longing in his eyes. "She's nice. Strict, but has a soft streak." He zeroed in on Kelsey's beautiful features. "Just like you."

She ignored the comment, which was probably good. "Do you get to see her much?"

Not enough. Maybe I could go down to Queens this weekend. . . . "I see her." He said it tersely, to get off the subject, and stood. "Look, I appreciate what you're tryin' to do, but you aren't gonna save me, Ms. C."

"No one can save you but yourself, Luke." She stood, too. In her heels she was only a few inches shorter than he.

"I'll keep that in mind." He raised his chin. "Can I ask *you* something?"

"You can ask me anything. I may or may not answer." Again, the twinkle in her eye.

What's going on with you and Mike Wolfe? "Your father. Are you close to him?"

"In some ways, I'm very close to him."

"Can you be honest with him?"

"Um . . . no. Not really."

Luke just stared at her.

"What about your father?" she asked.

All of a sudden, Luke felt claustrophobic, even though the March sunlight streamed through the windows and the room was bright and airy. "My father's dead."

She grasped his arm. "Oh, Luke, I'm sorry."

The heartache in his eyes was real.

"Did you get along with him?"

"Not until it was too late." He glanced at the clock, then back at her. Her hand stayed on his arm, squeezing comfortingly. The air between them crackled. "Speakin' of late, I gotta—"

"Luke?" The stern voice came from the doorway. "Aren't you supposed to be making up yesterday's Math class?" He turned to find Stonehouse in Kelsey's doorway. The man's color was high. His eyes focused on Kelsey's hand, which was still on his arm.

Shit.

JOE strode into Suzanna's office, clearly upset. "Sorry I'm late."

She glanced up at him, still bowled over by the revelations of last night. They'd planned to meet today, but couldn't schedule time together until almost four. "No problem." Leaning back in her chair, she studied him. His gray suit and light gray shirt were impeccable, as usual, but his striped tie was a bit askew and he looked more . . . rumpled than usual. "What's wrong?"

"I'm going to *kill* that kid!"

Rising, Suzanna circled the desk and closed the door, although anyone overhearing that particular comment would think it fit right into his cover of frustrated uncle. Even after mulling it over all night long, Suzanna still couldn't digest what was happening in her school.

As she sat down again, she watched him. "What's he done this time?" Now that she knew Luke wasn't a troubled kid, amusement tinged her voice.

"Showing off. Getting Kelsey Cunningham to feel sor—" Joe had been pacing like a commander with undisciplined troops; he stopped when he got a good look at Suzanna. "What's the matter?"

Smoothing down her teal suit—she'd picked it today because of its brightness—she asked, "The matter?"

Slowly, he crossed to the desk and leaned over, bracing his hands on the top. She had to keep herself from shrinking back. Covered in cashmere-soft wool, his shoulders looked huge from this angle. She could detect the growth of dark beard beginning to shadow his jaw by this time of day. "Your face is drawn, and your eyes are almost . . . haunted."

"Are all Secret Service agents so melodramatic?"

He didn't take the bait, the detour, the rerouting of their conversation. Instead, and shocking her, he reached over and grasped her chin, lifted it.

She would never have expected such gentleness in those strong fingers that pulled triggers and slapped on handcuffs. "*Suzanna.*"

"I . . . I didn't sleep last night."

"At all?"

She shook her head. The gesture dislodged his hand.

He dropped onto a chair across from her. "Why?"

Lawrence used to tell her she was cool as a cucumber in difficult situations, except for her eyes. They blazed amber fire, he'd said. Agent Stonehouse could get scorched by the look she gave him. "How can you ask that? I found out at ten o'clock last night that my school could be the next Columbine, there are two Secret Service agents playing *I Spy* in my building, and there's nothing in hell I can do about any of it."

As if choosing his words carefully, he waited to answer. "That's not true. You can be a big help to us."

"Then why didn't you let me in on the undercover plot at the outset?"

He said nothing. Just tented his hands and stared at her.

Finally she sank back in her chair. "All right, I know why." She smoothed down her hair, which was drawn into a tight knot at her neck, and fiddled with a silver hoop earring. "It doesn't matter, anyway. All that matters is that we get your help."

"It matters."

She held his gaze, said no more.

"You were better when I left last night. What's bothering you today?"

"The Secret Service Safe School Initiative, the FBI profile, and the Department of Education's analysis." She pointed to a pile of papers stacked haphazardly in front of her.

Angling his chin, he frowned. The hardened mask of his features frightened her, reminded her that this was a man who had probably killed people. "You asked me to get you the information."

"Yes, well, I figured you'd be asleep at 3 A.M. when I downloaded it from web sites."

"I wish you'd waited until I could go over it with you."

"Joe, I don't need to be protected from this!"

His green eyes flamed some fire of their own. He was a man used to protecting. "All right. Talk to me about what's upset you, other than my decision not to bring you on board right away."

Frustrated, she pushed back her chair, stood, and crossed to the coffeepot; the pretty pink carnations near it brightened the late afternoon. She stopped to inhale their scent. "Want some coffee?"

He nodded. "Black."

She fixed it as she talked. "Let's start with the fact that this is a no-win situation. First off, these articles describe elements of a safe school. And we do most of what they suggest at Fairholm." She came back to the desk, handed him his coffee, and sat down. She picked up a sheet from the pile of papers. "Focus on academics, promote good citizenship, offer help in dealing with kids' negative feelings and show them how to work out a solution."

"Yes, you do all that well. But it doesn't hurt to do more. Especially since 9/11."

"Still, we were singled out." She rapped her knuckles on the stack of papers. "Then, the Department of Education report indicates that in order to have a safe school, you need to have clear, fair rules that are reinforced by all personnel. But the FBI and Secret Service reports say that kids who bring guns to school often go after the people who meted out the discipline."

"Some of the information is contradictory. People are searching for answers, Suzanna."

"That same report tells you to be democratic with students and staff, to create a trusting environment where alienated kids can talk to their teachers. I've *done* all of that. I've tried to make this place open and flexible, and I still end up at risk."

He sipped and watched her. Most men would have interrupted by now, tried to tell her she wasn't looking at this clearly. His listening impressed her. She hoped he was as good with the kids.

"And those risk factors could apply to every student in school. Even Josh." Her voice wavered on his name. "His father died before he was thirteen. Christ, Joe, my son is no Dylan Klebold or Eric Harris."

He leaned forward in his seat. "No, and he wouldn't be pegged by us. One risk factor doesn't make him a candidate to be watched. Don't misunderstand the statistics, Suzanna. The reports are merely saying if there are a high number of risk factors evident in one student, he may be on a pathway to violence."

Her shoulders slumped and she sat back. "I suppose." She nodded to the stack of information. "That FBI report? It recommends Gestapo tactics, Joe."

He smiled. Again, she was . . . affected by what it did to his harsh features. "The FBI does tend to be heavy-handed. Unlike the Secret Service, which is fair and reasonable."

His levity drew a smile out of her. Then she sobered. "But anonymous reporting? Police officers in the school permanently? I'm not sure I can live that way."

When she said no more, he asked, "That's not all of it, though, is it?"

She shook her head.

"Tell me."

God, could anybody resist that coaxing tone? He probably got hardened criminals to make signed confessions.

"I'm worried about Josh."

"Because I said last night he could be in danger?"

"Partly. He *is* a popular kid. . . ." She could feel her face flush. "The FBI report noted, like you, that popular kids get targeted. What's more. . . ." Her throat worked convulsively. "That hit list. It just had Quinn on it. No first name." Now her eyes teared. "What if. . . ." Again she threw back her chair, rose, and went to look out the window. She swiped at her eyes. It was unthinkable. Obscene. Totally intolerable.

After a moment, she felt strong hands on her shoulders. For a brief space of time, she wanted to lean into those hands, against that broad wall of a chest, and let Joe comfort her. It had been a long time since a man had given her solace.

"Say it out loud, Suzanna. Fears that are spoken are easier to deal with."

"I'm afraid that Josh could be a target of somebody's violence. If I lost him . . . I got through Lawrence's death. I could never survive losing my child."

He went absolutely silent behind her. Just the slight tensing of his fingers on her shoulders alerted her. Oh, God, she'd forgotten about his niece. Immediately she turned around. His hands remained on her. "Joe, I'm sorry. I wasn't thinking."

Now his eyes were as bleak as a February dawn.

"You were close to her, weren't you?" she asked.

He nodded.

"It must have been horrible."

Bleak eyes got even bleaker.

"I'm so sorry."

"I won't let it happen to Josh." His voice was strong. Determined. Hoarse with emotion. "To any kids at Fairholm. I'll die protecting them."

She nodded. His hands flexed on her. Then he rubbed them up and down her arms. "Better now?"

"Yes."

He indicated the conference table. "Let's go sit there. I brought some information, including the report that made us target your school. The more you know, the better you'll feel."

Seated, he drew out glasses and put them on. He was . . . attractive in them.

The hours passed. He reviewed most of what she'd read, discussing it with her, explaining things she didn't understand or might have misunderstood. His clarification, and his disagreement with some of the tactics, helped calm her.

At eight o'clock, he glanced at his watch. She wondered if he had plans tonight. And suddenly, she wondered if he had a family. Was he married?

Stacking the papers, he drew off his glasses and said, "Suzanna, the fact that we're here should make you feel better. We can help *avert* an eruption of violence. Your situation isn't critical—yet. There's a difference between risk factors and imminent warning signs. We're just trying to figure out who's actually at risk here, and how to help them." He waited. "And when we leave, we'll have procedures and policies in place that will make you feel more secure."

"Like what?"

Again, he checked his watch. "It's complicated. Let's leave it for another time. When can we talk more about this."

"How about tomorrow?"

"All right."

Then she shook her head. "But the school will be a zoo. NYSSMA—New York State School Music Association—is having solo fest here. We won't have any privacy."

"And Josh will be at your house."

"Josh is away at an All State Student Court this weekend in Albany." She sighed. "I want to talk to you about him, too, as a parent. You can to come to my house if you like. Any time is fine."

He lazed back in his chair. "No plans for the weekend?"

"Tonight, my only plan is to go home and crawl into bed."

Steepling his hands, he stared back at her. Suzanna would have given up a week's pay to know what he was thinking.

ALONE? Joe wondered, staring at Suzanna. *Would she crawl into bed alone?* It was on the tip of his tongue to ask, but he caught himself in time. What the hell was he thinking? Not only did he need to stay focused in this operation—and not be distracted by personal feelings—but like most agents he led a solitary life, and didn't have the same needs, and opportunities to fulfill them, that normal men had.

Though right now, he felt those needs. Standing, he concentrated on his briefcase as if it were the lost Ark.

"Joe, you're scowling. Is something wrong?"

The thought of you in bed with another man is wrong.

"I didn't sleep well, either," he said glibly. He repacked his briefcase, then snapped it shut. Finally, he faced her. "I need to mention one more thing. This can't wait."

"All right, what?"

"Your safety. I don't want to alarm you, but this kind of thing—staying here till eight at night, walking out alone, going home by yourself—isn't acceptable. You can't do it anymore."

"Joe, I'm principal. I have night meetings."

"I know, but you have to take precautions."

"How?"

"Somebody needs to be with you. If there's a board meeting, I'll arrange for Maloney to accompany you to your car. On nights like this, I can be around."

"Do you really think this is necessary?"

"Yes. Along with other precautions we'll discuss tomorrow."

Her shoulders sagged. He'd added more weight to them, but it couldn't be helped. "Fine."

They left her office, locked up, and detoured to the counseling suite to get his coat; they were outside in minutes. The cold night swirled around them.

"Jesus, this city's freezing, even in March." He shielded her with his body, placing a hand on her back as they made their way to her car. She seemed small and slight next to him.

"Where do you live?" she asked.

"Washington."

"Of course."

They skirted the slush from a recent snowfall, and some splattered up on her stockinged legs. She should have worn boots. "It's warmer there this time of year, right?"

"Yes, it's. . . ." His voice trailed off as they reached the car she'd driven to school. She glanced at him, then tracked his gaze.

Josh's little silver Beetle sat in her usual spot. She'd taken it this morning because her BMW was in the shop and her son left for Albany today. At first glance, nothing seemed amiss. Then she looked down at the tires.

"Damn, that's all I need. A flat."

He grasped her arm and moved closer. "It isn't just a flat."

"No?" She leaned on him, wary.

He nodded to the front of the car. The front tire was also deflated. He drew her with him around the left side. Both of those tires were down, too. He'd bet his pension on what he'd find when he inspected the tires. "Son of a bitch."

She cleared her throat. "They've been vandalized."

"Yes. Slashed with a knife, is my guess."

She drew in a deep breath.

Would she fall apart? Would she cry?

Instead, she whipped out her cell phone and rummaged in her purse. Punched in a number she'd located in a directory. Waited. "This is Suzanna Quinn. I'm at the Fairholm High School parking lot. I need a tow truck."

He watched her, impressed. She clicked off the phone and raised her chin. "Triple A's coming to the rescue," she said.

After a moment, he added, "So's the Secret Service, Suzanna."

EIGHT

BRENDA Way couldn't wait for the weekend. Usually, she dreaded the hours alone in her condo on the hill, where the quiet made her more wired than usual. But she was up bright and early Saturday morning at her computer; still dressed in her pj's, she clicked into private files that nobody else could access. Conrad had taught her about computers. And about life.

She hadn't dared work on the project at the office, and she'd been out too late last night at Snoop's, the newsmen's hangout one town over, to start the project then. Sipping her almost bitter coffee, staring out at the rolling hills that overlooked the valley, she organized in her head how she'd approach this task. Not working from notes, she began with the title.

Under Cover/Above the Law?

Undercover. She thought about Conrad. He'd been killed when he'd been checking out a story and had innocently walked into an undercover operation orchestrated by the RICO task force, the government agency that investigates and prosecutes the mob. Not knowing the circumstances had cost him his life. Her heart still ached when she remembered how he'd been ruthlessly gunned down. He'd *want* her to stop this current breach of justice. And wasn't it fitting that she would be the one to benefit from one undercover operation when she'd lost so much because of another?

She went back to work. At this point she was considering an article maybe for *The New Yorker*, but who knew? Depending on how much information she could gather, she might turn it into a book, which she'd dedicate to Conrad. In either case, she'd show all those dickheads at the *Times* what they'd lost.

Someday she'd be as successful as Suzanna.

Whom Brenda had never told why she'd left New York's foremost newspaper.

How could she tell perfect Suzanna that her never-good-enough friend had a drinking problem and had neglected to check facts on an article about a day care scandal? Her faux pas had caused the *Times* to pay megabucks to prevent a lawsuit. Needless to say, Brenda had been fired. She still remembered the editor's words. . . .

"You're a tough broad, Brenda. And a good reporter. I'd keep you on if I could, but you blew it big-time. Get help with the drinking. Since Conrad's death you haven't been the same. . . ."

She'd gotten help. After several days in a bourbon haze, she'd gone to a recovery spa in Pennsylvania, endured the agony of drying out, then came to Fairholm because Suzanna was here. She'd started drinking again to avoid dying of boredom, but she had it under control.

She typed. *Is it ethical for the government to infiltrate schools? Is it the press's responsibility to make known what's happening? Can we allow these Nazi tactics?*

Conrad would answer, *We know it's not ethical, kiddo.*

Suzanna had said he was a father figure to her. Father. *We know about your father, Suzanna.* Brenda scribbled a note to find out what happened to Nathan Carson. She could probably get it out of Suzanna, but she didn't want to pressure her. Thursday night her friend had looked stunned and . . . fragile.

Now, how was Brenda going to document her facts?

Go on the Internet. Download Secret Service research.

Would she be able to get any background on Stonehouse and Ludzecky? Maybe she could hire a PI to find out about them. Spies spying on spies. It had a certain poetic justice to it. A section of the book could be on the men who go undercover and dupe the public. Maybe one of them had something juicy in his background.

Go to archives, get information on Spike Romano's arrest. The incident during which she'd met Stonehouse might say something about the mysterious agent.

By noon, Brenda had filled several pages with notes. She felt almost intoxicated with delight. "Hallelujah," she sang to the computer as she hit the Print button.

Brenda Way was once again on the road to being Brenda Starr. Nobody was going to stop her now.

"THAT'S it. Good. Good." The instructor scanned the high-ceilinged room with a bank of windows facing the class participants. Her gaze landed on Brenda. "Brenda, you're distracted. Steady your mind. Get fully in the present. Slowly ease the tension in your neck and stretch those calf muscles."

After another puzzled look from Suzanna, who sprawled out one mat over, Brenda tried to concentrate, tried to find her inner self, but she was jittery and needed a drink. All she could think about was what Suzanna had told her this morning when they'd driven to the Fairholm Community Center together.

She'd had to pick up her friend because Josh's car had been vandalized yesterday and Kelsey, who lived closer and often took the same yoga class, was out of town this weekend. . . .

"All four tires were slashed," Suzanna had said.

"Does Stonehouse think it's related to his business?"

"He thinks everything is. I have to be back by two." They usually went out for lunch after their class.

"Why?" Brenda had forced her eyes to stay on the road, and tried to lighten her grip on the steering wheel.

"Joe's coming to the house to go over more of the research with me. To show me the information that made the Secret Service target my school."

"Hmm." Brenda had wondered how she could crash the meeting. . . .

"Brenda!" Suzanna said, stretching out into a cobra position. "Get with it!"

Brenda snapped back to the present and elongated her body. Inhaled. Exhaled. Sometimes this yoga helped to calm her, and sometimes she had so much time to think during the class, she had to take a Valium when she got home.

After an interminable hour, the class ended. As they headed to the showers, Suzanna asked, "What was wrong with you today? You're normally high-strung, but rarely this bad."

Brenda said, "I'm distracted."

Suzanna arched a brow as she pulled open the locker room door. Her maroon Spandex leotard highlighted the color in her cheeks, though she looked tired today.

Inside, Brenda was assaulted by the smell of disinfectant, reminding her of her days as a hotel maid when she'd worked her way through college. "It's because of what we found out Thursday."

Her eyes wide, Suzanna scanned the lockers and benches. "Shh. I don't think we should talk about it here."

"Sorry."

But she wasn't sorry. The public had a right to know what the government was up to, and newspapers had made an implicit promise to the masses to inform them. It was Brenda's duty, no matter what the cost. It was the duty of all newspaper reporters.

"NO, it's not going to happen." Digging his hands into the khaki slacks he wore with a forest green crewneck sweater and a black T-shirt underneath, Joe Stonehouse stood in Suzanna's den and scowled darkly. He looked good, Brenda thought, dressed casually for a change. Sexy as a young Clint Eastwood.

Suzanna glanced at Brenda. Nervously, she stuck her own hands in the back pockets of the jeans she wore with a beige cashmere sweater and low-heeled boots. She'd been at a loss for words since Brenda had followed her in, and waited for Joe to show up. "I think—"

"It doesn't matter what you think, Suzanna," Joe interrupted, casting her an impatient glance. "I won't discuss the case with her here. What's more, you shouldn't be discussing it either."

"I'm here, Stonehouse. Don't talk about me as if I'm not." God, Brenda hated it when men did that to her. It had happened a lot at the *Times*.

"You won't be here long." The man was cool and unflappable. Did anything get him juiced up?

Brenda plopped down on one of the sofas in Suzanna's den and stared at the rows of bookshelves. She sipped her bottled water, wishing it was gin. "I think this should be Suzanna's call."

"You don't get it, do you?"

"Get what?"

"That I'm in charge here. Suzanna has no say in this."

"Yeah, you're doing a great job, Agent Stonehouse. Somebody slashed her tires last night right under your nose."

He whirled around and faced Suzanna, who leaned against her teak desk. "Did you tell her that?"

Suzanna raised her chin in a defiant gesture. "She's my best friend, Joe. I always confide in her when I'm upset."

"As of now, you confide in no one but me."

Brenda studied the guy. He looked ready to spring into action at any minute. He was tense, alert. But there was something about the way he was with Suzanna, a softening, that she'd noted on Thursday night, too.

Stonehouse's autocracy got Suzanna's back up, as Brenda knew it would. All she had to do was bait him, and she'd get what she wanted. Another thing Conrad had taught her.

"Isn't that a little extreme?" Suzanna's tone was irritated. "I still have a life, you know."

"Not until this whole operation is finished, you don't."

"*I* think it's extreme," Brenda put in. "You sound like we're on the verge of Armageddon, here."

"Ms. Way, I don't really care what you think."

You will.

She transferred her gaze to Suzanna. The woman looked

torn. It was only two in the afternoon, and she seemed about to collapse. A memory came to Brenda, of Suzanna staying up all night with her when Brenda had had an abortion in college and was sick from it.

She wouldn't make a sacrificial lamb out of her friend now. So she stood and grabbed her purse. "Never mind. I'll go."

"Brenda, I. . . ."

"It's okay, Suz. I'll call you later to see how you are." She faced Joe. "You could have given Hitler lessons, Stonehouse. But I'm not afraid of you. I'm leaving for Suzanna's sake."

Stonehouse glared at her.

Did he believe her? Now, or earlier, about her interest in the case? Brenda would have to be careful. Stonehouse wasn't a babe in the woods like Suzanna.

She left her friend with a peck on the cheek and a promise to call. Outside, she made a promise to herself. She was going to get back on top of her profession if it killed her.

SUZANNA held herself stiffly as she watched Brenda leave the house. She was trying desperately not to overreact because she had the safety of fourteen hundred kids, nearly two hundred staff members, and herself and her son to consider. She stood by the window and took deep breaths.

Joe Stonehouse was just doing his job. Though it didn't set well, she needed him. Getting angry would be counterproductive. As Lawrence always said, *Do what you have to do, love.*

So she turned to face the agent. The green sweater, stretched tautly across his chest, turned his eyes the color of wet grass. She wondered if the wool was as soft as it looked.

Jamming his hands in his pockets again, he leaned back on his heels. "You can let me have it any time." His words were sober, but tinged with something. Acceptance, maybe. She wondered if he was ever lonely.

"Do you have any family besides your sister, Joe?" she asked.

His jaw tightened almost imperceptibly. "Just her and her other two kids. Her husband, Al."

"Your parents are dead?"

"Yes. But they weren't. . . ." He shook his head. "Never mind."

Suzanna wanted to probe, but also wanted to know something else. "Did you ever marry?"

"Once. I'm divorced. She was a good woman, and it wasn't her fault. An agent's life isn't conducive to nurturing a relationship. Word on the street has it that the divorce rate for the Secret Service hovers around eighty-five percent." He stared over her shoulders, sadness etched on his strong features. "My niece who was killed was the closest thing to a daughter I'll ever have, I guess."

Wrapping her arms around her waist, Suzanna said, "My parents are dead, too."

"I know."

"Oh. Of course you do." They exchanged a meaningful stare. "Since my brother lives in Arizona, I don't see much of him. Lawrence was an only child." She glanced toward the window again. "Brenda's always been like family to me, especially since Lawrence died."

Awareness dawned in his eyes, darkening them. "I'm sorry she has to be cut out of this."

"And Kelsey, too. *She's* the daughter I never had. It's hard to deceive her. There are a lot of trust issues with her. . . ." She didn't finish the thought.

"It's an unfortunate situation all around. I'm sorry you have to go through this alone."

She turned back to the window. Though her cashmere sweater was warm, she felt chilled. "It's one of the worst things about being widowed at forty-three. Josh is going off to college this fall. I haven't been careful to build a wide circle of friends. Just Brenda and Kelsey, really."

"You've been busy running a school." His voice had taken on an edge. She recognized it, now, since she'd heard it before. It was protective. Defensive. Of her.

The thought warmed her, made her feel less alone.

"I don't want to hurt Brenda. Or lose her as a friend."

She felt, rather than heard, him come up behind her. "Don't you think that if she's really your friend, she'll understand this exclusion is necessary?"

Suzanna shrugged. "I don't know. Brenda's tough to figure out. She's had a hard life. She's had to scrap for everything—material things, grades, a good job. Nothing's come
easy for her, like it did for me." She smiled wistfully. "I always wondered why we stayed friends. We're so different.
Except for our belief in honesty and integrity."

"Anyone would be lucky to have you as a friend." His
voice grew tender.

That, more than anything, made her posture droop, her
body let down; fatigue washed over her. Had he seen it? Was
that why his hands came up to clasp her shoulders?

She should have startled at his touch. But, like yesterday,
it seemed familiar, seemed right, which she knew in her head
was crazy. But her heart was reacting. To let it, was even
crazier.

"Trust me, Suzanna." His mouth was close to her ear. "I
realize this is difficult. But we've got to do it my way. For
your safety. For the safety of hundreds."

"I know."

She shuddered, and his hands tightened on her.

"I can help," he said. "I can preclude a violent incident, if
you'll work with me. Do it my way. Please."

Biting her lip, backstopping the emotion, she whispered,
"I will. Of course I will."

For a moment, he drew her back against his body. It was
lean and muscled and very male. Swamped by his heat, by
his woodsy, masculine scent, she was drawn to him. He
squeezed her shoulders, then stepped back and crossed to the
other side of the room.

Her equilibrium spun off, the way it had once when she'd
gone on Space Mountain at Disney World with Josh. She
waited until the disorientation passed, then pivoted around.
His Secret Service mask was in place. His face was stony,
like his name.

"Where should we start?" she asked, more in control,
probably as much because of his demeanor as his physical
distance.

"Let's talk about the process here for a minute." He nodded toward his briefcase. "I think I can make you feel better

about all of it." He went to the couch, sat down, and patted the cushion. "Come on over here. I can use your help."

Studying him, she approached the sofa. "That's good to hear."

They sat side by side on the couch. He removed some literature from his briefcase and put on his glasses. "First, I want you to see what you're doing right. This list addresses the physical layout at Fairholm. It squares with the recommendations of the psychologists: no overcrowding, small classes, wide, lighted hallways." He held up the paper, and she read along with him.

"Oh, Joe. I can't do some of this."

"What, specifically?"

"Here. The Department of Education says to close the campus during lunch, have the kids wear uniforms, get police inside the building."

"I agree with the first one. Your students shouldn't be allowed to go off-site for lunch."

She sighed. "The faculty was divided on that, too."

"It's not safe, Suzanna. We have to discuss ways to rectify things like this." He smiled over at her. "Remember, I said that we'll put some things in place before we go."

"Uh-huh."

"That's one of the recommendations we'll make. And we'll want to in-service the staff. Talk openly about safe schools."

"Without telling them who you are?"

"Yes. Usually my cover is that I worked on a task force with the Department of Education, and you recently learned of my expertise. And since the state came out in 2001 with their Code of Conduct, and with other guidelines to effect a safe school, this shouldn't be too out of place."

"Sounds logical. What other changes should we be making?"

"Better monitoring in the halls and high-traffic areas."

"I'm always on the teachers to be in the halls between classes."

"Maybe if they see it as a safety issue, they'll do it more."

"What else?"

"Stagger dismissal times."

"That could be a nightmare."

"I've got software to help figure it out. We also have to establish areas where kids can go if a crisis occurs."

She drew in a breath. "It sounds so dramatic."

"You've already got a crisis evacuation plan in place. And the state is tending toward mandatory drills to practice the plan."

She buried her head in her hands. "Foolproof communication. Maneuvers, drills. It sounds like a police state."

He didn't say anything for a moment. Then he added, "And we need to talk about bullying. Your school should adopt a zero tolerance policy for it. I have an outline of what kids should do if they're bullied and what teachers can do to stop it."

Searching deep inside herself, she straightened. "All right. I'll consider anything to keep the kids safe." Taking the paper from him, she raised her chin. "Let's see how we do all this."

BY five, she'd had it. Joe had planned to review the risk factors and discuss the students he was targeting, but he decided Suzanna couldn't handle any more. When she excused herself to get coffee, he stood and crossed to the tall étagère on a far wall. Early evening shadows made crisscross patterns on the glass shelves, and he fingered their cool, smooth surface.

Frankly, he'd had it, too. Usually he reviewed the stats for administrators with professional detachment. But he couldn't summon a neutral attitude today.

One reason was because she'd asked him about his family. How ironic. He dug into everybody's background and knew their seediest secrets, yet no one knew his. Even he and Ruthie never talked about their unorthodox upbringing in the sixties culture.

A culture that had almost destroyed him.

Dragging his thoughts away from his own life, he concentrated on Suzanna's, partly displayed before him. But as he studied Josh's basketball trophies, as well as Suzanna's teaching degrees and commendations, his mind wasn't on the accolades. Instead he saw her pale face when she realized Josh's car had been vandalized, heard her struggle to be brave with the Triple A people, watched her go through the motions until he could drive her home.

They'd come straight here.

"Thanks," she'd said, reaching for the car door handle.

"I'm coming in for a minute. I want to check out the house."

If possible, her face got even paler. He was sorry for upsetting her further, but her safety was at stake. He'd entered the house first, checked all three floors, and made sure doors and windows were locked. "Put the alarm on as soon as I leave."

She nodded.

"What will you do now?" he'd asked.

"Take a bath and go to bed."

"All right. . . ."

But the images of her in the bath had haunted him on the short drive to his house. Thankfully, Ludzecky had gone to visit his family. So Joe had been alone. He'd allowed himself a manhattan and tried to work. But he was outlining a plan for her safety, and it was hard not to think about her while he did that. Did she use bubble bath? What would it smell like on her skin? What would she feel like warm and wet?

Trying to distract himself from repeating last night's musings, he picked up a picture of Lawrence. Her husband had been good-looking. Joe wondered what kind of sex life they'd had. Then he cursed a blue streak that he'd allowed that thought to surface.

"Joe? What's wrong?"

His back to her, he shook his head and set the picture down with a thump. His speculation was totally inappropriate. "Nothing," he said curtly.

"I brought some coffee."

"Fine."

He turned and faced her. She'd left her hair down after her yoga class, and it swirled in blond waves around her shoulders, skimming the cashmere, which looked almost as soft as her skin. Setting mugs on a table, she sat and smiled up at him.

He didn't smile back.

"Have I done something to upset you?"

"Of course not. You're handling this like a pro." He crossed to her and sat, weary himself. She handed him a mug. Their fingers touched, jarring him. "We might as well finish this part."

"You're concerned about my safety." She was smart, he'd give her that, and gutsy. He was glad she didn't avoid the facts.

"And Josh's."

Her gaze hardened. He'd expected a weepy reaction. "I had his car last night."

"Yes."

"So we don't know if the vandalism was meant for me or for him." She added hesitantly, "Just like the hit list."

"Right."

She stared at him with wide, frightened eyes.

"Suzanna, some procedures really have to be put in place to ensure Josh's safety along with yours."

"How can we do that? Josh doesn't know who you are."

"No, but I can still talk to him about safety. Tell him that I was with you when you found the car was vandalized. Talk to him about kids having grudges, taking them out on the principal and her family. And what that means to him."

"It sounds like a plan." She ran a restless hand through her hair, mussing it. His body reacted.

"I was going to ask you to talk to him anyway."

"So you said. About what?"

"Sex."

The mug slipped in his hands, but he caught it. "Excuse me?"

She chuckled. "My son's almost eighteen. He's got a steady girlfriend. I'm not naive, Joe. I know about young men's needs."

He didn't want to discuss this with her. Did she know about grown men's needs, too? "It's important to recognize what you're dealing with," he said neutrally.

She sipped her coffee. "He can't talk to me about it. I've tried to get him to open up. I think things are getting heavy with him and Heather. He needs a man to talk to . . . you're starting the Boys' Concerns group. I was hoping it would come up there."

"I'll make sure it does. Try to segue into a private meeting with him."

"Thanks. I appreciate it."

Without censoring his reaction, he reached over and grasped her hand. It was ice cold. Because of that, he told himself, he held it fully in his. "You know, Mom, guys have been going through puberty since time began. Josh will weather it."

"Yes, but will I?"

"It's hard to do everything alone."

"He would have talked to Lawrence."

Joe didn't want to hear this, either. "Were they close?"

"Very. I always thought . . . I didn't think I'd be left to deal with this issue myself." She shook herself out of the mood. "Anyway, I need help. With my son, just like with this whole school thing, I guess."

Your cue to let her hand go, Stonehouse. He squeezed her hand once, then released it. Reaching into his briefcase, he pulled out another sheet of paper.

"You're pretty good at lists."

He didn't tell her he'd made this one at 2 A.M. when he couldn't stop thinking about her. "Last night was no accident."

"I know. I'll be more careful."

"You need to do more."

She took the list, scanned it.

"All right, I'm making sure the alarm is on." She read further. "Josh shouldn't stay overnight anywhere? That's going to be a tough one to explain."

"We'll go at it from the 'your mother's a principal' angle."

She read on. "Not working late alone. This is going to take up a lot of your time, Joe. I have night meetings. Commitments."

"That's why I'm here."

"Don't you have any personal time when you're undercover?"

"No. It isn't a big deal. I take weeks, sometimes whole months, off in between assignments."

"No special woman to complain about that?"

He watched her carefully for the origin of the comment. He didn't see it. "No. As I said, this is an isolated life. Thankless, too, in many ways. It's harder on Ludzecky. He went to New York to visit his family last night."

She nodded.

"What about the last item on the list?"

She scanned it. Her eyes widened. "Do you really think that's necessary?"

"It would help."

"Josh has a black belt in karate. I won't be able to convince him to take the self-defense lessons with me." She blew out a breath. "And where will I find time for lessons?"

"You can replace your yoga class with them."

"I could. It's just that yoga centers me. Calms me. Self-defense lessons will stir me up."

Don't say it. "I could give you the instruction."

"Really?" She grinned, looked him up and down. "You're so big, you could crush me."

Oh, Lord.

"I'd be careful with you, Suzanna."

Her color heightened. Her lips parted. But she held his gaze. Finally she said, "I imagine you would."

NINE

———

THE Ludzecky household was the noisiest place Luke had ever been. As a kid, it drove him wild—the phone constantly ringing, a stereo blaring from each of the four bedrooms, and the girls chattering from dawn till dusk. His seven sisters could reach a decibel level that would surpass Chinese torture in the right circumstances. Often, he escaped to the solace of his bedroom, only to have them prance in on him, needing advice, some money, or even to borrow his shirts. The worst part was how they insisted on interfering in his love life; they'd put him in a million embarrassing positions. Still, he loved the girls, five of whom came home today at Donuta Ludzecky's command.

Caterina, the one who was closest to him and nearest his age, mimicked his mother's voice as she plopped down next to him at the scarred kitchen table in their cozy home in Queens. Her eyes, the exact hazel color of all eight of them, sparkled with mischief. "'You'll come home to see your brother unless you're sick or having a baby,' she told us all."

Luke smiled at the impersonation. "*Dobrze*, Cat. You're improving."

Actually, one of them *was* having a baby. Ana, two years younger than Luke, was about to give birth, so she'd been excused. Her impending motherhood made Luke feel like he was missing something in his life. Sofia was traveling in Europe with her doctor husband, so Donuta let her off the hook, too.

Luke held court with the other five girls while they waited for an early supper before he went back to Fairholm. "Can it, ladies. You know you love havin' me here."

"Yep," the youngest, Elizabeita, put in. She was sixteen, still in high school, and brighter than all of them put together. "It's like the pope's visiting whenever Lukasz breezes into town."

"Prosze!" he begged, and threw a napkin at her. She giggled adoringly.

From behind, Magdelana slid her arms around his neck, then placed a beer in front of him. "You know we love you, buddy."

Unbidden, another woman who'd recently called him that came to mind. *How are you, buddy?* Kelsey Cunningham had asked the day he was suspended for keeping her away from Webster's fists. Her dark eyes had been troubled, and her hand had stayed on his arm a long time.

"Hey, Lukasz, where'd you go?" Magdelana asked.

"Nowhere, Maggie." He grabbed her hand and kissed it. "It's good to see you."

Donuta bustled into the kitchen, carrying *golabki*, kielbasa, and his favorite, pierogi. The enticing aromas of his mother's specialties warmed him. Setting the food on the table, she stopped and took Luke's face in her hands. "My *bopchee*," she said, kissing him on the lips. *"Brakuje mi Ciebie."*

"I miss you, too, *Matka*."

Paulina and Antónia entered the room together, carrying the rest of the traditional Polish dishes. Identical twins, they were sophomores at Columbia. The girls bounced onto chairs after he and his mother sat; everybody looked to Luke. As the only man in the family, he led the prayer. "Dear God, thank you for bringing us together. Thank you for this wonderful food and for the gift of life."

Donuta put in, "And keep Lukasz safe."

His sisters stilled. They knew he worked undercover for the Secret Service, but nothing specific about his jobs.

Though they didn't belabor it, the recognition that their brother and son was often in danger sat heavily on his whole family. Because of it, Luke religiously called home every Monday night to let them know he was all right. He knew they waited for the reassurance.

Briefly he wondered how Stonehouse had done this job all these years. Must be he didn't have a family who worried about him. God, Luke hoped he didn't end up alone, like Joe.

"So," Paulie said in her usual glib manner, trying to defuse the moment, "how's the world of espionage?"

"You know your brother can't talk about that." Donuta patted his arm. "We're just grateful you could squeeze in a visit."

Which made Luke feel bad that he didn't come home often enough. Not that he could. Even getting away now was a risk, but he was too close—three hours away—to miss the opportunity. Stonehouse agreed he could go. "I'll try to get home more, *Matka*." He smiled at the women who were responsible for his love, respect, and awe of the female sex.

"Can you at least tell us where you're working?" Elizabeita asked. "We can't tell from those spiffy clothes you're wearing." He'd dressed up for his visit in navy slacks and a pressed pin-striped shirt. Sometimes he missed his real clothes; he wondered if Kelsey would like them.

"No, Lizzie, I can't tell you."

"Is it exciting?"

"Yeah, the work's interesting this time."

"Any new women on the horizon?" This from Caterina. He swore she could read his mind.

Which was why he tried to blank it of dark eyes and wispy bangs falling into them. *Luke, you have so much potential . . . let me help you . . . I could tutor you.*

"There *is* somebody." This from Toni.

"There's women where I'm working." He grinned. "They're gorgeous. And smart. Just like you, baby."

"Then they won't want anything to do with you," Elizabeita said haughtily.

"Quiet, Einstein," Luke teased. "Boys don't like girls who show off their IQ."

"Yeah, Lukasz, that's always been your problem." Caterina again. "The women who fall at your feet can't match your mind."

I'll bet you got straight A's in everything. Luke couldn't believe no one had scooped Kelsey up yet. The face of Mike Wolfe materialized before him. *I'll try to distract Ms. C. a little longer so you can beat her to class.* Luke had watched the man's hand slide to the feminine slope of her back, caress it gently. His own hands had fisted.

"Come on, Lukasz, share!"

"I'm *so* not gonna do that. You'll try to interfere like you always do. But I'll tell you a story about Bush's bodyguard."

Tales of the exploits of the uniforms had always intrigued the girls. He spent a lot of time entertaining them with allowable details. As they ate, his sisters got owl-eyed at yet another story about the president of the United States and forgot all about the women at his school.

Luke didn't forget as easily.

BEN'S fingers were nimble on the strings as he played one of his original songs. His hair was tinted green and he had it tied in about a dozen tiny pony tails on top of his head. He wore a thick green sweatshirt with symbols of the pagan holidays. When Luke had asked him about it, Ben said Morgan gave it to him for Yule, the pagan holiday at Christmas.

The words that left Ben's mouth were heartbreaking, even to a macho guy like Luke.

> You're a Super Freak
> screaming at 3 A.M.
> And you're a Super Freak
> just praying for the end.

Stoically, he let Ben finish the song as he sank back against his headboard in the upstairs bedroom of the house Joe had rented. Luke chose his words carefully. "Pretty heavy stuff, Franzi."

Ben shrugged, then frowned. "The English teachers at

school say people use poetry to vent their saddest feelings. Songs, too."

"Yeah, I do that." Picking up his Gibson, Luke strummed absently.

Ben fiddled with his own guitar. "You won't tell anybody about the lyrics, will you?"

"Like who?"

"Your uncle, for one. All I need is him on my ass."

"On your ass?"

"For *suicidal* feelings. My mom would freak if she was contacted by the school about *her son's depression.*"

"What's your mom like?"

"She's okay. She's a teacher and always hovering over me like I'm one of her little kids." He smiled. "I mostly like it, but it's suffocating sometimes."

"What does she think of your Wiccan stuff?"

Ben's head snapped up. "Why?"

"Hey, no offense. I'm just interested."

The boy settled down. "She lets me do it; she even takes an interest. Once when we were in the basement, doing a circle—"

"What's that?"

Ben explained how Wiccans believed in sectioning out a sacred space when they prayed or used magic. In a way, it was a mobile church. "Anyways, my mother came to the basement while we were praying and I yelled, 'Don't step in the circle.' She didn't wig out like most parents would have. She smiled, asked me to explain what we were doing, and left us alone."

"Nice lady."

"She's cool, even if she does make me go to church with her." He looked at Luke. "What's your mom like?"

Luke gave his worst bad boy scowl. "My mother can't handle me, that's why I'm here. With my shrink uncle." Luke rolled his eyes. "Don't worry about me tellin' him anything. Hell, we hardly ever talk. I can't stand him." He added, "Kids at school say he's a good counselor, though."

"Why aren't you living with your father instead of him?"

"My pa's dead."

Ben stared off into space. "My dad's dead, too."

Luke hummed a bit, giving Ben the opportunity to talk. When he didn't, Luke asked, "Was he as cool as your mom?"

"Yeah, he was a college teacher. Really with it. About guy things, you know." Luke could hear the emotion clog the boy's throat. Damn, Luke was no psychologist. He felt more equipped to deal with kids who said they wanted to kill their teachers than with those who had thoughts of killing themselves. At a loss, he decided to act like a friend. "I'm sorry."

Again, Ben shrugged.

"What did he die from?"

"A quick and dirty case of pneumonia." Ben drew in a breath. "He was gone in a week. Can we talk about something else?"

"Okay."

Luke thought about Ben's loss. "Can I ask you somethin'?"

"I guess."

"Were you friends with that kid, Zach, who killed himself?"

Dark eyes narrowed and filled with pain again. Ben nodded.

"Was he a nice guy?"

"Yeah. Got along with everybody. Even jerks like Duchamp and that scumbag Webster. That's why people were surprised when he offed himself."

"Were you?"

Ben shook his head, looked away, busied himself with a few chords. For a while, they picked at some songs together, then Ben glanced at the clock. "I gotta bounce by nine. I don't have my night driver's license."

"Why didn't you say something? I could've picked you up."

"I like my own wheels. Makes me feel I'm in control."

"Aren't you? In control."

"Nobody's in control of their life, Ludzecky; it's all an illusion." He grinned. "Hey, sounds like a song." His voice was mellow as he sang, "It's all an illusion, the life we lead."

Luke listened to the pain behind the words as well as the sad melody. It wasn't a good idea to jump to conclusions, but

Luke knew he had to talk to his *uncle* about the young boy before him.

Ben was packing up when he said to Luke, "I got tickets to see the Wild Strawberries tomorrow night."

Luke whistled. "The band's phat. And the lead singer's a hottie."

"Morgan can't go. She won't be back from Albany in time."

"*I'd* like to see them."

The broad hint made Ben smile. "Okay." They headed downstairs. "You can drive, 'cuz it'll get over late."

At the front door, Ben turned to Luke. "You won't talk to your uncle about me, right?"

"I promised I wouldn't." He hoped he sounded offended.

Ben gave him a mysterious smile. "Good, 'cuz I wouldn't wanna have to kill you."

Luke guessed Ben was kidding, but his Secret Service instincts urged him to react.

Then Ben punched Luke's shoulder. "Just kidding, Ludzecky."

"Oh, sure. I knew that." He punched Ben back. "'Bye, buddy."

"HE said *what?*"

Luke let out an exasperated breath. "He was just kidding."

"Damn it, Luke, you don't know that." Stonehouse paced the den where Luke had found him sipping a drink and staring at reruns of *The X-Files*. Something was bothering the guy. He'd been surly and antisocial since Luke had returned from his mother's.

"What's eatin' at you, Stonehouse?"

"Nothing."

"Yeah, that's obvious."

"Oh, hell. I don't know why I'm taking this out on you." Stonehouse stopped his nervous trek, then took a sip of his drink. "Somebody slashed Suzanna's tires."

"*What!*"

"Luckily, I was with her when she found it. I'm afraid she's in more danger than I thought."

"Well, we're making strides here."

"Yeah, but I don't feel good about all this. I can't pinpoint anything, really. She had Josh's car, so the violence could have been meant for him." Again, the agitation.

Luke studied the man. "You got something goin' with this woman?"

"No, of course not. Why the hell would you ask that?"

"You're pacin' like a worried suitor."

"I'm responsible for her safety. For everybody's safety."

Luke dropped onto the arm of the couch. "You really believe that, Joe?"

"Of course I do. I've got to keep her—all of them—out of harm's way."

"I wanna do that, too, but we aren't gods. We can't guarantee their safety. We just do our best to uncover problem areas in the school. And help the troubled kids, like Ben."

Joe frowned. "So, how's he doing overall?"

"He has a lot of risk factors. Recent loss. First his father, then Riley. Suicidal thoughts. And that Wiccan stuff."

"You said he's not into devil worship, right?"

"No. Wicca seems to be a healthy religion. The kids get on him about it, though."

"We should read up on it more. To be sure his version is accurate."

"I can go on the Net tonight."

"All right. That would help."

Luke stood and headed to the door.

"Luke?"

He pivoted around. "Yeah?"

"I'm sorry I bit your head off. Good work with Ben."

"Thanks."

An awkward silence fell, but Luke hung back.

"How was your visit with your mother?"

His grin was broad. "Great. My sisters were home, too." He hesitated. "You got any family?" It was amazing what people didn't know about each other.

"Yeah, a sister."

"You miss her?"

"Yes."

"Me, too. I mean, I miss mine." Another awkward pause. "This is a tough life, isn't it?"

"Most of the time." Joe sounded resigned. After a moment of strained silence, he turned away, as if embarrassed.

So did Luke. Hell, he didn't even like the guy. Why should he feel good at the compliment? At the solicitousness? Luke had lived all his life without male approval. He didn't need it now.

THE concert hall in downtown Fairholm was cavernous. Rows of seats crowded in together like stiff little soldiers. There were groups of Wild Strawberries fans standing in the back and along the sides. Which made it totally unexpected that Luke and Ben bumped into—literally—Mike Wolfe and Kelsey Cunningham.

Ben said, "Oh, sorry. Hey, Ms. C.!"

"Ben, hello." She smiled at the boy and turned her gaze to Luke. "Hi, Luke."

At first glimpse of her, Luke thought he might swallow his tongue. She was dressed in tight jeans which outlined every contour of hip and thigh. Boots made her a couple of inches taller. But, holy Jesus, the shirt she had on should be illegal! Black Spandex dipped low in the front and hugged the generous curves that Luke had speculated about but never seen in such . . . definition. The shirt was saved from being salacious by a fringed suede vest she'd worn over it. Dangly brown and black earrings completed the bohemian outfit.

She looked just about good enough to eat.

Wolfe apparently thought so, too. His eyes narrowed on Luke. "Close your mouth, Ludzecky."

Luke burned at the chastisement. But he forced himself to feign embarrassment.

"How are you, Luke?" Kelsey's voice was solicitous.

"Good." He didn't know why he added, "I got to see my mother this weekend."

She reached out and squeezed his arm. He felt her touch all the way to his toes. "How nice."

Wolfe drew her back. Kelsey tossed him a questioning look.

"I didn't know you were coming tonight," Ben put in. "When we talked about the concert, you didn't say anything."

"I didn't think I could get tickets." Kelsey gave her full attention to Ben.

"Glad you did," Ben said and smiled.

God, it was true that teachers could spark kids' self-confidence. Ben knew Kelsey liked him, and it made him feel good. It also looked like Ben had the makings of a big-time crush. Not that Luke blamed him.

Wolfe said, "Let's go, Kelsey. I want to get up front."

After quick good-byes, Luke watched them leave. Ben said, "Let's go down where they are."

Mutely, Luke followed Ben. He wasn't exactly sure why tonight had suddenly turned as grim as identifying a dead body. All he knew was seeing Wolfe with Kelsey put a damper on the evening.

An hour later, after the warm-up band finished, Luke's black mood darkened when he and Ben were maneuvered by the crowd to a spot behind the couple and Wolfe slid his arm around Kelsey, touching her waist intimately. So when a fellow fan bumped Luke's arm—and he was in the process of drinking a Coke—he didn't try to stop the trajectory. The liquid landed on Mike Wolfe's back, soaking his Guess sweatshirt.

"What the fuck—"

"Mike!" Kelsey admonished. "The kids are behind us."

Wolfe turned around. "Who the hell did that?"

"Sorry, Mr. Wolfe." Luke held up his hands, arrest-style. "Somebody hit my arm."

As he wrung out his sleeve, Wolfe continued to swear. "Jesus Christ, I'm soaked."

"Oh, geez," Kelsey finally said. "Just go buy a T-shirt and put it on. It'll only take a few minutes."

"I'll pay for it," Luke said, reaching for his wallet.

"No." Wolfe must have realized he was supposed to be the adult here. "It's no big deal." He glanced around. "Come with me, Kel. I don't want to leave you alone in this crowd."

"But the Strawberries are coming on soon. I'll miss their opening number."

"Concerts can get rough. They mosh."

"Not at a Strawberries concert. I'll be fine."

"We'll stay with her," Ben said.

Luke hid a grin. "Yeah, we'll protect her."

Kelsey rolled her eyes. "Go, I'll be fine. I'll stay right here with my bodyguards." She tweaked Ben's muscles. "See?"

Grumbling, Wolfe left. Ben and Luke flanked Kelsey like sentinels. Soon, the Wild Strawberries came on. Kelsey stuck her fingers in her mouth and let out a whistle.

Luke laughed out loud.

The lead singer, Roberta, thanked the crowd for coming, and made mention of the ponytails all the guys wore, their versions of her upswept hair. Then she began to sing. She had a sultry voice. It was smooth and sexy, and reminded Luke of hot nights and tangled sheets. Kelsey got a dreamy look on her face as she swayed to the bluesy words of love and loss and yearning.

Luke tried to concentrate on the performers.

He did, until they played a rowdy song that got everybody moving. And crowding. And pushing. Kelsey ended up in front of him, and Ben was herded several people down. In no time, everybody in the audience was packed in like the proverbial sardines.

It was hell.

It was heaven.

Kelsey was plastered against Luke. His hands came up and grasped her arms. To steady her. He could feel the indentation of her back, the soft swell of her hips, her nicely rounded fanny pressing against him. Short, dark hair that smelled like flowers tickled his cheek. They were pressed even closer; his hands slid to her rib cage.

Proximity combined with nature, and Luke became aroused. He swelled against her.

Please don't let her know.

She knew. Her body stiffened.

I'm sorry, he thought as an adult. But a kid would die before he'd acknowledge the reaction to a teacher.

Luke tried to ignore the shapely body pressed against him. His fingers itched to explore it. His mouth watered to taste it in all the right places.

And he cursed heaven, hell, and the Secret Service, because he knew this was the closest he'd ever get to Kelsey Cunningham.

TEN

"SON of a bitch!"

In an isolated corner of Fairholm's computer suite, Luke glanced over his shoulder at Max Duchamp, who sat back to back with him, cursing as he stared at the message that came across the screen. "*Access Denied?* What the hell is this?" Max asked no one in particular.

"Max, is something wrong?" the cute red-headed computer teacher called out from her desk. She looked like Molly Ringwald. Luke had heard that Max flirted with her, and if the lab wasn't busy, she let him in this room to play with the computers.

"No, ma'am." He shrugged his camouflage-covered shoulders. "I'm just working on a Psychology project and I can't get to the site I need."

She stood and crossed to him. Small and pretty, she had a few freckles on her pert nose. She leaned over Max and reached for the keys.

"Don't." Max's voice was harsh.

The teacher jumped back.

"Sorry. Ms. Cunningham says we have to do it ourselves."

Luke snorted, but didn't blow him in; Kelsey had said nothing of the sort. Max must be up to something else. If

Luke could help him, it might be the opening he needed to get into Duchamp's group.

"All right." The teacher headed back to her desk.

Max fiddled with the keys some more. After another five minutes, he gave up. "Shit," he mumbled under his breath.

Luke kept typing. Max stood and turned around to face Luke's computer station. Luke knew he'd see the *Screw 'Em All* web site on the screen.

The other boy was so surprised, he didn't censor his words. "Hell, Ludzecky. They'll crucify you if they see you in that site."

"Fuck 'em. They gotta catch me first." Luke glanced at the teacher. "Watch me rock." With a quick flip of his hand, another site came up: *Study Questions for U.S. Government.*

Max laughed. "How'd you do that?"

"State secret," Luke mumbled. When Max just stood there, Luke said, "Plant your ass if you want. We can dick around with this together."

For a few minutes, they read the lyrics of the shock rock web site. Some of it was funny. Some of it was sick. How Duchamp reacted would tell Luke a lot. When the description of cutting off little kids' fingers scrolled by, Max cringed. "This sucks."

"Yeah." Luke waited a beat. "Where you tryin' to get to? I'm an expert hack."

"Somewhere."

"Suit yourself." Luke glanced at the clock. "Got Psychology in a few minutes anyway." Where he definitely did not want to go and face the beautiful Ms. Cunningham again. Life had been hell since the concert three days ago, and he didn't want to think about any of it.

Max shrugged. "You got issues with Webster, don't you?"

Play it cool. "Not as much as it might look like. But, hell, Duchamp, everybody's got issues with the guy. He's a loose cannon."

"I guess. He bugs me sometimes. He crashed at my house for days last week. My father wasn't there, so it didn't matter much. I hate it when he comes around when my dad's home."

Luke filed away that piece of information.

After a moment, Max said in a hushed tone, "I got a site. Nobody can know."

"Yeah, who am I gonna blab to?"

"Your uncle."

Luke laughed. "In case you can't tell, he and I ain't exactly pals."

"I can tell." Max smiled wickedly. "Okay. But I couldn't get in it today from school. That never happened before."

"How come?"

"Dunno. Maybe they slapped on some new controls." The bell rang. Max said, "Wanna skip Psychology? If you help me get in, I'll show you my site."

Luke shrugged. It would fit right into his plan. "Sure. I'm so not with that class anymore."

"You the man!" Max said and high-fived Luke. He shot a glance toward the desk. "First I gotta charm the lady into letting us stay."

While Max went to *charm the lady,* Luke tried to occupy himself with the computer. But his mind drifted back to his contact with Kelsey this week. Since the concert.

Monday in class. . . .

"Luke, what do you think about personality disorders?" She'd been perched on that damn desk again, her green skirt tucked over her knees, but still showing some shapely calf.

"I think sometimes I'm Jekyll and Hyde." He gave her legs a leer. "Not too shabby lettin' your bad side come out."

She'd stumbled over her next question.

Tuesday, he'd come in late. . . .

"Where were you?" she'd asked after class.

"I needed a smoke." He shrugged inside the nasty coat he'd found at a thrift store.

"There's no smoking on school grounds, Luke."

"Come on, don't be a Goody Two-shoes. Kids smoke."

"Luke, smoking's—"

"Don't lecture me," he'd snapped.

"And don't raise your voice to me, young man."

He'd given her a surly apology and stalked out.

Today, he'd almost completely alienated her by making a

lewd joke in class. Afterward, she addressed the issue of his behavior directly. "Luke, why are you doing this?"

He remembered thinking, *Because I get hard just looking at you, lady. Because at the concert, I almost forgot who I was and what I was doing there.* Geez, Stonehouse would have a fit. Right then Luke had known what he had to do. And it fit in with his cover perfectly.

Max strolled back. "She says we can stay."

"Tell me where to go." Luke's hands were poised on the keyboard.

Max gave him the directions, and the keys clicked nonstop. After five minutes, Luke shook his head. "Geez, Duchamp, this thing is buried deeper than shit. What you got in here?"

"You'll see." Max watched the screen as various icons and symbols came up. "This is where I got to. I couldn't go further."

"Yeah?" Luke played with the keys.

"Hell, your hands are quicker than a horny john's."

Luke didn't answer. Instead, he scowled. Said, "Man, this is fuckin' deep," and clicked keys some more. Finally he smiled. "I'm past it."

"Jesus Christ! How'd you learn to bypass that stuff?"

Oh, hell. Can't very well tell him several government specialists taught me. "Some babe I humped worked for a computer company; she showed me. I need passwords from here."

Max frowned. "Only Webster knows the passwords."

"Hey, it's cool. I won't look." Luke stood and turned away, pretending to read something posted on the wall in front of him.

Just as Max reached for the keyboard, Luke heard from the doorway, "What are you guys doing in here?"

KELSEY stared at the two boys who were skipping her class. Though she wasn't surprised about Max, Luke Ludzecky disappointed her. No news there! Since the concert, he'd been acting strangely, even wearing different clothes. Today, he sported grungy jeans and a sweatshirt with

Do Me!, a marginally acceptable saying at best, on it. "Luke? Max? Why aren't you in class? The counselors are in there to talk about psychology courses in college."

Max turned around in his chair and ducked his head. "Is it last period already?"

Her eyes narrowed; she dug her hands into the pockets of her loose green dress. "Don't give me that. If you're skipping, at least be man enough to admit it."

Luke shifted and his face reddened, but he said nothing.

Max's eyes turned dark. "I'm bouncin'. I don't need this fucking shit from no woman." He stood and stomped out, the clomp of his army boots echoing in the large room.

Kelsey let him go; she'd deal with him later. She faced Luke; he leaned against a desk and crossed his arms over his wide chest.

"Nothing to say for yourself?"

His face blank, he held her gaze. "I skipped your class."

Hesitating, she walked toward him. Up close, she could see his beard beginning to fill in. "Why are you hanging around with Duchamp?"

"Max is okay."

"It's not good to surround yourself with troublemakers." She motioned to the room. "This, for instance. As far as I know, you never skipped class before."

"It isn't Max's fault. We were on the Web and just got caught up in it." He jutted his chin out. "I didn't plan to skip."

She glanced over his shoulder. "What were you doing?"

Briefly, he looked back, as if to check out the screen, which was blank. "Max wanted to show me a web site. No big deal."

"Big enough to skip my class."

"Chill, Ms. C., it isn't the end of the world."

She could feel her face flush. "I'm going to write you up."

He rolled his eyes. "Do what you gotta do, lady."

Kelsey couldn't fathom why his insolence hurt. Kids acted like kids sometimes. They skipped class. They were defensive when cornered. She'd never taken it personally before. Yet right from the beginning, things had been different with this boy. Her heart contracted at his cavalier attitude toward her.

Suddenly, she was bombarded by memories of last Sunday night, when they'd been pressed against each other in the crowd at the Wild Strawberries concert. She tried to tell herself it was no big deal. Teenage boys were sexual creatures. They *reacted* to women. But the whole episode had made her so uncomfortable, she'd pushed away the memory of it all week long. She tried to do so again. "I guess I thought we were . . . closer than this."

He stared at her hard. "Yeah, well, things aren't always what they seem."

"Oh." Defensively, she clasped her arms around her waist, the sinking sensation inside her increasing. "I see. Well, I guess you'll have to deal with the consequences."

He shrugged.

"Your uncle will be upset."

"He'll probably beat the crap outta me."

"What?"

He shook his head. "I was exaggeratin'."

For some reason, she was struggling with a clear-cut case of skipping. "Luke, I—"

"Look, Ms. Cunningham. Just report me. I told you once before you couldn't save me."

"But you've been doing so well."

"I'll be fine." He turned; she watched him swagger to the door.

Before he was out of sight, she called to him. "Luke?"

He stopped but didn't turn around.

"I'm sorry for whatever's making you do this. I wish I could help."

His fists clenched, but he didn't say anything. He just walked out the door.

And Kelsey just watched him, feeling miserable. For the life of her, she couldn't figure out why.

AT the end of the day, Kelsey approached Suzanna's office. She'd been preoccupied the rest of the afternoon with Luke's behavior, and needed to talk to someone. Just as when she was sixteen and struggling with prom dresses and boys, there was only one person she wanted to confide in. It was almost five o'clock, and she hoped Suzanna hadn't left.

Kelsey found her friend in her office, poring over some documents. Suzanna looked sophisticated and chic in a red suit they'd picked out together one day, her blond hair in its usual knot, hammered gold adorning her ears and throat. She wore the glasses she donned only when she was tired. Knocking on the open door, Kelsey said, "Hey, lady, got a minute?"

Suzanna's head snapped up; she stiffened slightly, then shoved whatever she was reading under a book and smiled. The gesture seemed affected. Suzanna was stressed.

"Are you all right?" Kelsey asked, coming inside. "You seem tense. And you look exhausted."

"Sit. I'm all right. It's just been a long couple of weeks."

"Yeah, spring break can't come fast enough."

Leaning back in her chair, Suzanna sighed. "I wish I was going with Josh to Italy." The Italian Club was sponsoring a trip to Italy, and Josh, president of the club, had helped organize it. Suzanna could have tagged along to chaperone, but she wanted to give her son space. She was the epitome of a good mother, and Kelsey had been lucky to have her in her life.

"Heather going, too?" Kelsey asked.

Suzanna rolled her eyes. "I'm afraid so." She frowned. "I'm worried about that."

Kelsey remembered the makeout session she witnessed in the hall. She crossed her legs and fiddled with the nickel-size buttons on her dress. "Does he talk to you about it?"

"He says he can't. Does he ever talk to you?" Suzanna knew Josh and Kelsey had gotten close again after she'd moved back to Fairholm.

Kelsey said, "Not about that."

"I'm hoping Joe Stonehouse makes some headway in the Boys' Concerns group. They had their first session Monday, and Josh says it was *mad-cool*. The guys were so interested, they're meeting again tomorrow."

"I wish Stonehouse could help his nephew. It's the old *cobbler whose kid had no shoes* story, isn't it?"

Suzanna adjusted the paisley silk scarf draped over a beige collarless blouse. Kelsey had given her the accessory for Christmas. "Are you having trouble with Luke?"

"Yes." Kelsey noticed her foot bouncing, and stopped the nervous gesture.

"I thought you and he had a good relationship."

"We did. Until this week. He's turned into Mr. Hyde."

"Kids are funny, Kel. They run hot and cold."

"No. It's something different with Luke." Kelsey stared at the tulips on Suzanna's credenza. "It's what I wanted to talk to you about."

"All right." Suzanna looked . . . uncomfortable.

Kelsey cocked her head. "Suzanna, don't you like Luke?"

"What's not to like?"

She chuckled. "He is a handful." She watched Suzanna. "You seem a little jumpy when we discuss him."

"Do I? I don't mean to."

An odd answer.

"Tell me what's going on," Suzanna coaxed.

Kelsey recounted the boy's surly attitude all week. The unusual comebacks. Even how he was dressed.

"Did anything happen to precipitate this?"

"Well, I saw him at the concert Sunday night. I was with Mike Wolfe and—"

"You're seeing Mike Wolfe socially?" Suzanna had a protective streak a mile long.

"Back off, mother hen. I wanted to go to the Wild Strawberries concert. He asked. No big deal."

"I hope not. That ego of his needs constant feeding."

"He's okay. A little immature." She remembered why she was here. "Contrary to Mr. Ludzecky, who's very mature for his age."

Suzanna folded her hands on the desk and leaned over. "Anything happen at the concert?"

Oh, God, did it. She reexperienced the feel of him up against her, aroused, and she shivered.

"Kelsey?"

"Nothing happened." She couldn't articulate this, not even to Suzanna. She was barely able to think about it.

"Then what?"

"He seemed, I don't know, maybe upset to see me and Mike."

Suzanna's eyebrows furrowed. "Kids get crushes," she said. "You've been nice to him. Maybe he was jealous."

"He's a student, Suzanna."

"As you said, he's a mature guy; and you're a beautiful young woman." At Kelsey's frown, Suzanna said, "Sweetie, you know kids get crushes on teachers. Their positive feelings help them work out their relationships with the opposite sex. Just so long as the teacher handles it well, it's perfectly healthy."

Relieved by the simplicity of Suzanna's response, Kelsey threw back her shoulders. "I know. I guess it just seems like Luke's too old to have a crush. But he's only what, eighteen?"

"Nineteen. He failed a grade."

"Why would he skip my class if he has a crush on me?"

"Trying to get your attention?"

"He has my attention. He's had it all along."

"Then it must be a phase. Maybe he broke up with his girlfriend or something."

"He has a girlfriend?"

Suzanna stared hard at Kelsey. "I don't know. It was just an example." When Kelsey said no more, Suzanna asked, "Kel, is there something you're not telling me?"

"No. Of course not."

"You can tell me anything, you know."

Kelsey smiled. "I know. I'm just sad about not being able to trust Luke anymore." Surely that's all it was. Because trust was important to her, in all relationships.

With a slight smile, Suzanna shook her head. "You've got to toughen up, young lady."

"So you keep saying." She stood. "I'd better go."

"Okay. Want to do lunch this weekend?"

"I'd love to."

"Saturday after yoga?"

"Yep. Would Brenda want to come?"

"No, she's going to New York right after class."

Kelsey left, and headed toward her classroom. She was unnerved, mostly at having withheld something from Suzanna. Her friend was such a stickler for honesty. She'd be disappointed that Kelsey had concealed what had happened at the concert.

Why hadn't Kelsey told her?

Was she embarrassed? Or was it something more?

"Oh, Lord," she muttered and hurried down the hall.

LUKE put his head down on the desk in the in-school suspension room and thought about his "uncle's" words yesterday . . .

"Suspended? Because of Duchamp? Terrific." But there was no sarcasm in Stonehouse's tone.

Despite his vow not to care, Luke was pleased at the compliment. "It'll make us tighter."

"I know. Good work. Tell me about his site."

"We never got in. Kelsey stopped us before Duchamp got to use the passwords." Luke had drawn a paper out of his pocket. *"Here's the steps we went through. If he'd typed the passwords, I could've gotten them off the computer later. But she interrupted us."*

"Could you have gotten the passwords so easily?"

He shrugged. "Yeah. Sure."

Stonehouse studied Luke's notes. When he looked up, he smiled. "You have a good memory."

"Photographic. It's why the Secret Service wanted me."

The older man had watched him carefully. "I'm beginning to think there are more reasons than that. This is substantial progress, Luke. You've made strides here."

Again Luke had basked in Stonehouse's words, as if he'd gotten praise from the president himself. . . .

Well, at least Stonehouse was happy. Luke *wasn't* happy about what he'd done this week to Kelsey. The look in her eyes when she said *I guess I thought we were closer than this* still made him sick inside. It was the same feeling he got when he did something bad to his mother or yelled at his sisters. His stomach always started to hurt, and stayed that way until he made amends. Donuta Ludzecky told him maybe God was a woman and it was her way of keeping him in line.

"Mr. Ludzecky. It's not allowed to put your head down during in-school suspension." The monitor who ran "The Jail" fit every stereotype in the book. She wore thick-soled shoes, drab clothes, and Coke-bottle glasses. He expected her to pull out handcuffs any minute.

From the other side of the room, Max, who was also corralled there, snorted. The monitor sent him the evil eye.

Sluggishly, Luke sat up. He said, "Yes, ma'am," and saluted.

A chuckle from Duchamp drifted over.

"Do the work that was sent down for you."

Luke glanced at the pile of assignments teachers were required to provide if a student was in ISS. Geez, how did the staff have time to teach when they had to do all this shit? Listlessly, he picked up the top sheet.

In pretty feminine script were his Psychology and Government assignments. Just seeing Kelsey's handwriting made him feel bad. The note read, "Luke—Write an essay for Psychology on why people don't live up to their potential. Why they purposely mess up their lives. Why they do everything possible to make themselves miscrable. I want to see it today after school. I'll be working out with the track team in the weight room from four to five, so come to my classroom either before or after."

Damn, the woman didn't let up.

Reluctantly, he picked up the pen to do her freakin' assignment. Hmm. If he handled this right . . . oh, God, there went his stomach again. It clenched into Boy Scout knots at the thought of writing something offensive.

"Luke."

He looked up and scowled at Suzanna, though inside he was grateful she'd come. "Oh, no. The big guns."

"I'd like to see you." She nodded to the supervisor. "Marlene, I'm taking Mr. Ludzecky to my office for a bit."

Slowly, Luke rose; when he passed Marlene the Monitor, he winked at her. He thought he saw Suzanna hide a smile. They said nothing until they were ensconced in her office, a few rooms down from ISS. Door closed, Suzanna took the chair behind her desk. "You can sit, Luke."

"I'd rather stand, okay? I been sittin' at that damn desk all day." He arched his back. "I'm too old for this."

She smiled, but it was perfunctory.

"Something wrong?"

"Kelsey Cunningham came to see me yesterday. About you."

His stomach ache intensified. This time jet planes rammed against its walls.

"She's upset by your actions this week."

Stalling for time, he blew out a breath. What had Kelsey told her? "I'm sorry about that. But I need a way to get tight with Duchamp." Luke knew that Joe had outlined for Suzanna which kids they were trying to buddy up with.

"By talking back to Kelsey? By skipping her class and being rude about it?"

"I was worried that Duchamp thought I was too nice to her."

"Ben Franzi likes her. And Joe said you were getting close to him. He won't appreciate this."

"He wasn't around when I was dissin' her."

"Are you sure that's all it was with Kelsey?"

"Did she say there was more?"

Suzanna's eyes narrowed. "No, she hasn't a clue why you're suddenly being obstreperous."

He blew out a heavy breath. "I should have been worse right from the beginning. I don't usually do this back-and-forth thing, but there was more than one group to get in with this time."

"You're quite charming when you want to be."

"Did Kelsey say that?"

"Not in so many words. She did mention you seemed upset at the concert."

The concert. Uh-oh. "Upset?" His voice was a croak.

"To see her with Mike Wolfe, maybe?"

"You know, you oughta warn her about the guy. The kids say he has a mean rep with women. She shouldn't be another one of his conquests."

"She isn't. But Luke, that's none of your business."

"I'm not a student, Suzanna."

"Kelsey thinks you are."

Digging his hands in his pockets, he gave her a smile with some of that charm she had mentioned. "What am I saying? You're right. It must be that Polish gene I got to protect women. Look, I'll try to play this a little better so she isn't affected as much by what I have to do. But my main concern now is gettin' in with Duchamp and Webster and Morton."

"Does Kelsey have to get hurt in the process?"

Oh, fuck. "For the greater good, maybe."

"You sound like Joe."

He narrowed his eyes. "No need to insult me, Suzanna."

She smiled. "He's not so bad."

Luke studied her. There was something about the way she said that. . . .

"You can go now," she told him. "I just wanted your take on this thing with Kelsey."

"I don't mean to hurt her. Honest."

"I know you don't." She came around the desk.

When she pulled open the door, he said cockily, "Thanks for springin' me for a while, Mrs. Q."

"Remember what I said, Luke. You're on thin ice."

"Yeah, sure. See ya."

He headed out the door, hoping the ice held for just a little while longer.

THE weight room smelled like day-old socks and stale sweat. No matter where Luke went—schools, private gyms, the Secret Service Fitness Center—the odor was the same. He glanced around at the girls who were pumping iron and thought of his sister Lizzie, who was a lifter and on the track team. He hoped he could get to one of her meets.

Where would he be this spring? he wondered as the girls began to file out, calling to Kelsey. Was he going to stay in the Secret Service after his time at Fairholm was up?

"Bye, Ms. C."

"Thanks."

"Have a nice weekend."

From a corner of the room, he heard, "Thanks, ladies. You, too."

Luke gripped the essay in his hands.

Kelsey was sprawled out on the weight bench doing arm presses. Luke crossed to the corner, his sneakers quiet on the polished hardwood floor. The door slammed as the last girl left, and light from the high windows bathed the area in a mellow glow. When he reached Kelsey, he saw that she had her eyes closed, so she didn't know he was there.

He seized the opportunity to watch her. She wore short blue gym trunks that revealed a long expanse of toned muscle and silky skin. A gray T-shirt, damp with sweat, hugged her upper body and made his mouth go dry. Her face was crimson with effort as she lifted the bar. When he checked beyond her to the weights, he saw why. "You shouldn't be doin' this without a spotter."

The heavy stack of weights clanked when she let go of the bar. Quickly she sat up. "You, um, don't need a spotter when you're using a universal gym."

"It's not a good idea to work out alone."

Reaching over, she grabbed a towel and wiped the sweat from her face. Her damp hair clung to her scalp. "What are you doing here? I said I'd be back in my room by five."

He glanced at the clock. Foolishly, he hadn't wanted to be alone with her, and thought if he dropped the essay off in the weight room, they'd have forty girls as chaperones.

"I, um, got a date at five and need to do some stuff before."

It was just a moment's hesitation, but she stilled. Then she bent over and fished in a blue duffel on the floor and took out a bottle of water, unscrewed it, and sipped.

The action seemed to calm her. Watching as the water went down her slender throat did not have the same effect on Luke. The bench was still wedged between her legs. He forced his eyes away from the view of her thighs and crotch, wishing like hell she'd put sweat pants on. To distract himself, he scanned the suite. "Nice workout area. Expensive equipment." God, did his voice sound hoarse?

"Yeah, it's new."

"Jocks are important at Fairholm."

"All kids are. We got a new music suite when this was built."

"Oh. Good."

"Are you going to go out for Mr. Wolfe's baseball team?"

Luke felt his fist curl. He deliberately relaxed it. "Maybe." He dropped down on the bench across from her. "What's he like?"

"The kids say he's a great coach."

"I heard he has a rep with women."

She gripped the bottle tightly. "I don't think that's an appropriate topic for a student and a teacher to discuss." She wouldn't look at him. Instead, her eyes fixed on something behind him.

"Sure. Whatever." He held out the essay. "Here. Read it and weep." Abruptly he stood and started to walk away.

She grabbed his wrist. "Wait."

Oh, God, her hand felt so good on him, *he* wanted to weep.

No, what he really wanted was to throw her down on that bench, climb on top of her and drive into her with all the passion that he felt for her. With all the passion of a man.

His back half turned away, he said under his breath, "Goddamn it."

"Don't swear, Luke."

Surly and out of patience—it wasn't an act this time—he glanced back at her. "Ms. C., why do you keep doin' this? How'd I become your pet project?"

She dropped her hand and drew in a breath. Her eyes told him he had hit the target. There went his stomach again. It kicked like a baby elephant was dancing inside him.

"Why are you being so mean all of a sudden?" she blurted out. "It's as if you've decided to hurt me intentionally."

Bingo. "I'd never do that." *If I had a choice.*

"Luke, why can't we go back to the way it was before. . . ."

He rounded on her. "Before the concert?"

"Is that what this is all about?"

Oh, God, he couldn't do this. He just couldn't. Furious with himself and the whole situation with Kelsey, he jammed his hand through his hair. "No, it's not about the concert." He nodded to the essay. "It's about what I wrote in there."

"Sit down, then, let me read it now."

He hesitated.

"Please."

Sighing, he sank back down on the bench, feeling like a falling man who couldn't gain purchase.

Her forehead furrowed as she read his paper. She bit her lip. He couldn't wrest his gaze from the sight of her teeth worrying those full, lush lips. When she looked up, there were tears in her eyes.

Aw, shit.

"Oh, Luke."

"He's been dead a long time. But it gets all stirred up whenever I see my mother, like last weekend."

"He put a lot of pressure on you, as the only boy in a big Polish family."

Well, much of what he'd written was true. "Yeah, I never lived up to his expectations."

"How long ago did he die?"

"Te—two years ago." Damn it, he almost said ten. He lost his mind around this woman.

She reached out and clasped his arm with strong fingers. Leaned toward him. "I'm sorry life has been difficult for you."

He swallowed hard, not feigning the emotion. He leaned closer, too. "Did you ever wish you could just change some things? Like how stupid you were? How bad you acted?"

"Not that. But I've wished I could change some things about my relationship with my father. So I sort of know how you feel."

"Yeah?" Suddenly he wanted to know. He flipped through the files of his memory. *Close to father. Shares a lot of interests.* "You talk like you're close to him."

She shook her head. "I am. But I let him walk all over me. It hasn't been good for our relationship. I need to take a stand more often with him, be firmer in my decisions."

"Least he's alive. You could change that. Now."

She peered closely at him. "You know, sometimes you have the wisdom of a man much older."

Jesus! What was he doing? He drew back from her, to where he couldn't smell her, couldn't see the way her eyes darkened like they might when she made love.

"Yeah, so my uncle says. Only not so nice. It was more like me being too big for my britches."

"Is he mad about the suspension?"

"PO-ed big time."

"I'm sorry."

"Ms. C., it's my fault." He nodded to the paper she held. "It's like that says. I get down about my father, then about my mother not wantin' me now, and I act dumb." As he gazed at her, his heart skipped several beats. "I'm sorry I hurt you."

She swallowed convulsively. He could see her chest rise and fall inside the T-shirt. Her face flushed even more.

He had to get out of here.

He stood. "I gotta go. I can't promise I'll be Josh Quinn from now on, but I'll try to control myself around you." *Understatement of the year.*

Her shoulders straightened. She drew in a breath. "It's a deal." She held out her hand.

He knew he shouldn't, but he did anyway. He reached out and meant to give her a quick shake. But the electricity that arced between them turned the clasp into a tight, compulsive grip. Both stared down at their linked hands. His was big, male, adult; her slender, feminine one nestled inside it. Just the way God meant things to be.

He couldn't move, and felt his breath come in heavy pants. When he looked over at her, she was trying to take in more air, too.

And then the distinctive sound of the gym door rattled through the weight room. Keys jangled. Luke turned in time to see Mr. Wolfe-in-Polo-clothing plop his hands on his hips and say, "Hi, guys. Is this a private party, or can I join in?"

ELEVEN

———

"SEX is important to everybody, whether they admit it or not." Joe sat in one of the lounge chairs in the meeting room of the counseling suite, and opened up the second Boys' Concerns group with what he knew was an attention getter.

Under-the-breath adolescent remarks rumbled out of the guys who occupied several overstuffed couches, slouched on some of the padded straight chairs, and sprawled in beanbag sacks on the floor. Sitting on a table in the corner, Josh quietly surveyed the scene.

"Yeah, yeah, I know," Joe added. "It's uncomfortable to talk about this, but you guys were the ones who put it on the list Monday and chose it for your first topic."

Which, Joe thought, would have been the last topic *he'd* have picked right about now. He was already thinking about sex too much.

I'd be careful with you, Suzanna.
I imagine you would.

"We wanna talk about it," a football player with Schwarzenegger muscles put in. "This is all private, right?"

"Of course. I'm expecting nothing to leave this room."

"Even if we tell you"—the kid's face turned bright red, yet he finished—"we're doin' stuff, you won't narc on us to our parents?"

"You have my word." He directed a glance at Josh.

I'll talk to him, Suzanna, but I won't tell you anything unless he's in danger of hurting himself.

I wouldn't expect you to.

Of course she wouldn't; openness and honesty were too important to her, which was why his being at Fairholm was so hard for her to handle. He wanted more than anything to do some good while he was ferreting out the danger. For her peace of mind. And he wanted to help her son.

"I already explained my position on that, men. But, if you're still concerned, let's go about it like this." He picked up a pad of paper. "Everybody rip off a sheet. Josh, pass around those pens in the cup on the table. All of you, write out one thing you want addressed today, one thing you need to talk about. That way we won't know who the concern came from."

The boys looked relieved—from the football player, to Josh, to Smurf, who sat alone in a corner and seemed to be trying to stay unnoticed. They represented many of the cliques in school, which was exactly what Joe had wanted.

As materials were passed out, they joked around, but finally settled down to write. As the boys wrote, Suzanna's image stuck in Joe's mind. All that glorious hair . . . how she looked in form-fitting jeans . . . how her hand flew to her slender throat, indicating she was skittish around him.

Yep, sex *was* a concern to everybody, even if you didn't admit it.

After five minutes, Joe collected the boys' writings. "I'll start with the top one." He donned his glasses. Knowing his attitude would set the tone, he sat back in his chair and crossed a leg to settle his ankle on his knee. Ruthlessly, he suppressed the knowledge that, given his upbringing, he wasn't quite as comfortable with the issue of sex as he seemed. But damn it, if he could help young boys, he would. "If I have sex with my girlfriend, I'm afraid she'll expect me to marry her." He looked up. "What you're getting at here is sometimes women connect sex with commitment, and guys don't see it that way." He waited. "Should guys have sex without commitment? That's the issue."

"We're only seventeen, or eighteen." This from the football player again. "We're not ready for the ball and chain."

"Then are you ready for sex?"

"We're always ready for sex," said the athlete's buddy.

Joe smiled. "Now, that's a problem, isn't it? Guys have a natural inclination for sex. I know how it is. It can drive you crazy and can be all you think about. Fantasize about."

Suzanna's unbuttoned pink blouse and lacy bra had played a starring role in *his* fantasies this week.

"So, if you aren't ready for commitment, what do you do?" Joe asked pointedly.

"It's a *hard* question." This from the jock. Joe laughed along with the guys at the pun. The boys would relax with the teasing and by seeing that Joe didn't shy away from anything.

They talked about responsibility and selfishness, and when there seemed no concrete answers, Joe said, "You know, there aren't going to be a lot of answers here. It's important to explore the issues, though."

He went on to the next paper. "We have sex. She doesn't like it much." Well, this was bound to come up. "Women are different from men. You've all heard about foreplay." He grinned at the athletes. "And it has nothing to do with football, guys. Women like to be touched and caressed in different ways from men."

Where would Suzanna like to be touched?

"Um, how do you know? What to do, I mean?" The young man in the corner hadn't spoken before.

"Each woman's different." Again Joe smiled.

"Then how do you know?" asked a pink-cheeked, blond soccer player.

"You could ask her." But Joe wouldn't ask Suzanna . . . he'd explore every single inch . . . Damn, what was he *doing?*

Joe managed to keep focused for another half-hour, without letting his own fantasies intrude. Though the discussion became more open, he noticed Josh said almost nothing.

"Well, here's a common comment. 'I'm embarrassed to buy condoms.' "

Joe wondered briefly if he had any on hand.

"This is a crucial point, guys. We aren't just talking pregnancy here, like we were when I was young. We're talking life and death. Nobody can afford to ignore safe sex."

Josh sank lower into the seat. This was a small town. His mother was principal. Could the boy just walk into a drugstore . . . ?

"There are ways to get condoms if you're embarrassed or afraid somebody might see you. Let's talk about that now."

That discussion took the rest of the time. Joe had gotten through only a few sheets, but he was pleased with the outcome. "Before you go, I'd like to reiterate our agreement here. None of what was said should leave the room. Not even who was here. It's private, and this group will work only if we trust each other." He zeroed in on each of the young male faces, some still embarrassed, some a little fearful. No boredom, though. "Agreed?"

There was a chorus of yeses.

"And I hope you'll all come back next week."

As everybody filed out, Josh stayed behind. Joe pretended to be packing up. Casually, he leafed through the rest of the questions. Sure enough, the boy came over to him when everyone was gone.

"You mean it?" Josh asked without preamble.

"Do I mean what?"

"This is private."

"Yes."

Brown eyes assessed him. He'd seen that look from Suzanna.

"I give you my word I won't say anything about this to your mother, if that's what you're worried about."

"She's the principal. She'll wanna have a handle on what goes on in this group."

"I'll talk in vague terms, then. She already knows you're attending. She *wants* you to come here. But I'll keep what we say private, like I promised."

Josh sighed.

"You can trust me, Josh." Joe winced inwardly, thinking about the undercover work. "I mean it."

"I guess."

"And if you want to talk specifically about you and that girl I always see you with, I'm here."

He thought he saw relief on Josh's face. "Maybe." He turned to go. "Thanks." Then he smiled Suzanna's smile. "It's good to have you in this school, Dr. Stonehouse."

For a moment, Joe felt a fleeting sense of connection, a bond that he hadn't experienced with a teenager since Josie died. It was quickly followed by guilt—prickly and uncomfortable. When Josh left, Joe sank into the chair, drew off his glasses, and rubbed his eyes. It wasn't good to get attached here. He wasn't going to be at Fairholm long. He had a job to do for the government, and though it was satisfying that he could help out the kids, he shouldn't get fooled into thinking any of them could mean something to him.

It's good to have you in this school, Dr. Stonehouse.
It's nice to know I'm not in this alone.
Damn it, things were getting complicated.

JOE opened the door to Suzanna at seven o'clock that night. She smiled at the picture he made. "Wow, this is a switch."

Standing before her in gray fleece shorts, sneakers, and a navy T-shirt that hugged all his muscles, his eyes twinkled. "Did you expect me to work out in a suit?"

"Frankly, I never know what to expect of you."

"Come on in."

She stepped into the foyer of the house. To the left sprawled a big family room and a dining room off that, a study to the right, and stairs to the second floor. Everything was in earth tones, clean and homey. "This is nice."

"You sound surprised."

"I guess I've seen too many movies."

At his questioning look, she smiled. "You know, safe houses with no windows, bars on the doors."

His innocent look was almost comical. "We're just an average uncle and nephew trying to finish out the school year."

"Still, this is comfortable. The government has invested a lot of money in STAT, haven't they?"

He leaned back against the foyer wall and crossed powerful arms over his chest. "What's the price of a kid's life, Suzanna?"

She smiled her approval. "Yes, I agree. The money's well spent. But you know that the public would probably protest. Like they do about most school expenditures."

"The public will never know about this." He stepped forward. "Let me take your coat."

Underneath the heavy quilted jacket she wore a sweatsuit.

"You'll be warm," he said scanning the gray and red fleece outfit Josh had bought her for her birthday.

"I've got shorts and a T-shirt underneath."

"We should get started, then." He didn't move. "You look tired."

"Not sleeping well," she said dismissively. "Where to?"

Without further comment, he led her to the kitchen, an L-shaped space that seemed well used. She caught the hint of spaghetti sauce and wondered if he cooked. More likely Luke did. Joe opened the basement door and trundled down the steps.

Following him, Suzanna didn't know what she expected, but it wasn't the state-of-the-art workout room he led her into. "This is great." The floor was carpeted, with a twelve-by-twelve mat at one end, and knotty pine covered the walls. An expensive-looking entertainment system with a TV and stereo took up the space across from a sleek treadmill. Adjacent to it were a punching bag and a futuristic-looking weight machine.

"The room was here. I insisted on top-of-the-line equipment." He grinned, and her stomach contracted. "We old guys gotta stay in shape."

"You look better than half the PE teachers at school."

His mouth curved up. "Think so?"

She frowned, picturing Mike Wolfe.

"What is it?"

"Nothing. Let's start."

He watched her, deciding, she knew, whether to pursue the cause of her reaction. God, he was alert. And astute.

You like smart men, Suzanna. Good thing I have a Ph.D. She'd chuckled at Lawrence's comment. But it was true.

"All right. Stretch first, over there on the mat. Use some of your yoga techniques."

Suzanna dropped to the floor while Joe crossed to the empty wall, braced his arms on it, and extended one leg to stretch his calf the way Josh often did. His leg muscles were corded and dusted with hair darker than that on his head. She wondered what his chest looked like. Kelsey said he had a nice butt. . . .

"Suzanna?"

She looked up to his face. He was staring at her. "You frowned again."

Bending at the waist, she touched her toes. "I was thinking about something."

He came to stand before her, then squatted down. "Keep stretching, but tell me why you're so preoccupied."

She shook her head.

"Did something happen you're not telling me about?"

Close up, he smelled so male, her heart pushed against her rib cage. "Not the way you mean."

"What, then?"

How not to answer him?

He sat down on the floor and waited till she looked at him. "I thought we were becoming friends."

She smiled, sadly. "I'm worried about Kelsey."

"Why?" His eyes narrowed. "Did Ludzecky do something else?"

"In a way."

"If you tell me, I'll give you a report on my Boys' Concerns group. The one with your son in it."

"Bribary is against the law."

"Bring in the Feds."

She laughed aloud.

Spontaneously, he grazed her cheek with his knuckles. "It's good to hear you laugh." After a moment, he dropped his hand.

When she got her breath back, she said hoarsely, "Not much to laugh about these days."

"Hopefully, the outcome of our stint here will make you smile for a long time." He arched a brow. "Kelsey?"

"She's upset about Luke's changed behavior."

Knees bent, Joe dangled his hands between them. "He's doing his best, but he needs to get in with Duchamp."

"I know. It's just that she's getting hurt in the process."

"How?"

"Kids have power over teachers, Joe. Just like they have power over their parents. You invest in them, worry about them, and when they let you down, it hurts."

She bent to the side to stretch again.

He did a few leg extensions. "I'm sorry."

"I want to tell her."

His movements stilled. "Tell her what?"

"About the undercover."

"Absolutely not."

"Just her."

"No."

"Can't we discuss it?"

"No, it's nonnegotiable."

"Look, Joe, you just don't understand what's at stake here. Kelsey's got issues with trust. She depends on me to be straight with her. By deceiving her this way, I'm undermining something that's bound us together for years."

"I'm sorry to hear that. But it doesn't change my decision on this."

"What's the harm in her knowing?"

His face reddened. He was a man not used to explaining himself. "I've already gone through this with you, Suzanna."

She didn't say anything.

As calmly as he could, he reiterated all the things he'd told her about the importance of secrecy. He ended with "And specifically, what we're doing now is tricky. We have to make Duchamp and some of the other kids believe Luke's a punk, willing to piss off the teacher who likes him. If Kelsey knows, she won't react as she should. She's a teacher, not an actress. Kids sense things more than you imagine."

"Then can I tell her after you're all done? She'll have trouble with the deception, but if I could explain it all to her then, it might be okay."

"No. Like I've said before, we'll go on to another school with no one the wiser."

"Brenda Way knows."

"Which is something that concerns me. You have no idea how many nights I've been up worrying that this operation won't stay secret, that it will leak out." His face was grave. "It would shut us down."

"I'm sorry this upsets you. But I have to protect Kelsey. She'll not only think she failed with Luke when you leave, but if she ever found out by accident what I've kept from her, it would hurt our relationship."

"But she'll be safe. So will you, and all your kids."

Staring down, she slapped the mat with her hand, the sound echoing in the basement. "I hate this."

"I know." After a charged silence, he rolled to his feet. "Let's start. You can channel that anger into the maneuvers."

She stood, too. Quickly, she removed her sweats and pulled her hair into a loose ponytail. When she faced him again, the Secret Service mask was back. Only his usually hard-as-jade eyes betrayed the man inside the agent. They took in her shorts and coral T-shirt with a very male perusal.

She raised her chin. "I'm ready."

"We're going to concentrate on two techniques." His voice was after-sex hoarse. He coughed to clear it. "An attacker can come at you from the back or front; you have to be prepared for both."

"All right."

"Always aim for the vital areas in either case. I'll show you first. Lunge at me."

"You, um, aren't gonna hit any vital areas on me, are you?"

His eyes focused on hers briefly, a spark of amusement in his. "I wouldn't dream of it." Then he added, "I told you I'd be careful with you, Suzanna."

She'd had dreams of him saying that, in a different context.

"Let's walk through this first." He stood still, his arms loose at his sides, his feet spread far apart. "Raise your arm at a right angle like this." He lifted up her arm. "This is called a side block."

His other hand fell to her hip; his fingers flexed on her. Suzanna's chest tightened. His rose and fell.

"Stay where you are. As the victim, *I'd* step aside, lift my other arm"—he raised his hand—"and go for the attacker's mouth"—supple fingers swiped her lips—"or eyes"—he traced a brow—"or the bridge of the nose." His knuckles grazed there.

Her breathing escalated like she'd run a marathon. Then she felt the world go out from underneath her.

Literally.

She fell to the mat, though Joe cushioned the fall by holding onto her arm.

"What the hell was that?" she asked.

He smiled down at her. "I brought my foot behind you and took you down, lady. Just like you'd do to your garden variety attacker." Amused, he squatted. "I didn't hurt you, did I?"

She shook her head. "Just surprised me."

"It's good to surprise an attacker."

She gave him a withering look.

"We have to practice this. A lot, so it becomes second nature. If you have to think about the move, you won't be able to do it." He stood, held out his hand and drew her up. They faced each other like boxers in the ring.

An hour later, Suzanna was dripping with sweat. Every muscle screamed for her to stop.

"You did great," he said from the mat where she'd thrown him.

"Did you let me best you?"

"No."

She smiled and dropped down beside him.

"I think that's enough for tonight."

She stuck out her legs, leaned over at the waist to stretch, and moaned. "I'll be too sore for yoga tomorrow."

Joe's eyes darkened. "You go with Kelsey, don't you?"

"And Brenda."

"Remember what we talked about earlier."

Irritated, she didn't say anything.

"About the importance of secrecy."

"I remember."

"I want your word, Suzanna. That you won't now, or ever, reveal this operation to anybody."

She stiffened. "You have it." Angry, she sprang to her

feet. He came up behind her and turned her around. She was only as tall as his chin, and he was so big, so male, she felt encompassed by him. Her eyes were glued to his chest. She lifted her hand and touched it. The muscles beneath her fingers contracted, and he sucked in a breath. His hands went to her shoulders, slid to her biceps.

And then he drew her to him.

He was a wall of muscle, hard, damp, and very safe. Suzanna couldn't remember when she'd felt this safe. Arms of steel banded around her. One hand splayed against her back, bringing her closer. Another went to her hair, tugged, released the ponytail. His fingers threaded through the heavy mass.

His touch zinged all the way to her toes.

"I'm sorry, sweetheart."

She didn't ask about what. She didn't comment on how naturally the endearment fell from his lips.

"That things can't be the way you want them."

Instead of answering, she buried her nose in his shirt.

He finished, "The way I want them."

She nodded. She knew he meant that he'd leave here when he was done and, for the sake of the operation, have no contact with her ever again. That he was sorry about that.

Another hug. "You'd better go," he said harshly.

At first, she didn't answer, then finally said, "I'd better."

TWELVE

———

NOTHING was quite like the inside of a New York City newsroom—the smell of stale coffee and ink, the clatter of the computers, even the buzz of excitement. Though today, Sunday, not much was happening in the desk-cramped room. It was one of the reasons Jerry Wakefield had agreed to meet Brenda here. *Though I don't know why the hell you'd want to come back,* he'd barked. Sometimes he was as gruff as his old friend Conrad used to be.

But Brenda knew why she'd returned. She needed the reinforcement today. She needed to remember why she'd started on this rocky path back to the top. After what she'd found out about Joe Stonehouse yesterday—and, hopefully, what the private investigator would tell her tonight—she needed the reminder.

Slowly she crossed to the feature editor's office. Through the window she could see the battered desk. A worn leather chair. She could still see Conrad leaning back, feet propped up, his brown eyes sparkling. *You can be the best, kiddo. Win that Pulitzer. Prove to them you can do it.*

Juxtaposed to that she heard her mother's whiny voice. *You're just like your old man. Always have to be right. Always have to prove yourself.*

"Brenda?"

Turning, she found Jerry behind her. He'd gotten a gut, and lost more of his hair in the five years since she left, but his kind blue eyes still smiled at her fondly. He nodded to the office. "Hard to see this again?"

"Nah." She stared ahead. "Remember when he got the promotion? He was so excited."

"We celebrated all weekend."

In some ways, their coworkers had been their families. Certainly, for Brenda, Conrad and the newspaper people were the only real family she'd ever had. He'd even left her all his money in his will. She'd been surprised by the legacy and shocked to find out what was in his stock portfolio.

He was her family in every sense of the word, just like Suzanna.

"Why'd you want to come here? We could have met at the restaurant."

"Nostalgia, I guess."

"You wanna come back, kiddo?"

Tears sprang to her eyes. Conrad had always called her that. "Maybe. I got a story I'm working on that's going to shoot me to the top."

He smiled. "You're just like him."

Linking her arm with his, she said, "Thanks for the compliment."

Jerry turned as grim as a pallbearer when they slid into a booth at Perry White's, a narrow, dark newspaper hangout and she ordered a glass of wine. "I thought you were off the booze, Brend."

"I am. I indulge once in a while, on special occasions." She gave him the once-over. "It's so good to see you."

He wasn't derailed. "You know, he always saw you as the daughter he never had."

Uncomfortable, she drew out a cigarette. "He'd hate that I was let go from the *Times*."

Jerry frowned. "He'd hate the booze and butts thing."

"I'll be back, though," she went on, as if he hadn't spoken. "I'll make him proud, in a way that's perfect poetic justice."

By exposing, she thought to herself as she took a long

drag on the Marlboro and sipped her Merlot, *exactly the kind of thing that got Conrad killed.*

BRENDA was still drinking five hours later. She'd wandered around the city, taken in a Monet exhibit at the Met, and waited for her seven o'clock appointment with the PI. The Big Apple turned cool when the sun went down, and she shivered in her raincoat.

The wine she sipped, as she took in the dark mahogany walls and sawdust covered floor of Dresden's, warmed her. A seedy Times Square bar, it seemed suitable for her meeting with the PI she'd had occasion to work with years ago. She was hyped about what he'd told her on the phone Friday, so hyped she said she couldn't wait for the written report and wanted to meet with him tonight.

She was also hyped about what she'd learned yesterday afternoon, thanks to her best friend's slip after yoga class. Brenda hadn't let herself think about it when she was with Jerry. She was very good at compartmentalizing her life that way. But now, ensconced in a booth with a drink and another cig, as she waited for more ammunition, her mind drifted back to Suzanna. . . .

"You look like shit, Suz," Brenda had said as they shared coffee before class in a new bistro that had just opened in downtown Fairholm.

"I'm exhausted and sore as hell."

"How come?"

She'd rubbed the bridge of her nose with thumb and forefinger. "Agent Stonehouse is giving me self-defense lessons."

Brenda had stilled. "Does he think you're in that much danger?"

"It's precautionary, I guess."

"I don't like this, Suzanna. If you went public with the hit list and tire slashing, you could get protection openly, round up these kids he suspects, and quash the danger before it has a chance to erupt." Brenda's words were out of her mouth before she realized that her own agenda would be seriously altered if Suzanna did what she advised. *But if Suzanna was really in danger*, she remembered thinking, *so what?*

Suzanna had smiled in that nurturing way of hers, and shaken her head. "Thanks for the concern. I love how you worry about me. You're such a good friend."

"Don't try to distract me."

"Joe thinks this is the best way to proceed."

"Yeah, the expert on school shootings. It's impersonal to him, Suz. He doesn't have the investment here you have. It's just a job to him."

Suzanna's defense of the man had come out of nowhere, like a damn bursting. And it had all the force of a renegade flood. "No, you're wrong. It's very personal to him. He loves the kids. . . ." At Brenda's roll of the eyes, she said, "His niece was shot. . . ." Suzanna's voice trailed off then.

"His *niece* was shot?"

Eyes wide with horror at her revelation, Suzanna reached for her coffee; her hands shook as she held the cup. "Oh, God, I can't believe I said that. I'm not supposed to tell you any of this. If I wasn't so tired, it wouldn't have slipped out."

Brenda stared hard at her friend. "His niece was killed in a school shooting? When?"

"Brenda, please."

"Suz, you already told me this much. I want the details."

"I don't know them. All I know is it was his sister's daughter. It happened a few years ago, I think he said."

"How many?"

"Three or four."

Brenda had tried to calm herself, but couldn't wait to get home and onto the Net. From there, it wasn't hard to track down what school shootings happened a few years ago. She read the account with horror. Seventeen-year-old Josie Callahan, shot by a fellow honor student who felt too much pressure and had exhibited suicidal tendencies. The shooter had killed himself after he'd gruesomely gunned down four others. Survived by mother, Ruth Ann; two siblings, Mark and Shelly; father, Al; and a beloved uncle, Joseph.

There were myriad pictures, just like with Columbine, and even one of Joe; Brenda recognized the broad expanse of his back in the fitted Italian suit, though he'd covered his face with one hand and grasped his sister with the other. . . .

Exhaling smoke into puffy rings, Brenda retrieved a notebook she always carried with her. Suzanna had given it to her, saying it was just the right size for her purse, and was for sudden inspirations. She wrote: *section devoted to the life of a Secret Service agent. What goes on behind the scenes? Personal history.*

She cringed. The family's grief would be flaunted for all to see. Okay, so she wouldn't use names. But anyone could piece it together as she had.

And Joe would blame Suzanna.

Maybe that wasn't half bad. Doodling on the pad, Brenda thought back to the events of the weekend. She'd been disturbed by Suzanna's strong defense of the man. By how her face softened and she got all dreamy-eyed when she talked about him. Brenda was afraid Suzanna was falling for the guy. And that was not a good idea. He'd make her miserable. He wasn't her type. He was tough, like Brenda; hard-nosed. Street-smart.

And, she thought as Harvey Meachum ambled through the door, she was about to find out why.

A wiry little man with eyes like a beetle's, Meachum slid into the booth. "Jesus, Brenda, this is damn inconvenient for me."

She signaled the waiter. "I told you there was an extra hundred in it if you'd meet me tonight for a prelim report."

"Yeah. It's the only reason I left Bambi's bed."

"Bambi? Oh, God, Harvey, you really are out of a grade B movie."

They ordered drinks. Brenda said, "So, spill it. Where did Agent Stonehouse and Agent Ludzecky come from?"

Harvey drew a notebook out of his jacket pocket and peeled back the cover; he squinted in the dim light. "The kid's a bust. Normal family life. They live in Queens."

Hmm. Not far. Maybe she could get a peek at them.

"Seven sisters. Mother alive, father dead." Harvey took a swig of his Molson's when it arrived. "Don't know how the guy survived living with all those women."

It sounded like heaven to Brenda, who'd grown up with no siblings, an alcoholic mother, and an absent father.

"He's twenty-six, graduated summa cum laude from Columbia in political science, applied to law school, got in but never went. He joined the Secret Service at twenty-one."

She shrugged. So the adorable Agent L. was smart. Who would have guessed?

But she wanted the meat. "Tell me about Stonehouse."

"That was tougher. His shit was buried deep."

She rubbed mental hands together. "Why, has he done something?"

Scowling, Harvey shook his head. "Not like you mean. His record's squeaky clean. What I could get of that. The government files were hard to access. But the personal stuff came up."

"What?"

"He had the screwiest background. Was raised in the sixties in Pennsylvania."

"Don't tell me he was a Quaker. Though it would fit his no-nonsense demeanor."

"Nope, just the opposite. He lived in a commune."

"A what?"

"A commune. You know how the sixties were. Back to the earth. Make love, not war. His parents were honest-to-goodness hippies. He was brought up by a whole group of 'em."

"Wow. How come he turned so straight, I wonder?"

Harvey's face darkened. "You know what happened in some of them communes?"

"No, do you?"

"Yeah. I had a hunch and ran down this one. A few of the original members are still alive."

"His parents?"

"No. But I got an earful from the others. The little old couple who talked to me sure don't look like swingers."

"Swingers?"

He nodded. "According to them, that free love stuff was all it's cracked up to be."

"And?" Her newspaper instincts went on red alert. Harvey knew something sensational.

"For the kids, too."

"The kids?"

"Uh-huh. The adults figured it was their responsibility to rid their kids of their sexual hangups at an early age."

Brenda's stomach lurched. "That's perverted."

"Maybe, but they didn't think so. Apparently they initiated both the boys and girls ASAP."

Oh, God. "Was . . . was it incest?"

"No, thank God, it wasn't. But still, Stonehouse and his little sister grew up pretty fast."

"How old were they?" she asked tightly.

"He was ten when they joined. She was six."

"How long did the family live there?"

"The parents died there. Stonehouse and the girl disappeared when they were fourteen and ten."

"Disappeared?"

"They ran away. Never saw their parents again. Or anybody else from Sweet Times Farm. The old couple says they were missed."

Brenda could just picture it. "I'll bet." No wonder he'd gone after that child porn guy.

"Sick, isn't it?" Harvey asked.

"Yeah. It's sick." And it explained a lot. A whole lot about Joseph B. Stonehouse. Secret Service agent. Beloved uncle.

And abused child.

THIRTEEN

———

THOUGH it didn't happen often, Kelsey had been depressed all week. She'd had a tedious conversation with her father when he'd tried once again to convince her to come to Yale to teach. She was really getting tired of his overbearingness, and knew she should deal with it head-on. He was stopping over to see her this weekend on his way to do research in D.C., and she feared she'd be subjected to his continued tirade, which she didn't seem to be able to stem.

Maybe I should leave the high school, she thought as she entered her classroom after cafeteria duty. There'd been a fight during lunch, which she'd broken up; in the process, she'd gotten slammed against the wall and her shoulder was sore. But it wasn't only that. This morning, when she'd gotten to school, her identification badge, which had been in her desk drawer, had been cut in half—right through her face. Security guessed someone must have broken into her classroom. It was frightening.

To top it off, the results of the Government midterm she'd graded last night were dismal. Then, Ben Franzi had written a disturbing essay for Psychology about aberrant behavior being a good thing and, when she tried to talk to him, he'd blown her off.

As she reached the door, she came face-to-face with one

of her biggest problems. "Ms. Cunningham," Luke Ludzecky said as he accompanied Morgan Kane through the door.

Luke had been excruciatingly polite and purposely distant all week. At least he hadn't been bad, contrary to the next boy who followed him in. Rush Webster traipsed into class wearing headphones, brashly ignoring school policy, which prohibited musical devices, pagers, and cell phones.

"Ditch the headphones, Rush," she said as she set down her leather bag and removed her jacket. She'd fussed with her appearance today, selecting a soft beige blouse and long raw silk skirt and jacket to match. She'd put on her prettiest earrings—dangling copper with abalone shell in the middle of them.

Rush trudged to his seat without acknowledging her comment. He slouched in a desk in the back and closed his eyes so that when she crossed the room to stand before him, he could neither see nor hear her. Typical ploy on his part.

In no mood for rebellion today, she yanked the headphones off. He sat up straighter. "What the fu—" He cut himself off. "Don't touch me, lady. Or my stuff."

"Then keep your eyes open and follow the school rules. Get rid of the headphones." Not waiting for an answer, she turned her back. It was a signal that she expected to be obeyed.

Under his breath, Rush mumbled, "Bitch."

She circled around. "Got something to say to me face-to-face, Rush?"

His eyes narrowed into slits. He stared her down.

Despite her impulse to step back, she held his gaze for long seconds. "I expect an answer, young man."

He shook his head. It was enough. Pivoting, she headed for her desk. From the corner of her eye, she saw Luke, poised on the edge of his seat. His entire body was ready to spring, reminding her of the young jaguars she had seen on a wildlife show her father watched. She gave Luke a stern look. He didn't relax. She shook her head slightly, and he sat back. Just what she needed. A knight in shining, though somewhat tarnished, armor.

The rest of the class went downhill from there.

Kelsey picked up the test papers. "These weren't good, guys. Look at the screen." She'd done an item analysis on the computer, which she hooked up to the TV; she called up the results.

The kids groaned.

"My sentiments exactly." Only five students had passed, and just one scored in the nineties. "These results are unsatisfactory for a midterm exam. Any thoughts on how to proceed? I can't very well reteach everything."

"Can we see our own papers first?" Morgan asked. "Maybe we can tell from them what we should do."

"All right." The room was quiet, except for her heels clattering on the floor as she returned the exams.

She tried not to watch Luke as he scanned his paper. She was surprised he'd failed the test; although he hadn't been in her class the whole semester, he should have passed. He had a bright, incisive mind and picked up everything quickly.

His hazel eyes narrowed, and he winced when he saw the grade.

"Uncle Joe ain't gonna like this one."

From behind, Morgan leaned over his shoulder. She'd gotten the highest grade. "I could tutor you," she whispered.

Kelsey felt something shift inside her. It only added to the confusion she'd been feeling all week.

Rush wouldn't take his paper when she got to him, so she set it on the desk and returned to the front of the room.

Addressing the class, she said, "What I'd like you to do is get into groups and brainstorm how to deal with these bad results. Come up with ideas on how to review this material; what, if anything, we can do to improve your term averages; and generally, what's going wrong in class that the grades are abysmal." She smiled at Morgan. "Peer tutoring by those who passed is an example of how we might compensate."

As the kids formed groups, Kelsey took attendance. She noticed Smurf was missing, for the third day in a row; Luke had volunteered yesterday to bring some work home to him this afternoon. She also noticed that Webster sat staring at his paper, which bore the grade of 20, while the rest of the kids formed groups.

Let it go, she told herself. *It'll just be another scene.* But one of Kelsey's cardinal rules was not to allow the kids to veg. More than once, if a kid refused to work, she'd kicked him or her out. Why let Mr. Sourpuss change that?

She approached his desk. "You need to get into a group, Rush."

He purposely turned his head and stared out the window.

Oh, hell. Maybe she'd give it one more try. "If you're upset about your grade, we could talk about getting you some help."

His body tensed, but he continued to face the windows.

Her temper spiked, aided by a sleepless night and dreams she couldn't remember when she did catch some z's. "Look at me, Rush."

He didn't.

"You have to participate in group work like everybody else."

Still no answer.

"Have it your way." She went to her desk, found a disciplinary referral, and wrote him up. She could tell by the silence that the rest of the kids were watching. When she finished, she walked back to his desk and held out the note. Still, no response. This time she tossed the paper onto the desk. "Pick it up, get up, and leave the classroom."

Nothing.

"*Now!*" She raised her voice.

Slowly, his head turned and he raised his chin. The contempt in his eyes made her heart trip in her chest. What had she done to deserve that? "Don't yell at me, lady."

"Then don't ignore me. Get up and go to the office, now."

Again, he refused to obey and just stared at her. Finally he spat out, "I go where I want, in my own time."

"Not in this school you don't." She strode to the front of the row and pointed to the door. "Leave, or I'll call the office and have security come to get you."

An interminable minute later, he stood. She moved out of his way as he reached the top of the row. Instead of heading for the door, he stopped before her.

Don't ever face down kids. Just get them to leave. It had been sound advice during practice teaching. But she'd be damned if she'd let Rush Webster intimidate her. She held her ground, even though she had to look up at him.

The class had gone still. She heard a shuffle and then Morgan's worried voice, "Don't, Luke, you'll get suspended again. Ms. C. can handle it."

Kelsey took the time to glance at the class. "I can deal with this. Everyone stay put." She returned a steely gaze to Webster.

The remark seemed to inflame him. He stepped forward. Loomed over her now. He was so close she could smell something on him . . . pot, maybe. His eyes were bloodshot; his throat worked convulsively.

And Kelsey was afraid.

She inched back and circled her desk. Picking up the black phone, she scanned the kids. Luke was out of his seat, held back by Morgan's hand on his arm. Again, she shook her head at him as she dialed zero and spoke into the phone. "I need someone in 435 right away."

Webster headed to the door. But she didn't even have time to breathe easily before he turned around and stalked back. With a lethal glare, then a grunt, he heaved her desk up and over. Papers flew, pens and scissors banged on the floor, and books slammed against the wall.

Since Kelsey stood close behind the desk, the edge hit her knee and she went down.

LUKE leaped over a student desk and flew to the front of the room. Webster had sprinted out the door, but Luke didn't spare him a glance. All he could think about was getting to Kelsey.

She was in a heap on the floor, wedged between the wall and the desk; he couldn't tell if she was hurt. "Somebody help out here," he yelled. Two football players rushed to the front to right the desk with him. He circled around it fast. Bending down, he saw her clasping her knee and moaning.

"Where are you hurt?" he asked hoarsely.

"My knee. The desk hit it."

Shielding her with his body from the kids who'd gathered around, he lifted her pretty skirt. Her stocking had a gaping hole in it, with tiny runs fanning out; her knee was already discolored and beginning to swell. And she was shaking badly.

He put his hand on her neck, whispered, "Shh, Kelsey, it's all right," and turned to face the kids.

"Morgan, run to the health office and get some cold packs. This has to be iced down right away."

He turned back to Kelsey. Her face was chalk white, her lips trembling.

In that second, Luke wanted to murder Rush Webster.

"You're safe," he said softly. It took every ounce of his willpower not to pull her to his chest.

"Oh, God," he heard behind him. Suzanna hurried in the door, a security guard close behind her; she was at Kelsey's side in seconds. Kneeling, she looked at Luke. "Is she all right?"

"Her knee got banged up. I sent for cold packs."

Suzanna took one good look at Kelsey and tugged her into her arms. Kelsey buried her face in Suzanna's shoulder and hung on. More than he wanted his next breath, Luke wished that she was clinging to him. But, good agent that he was, he stood and stepped back.

Stonehouse came running through the door. "What happened?" The kids all started talking at once. Joe said calmly, "Shh, guys, one at a time." He looked to Luke.

"Webster got out of line again."

Joe raised his brows.

A young girl must have interpreted it as chastisement. "Ms. C. wanted to handle it herself, Dr. Stonehouse. She told us all to back off."

Nodding, Joe seemed to approve.

It didn't make Luke feel a whit better.

Morgan returned with the cold packs. There was a flurry of activity, then the nurse came in with a wheelchair.

While they tended to Kelsey, Joe went to the phone. Luke followed him. "Security. This is Age—Dr. Stonehouse. There's been an altercation in room 435. Get your personnel out looking for a student named Rush Webster. About six feet, dark hair and eyes, wearing. . . ." Again he looked to Luke.

"Black leather jacket, army boots, and blue jeans."

As Joe related a description of the guy, Luke's hands fisted. A million things were running through his mind. Should he have helped? Would he have blown his cover? He was a mass of conflicting emotions as the wheelchair was pushed out of the classroom to the nurse's office. Accompanying Kelsey, Suzanna blocked Luke's view of her. He started to follow them.

Joe grabbed his arm at the door. "Luke, stay."

"Not on your life," he mumbled, shook himself free, and trailed the entourage down the hall.

They wouldn't let him in the inner sanctum of the nurse's office, and he backed off once he realized how inappropriate it was for him to even ask to go in. He paced the outer area that was filled with cots, a desk, and several filing cabinets. The room smelled like antiseptic.

Suzanna came out interminable minutes later. She crossed to Luke. Her face was drained of color, but her eyes were flaming. Dragging him aside so no one could hear, she asked tightly, "Why didn't you stop Webster?"

What could he say? That he didn't want to blow his cover? That he jumped in headfirst on the last job and almost ruined the operation? Or the truth—that he knew he was too involved with Kelsey already, and that wariness had overridden good judgment?

"It happened so fast . . . she seemed to be handling it. . . ."

Suzanna's eyes said those were stupid answers.

They were.

"Can I see her?"

The principal drew in a breath. "I don't think that's a good idea."

He straightened. "Is her injury bad?"

"No. She's mostly just shaken. Her knee's swollen, though. The school physician says she'll need to stay off it for a few days. I'm taking her to her own doctor, just to be sure."

Stonehouse came through the door. "Webster's nowhere to be found on school grounds. Security can't do much more."

"We should call the police." Suzanna was upset.

"I'll do it," Joe said. "I'll call Captain Caruso, my contact."

"Joe, I—"

Before she could finish, Mike Wolfe bulldozed into the office, his face flushed. "I just heard. Where is she?"

Suzanna straightened. "In there, but I—"

He didn't wait. Instead, he barged through the door, letting it bang shut behind him.

Luke stared after the man, his fists curling at his sides. "Son of a bitch," he said, and stalked out of the office.

SO this was Suzanna mad! Really mad! Throw-things, swearing mad. She didn't know she was being watched and, as he stared into the house through the glass doors off her back deck, Joe was mesmerized by her loss of control.

He wondered if this was how she was in bed.

An end-of-March cold front had blown into Fairholm, and he could see the puffs of air coming from his mouth. He'd been waiting in his car for her to return from Kelsey's, and after she'd pulled up and stomped from the garage into the house, he decided to check her out to see if she was all right. Knowing he'd be the last one she wanted to see tonight, he'd circled around back, guessing she'd go out into the kitchen.

She did. She ripped off her coat and flung it to a chair; it slid to the floor. Then, she yanked open a cupboard door, pulled out a box, and slammed the door shut. She dragged open the refrigerator, removed milk, slammed that door, too. She tried to pry open the box, and when it stuck, she hurled it to the floor, where it bounced on the area rug. For good measure, she kicked it hard; it banged against the baseboard.

Then she paced. Her glorious hair flew around her shoulders in wild disarray, falling into eyes he knew were blazing. She strode back and forth. Then, unexpectedly, she sank onto a chair and buried her face in her hands.

His heart clutched in his chest, squeezed even harder as he saw her wipe away a tear; it began to punch against his rib cage as she pillowed her arms on the table and buried her head in them.

He wasn't thinking straight when he inched up close to the glass and knocked. She practically ricocheted off the chair. After she recognized who was there in the dark of night, she stared at him for a moment, eyes narrowed, mouth tight. At least his presence brought color to her face. Slowly, she rose, crossed the room, unlatched the lock, and slid the door open. "Standard procedure for the Secret Service, Agent Stonehouse? Lurking in the dark, watching people?"

He jammed his gloved hands into his pockets. "Sometimes."

"What do you want?"

"To see if you're all right."

A flush crept up her neck. "Of course I'm not all right. A kid assaulted a teacher today, I've got spies in my school—one of whom just stood by and watched the entire incident—then the superintendent, and you, I might add, kept telling me to stay cool. Well, I'm *not* cool."

He glanced toward the box that lay on the floor, noted it was Hershey's cocoa. "No, I see you're not."

She looked down, closed her eyes briefly. "It was childish."

"It was human. I don't blame you for being upset."

"You want to come in?" She scanned him up and down. "You look different." He wore jeans with an L.L. Bean jacket, a green sweatshirt underneath, and boots.

Stepping inside, he said, "I'm going out of town." He glanced over her shoulder at a pretty starburst teak clock on the far wall. "I was just waiting for you to get home, to see if you were all right, before I left."

"You're leaving town?" Her voice quavered. The small show of anxiety made his gut clench.

"For the weekend. It's been planned a while. It's personal."

Her arms banded around her waist. "Oh."

His hands fisted. "Ludzecky will check up on you." He looked into the dark house. "Josh out for the night?"

"Josh went skiing with Heather's family for the weekend."

"*What?* I talked with him about sticking close to home."

Releasing a heavy breath, she shrugged. "I know. I forced the issue. He'd had this ski trip planned for a long time, and was going to cancel it." She raised her chin. "I wouldn't let him."

"I don't like you being alone here with Webster on the loose."

Her eyes widened. "Do you think I'm in danger?"

Unzipping his jacket, he said, "I don't know what to think anymore." He nodded to a kitchen chair. "May I?"

"Yes, of course." She darted a glance at the stove. "Would you like something before you leave? Coffee, maybe?"

His grin was brief. "I haven't had hot chocolate in a while."

She smiled, then turned, crossed to the box, and bent over to pick it up. Her beige skirt was calf-length, and she wore it with boots and a matching sweater, but the action made his blood pump faster just the same. Returning to the table, she handed him the box. "If you'll open it, I'll heat the milk."

He removed his coat while she poured milk into a pan. He took a spoon, which lay on the table, and pried open the top of the box. "See, Secret Service agents are good for something."

Glancing over her shoulder, she gave him a wry look. "I'm sorry about what I said today."

"Which part? That we were bumbling idiots or that we were total incompetents if we couldn't even protect your teachers?"

Her face was flushed from the heat of the stove. And from embarrassment, he guessed. "Both. I was upset about Kelsey."

Kelsey again. She was so close to the girl. No wonder she was so upset.

He brought her the chocolate. The milk smelled sweet, and made him remember fixing the drink for Josie when she was little and couldn't sleep. He set the box down and turned away to squelch the memory of all he'd lost.

"Kelsey's okay," Suzanna said.

Joe crossed to the doors and, sticking his hands into his back pockets, stared out at the the yard. Light snowflakes danced in the wind. "Yes, I know. I called her after you left her house."

"You called her?"

"As a counselor checking up on his colleague." He shook his head. "Ludzecky was like a caged tiger when he got home. He wanted to storm right over there and see how she was. I calmed him down, then called to see how she was doing." Joe shook his head. "She asked if she could talk to him. She's something else."

Still stirring, Suzanna sighed. "I know she was worried about his reaction. She says she explicitly told him not to intervene. Of course, she thinks he's just a kid."

Joe faced her. "He shouldn't have intervened, Suzanna. He could have blown our cover."

"Kelsey got hurt, damn it."

"She would have gotten hurt if we weren't here."

"But you *are* here. Luke could have stopped it. And it wouldn't have blown your cover. He's already established himself as Sir Galahad."

"It's my fault."

She faced him. "Why?"

"I've been on his ass—" Joe sighed. "On him about controlling his behavior." He rubbed his arm. "I got shot the last time we worked together because he jumped into something like this. I think he misread the situation, though he doesn't believe he did. In any case, he was formally reprimanded. I've tried to convince him to not interfere unless absolutely necessary."

Suzanna's gaze rested on his arm, then her eyes met his. Hers were full of a woman's sympathy.

"She's okay, anyway, isn't she? Just a swollen knee."

"Yes."

Frowning, he scanned the room. "Maybe you should go stay with her for the weekend. Help her out."

"No. She was exhausted tonight and just wanted to sleep. Plus her father's coming tomorrow. Though he'll get on her about how she got hurt, he loves her and he'll take care of her."

"You could still go over there."

She shook her head. Swirls of honey blond hair distracted

him. "Reynolds Cunningham and I don't get along. We haven't since I 'got his daughter into high school teaching, for Christ's sake.'"

Joe chuckled at her imitation of Kelsey's father.

"And he resents my interference in her life."

"Tell me about that. Why it bothers you so much that you're keeping secrets from her."

Suzanna turned back to the stove; she stirred the hot chocolate as she filled him in on her long-standing relationship with Kelsey and the young woman's need for trust.

"Thanks for sharing that," he said when she finished. "I understand your issues with the undercover more, now. But I'm sorry, it still has to stay covert."

"I know." Her tone was so resigned, it made his heart constrict. When she finished with the cocoa, she poured it into mugs and brought it to the table. The liquid steamed as she set down the mugs, and he noticed little tendrils of her hair curled from the heat. "Come drink this. You're probably anxious to get going."

God, she was beautiful in the dim light, her hair loose around her face, little pearl earrings peeking out from beneath it. As they sat together, she sipped her hot chocolate delicately. She reminded him of a fragile porcelain doll. Thinking about her tantrum earlier, he knew she was tougher than she looked. Still, her staying alone for the weekend when he wasn't in town was unacceptable.

"Where are you going?" she asked, as if reading his mind. "Or can't you tell me?"

I can't tell you. "To my sister's." A long pause. "It's the anniversary of Josie's death."

"Josie?" Her hand slid over to cover his. "Oh, Joe. She was named after you."

He nodded and held on to her. "My family's better. They have strong religious faith, and their church has helped them cope with her death. Still, no matter what, wherever I am, I manage to get home for . . . this."

"Home?"

Briefly he squeezed her fingers, then let go. It felt too good, gave him too much comfort. And he was a man who didn't take comfort well, had taught himself not to need it. "I guess I see their place as my home, not my brownstone in D.C. I have a suite of rooms at their house." He smiled. "They live in this sprawling farmhouse on acres of land." He glanced out the window. "There might even be sledding with my niece and nephew this weekend."

"I'll bet they love having Uncle Joe there." Her voice was wistful.

My brother's in Arizona . . . Brenda and Kelsey are the only family I have. . . .

"I think, because Josie and I were close, my being around makes them all feel better."

"And you? Do you feel better when you're there?"

He studied the chocolate as if it were tea leaves and revealed the secrets of life. "Yes."

They drank in silence. Did her thoughts mirror his? That he wished like hell they were here under different circumstances. That he had the right to throw back his chair, drag her onto his lap, and kiss away the worry on her face. He'd slipped up the other night, and called her sweetheart. With a flash of insight, he wanted the right to all kinds of intimacies with her.

"I wish things were different," she said softly.

He couldn't let her verbalize it, or he'd do something stupid. "I do too, Suzanna." Even to his own ears, her name sounded like a caress.

For a while they sipped the cocoa and made small talk. Then she glanced at the clock. "You should go before it gets too late."

"All right."

The scrape of their chairs was loud, echoing in the silence of so much left unsaid. Crossing to the doors, he rattled them.

"I'll turn the alarm on when you leave, Joe. All the doors and windows are wired."

"I know." He pivoted. "Walk me out the front so you can set the security system when I leave."

Together they walked through the kitchen, down the corridor, to the foyer. The living room was dark, and a tree batted against the window. She jumped back. His eyes narrowed on her.

"I'm a little skittish, I guess."

"Call Ludzecky if you get scared. He'd love to play rescuer, since his pride's been bruised by today." That wasn't enough, though. "And if anything happens, call the police."

Suzanna gave him a brave smile.

"Promise?"

"I promise."

Next to her, on the hall table, was a bunch of daisies. They suited her perfectly. He glanced up the steps behind her. "Will you take a bath now?"

She looked away, and he wondered again what she was thinking. "Maybe."

"Suzanna, I—"

Gently, she raised her hand to his lips. His entire body warmed at her touch. "Shh. Go. Your family needs you."

So do you, he wanted to shout, feeling more torn than he could ever remember. What if something happened to her when he was gone? Could he live with that? He grasped her upper arms.

She leaned in close to him, so her forehead touched his chest. "Joe, please, just go."

Releasing her, he turned. He reached for the door and clasped the cold knob, but he didn't twist it.

Agent Stonehouse warred viciously with the man inside him.

Whirling around, he looked into amber eyes as conflicted as his must be. "Come with me, Suzanna."

FOURTEEN

SUZANNA couldn't believe she was sitting in the Callahans' warm cocoon of a family room in Connecticut at eleven o'clock on Friday night. She was surrounded by Joe; his sister, Ruth, who sat on his right and kept touching his arm; and Al, lounging in a chair and looking eternally grateful to see his brother-in-law. High school senior Mark sprawled at Joe's feet and ten-year-old Shelly sleepily leaned on her uncle's shoulder.

When he'd asked Suzanna to come here, she'd protested, albeit weakly. . . .

Joe, I can't go with you. It's got to be against the rules.

Mr. Straight Arrow himself had said, *Screw the rules. We'll talk about how to handle my family on the drive up.*

Joe, I—

Please, Suzanna. I want you with me.

It was the phrasing that had persuaded her. It was personal, possessive. Like the other night when he'd held her close and called her sweetheart. Neither of them had mentioned that slip.

"More wine, Suzanna?" Ruth resembled Joe with her green eyes, classic features, and dark hair. Dressed in navy slacks and sweater, she smiled warmly at her surprise company.

Suzanna tugged at the cowl of the white sweater she'd put on, with black jeans, for the trip. "No, thanks, Ruth. I'm having trouble keeping my eyes open as it is."

"Even though you slept on the way up?" Joe teased.

Delighted at this new side of him, Suzanna smiled. Primarily, she was stunned at the man who came out from inside the agent, though she'd caught glimpses before. She *had* slept on and off, but overheard the calls he made from his cell phone. . . .

Ruthie, I'm bringing someone with me. A pause. *Yes, a woman, but it's not like that.* Another pause. *No, not in my rooms. Make up the guest room.* A chuckle. Then, soberly, he said, *You can't ask her anything, not even what she does for a living. She's connected with the case. Tell the kids.* A big-brother sigh. *Yes, she's very pretty.*

Feigning sleep, Suzanna had been warmed by the compliment and nestled into the blanket and pillow he'd provided.

His call to Ludzecky was equally interesting.

I've got Suzanna with me. Luke reacted; she could hear his elevated voice over the phone. *I know, and frankly, I don't give a shit.* Again, a comment. *Yes, you could have watched her, Luke. I'd trust you to do that. But it's . . . complicated. We'll talk about it when I get back.*

His conversations weren't the only things that had intrigued her. The closer they got to his family's house, the more he seemed to unwind. When she'd awakened, they chatted about how to handle her being with his family, but mostly they talked about normal things, like normal people.

His reaction when they arrived had emphasized the change. Before her eyes, he'd behaved like a completely different man. An honest, passionate, flesh-and-blood man— hugging his sister till Suzanna thought Ruth's ribs might crack; unabashedly embracing Al; letting Mark make the first move to hug him. And Shelly had not let go of her uncle once in the two hours they'd been here.

"Somebody else is sleepy." Al indicated his daughter. "Want me to help you to bed, princess?"

Joe stood and scooped her up. "I'll do it." He held the

long-legged child in his arms as he smiled at Suzanna. "You okay?"

She nodded.

Mark said, "I'm going up, too." He was a gangly teenager who took after his soft-spoken father. "Dad, wanna see what I did on our web site before I crash?" He and Al were working on a web page for Mark.

Al yawned. "Yeah, then I'm turning in." He stood and smiled at Suzanna. "They keep you young. See you in the morning." He crossed to his wife and kissed her soundly on the mouth. "Don't stay up all night with Joey. You won't enjoy the rest of his visit."

Joey.

"I won't."

And then she and Ruth were left alone. Suzanna, the mystery woman, and Joe's very close sister.

"He's never brought anybody here before, you know." Ruth had her brother's no-nonsense way about her, though she relaxed back onto the nubby beige couch.

Suzanna shook her head. The other woman's honesty called forth her own. "I *don't* know, Ruth. I don't know much about him."

"Would you like to?"

"You mean about how you grew up and everything?"

Her face shut down quicker than a door slamming in your face. "No, we never talk about how we grew up." She brightened. "I mean other things."

"I'm not sure he'd want me to know more."

"Because you're part of the case."

"Yes."

"So you'll be out of his life after whatever he's doing with you is over?"

Pierced deeply by the thought, Suzanna nodded. "He's different here," she said quietly.

"Never seen him in jeans?"

"Not just that. He's softer, more vulnerable."

Ruth said quietly, "I worry so much about him. I hate the Secret Service lifestyle. All the agents live such a lonely existence." She swallowed hard. "And, of course, I live in terror that something will happen to him."

It was a fear that Suzanna hadn't allowed herself to entertain. But reality came crashing in—an unwanted guest at a very private party—and she admitted, for the first time since this whole thing began, that Joe—and Luke, too—were risking their lives in Fairholm.

I'll die protecting them.

Oh, God.

"Well, no story." Joe's voice was a deep rumble from the doorway. "She fell asleep without asking."

Ruth laughed, and Suzanna tried to cover the horrible realization she'd just had by yawning.

"Tired?" he said solicitously.

Don't stay up all night with Joey. These two needed time together.

"Yes, as a matter of fact, I am."

"Come on, I'll take you to your room."

No, he couldn't do that. It was too intimate. Just as showing her his suite earlier had been.

His own private space was different from what she'd expected. Lightly stained oak walls. A huge bed with Indian print covers. A den off that, and a bathroom, all decorated in soft browns and greens which highlighted his cat eyes.

She stood. "I can find the way this time."

"Good night, Suzanna," Ruth said.

"Good night, Ruth." She faced Joe, and her insides turned soft. "Thanks for bringing me here."

She was halfway up the steps when she remembered she'd left her purse by the couch. Backtracking, she made it to the doorway unseen when she heard Ruth say, "This is so unlike you, Joey. What's going on?"

"You know I can't tell you that, honey."

"I don't mean the undercover work. I mean *her.* You're breaking every policy in the Secret Service handbook by bringing her here."

"I am. And I could get called on the carpet for it."

"Are you that worried about her safety?"

"The truth?"

"Nothing but . . . like we agreed."

"It's more than the case. I wanted her with me."

"Why?"

"I can't answer that. I won't."

"Joey—"

"No, honey, drop it. Let me just enjoy this weekend with you and the kids. And her. I . . . need it."

"Okay." Quiet. "I need it, too."

Suzanna pivoted, abandoning the purse. Her heart was racing as she quietly crept back to her room. Though the guest accommodations were homey, and the bed comfortable, it took her a long time to fall asleep.

SUZANNA was awakened by squeals and laughter. She turned over in her bed, trying to block out the sound. But it kept up, grew louder. When she came fully awake, she heard voices outside her window—high, feminine shrills and low, masculine shouts.

Sleepily, she glanced at the clock and was startled. When was the last time she'd slept until 10 A.M.? Burrowing into sunny yellow pillowcases that smelled like detergent, she listened to what was happening outside. The sounds reminded her of Josh and Lawrence and how they used to play outdoors in the winter. An acute pang of loneliness ambushed her.

She eased out of bed and crossed to the window. It had snowed last night, and all the Callahans and Joe were engaged in a snowball fight. It was Ruth and Joe against the rest of them—as if they'd been doing that all their lives, siding against the world.

We don't talk about our childhood.

Rapt, she watched Joe's bullet-like throw at Mark, which hit him square on the back. The boy and his sister responded with several lobs at him; one caught him in the face. She wondered if it stung. From here, she could see his cheeks were red.

He advanced on the kids as the other two adults went off to the side. Shelly started screaming, and running, and Joe darted after her. When he caught up with her, Mark sneaked up behind him and jumped on his back. Joe's cap was dislodged. The three of them fell to the ground, and the kids proceeded to bury Joe in the snow.

She had to turn away from the sight. This was a man who could mean . . . too much to her. And she wouldn't let herself go there. As she showered in the bathroom adjacent to her room, she tried to forget the sight of him outside with his family.

But she remembered his words. . . .

First from three nights ago, *I know, sweetheart.*

Then from last night, *It's more than the case. I wanted her with me.*

Get a grip, girl, she told herself. *He isn't going to be in Fairholm forever. He's only doing his job. One you shouldn't distract him from with a romantic interest.* Besides, he'd made it clear that his lifestyle had no room for women in it.

By the time she was dressed in jeans and a heavy blue angora sweater, socks, and boots, she'd almost convinced herself. Downstairs, she was sipping coffee in a windowed breakfast nook when the back door opened and someone came into the mud room.

Murmurs, a soft laugh, and suspicious rustles. ". . . in the laundry room, lady. We did it here before."

Ruth and Al.

Purposely, she made noise to let them know she was up. A few minutes later, they came down the corridor.

"There she is," Al said, flushed from being outdoors—and probably the suggestive remarks he'd made to his wife. He seemed younger today in a beige chamois shirt and brown slacks.

Looking rested in a red sweatsuit, Ruth was holding onto Al's arm. Suzanna had been shocked to see Joe turn into a toucher up here, too. "Good morning."

"Good morning." Suzanna nodded outside. "They have stamina, don't they?"

"Yeah." Al poured mugs of coffee and fixed Ruth's with sugar and cream. "He'll be dragging by the time he leaves. The kids don't let up on him."

"It's because. . . ." Ruth stopped, her eyes rounded. Al stiffened. They both glanced worriedly at Suzanna.

"Ruth, I know what this weekend is. You don't have to watch what you say around me. About Josie, at least."

Ruth's eyes widened further. "He told you?"

Suzanna nodded.

Al took a seat and glanced out the window. "Sometimes I think he suffers more than us. He doesn't have anybody to share his grief with."

Ruth grasped Al's hand. "They were so close."

"I'm sorry," Suzanna said. "About your daughter."

"Thanks." Ruth looked toward the window, too. "It was senseless. Such a waste." She swallowed hard. "Kids are so precious. You never know how much until. . . ."

Suzanna waited a moment, then said, "I have a son. I know how precious children are." Sighing, she added, "And his father died five years ago. It's hard to lose someone you love."

Nodding, Ruth stared outside. "Oh, no, look."

Suzanna recognized the change of subject for what it was. "Oh, Lord."

Uncle, niece, and nephew had trudged up the hill behind the house. Each was seated in a saucer-like sled at the top. They sped down the hill. Suzanna smiled as the kids purposely maneuvered their sleds right into Joe's. The crash upended them all, and they fell into a heap on the slope.

Ruth's eyes teared. "He's so good with them."

"I can't believe it," Suzanna said. "He's so different here."

"This is the real Joe, Suzanna."

"Is it?"

"Yes," Ruth said firmly. "It is."

JOE tossed in his bed, unable to settle down. The new print comforter and pretty beige sheets Ruthie has picked out were in a tangle. Through the skylights, he studied the stars, which he never got a chance to see in his city dwelling. They twinkled and winked and made him think about life as it could have been.

Turning over, he punched the pillow. Was she asleep? He glared at the red numbers on the clock. Only 11 P.M. Everybody had turned in early because of the active day, heavy Italian dinner, and a little too much wine for the adults. Suzanna hadn't seemed tired, though she'd gone to her room when everybody else did. He'd had a quick fantasy of the two of them going to bed hand in hand, tucking in a kid or two, holding each other through the night.

That was never to be. Tomorrow they would go back. He'd turn into Agent Stonehouse and have to face the complete breach of professional conduct he'd made for the first time in his career by bringing a client into his personal life.

But he didn't regret it.

You're different here, she'd said as they cleaned up the dishes. She'd offered to do it alone, but Joe had joined her to help.

I am.

I like both, she told him.

Both?

The Secret Service agent and the man.

He'd had all he could do to keep from sidling up behind her at the sink, trapping her between his body and the counter, and drawing her to him. He'd have turned her around, taken her mouth—she'd taste sweet and sexy—and touched her intimately.

Arrgh. . . . He groaned into the darkness.

Disgusted with his ruminations and the effect they were having on him, he snapped off the covers and rolled out of bed. He'd go downstairs. Maybe hit the hot tub. Anything but lie here and think about . . . making love to her. Finally, he admitted it. He wanted Suzanna, more than he could remember wanting a woman in his life.

Throwing on gym shorts, a sweatshirt, and a pair of Docksiders, he opened his door. He crept down the hall and found his way in the dark to the back of the house and out to the deck. As he was uncovering and turning on the Jacuzzi, he saw the light from her window above.

Don't do it, he ordered himself.

But the agent was not in control this weekend. And the man took over. Cursing himself all the way, he stopped in the changing room off the deck, grabbed one of Ruthie's suits and his bathrobe that was hanging there from the last time he visited, and made his way up to Suzanna.

She answered on the first knock. Briefly, he closed his

eyes at the sight of her, dressed in icy blue satin pajamas. He could see the outline of her breasts through the top.

"Joe?" she asked quietly. "Is something wrong?"

"No, I couldn't sleep." He glanced behind her, saw the lit reading lamp and a book resting along with her glasses on a table. "You, too?"

She shook her head, sending wild hair flying.

"Come with me?" he asked hoarsely.

"Where?"

He thrust out the bathrobe and suit. "To the hot tub."

"Are you kidding? It's freezing outside."

"But the water's warm. The kids used the tub today."

"No way."

"The high school principal's afraid of a little cold?"

Her eyes narrowed.

"Come on, Suzie Q, I dare you."

Her beautiful, luscious mouth literally dropped open with the nickname he'd called her only in his mind. But then, without a word, she grabbed the clothes from him and closed the door. He chuckled at her reaction all the way to the tub. He was already in the steaming water when she appeared in the doorway.

And, at that moment, the agent inside the man surrendered completely.

She stood clothed in his bathrobe like she belonged to him. The white terry cloth skimmed her ankles, and the sleeves reached way past her hands. She raised them to the lapels, and pulled the top close around her neck.

He couldn't speak for how utterly sexy she looked. Vivid fantasies of what might have preceded her wearing his robe, or what might follow her donning it, flicked fast-forward through his mind. He was grateful that his body was covered by the water.

"Joe?"

Her whispered word brought some sanity back. He ordered his wayward libido to quiet. "Come in. It's nice and hot."

Stepping outside, she raced the short distance to the tub and hung the robe on an outdoor coat tree. He got only a quick peek at womanly curves and feminine flesh before he took her hand so she could climb in the tub safely. He meant to let go, really he did, but once she was in, somehow he couldn't. He held on, thinking, *Let me have this much. Just for tonight.*

She plopped down beside him. Joe laced their fingers, the gesture intimate. After a moment, she grasped his hand more tightly. They watched the stars for a few minutes. The steam was thick off the water, dissipating into the crisp night air.

At one point, she turned and laid her head on his shoulder. It was better than cotton candy, Christmas, and the Fourth of July parade in Washington. He angled his body so he could take some of her weight and kiss her hair. Eyes closed, she sighed.

They stayed that way for a long time, and Joe knew that, for as long as he lived, no matter where he traveled in the world to do his godforsaken job, he'd never feel as he did on this crystal-clear night, at this isolated farmhouse in Connecticut, with this very precious woman beside him.

FIFTEEN

———

WELL, Luke figured philosophically, if Stonehouse had stayed put, Luke wouldn't be sitting in his battered Ford at eleven o'clock at night, staking out Kelsey Cunningham's house, because he was so hung up on her. But no, the big guy had to leave town this weekend, when Luke's self-control was zilch. It was something personal with Joe, something he wouldn't share with Luke.

And you're surprised at that because. . . .

No, he wasn't surprised. Just concerned. Joe looked pained about something. When he told Luke it was personal, he'd been as rigid as a gun barrel and, paradoxically, more emotional than Luke had ever seen him. Luke had wanted to probe, but Joe had turned away and the opportunity was lost.

Then there was that phone call from him later, saying he was taking Suzanna with him on the pilgrimage. Now *that* was screwy.

Or was it?

Hmm. Luke wondered if they were getting it on. He laughed out loud in the quiet of his car. Like teenagers thinking about their parents having sex, Luke just couldn't imagine old Joe and Suzanna doing it. Besides, the Ice Man wouldn't break Secret Service rules if the Cabinet ordered him to.

Now, Luke—he'd break every rule in the book for Kelsey. He pounded the steering wheel and stared hard at her house—a small two-story just outside of the main downtown area. Painted a pretty gray with black shutters, it was a typical suburban home, something Luke could have sworn he'd never want. But tonight, in the cold of March that surrounded him, he could picture himself sharing a house like that with Kelsey. Hell, he'd live in a pup tent if he could have her.

He laid his head down on the steering wheel. Oh, hell! He was really losing it. How many times did he have to tell himself that she was off-limits? That when the undercover was over, he had to leave Fairholm and sever all contact with all of the people here, in order to continue with the operation. There was simply no way out of it. For him, or for Joe. Suddenly Luke hoped Joe wasn't getting into any kind of relationship with Suzanna.

The soul-searching knocked some sense into Luke's thick skull and made him reach to start the engine—until a black Camaro pulled into Kelsey's driveway. He knew that car. He'd seen Mike Wolfe swagger to it, rub smudges off its shiny exterior, and slide in it like Mr. I'm-Too-Sexy-for-the-World. To release the pressure in his chest, he spat out, "Goddamn fucking son of a bitch." But he didn't drive away.

Kelsey's front door opened, and a shadowy figure let Wolfe in. Luke waited a half-hour for him to leave. Geez, she'd be tired tonight. What the hell was the guy doing, coming this late, overstaying his welcome?

Well, just maybe Luke was going to have to find out. He stormed out of his car and headed for the house. He had a pretty good idea, from the lights that were on, where she'd been all night. Slowly, he crept up the lawn, cursing the crunch of the snow under his boots. He was glad when the wind picked up and blocked out any sound he made, even if it was getting colder. His ears stung, and he slipped on his gloves. The air sliced right through his bomber jacket, so he zipped it up. Sneaking around to the side of the house, he scoped out the windows. There were two of them, on either side of the fireplace. The blinds on one were closed. He jogged to the other window.

Open blinds. Shit, she should be more careful. Unsavory characters could be looking in on her—not somebody like Luke, who was concerned about the Big Bad Wolfe inside. He found a position where he could peer into the room but not be seen from the house.

They were there, sitting on a couch. She was scrunched into the corner, surrounded by bed pillows, as if she'd sidled as far away from him as she could get. She wore a thermal shirt and pj bottoms; her leg was elevated on the coffee table. Wolfe was holding her hand, inching closer, talking to her, sliding his fingers up and down her leg. Luke couldn't hear what the creep had to say, but he saw Kelsey shake her head.

Wolfe's bodybuilder chest leaned into her. Luke's heart began to hurt.

Wolfe's mouth grazed that lovely hair; Luke had wondered a million times what it felt like. Remembered vividly what it smelled like.

The jerk worked his way down, kissed her nose. Luke's throat closed up.

The guy put his lips on her cheek. Then took her mouth. Luke felt his insides knot.

Wolfe's hand came up and clasped her throat. When it headed south, for her breast, Luke looked away.

He wanted to die.

He was just about to leave, unable to tolerate watching some other man touch Kelsey intimately, when he felt a hand collar him. "Okay, kid. What're you doing here?"

CHRIST, the man was an octopus; Kelsey was trapped between the pillows and Mike Wolfe's hard body. She'd tried to push him away, but he wouldn't budge. When his mouth worked its way down to hers, she thought, *Why not?* He'd kissed her before, though she hadn't found his practiced technique particularly stimulating.

He wanted more than a kiss. Pumped up on drugs for her knee, still disturbed by the events of the day before—and thinking about Luke Ludzecky, of all things—she let Mike's hand go to her throat. It was big and warm, but felt vaguely foreign, somehow not right. So when he went for her breast, she grabbed his wrist.

He drew back. "What is it?"

"Well, a lot of things." She studied his face. His expression was that of a man aroused. Since she didn't feel the same, she said, "For one, we haven't been dating very long."

"A few weeks." He glanced at her chest. "Enough for this."

"I'm not sure I agree. But second, I'm in pain, Mike. I just took a Percocet, I've been on muscle relaxants for two days, and I'm woozy."

"Oh, uh, sorry." His eyes lit up. "I could ease the pain."

"No thanks." She was about out of patience. The incident yesterday had drained her; what the confrontation with Webster hadn't taken out of her, the medicine had.

Because of that, she'd called her father and asked him not to come down today but wait until tomorrow. She hadn't wanted any company, including Mike. "Look, Mike, maybe you misunderstand our whole—" The doorbell halted her when she was about to tell him that continuing to date him was probably not such a hot idea.

"I need to see who's at the door." When he didn't move, Kelsey pulled her princess routine. It worked like a charm on most men. "Let me up, please."

"I could, um, get it."

"No, thanks. I'd like to do it myself." Shakily, she rose, grabbing onto the table to steady herself. For a moment, the world tilted, then righted itself. She took the crutches and hobbled to the foyer, breathing in to clear her head. After checking the peephole, she pulled open the door.

A police officer and Luke Ludzecky stood on her porch. The blast of cold air momentarily revived her. "Hi," she said to Luke. Then she looked at the officer. "What's going on?"

"We caught this kid outside your window, playing Peeping Tom."

"*What?*" Her stomach dropped at the thought of what Luke might have witnessed between her and Mike.

"He says he was checking to see if you were up; he didn't want to wake you if he rang the bell and you were asleep. He says you had some kind of accident yesterday and he wanted to see if you were all right."

She lifted a crutch. "He's right about that." The dizziness returned full force. She had to blink to keep the cop in focus.

"Look, we got an order to watch your house this weekend. That maybe some kid from school might bother you. I say we caught him."

"I say so, too." Mike appeared in the doorway. Sparing him a glance, Kelsey could see the flush on his face.

She said, "Whoever ordered you to come here wasn't after Luke. If he says he was checking to see if I was awake, then he was." She smiled at Luke. "Come on in." She donned her princess look again. "Thank you, Officer. This young man is fine with me. He's one of my students."

"I don't think it's a very good idea—" Mike put in.

"Why don't you leave with the officer, Mike? I'd like to talk to Luke alone."

Mike straightened to his full six feet and postured almost comically. "The hell I will."

"Surely you don't mean you're refusing to leave my home when I ask you to."

Wolfe glanced from her to Luke and back again. "I don't like this, Kelsey." He regarded the young man intently. "First I catch you two alone in the weight room. Then he was in the nurse's—"

She interrupted. "Good night, Mike."

Mumbling, he grabbed his jacket off the coat tree and stalked out, followed quickly by the police. When she closed the door, she found herself leaning heavily on the knob. Finally she was able to draw back and face her visitor. "Well, this is a surprise."

Luke removed his gloves, jammed his hands in his pockets, and watched her, as if assessing her. Kelsey swallowed hard. They were alone. In her house. Her heart, which had slowed to molasses when Mike had kissed her, began to thump in her chest.

Luke looked older tonight. He had on a beautiful hand-knitted sweater that she'd never seen before, and the color brought out the green flecks in his hazel eyes. He seemed taller, too; bigger.

On the crutches, she swayed toward him, suddenly overcome with the lethargy that had been chasing after her all day. Luke's hands shot out to grab her. "What's wrong?"

"Nothing. I'm just a little tired, I guess. And I took a lot of medicine."

He seemed torn for moment, then said, "Oh, hell," and dispensed with her crutches with one hand while he anchored her shoulder with the other. In a lightning quick move that made her head spin, he swung her up in his arms and drew her close.

Against her will, she nestled her face in his chest. The wool of his sweater *was* soft, and he felt big and strong and very male. He smelled like some expensive cologne. Kelsey breathed him in before she realized what she was doing. This was a *kid*. One of her students. *Oh, my God.* "Luke, don't. Put me down."

He cleared his throat. "Okay. But you're not walkin'."

He strode into the living room and over to the couch. Gently, he set her down and lifted her leg to the table. Then he took the blanket and tucked it around her. She watched him through heavy lids.

"There." He gave her a half-smile. "You're down."

"Luke, what are you doing here?" Her words sounded slurred. "What were you doing out there?" She nodded to the windows.

His expression was innocence personified. "Just like I told the cop, I was worried about wakin' you."

"Why are you here this late at night?"

He seemed to think about that one. "I, um, oh, hell, I still feel bad about yesterday. Like I should've done something. I wanted to see if you were okay."

Frowning, she tried to order her thoughts, but they were getting jumbled. "Oh, Luke, I told you it wasn't your place to stop Webster or to protect me." She yawned now. "You're just a kid."

"So you keep tellin' me."

"What?" Her head must be fuzzier than she realized. "I don't understand that comment."

"No, you wouldn't. Listen, it's ingrained in me. I

should've tackled Webster when I had the chance." He nodded to her leg. "Instead you got hurt."

Lying back against the couch, she closed her eyes. God, she was tired. And though she'd taken a Percocet, her leg still hurt.

He said, "I'm sorry. You're exhausted. I shouldn't have come at all, started this commotion."

"No, it's okay. I appreciate your concern. It's just that it's been a long week."

When she opened her eyes, he'd squatted down in front of her. "Want me to help you to bed?"

"No."

"Wanna lie down here?"

She was so tired. "Maybe."

He plumped the pillows and drew off the blanket. She stretched out, and he put more pillows under her leg to elevate it. Then he covered her up, this time with a heavy quilt that was on the floor by the couch. "Go to sleep. I'll let myself out. And lock the door."

"Luke, I . . . we need to talk." Her eyes were closing. "It's not your fault . . . but you shouldn't be here . . . and in school, you called me Kelsey. . . ."

She was half asleep when she felt something brush her forehead. But it was gone before she could determine what it was, and then the world faded to black.

AW, hell, his ass was grass now. He'd only meant to watch her for a few minutes to make sure she was asleep. He'd turned off all but one light in the corner, removed his coat, and dropped down on a chair opposite her. After being cramped in his car all night, he'd stretched his legs out on an ottoman. The next thing he knew, freakin' birds were chirping outside her windows.

He blinked to clear his mind and assess the damage. His car was on the road, down a ways, parked under a tree. Conceivably, it could go unnoticed. Maybe he'd be able to sneak out without her realizing he'd stayed.

He sat up. She was on the couch, sound asleep. Her arm was thrown over her head, and her lips were slightly parted.

The cover had slipped down, and he crossed to her to draw it up; as he bent over, he saw that two buttons on her thermal top had come open. The upper curve of her breast was visible, and the nipple poked against the top.

He froze, unable to tear himself away from the sight.

She moaned. A sexy moan. A purely female moan.

Then she grabbed his hand.

His blood pressure skyrocketed as he waited to see what she'd do. She drew his hand toward her chest. Placed it over her breast. Of their own volition, his fingers flexed on her. The blood pounded in his ears and his pulse rate tripled. Never in his life had he felt anything so wonderful.

She whispered, "Luke," and her sexy utterance back-stopped his breath. His eyes flew to her face. Huh? She was still asleep? He couldn't help the grin that split his face. She was dreaming about him! It made him rock hard. He took only a moment's pleasure in her reaction. But then, because he was a man of honor, not a boy who'd cop a cheap feel, he drew his hand away. "Me, too, honey," he whispered and straightened.

He grabbed his coat and headed to the back door to let himself out. He circled around the side, and was approaching the front of the house when he looked up. A car pulled into the driveway and braked abruptly.

A man leaped out of the vehicle. He was big, with gray hair and dark brown eyes that looked familiar. "Who the hell are you?"

Aw, fuck, not again. Could this get any worse?

"Are you the lunatic who attacked my daughter?"

Yep, Luke thought as he faced Kelsey's father, *it could. It just got worse. A lot worse.*

ON Sunday night, Joe stood in Suzanna's foyer and, as had happened all weekend, the agent warred with the man. "I don't want to leave." Simple words, with a very complicated message.

Sitting on the stairs facing him, dressed in jeans again and a pretty rust sweater, she propped her elbows on her knees and her chin on her hands. "I'm fine here. You checked the house, and Josh is on his way home."

He wore his coat, ready to go. Purposely, he left it on so he wouldn't stay. "It's not that." Though, of course, he'd made sure she was safe.

"I know. It was a nice weekend."

It had been wonderful since last night, when they'd wordlessly shared the hot tub and their closeness had been palpable. He didn't know exactly when and how that had happened—over a period of time, he'd guess—but they *had* gotten close. Too close. It felt damn good, even if it was against the rules.

"You're thinking you shouldn't have taken me to Connecticut."

"It was probably unwise."

Suzanna threaded back the heavy fall of hair from her forehead. "Probably. Do you regret it?"

He thought about having coffee with her this morning, alone, when the Callahans went to church, and how the winter sun in his sister's breakfast room had sparkled off that honey-colored hair. He thought about her sidling close to him, seeking his body warmth, as they watched the kids ice-skate on the pond later that morning. He remembered her nearness in the car on the drive home, the way her perfume filled his head.

He'd kept her as close to him all day as he could, even when they'd all gone to lunch at a local diner and Suzanna had insisted on treating. "No, Suzanna, I don't regret it."

Gently, he pulled her up off the steps and rested his hands on her shoulders. "I have to go."

"All right." A woman's eyes stared up at him. They said, *I wish you could stay. The night.*

"Suzanna." He breathed the word.

She raised her hand. Smoothed his cheek with her knuckles. It was scratchy against her soft skin. "Go."

He would. But he grasped her hand first, opened her palm, and turned his mouth to it. The butterfly-soft kiss he planted there made her draw in her breath.

Before he could do any more damage, he turned and opened the door. He didn't look back. Just said, "Lock it," and closed it with a soft *snick*. He waited on the porch to hear the lock engage. He pictured what she was doing, where she'd go. It was a few minutes before he could make himself move.

On the drive to his house, he forced himself into work mode. Into government mode. Into the robotic mode that he'd functioned in for what seemed his whole life.

Man, he was tired of this. Tired of his world revolving around catching thieves and smugglers and people who wanted to kill innocent victims. He'd been tired of it for a long time. Laymen had no idea how nomadic and isolating the Secret Service was—one year he'd had forty-two separate out-of-town trips. But he didn't let himself dwell on that. His time with Ruthie always made him introspective, he guessed, though this weekend, he'd been even more reflective. Because of Suzanna.

"Ah, Suzie Q," he said aloud. "What am I going to do?"

His trained, disciplined mind answered him.

Absolutely nothing. You will finish here. You will leave and never see her again.

Angina-like pain gripped his heart. Because he knew that, indeed, he *would* do absolutely nothing.

Pulling into his driveway, he saw Luke's car. Good. They could talk about the case. They could plan and strategize. They could try to bring this operation to the next level.

He wondered what the kid had done this weekend.

LUKE let the rhythm of the Wild Strawberries consume him. Lying on his bed, he closed his eyes and got into Roberta's soulful tale of lost love.

There was a knock on the door. He drew in a breath and yelled, "Come in."

Stonehouse stood in the doorway. Luke eyed him carefully. He'd never seen the guy so relaxed. Damned if he didn't look like he'd gotten laid; but he'd had Suzanna with him all weekend. Unless Luke's earlier musings had been accurate. Were they involved?

"Can you turn it down?" Joe nodded to the stereo.

Luke picked up the remote and silenced the band he'd seen with Kelsey. "Hi. Have a nice weekend?"

Joe's face got . . . all soft and goofy. *Jesus.* "Yeah. You?"

"Not exactly."

Stonehouse's eyes narrowed. "Did something happen?"

"Not in the way you mean."

Staring at him, Joe said, "Do I need to sit down for this?"

"Maybe. A year of rest might do it."

Joe crossed the room and straddled the desk chair. "Shoot."

"I stirred some waters this weekend."

"Now why doesn't that surprise me?" No rancor, Luke thought. The guy really *was* mellow. Thank God for small favors.

"I, um, wanted to check up on Kelsey last night."

Joe winced. "Tell me you didn't go to a teacher's house on a Saturday night."

"I just meant to make sure she was safe. Webster's on the loose, she'd been hurt."

"I told you her father was coming to stay with her."

"Yeah, well, he didn't get here until Sunday morning."

"How would you know that?"

He caught me sneaking out of her house at 8 A.M.

Luke had to struggle not to close his eyes in disgust. Talk about inept. He should be stripped of his badge. "I met up with him as I was leaving her house."

"You watched her all night?" The coldness was blowing back into Stonehouse's voice like a relentless February storm.

Bolting up off the bed, Luke stalked to the dresser and opened the drawer. He pulled out a cigarette and lit it.

"You shouldn't do that, Luke. It'll kill you."

The drag on the smoke calmed him. "If you don't kill me first."

"Tell me all of it."

He faced Joe. "I got caught, twice." He paced. Smoked. "I was stakin' out the place; I was worried about her, and wanted to make sure she was okay. Then Wolfe showed up. He came over, and I. . . ." He ran a hand through his hair. "I spied on them through the window."

"Why?"

'Cuz I wanted to see what he was doing to her. "I'm not exactly sure."

"They heard you?"

"No, the cops collared me."

"What?"

"You didn't tell me you were havin' her place watched."

"I didn't know I had to clear everything with you, Agent Ludzecky."

"Look, you're right to be pissed. I blew it. I think I covered pretty well with Wolfe, although he stormed out mad as a hornet because Kelsey wanted to talk to me alone and wouldn't let the police cart me away."

"Why don't I think this is the worst of it?"

"Because it's not."

Luke finished the cigarette and leaned against the desk. For a brief second, he wanted to confide in Joe, share his confusion and guilt. Life as an agent hadn't let him make many close friends, and he really needed to talk to someone now.

"All right," he said instead. "Here's the worst of it."

He told Joe about carrying Kelsey to the couch.

He left out how she cuddled into him as if she belonged there against his heart. In it.

He told Joe how she'd fallen asleep and he was going to stay just a while to make sure she was okay.

He left out that he'd been unable to tear his eyes off of her, unable to leave because that was probably the only chance he'd ever get to watch her sleep.

He told Joe that he'd awakened and was about to make a clean getaway.

But wartime torture couldn't make him reveal that Kelsey had obviously been dreaming about him, that he'd touched her, even if she did initiate it, and that he'd almost come apart with his first, intimate contact with her.

"I left, of course, but um, good old Dad came pullin' into the driveway just as I came around the back of the house."

"No, Luke, tell me that didn't happen."

"I'm afraid it did." Luke shook his head. "He was suspicious, of course. Dragged me back inside and woke her up."

"What did she do?"

"Well, she was groggy as hell, and he didn't seem to care. He got on her about what I was doin' there."

"Did he know you'd spent the night?"

"*She* didn't know. I lied and said I'd come back to check up on her."

"Did he believe it?"

"I think so." He shook his head. "I'm mostly worried about the shit he gave her when I left. She wasn't feelin' well at all."

"You should be worried about our cover."

Luke nodded. "I know. I didn't mean for this to happen."

"Do you ever?" Stonehouse stood.

Luke had expected explosive anger. This cold reaction was worse. It was just like it had been when he disappointed his father.

"Maybe I can do some damage control here," Joe said.

"What are you going to do?"

"Call Kelsey first. See what I can do about that part. And then have my contact in the Fairholm police make sure everything's square on that end."

Luke felt like a first-class bumbling idiot. Exactly what Suzanna had called them Friday. Joe strode to the door.

"Joe?"

Gripping the doorknob, Joe didn't face him. He was probably trying to keep himself from strangling Luke. His shoulders were all stiff again, and stupidly, Luke regretted ruining the guy's earlier good mood.

"You can take me off the case, if you want. This . . . well, as I said, I blew it."

Joe nodded. "Yes, you did. I'll let you know what I'm going to do."

A huge lump formed in Luke's throat. How many times had he heard Stash Ludzecky say something similar, in exactly that tone?

"HI. It's Joe."

"I recognize your voice." Suzanna's tone was amused, as if it was silly for him to identify himself.

He sighed and stretched out on his bed, still dressed in his tan jeans and sweater. "Is it too late to call?"

"No, I was just getting into bed to read."

Joe bit back a moan. What would Suzanna wear to sleep in tonight? Silk? If she was his, he'd buy her something sexy, the color of fall leaves to accent her eyes. Sliding further down on the pillows, he shook his head. *This* was not good.

"Joe?" His silence had been prolonged.

"I just wanted to make sure Josh got home all right."

"He did." A rustle. A whisper of sheets, maybe, sheets that would smell like her. "He's asleep now."

"I'm keeping you up."

"No, I'm not sleepy."

"Me neither."

He couldn't stop himself. "A hot tub would relax you."

Her laugh was sultry, sexy. He hadn't talked to her much on the phone, and was surprised at how deep her voice sounded over the wires. "It would feel great." She waited. "It was nice last night, sharing that with you."

"I know." His body hardened at the thought of her so close to him, all warm and wet. To distract himself, he said, "There were some problems here this weekend."

"Really?" Tension crept into her voice. "Kelsey's okay isn't she? When I called over there, Reynolds answered and said she was napping."

"Her father still there?"

"Yes, he's leaving late tonight. Flying off to Washington, I think. He sounded more angry at me than usual. He told me I should be able to control those boys at school. I assume he meant Webster."

"And Luke."

A pause. "What does he know about Luke?"

Sighing, Joe released a pent-up breath. He realized he'd called to tell her the whole story. And to get some help. He was feeling deeply conflicted about the kid. As his boss, Joe wanted to strangle Ludzecky for bungling this. In a fatherly way, he wanted to help Luke deal with his feelings for Kelsey, which were getting more obvious every day. Succinctly, he described Ludzecky's escapades this weekend.

Much to his surprise, Suzanna laughed. It eased some of

the tension in Joe's body. Maybe this wasn't as bad as it had appeared. "I'll bet your young Secret Service agent is embarrassed by all that."

"As well he should be."

"You're upset."

"I am."

"Joe, the kid made a mistake. But it was a heartfelt one. He was worried about Kelsey."

Shifting the phone to his other ear, Joe said, "He worries about Kelsey too much."

"What do you mean?"

"I . . . I think he has feelings for her." He waited. "A man's feelings."

Suzanna drew in a breath. "I think she has feelings for him, too."

He didn't like hearing that confirmed. He sat up straighter.

"It's one of the reasons I want to tell her you and Luke are undercover. Please, can't we. . . ."

"No."

She hesitated, then said, "All right. I won't push it now."

"This thing between them isn't good, Suzanna. An agent can't afford to get personally involved."

No response. He swung his legs off the bed.

"We're trained to stay focused. To stay detached."

Still no answer. He stood.

"When we leave here, we can't have contact with anyone."

Absolute silence on the other end. He began to pace.

"No matter how much we want to."

Finally, she said, "I know all that, Joe. I . . . accept it."

He dropped down onto the bed.

After another significant pause, she said, "Take it easy on Luke. It's not always possible to control your feelings about someone."

"No, but you can control what you do. How much time you spend with that person. How much time you think about her."

"Can you?"

The conversation had gotten out of hand. He had to stop it. "I have to go."

"All right."

"I'll talk to you tomorrow."

"Sleep well, Joe." When he didn't hang up, she said, "And thanks for calling."

She hung up first. He stared at the receiver.

Son of a bitch!

SIXTEEN

———

SUZANNA went in to school early Monday morning to take care of some business, then left at ten to visit Kelsey. She cooked her young friend breakfast, straightened up the house, and was about to leave when Kelsey said from her nest of pillows on the couch, "Don't go yet. I need to talk to you about something."

Taking one look at Kelsey's drawn face and compressed lips, Suzanna crossed the room and sank onto the edge of the couch. The girl had been quiet all morning, and Suzanna had chalked it up to pain and the medication she was on. "What is it, sweetie?"

Kelsey looked away, as if she was about to confess to high treason. "Something's happening to me."

"Are you in too much pain? I'll call the doctor."

"Not in my leg. In my head. My heart." She scanned the room, her eyes suspiciously bright. Kelsey was tough, but sometimes teachers had uncharacteristic reactions when assaulted by a student. Symptoms similar to post-traumatic stress.

"That's not unusual after what you've been through. Are you afraid now?"

"It's not that. I'm pissed at Webster and could wring his neck, but I'm not wigging out about *that*."

"What *are* you wigging out about?"

Nervously Kelsey bit her lip. "Remember when I told you a few weeks ago that Luke was acting out in class?"

"Yes, of course."

"And you said he had a crush on me?"

"Uh-huh." Suzanna's stomach knotted. She was afraid she knew what was coming.

I think he has feelings for her. A man's feelings.

I think she has feelings for him, too.

"Suzanna, I have feelings for Luke, too."

Damn. She had to find some way to defuse this without tipping Kelsey off that the "boy" she was attracted to was a twenty-six-year-old man. She looked guilty. So guilty, Suzanna cringed. "He came over Saturday night," Kelsey explained. "Then again Sunday morning. My father caught him here. And it hit me in the midst of Dad's tirade that things aren't exactly right with Luke."

"Reynolds tends to exaggerate everything, Kel."

"I know, and I have to deal with him, sometime, about that and a lot of things. But he wasn't exaggerating about *this*. I do have inappropriate feelings for Luke. I have to admit it to myself."

"Sexual feelings?"

"Well, male/female feelings, at least; I'm . . . attracted to him." She closed her eyes, battling back tears. "I can't believe that I'm saying this to you. Am I some kind of a pervert? Like that woman who slept with that elementary school boy? Had his kid?"

Suzanna asked carefully, "Nothing's happened between you and Luke, has it?"

Kelsey shook her head. "But my feelings are wrong. . . ."

"No, sweetie. They aren't."

"They feel wrong."

Damn, all Suzanna had to do was tell her the truth. Motherly instincts warred with the promises she'd made to Joe. Her pledges to the girl she loved like a daughter conflicted with her vows to a man she was coming to care for, too much.

I want to tell Kelsey.

No . . . I want your word, Suzanna.

"Look, Kel, we can't help the feelings we have." She thought of Joe in Connecticut this weekend—in the hot tub, his hair sexily disheveled, the broad expanse of his sweat-soaked chest. "The only thing we have control over is what we do about them."

"Do you really believe that?" The little-girl hope in Kelsey's voice cut Sûzanna to the quick. God, she hated this deception.

"Of course. These aren't bad feelings. They're just ones that are inappropriate to act on. I know you. You won't let anything happen with Luke." *Please, don't.*

"Are you saying this as the woman who was a mother to me, or as a principal?"

"As both. I'd tell this to any young teacher in your position." At least that was true. She brushed back Kelsey's hair. "I love you as if you were my daughter, Kelsey. And I respect you as a teacher. I won't let you feel guilty for emotions that are human. You're a good person. You'll do what's right. You won't let anything unethical happen between you and Luke."

Kelsey glanced away. "I know that." She didn't sound sure. "I just . . . I. . . ."

"What?"

"Do you want to take him out of my classes?"

Suzanna hesitated. What would Joe prefer? "Do you want me to?"

"I don't know."

"Well, think about it. But my money's on you. This will blow over."

Before Suzanna left, Kelsey grabbed her hand. "What would I do without you? You always have my best interests at heart. I can trust you to help me with everything, even something as sensitive as this."

Suzanna smiled weakly.

"I love you, Suzanna. Thanks."

"I love you, too. Now stop worrying and get some rest."

AFTER much soul-searching, Suzanna decided to tell Joe about Kelsey's confession. Though in some ways it felt like the worst kind of betrayal, she didn't know how else to handle what she'd learned. And she hoped it would make Joe see they needed to tell Kelsey right away that Luke was not one of her students.

Instead, the situation made him furious. "Son of a bitch. I knew something like this would happen. That kid can't control himself." Gone was the tender, sensitive man of the weekend. Joe was every inch the agent this afternoon as he loomed over her desk. The very angry agent.

He began to pace, which he did when he was frustrated.

"Joe, they're young, healthy people. It's no shock that this would happen."

"Luke should have been more circumspect."

"I doubt he knows the meaning of the word."

Scowling, Joe stopped midstride. "He's smart, Suzanna."

"I wasn't insulting his intelligence. I meant his personality is such that he's probably never learned to be careful about what he does."

Joe rubbed his arm. "You can say that again."

Slowly she rose from her desk, came around it, and leaned against the edge. "You must see now that we have to tell Kelsey who Luke really is. What you two are doing here."

Joe ran a hand through his hair. "No."

"No?"

He stared down at her, his face hard. "I've made this clear before. No one else can know about our undercover work. It makes me more than nervous that Brenda Way is in on it. I won't jeopardize this operation any further to spare somebody hurt feelings."

Suzanna felt her temper spike. "It's more than hurt feelings. She's questioning her whole moral makeup. She thinks she's a pervert."

"You can change her mind about that. She idolizes you. She'll listen to you."

"She'll be devastated if she ever learns I've lied to her. Even more so now that's she's confided in me about her feelings. I know Kelsey. Where she's come from. If she finds out who he is, that I *knew* who he was when she told me how she felt about him, it will look like an unconscionable breach of trust on my part that I didn't tell her." She swallowed hard. "I'm not sure it isn't that, Joe."

"All the more reason not to tell her."

"Please, I think. . . ."

"*No!*" His voice had risen.

She drew back, her eyes wide.

"I'm sorry. I don't mean to yell at you."

Suzanna didn't know what to say. Though she was coming to care for this man, there was so much she didn't know about him.

He glanced at his watch. "Get Ludzecky down here. We'll tell him about this. Make him toe the line. He's hardheaded sometimes, but he's got a good heart."

Tears formed behind Suzanna's eyelids. "Oh, no, Joe, we can't tell Luke about her feelings. That would be an even bigger betrayal of Kelsey."

"It will protect her in the long run."

"Joe, please, don't do this."

"I don't have a choice!" he yelled. "Neither do you." He turned his back to her. "Get Ludzecky."

After a long hesitation, Suzanna asked her secretary to call Luke down to her office.

She and Joe were sipping coffee in a strained silence when Luke knocked on the door. She opened it and he said, "What'd I do this time, Mrs. Q.?"

"Come on in, young man." She was getting tired of playing this part. She wanted her school back, safe and sound.

Once inside, Luke saw Joe. His eyes sharpened. Became wary. "What?"

"We have to discuss something," Joe said.

"Is Kelsey all right?"

Suzanna and Joe exchanged a look. Joe said, "She's upset. About your visits this weekend."

Visibly the young man deflated. He faced Suzanna. "I'm sorry, Suzanna. I blew it."

She reached out and grasped his arm. "It's not just that. I went to see her today."

Panic flashed in his eyes. Oh, God, he had it bad. "Is she all right?"

"She's upset. Really upset."

Disgustedly, he shook his head. "I shouldn't have gone over there." He faced Joe. "Do you want me off this case?"

"No. But I want you to stay away from Kelsey."

Luke cocked his head, sensing something. "What's going on? What else happened?"

With a glass-cutting edge to his voice, Joe said, "Suzanna talked to Kelsey today. There's something you should know."

Luke's hands fisted. "You said she was all right."

"She is. Physically. Emotionally, she's overwrought because she has *feelings* for one of her male students. *You.*"

Suzanna's stomach soured as she listened to Kelsey's confidences being related so starkly. That she felt a little like Senator Joseph McCarthy with his underhanded tactics made her even more ill. How could she be doing this to Kelsey?

And there was more. As Joe told Luke the story, a flash of pleasure lit the young agent's face. It quickly turned to concern. The feelings were definitely mutual between the two, something Suzanna had suspected for a long time. Something that was bound to hurt them both, badly. "She must be hurting."

"She is. It's . . . unfortunate." Joe's tone was softer than Suzanna expected it to be.

Luke said, "Well, this clinches it. We have to tell her about the operation. I won't let her think she's some kind of lowlife."

Wearily, Joe shook his head. "No."

"Jesus Christ, Joe. You don't mean that, not now. Not after what she told Suzanna."

"I mean it even more."

"She'll carry this around all her life. She'll—"

"No."

Luke bristled visibly. "What if I tell her anyway?"

Joe didn't even hesitate. "I'll have you tossed out of the Secret Service so fast your head will spin."

He shrugged. "Might not be so bad."

"I'll bring you up on charges of insubordination."

"This isn't the army. What's the worst that can happen?"

"Your family will end up ashamed of you."

Luke's eyes flared. Suzanna watched, mesmerized, as he struggled to get himself under control. "That's a low blow." But one, nonetheless, that made Luke pause. Then, he looked to her for help. "At least take me out of Kelsey's classes."

Joe answered. "No, we can't do that, either. You need contact with Smurf, Ben, and Max."

"I've established contact already. I can keep it up without being in Kelsey's classes."

"No, constant contact is necessary. You'll stay in the classes."

"What about Kelsey?"

"Stay the *hell* away from her."

Luke's hands fisted and his face flushed. "You're a cold-hearted bastard, Stonehouse."

Suzanna's gaze went to Joe. A muscle clenched in his jaw. She suspected he was coming to care for Luke like a son, and this disagreement hurt. "In these kinds of operations, Agent Ludzecky, you've got to be a bastard."

Luke glared at Joe. "You know, if you're an example of what the Secret Service does to men, I'm not sure I *want* to stay in it." Without a word, he opened the door and stalked out.

Suzanna waited a moment, then got up, closed the door, and leaned heavily against the wood. In her heart, she wanted to help the man suffering before her. But her loyalties lay with Kelsey. "There's not much you can do to keep me from telling her, Joe. You have no control over me." Which wasn't exactly true. He had emotional leverage that he could wield. Did he know that?

His face blanked. He swallowed hard. She realized this was another blow to him, like Luke's accusations. "You gave me your word you wouldn't tell Kelsey."

"Joe, please reconsider."

"I can't, Suzanna. Too many lives are at stake. If people keep finding out, it will compromise this operation and any future ones. Hundreds of students across the country could be affected. It isn't just about Kelsey and Luke. She has to treat him like a kid to keep up the ruse." He crossed to her and grasped her arms gently. His green eyes were hot with emotion. "Please, trust me on this. I know what I'm doing."

It stunned her to realize she did trust him. "All right. For now, at least. Maybe it's not as bad as it seems."

"I'll talk to Luke again about keeping his distance. Alienating her, maybe."

"He's tried that."

"He'll have to try harder."

"I guess we all will."

"What does that mean?"

"Nothing. Nothing at all." Suddenly the weekend in Connecticut seemed light-years away.

ON Monday night, Brenda sat across from Suzanna in the bay window of Brenda's kitchen, both of them staring out at the snow-dusted lawn that sprawled around her condo. The security lighting cast the backyard in an eerie glow. "Christ, you think it's ever going to get warm?"

Suzanna pushed her plate away. She'd only picked at the spicy lasagna Brenda had made for her before the school's biweekly board meeting, which they regularly attended together. "No. It's going to be like Noah's Ark, only with snow." She smiled as if she'd thought of something pleasant.

Sipping her Chianti, Brenda watched her friend. "Hey, Suz, what's going on with you? You've been preoccupied all night."

"I have?" Innocence personified, Suzanna daintily wiped her mouth with a napkin.

"Yeah." Brenda remembered the first time Suzanna slept with a guy. She didn't tell Brenda about it right away, but looked all smirky and mysterious for days afterward. "Where'd you go last weekend, anyway? You never said."

"I took a little retreat out of town." She shrugged, picked up her wineglass. "I needed to get away after that thing with Rush Webster." She bit her lip. "He's still missing. Nobody knows where he is."

Suzanna didn't want to tell Brenda where she'd gone. *Hmm.* Brenda wondered why. "Are you worried?" she asked, twisting her glass in her hand. Light from the modern chandelier overhead sparkled in the ruby liquid.

"No, Joe and Luke have kept pretty good tabs on me."

"The Men from U.N.C.L.E." Brenda's tone was dry. At Suzanna's questioning look, Brenda rolled her eyes. "Don't you ever watch the Nick at Nite channel? They have all the old TV shows on. That was a spy show." She sighed. "It was Conrad's favorite when it first came out."

"You miss him, don't you?"

"Yeah. He's been dead seven years."

"Oh, Brend, I'm sorry. I never really made the connection with Conrad's walking into that undercover sting and what's going on in my school."

"No big deal."

Suzanna reached out and clasped Brenda's hand. Not one for physical demonstrativeness, Brenda was tempted to pull back. But this kind of gesture was so natural for Suzanna, Brenda allowed the comfort. When she did, it felt good. "It *is* a big deal," Suzanna said. "I know Conrad was like your father."

"I never had a father."

"That's why you're such a loner, I think. I worry about you all the time."

Drawing back, Brenda played with her fork. "Don't worry about me. I can take care of myself."

"You and Kelsey are my best friends. I'm entitled to worry about both of you."

A good change of subject and back to the matter that most intrigued her now. "How *is* Miss America?" Brenda liked the young teacher, but often teased her about her pageant-worthy looks.

Suzanna scowled. "Hobbling around on crutches. She's coming back to school on Wednesday. I can't get her to stay out longer."

"Not to worry. The young Agent Ludzecky will carry her books for her, I'm sure."

Suzanna fidgeted in her seat. "Why would you say that?"

"It's obvious he has a major crush on her. And you said he almost blew the operation when that punk assaulted her."

Suzanna shook her head; skeins of hair swirled around

her shoulders. "Joe's right, I shouldn't be talking about this."

Feigning umbrage, Brenda got up and poured them more wine. "Yeah, right, like I'm going to do something with it."

"No, it's just that Joe's such a stickler for rules."

And Brenda knew why.

The adults figured they could rid their kids of their sexual hangups at an early age . . . they initiated both the boys and girls ASAP . . . he was ten . . . she was six.

"Brend? What is it?"

"Nothing."

Suzanna stared at her a minute, then started when her cell phone rang. "I've got to get that. It might be Josh."

"Always the mommy."

Suzanna fished in her purse, found the phone, and clicked it on. "Hello." Pause. "Oh, hi." A longer pause. "Yes. I won't be alone. I'm going with Brenda." She stood and covered the mouthpiece. "I'll take this in there."

Ah, more secrets. Must be the hunky Secret Service agent was worried about Suzanna's safety. "Go, I'll clean up."

As Suzanna stood, she knocked her purse to the floor.

"I'll get it. Go." Rounding up the contents of Suzanna's purse, which had spilled out onto the tile, Brenda glanced at the stuff. Suzanna's wallet had fallen open. A few receipts escaped from it. Brenda scooped those up along with a brush, lipstick and a bunch of pens. As she was stuffing the assorted paraphernalia back into Suzanna's purse, a yellow charge slip caught her eye. For some reason, Brenda opened it and read it. A diner bill. For lunch yesterday. In Concord, Connecticut.

Concord, Connecticut.

Where had Brenda seen the name of the town before? She glanced up. Suzanna was in the living room, which was visible from the eating nook. She spoke softly into the phone. Laughed easily. Paced. Once again, Brenda remembered her friend in college. Suzanna was *flirting*.

With Joe Stonehouse.

Things clicked into focus then, like the lens of a camera zeroing in on its subject. Brenda had run across Concord,

Connecticut, in the Internet report of the school shooting three years ago in that state.

It was the town where Stonehouse's sister lived.

THE next afternoon, Brenda slid her notebook out of her purse and set it on the surface of the diner's table. Hidden from view by other booths and some strategically placed plants, Brenda uncapped a Mont Blanc pen Conrad had given her for graduation from college and wrote:

Callahans' house in the middle of nowhere . . . hid car in trees until got a glimpse of her . . . looks dramatically like brother . . . left house . . . met husband at diner for lunch.

Brenda glanced at the couple. As she stared at the Callahans, watching them enjoy their lunch, a pang of longing shot through her. Brenda remembered a passed-up opportunity. Peter from grad school had wanted to marry her. But Brenda had had stars in her eyes and bright lights in her future. Sometimes she wished she'd chosen the other path, had a husband to meet in town for lunch. Instead, Brenda had the dubious honor of spying on the scene to write about it.

Just like her whole life: on the outside looking in.

To distract herself from that grim thought, Brenda drew out of her notebook a picture of the Callahans' dead daughter, Josie. The photo was from a newspaper and had probably been her senior picture. Familiar green eyes peered out of a trusting, smiling face. She looked like her uncle, was named after him. In the book—and it was going to be a book, now—Brenda would milk the namesake and physical similarities.

A burst of laughter came from Ruth. Seated on the same side of the booth like teenagers, the Callahans cuddled close. Al ruffled his wife's hair, then leaned down to kiss her on the nose.

Brenda wrote, *Does Al know his wife's sordid past?*

If he did know, he didn't seem to care. Brenda wondered what that kind of unconditional love felt like. Then she was hit by an unpleasant thought. If Al Callahan didn't know about the early sexual history of his wife, what would finding out do to the way he felt about her?

What would their kids think of their mother when they read the book? Brenda's conscience prickled at that thought. It wasn't just Joe and Ruth and Al who would be affected by her exposé. How would the younger Callahans be able to hold their heads up in school when their mother's sexual experience as a young child was broadcast for all to see?

Tough shit, Brenda wrote in her notebook. Had anyone cared about her when they let her live with an abusive, alcoholic mother? Had anybody cared about her when Conrad died?

Suzanna had. She'd taken Brenda home with her for vacations in college when Brenda couldn't bear to be with her mother again. She missed days of work to spend with Brenda during Conrad's wake and funeral.

Suddenly, Brenda couldn't breathe. She had to get out of here. She'd gotten what she came for—confirmation that the Callahans still lived in Connecticut, a quick check of the diner where Suzanna had gone for lunch; proof that Suzanna had come up here with Stonehouse last weekend.

As a bonus, she got a real-life glimpse of the people tragedy had struck; seeing them, hearing them laugh, would make her prose come alive when she wrote about them.

And gave Brenda concrete images of the people who would be affected if she did this book.

Standing, she stuffed her belongings in her purse, threw some bills on the table, and hurried from the diner.

Outside, she could breathe better.

THE roads were slippery with wet drizzle from Connecticut to Queens, but *in for a penny, in for a pound.* As long as Brenda was playing spy, she might as well finish the job. She reached the Ludzecky house, a small, two-story on a nondescript street, at about five on Tuesday afternoon and had to wait only an hour until three people exited.

Hell, even if the investigator hadn't included Ludzecky's address in the report, she'd know these girls anywhere. They were female versions of Luke. And one was more gorgeous than the next. The two with the long bouncy hair down to their waists were identical. The other, with chin-length hair the exact same shade as the duo, looked younger. Brenda checked her notes. The twins were Paulina and Antonia. The youngest was Elizabeita. They sounded like the goddamn Trapp Family Singers.

The girls piled into a battered Blazer and took off down the street. Brenda followed at a discreet distance. They swerved to park at a local diner, jumped out of the car, and disappeared inside. After a decent amount of time, Brenda followed. Luck was with her; she snagged an empty booth right behind Luke's sisters.

She didn't know exactly what she was after here—what spin she'd take on Ludzecky for the book. But she'd been restless after she'd left Concord, and had the documentation on Luke with her, so what the hell? It was only another three-hour drive. As she sat down and removed her coat, she figured this little exposure to his family life might give her a tack to take on the young agent.

Not daring to make notes, she drew a book out of her purse and pretended to read. The Ludzecky women were oblivious to her presence. They made small talk about college and high school stuff. They ordered meals, as did Brenda. She'd just been served her salad when something came up at the next booth.

"*Matka* will kill us, Lizzie," one of the twins said, picking up a fork.

"You guys are wimps. If Lukasz was here, he'd do it with me."

Mental note #1: family calls him Lukasz.

"I wonder what's going on with him," the other twin mused, around a bite of hamburger. "Two visits in a few weeks."

"He seemed sad to me." Elizabeita frowned. It marred the perfection of her face.

"I know." A twin. "Girl-sad."

"Yeah." The other twin.

"Wish we could help."

"He told us last time if we interfere in his love life one

more time, he'll call up all our boyfriends and terrorize them."

Mental note #2: sisters meddle in love life (how cute!).

Elizabeita, definitely the most chatty of the three, went on, "I think he's getting tired of—"

"Shh." Both twins admonished her at the same time. One said, "Don't say anything. We shouldn't even be talking about him."

"Okay, he's getting tired of being a you-know-what." Elizabeita's eyes danced at her cleverness.

"Probably."

"Think he'll ever get married?"

"Not until he proves to himself he wasn't what Papa thought he was. That's why he joined that stupid Sec—*place* to begin with." The twin preened at her adept psychological comment.

"Cat says Papa was crazy about Lukasz. That Luke only thought he was disappointed. But he wasn't."

Mental note #3: son trying to live up to father's expectations. Maybe that was the angle for Brenda. How could she get more information on Luke's relationship with his father? Was there a way to connect Luke's father complex to Stonehouse? The two agents always seemed at each other's throats.

"I wish he'd quit that . . . job so we could see him more."

"Yeah, me too."

Mental note #4: sisters worry about him.

He was so lucky. Brenda would bet that his whole family loved him like these three. Again she was assaulted by guilt. What would her best-seller do to these girls when their identities and their hero worship were displayed for the world to see? Along with—if she could find more on this somehow—Lukasz's zeal to prove something to his dead father?

Upset by the thought, Brenda choked on the salad she was chewing. The lettuce wouldn't dislodge. She coughed, calling attention to herself. *Shit!*

Before she knew it, there was someone behind her, patting her back, saying calmly, "Put your arms up. It'll help."

Oh, just great. She was gonna get CPR from one of the Ludzeckys. The little one.

When the coughing abated, Elizabeita cocked her head at Brenda. "Hi, I'm Lizzie. You new around here? I don't think I've ever seen you before."

Brenda almost groaned. *Fine Lois Lane you make,* she chided herself as she tried to explain her presence at this little neighborhood diner in Queens.

SEVENTEEN

LUKE pounded up the steps to the Smurfellas' porch, carrying Smurf's assignments in his backpack. He'd volunteered to bring the kid homework—it would be a perfect opening to get into Smurf's personal life. After he left here, Luke was off to Max's to play on the computer, maybe get into that web site Duchamp boasted about. When Stonehouse first heard about these plans, he'd been pleased that Luke was making progress in diagnosing which kids were dangerous. Then yesterday happened. God knew what Joe would do after Suzanna's information about Kelsey's confession. A confession, if Luke was honest with himself, he savored sweetly in his heart. God, he wanted to tell her who he really was.

The wind picked up, and Luke raised the collar of his bomber jacket against the chill. Ringing the doorbell, he let thoughts of Kelsey's sleeping face and delicious body warm him. His hand flexed as he recalled touching her. Geez, he had to stop thinking about this. He had to get a grip if he was to finish this operation and get away unscathed.

Once again, he pushed on the doorbell and concentrated on Smurf. The house was huge, a brick Colonial in an exclusive area at the edge of town. Smurf's father was a VP at the local IBM plant, and they were definitely upper crust.

An older woman wearing a chic dress and enough gold to set off a metal detector answered the door. "Hello. Luke, is it?"

"Yeah, I got Smur—Jimmy's homework."

"Please, come in." A vein-lined hand fluttered to her neck. "I'm Mrs. Smurfella."

So this was Smurf's mother. Luke thought about his own down-to-earth *Matka*, always dressed in plain cotton house dresses and sensible shoes, smelling like vanilla.

"He's got cabin fever from being cooped up here," Mrs. Smurfella said. "He'd like to see a friend."

Once again, Luke felt sorry for Smurf, the guy everybody picked on. Nobody, except maybe Franzi, wanted to spend time with him.

"I'm sorry you had to come way out here," the woman continued. "My daughter was supposed to get his work, but she kept forgetting."

Mrs. Smurfella's face reddened. Her *daughter* was a first-class snob who ignored Smurf's existence. Though Luke's own sisters interfered in his love life all the time and were a general pain in the butt, the thought of the girls treating him like Ms. Valedictorian treated Smurf made Luke wince inwardly.

"He's not contagious." Mrs. Smurfella led Luke around a corner to a wing of the house. "He had the flu, but he's over it. The doctor said he can go back to school soon." She frowned. "He doesn't seem particularly anxious to return, though."

"Hmm" was all Luke said, but he was thinking, *Why? Because of the bullying?* They made their way to Smurf's room, through winding corridors, over thick carpet, under a gazillion skylights. Smurf's door was locked when his mother knocked and tried to open it.

On the second knock, Smurf pulled it open. "Damn it, Ma, could you—" The boy's face lit when he saw his mother had company. "Hey, Luke, how ya doing?"

"Great." Luke held up his backpack. "Don't look so happy to see me. I got your work."

Behind the thick glasses, Smurf's eyes flicked with something—suspicion, maybe? "It's okay. I wanted it."

"I'll just leave you two boys alone. Would you like something to drink, Luke?"

"No, thank you, ma'am."

"Well, stay a while. Jimmy could use the company."

Luke smiled warmly. It turned into a gape when he stepped inside Smurf's room. "Holy shit, Smurf, this is a goddamn palace." The area was really a suite; the bedroom itself had to be twenty feet square. Skylights dotted the high, slanted ceiling and there were several windows. A whole row of closets took up one wall. Off to the side was a hallway, and Luke could see a bathroom through the open doorway. A king-size bed with a fan-shaped headboard faced the biggest entertainment center Luke had ever seen. It held every gadget imaginable. He wandered over to it. "You got a DVD player *and* a VCR?"

Smurf shrugged.

Luke studied the lower half. "This a fridge?"

"Uh-huh."

"That is phat, buddy. Mad-phat."

"My new machine's the best." He nodded to the far end of the room. Really, it was a little alcove by itself. About five by eight, it sported the same skylights and windows, and held a computer system that could have come from a science fiction movie.

Luke crossed to it, Smurf following him. "That's an understatement."

"This baby can do everything. Sit," Smurf said, indicating the real leather chair in front of it.

"A man after my own heart, Smurfy boy. I love these things."

Luke dropped down, and Smurf pulled up another chair. "You like music; I got some sites bookmarked."

"Great." For a half-hour they played on the Net. It was fun, and distracted Luke, at least momentarily, from what Kelsey had told Suzanna about her feelings for him.

When Smurf went to get them something to eat, Luke seized the opportunity to check things out. The closets were full of clothes. The hallway off the main area led to a huge bathroom that even had a damned Jacuzzi. There was another door to the left—it was locked. *Hmm.* At the end of the hallway was a private entrance. Luke had just come back into the main room when the chime for an instant message pinged from the computer screen. He crossed to the machine.

The message was from a sender called Cassius. It read, "PBBs beware. Caesar's army is out in droves. Bury your site and don't visit the Colosseum until you hear from me."

Luke stared at the message, wondering what kind of game Smurf was into. There were armies of weirdos on the Net, and some of them were dangerous.

"What's that?" Smurf asked from behind.

"An instant message." Luke tried to look bored. "I got no idea what it means."

Smurf's eyes turned cold after he read it. "Means nothing." He flicked a few keys and the message was gone.

All traces of it.

Luke's Secret Service instincts surfaced. What the hell were PBBs?

THINKING he was too old for this kind of thing, Luke once again hid behind a tree; this time he was at Max Duchamp's, dodging Rush Webster. The punk exited the house through the walkout basement door in the back. His shoulders were stooped, and a day-old beard shadowed his face. Though he wanted to tackle Webster and beat the shit out of him for what the guy had done to Kelsey, Luke let him go.

Try to control your behavior, will you? Stonehouse had said. So he was trying. He let Webster get in his battered van and drive away, scot-free. Luke waited some, then headed to the private entrance and knocked on the heavy metal door.

"Yo, enter," Max called out.

As Luke walked in, Max looked up from his bed.

The girl next to him in the tangled camouflage sheets peered over her shoulder and tried to focus. "What, another one?"

Luke was startled to see a naked girl here. He'd guessed Max was hookin' up with girls, but . . . did he *share,* with Webster? The thought turned his stomach. Sometimes, he wished he could teach these kids, too, and help stop this kind of dangerous behavior.

"Ah, I can come back," Luke said.

"No, need." He patted the girl's ass. "Go wait in the pool room, Mel."

Sliding out of bed, she pouted as she picked up a T-shirt and tugged it over her head, casually dropping an obscenity when her bleached hair caught in the material. As she passed Luke, she scraped a fingernail down his arm. "You're a cutie," she purred, and left them alone.

Max picked up a cigarette pack from the table, knocked one out, and lit it. "You want a smoke?"

"I got my own." Luke fished in his pocket and lit up.

"How ya doing, buddy?" Max asked.

"Happy as a pig in shit."

Max studied him. "You pissed off about something?"

"No." Hell, Luke was losing it. He blew out gray rings and tossed a lascivious glance after Mel. "I thought you might share, is all."

"Nah. Not my thing."

Luke dropped down into a chair. "No fair." He scanned the room. "Saw Webster leavin'."

Easing out of bed, Max put the cigarette in an ashtray, stood, and shrugged into boxers that had rifles on them. He strolled to the fridge and snared some beer. "Webster's taking off."

"Takin' off?"

"Going to the city."

"He quittin' school?"

"Temporarily."

Well, this was news. Good news.

Pretending disinterest, Luke nodded toward the computer table where a yearbook was lying. "What you doin' with one of those things? You gettin' school spirit all of a sudden?"

"When my dick goes limp." Max opened two bottles and set one beside Luke. He took a long, cool slug, then nodded at the yearbook. "I stole it from the library."

"Yeah, why?"

"Wanted some names, that's all."

"Names?" *Like for a hit list?*

Scowling, Max sank back on the mattress and picked up the Marlboro. Did he suspect something?

"You got any weed?" Might as well see what else Max was into *and* change the subject.

"Not anymore. Me and Mel smoked the last of the shit I had before we boinked." He grinned lecherously. "It was good stuff. I thought the top of my head was gonna blow off when I came."

For some reason, Max's crudeness about sex made Luke's stomach knot. He thought of Kelsey and how he'd tucked her into the couch, pulled up the covers, and kissed her forehead. If they ever got to physical intimacy, they certainly wouldn't *boink*. He'd make love to her real slow, and savor every minute.

"Where'd you go, Ludzecky?"

Luke scanned the room for something that might have distracted him. "Don't it give you the willies havin' all those eyes lookin' at you when you sleep?"

Max studied the heads that adorned the walls—bear, elk, and even a doe. "No. I like 'em. They my buddies. I gave 'em all names." He grinned. "My father thinks that's funny."

Luke's gaze narrowed in on the gun rack. "Those loaded?"

"Not now, they aren't, but my dad has ammo." He preened. "I know where to get it."

"Hmm."

"You ever shoot a gun?"

Luke gave him a disgusted look. "Is the pope Catholic?"

Max laughed. "Wanna go to the shooting range with me sometime? My dad's president of the Fairholm Gun Club."

"You name the date, Max." As casually as he could, Luke said, "So, can I see this big, dark, secret web site you got?"

"Yeah. Sure."

Luke glanced out the door. "What about the squeeze?"

"She'll wait." He puffed out his chest. "I'm that good."

"Bite me."

Abruptly, Max stood and nodded to the computer. "I gotta take a leak before we do that."

As Max hit the head right off his room, Luke rose and

crossed to the desk. He reached to move the yearbook out of the way.

The book was open to Junior Prom stuff. Luke remembered his own special night and how sexy Marcy Wilkins had looked in a strapless green number that sent his adolescent hormones into overdrive. What would Kelsey look like all dressed up?

He focused on the page. In the center was a picture of the king and queen of the prom. Luke stared hard at it. In black marker, someone had circled the face of the king.

It was Josh Quinn.

SUZANNA was getting ready for bed when the doorbell rang. Hurriedly pulling her Fairholm sweatshirt and jeans back on, she headed downstairs in socked feet. "I'll get it," she called out to Josh as she passed his room.

From behind his closed door, Josh yelled, "Don't answer it until you see who's there."

Switching on a hall light, she took the stairs to the foyer; after checking the peephole and disarming the security system, she pulled open the door. Luke and Joe stood on the porch, looking grim. Her heart began to pound. "Has something happened?"

"Not like you mean." Joe hunched his shoulders against the rain. He nodded into the house. "Is Josh here?"

"Yes, he's in his room. Do you want to see him?"

"No, we want to see you." Joe's voice was raspy and his eyes concerned. "But he shouldn't go out."

She peered over Joe's shoulder at the dark, misty street. "He's not going out; we were both ready for bed."

Without invitation, Joe stepped inside and Luke followed. Suzanna closed the door. Luke rubbed his arms to warm himself.

"Can we talk somewhere?" Joe asked. "Without being overheard?"

Distressed, but holding it back, she said, "Go into the den. I'll tell Josh we can't be disturbed. He's used to this kind of thing."

Reaching out, Joe touched her shoulder. Luke smiled at

her, then followed Joe down the corridor. They'd both removed their jackets and were standing in front of the floor-
to-ceiling bookshelves when Suzanna entered the den. Their
bodies were braced like soldiers waiting for their next command. A light burned low in the corner, creating a cozy atmosphere in the room. Still, she felt chilled.

"Sit down," Joe said curtly.

Luke crossed to her and squeezed her arm. "It's okay. We
have some more information you need to hear." He tossed a
knowing look at Joe. "The old man's just worried about
you."

She smiled weakly at Luke and sank onto a chair. Both of
the men remained standing. Joe spoke first.

"Luke spent the evening with Max Duchamp. He found
two disturbing things. One was a picture of Josh in a yearbook Max had lying around; Josh's face was circled in black
marker."

At first Suzanna didn't get it. *Why would Max . . .* then
the significance of it hit her. "Oh, no."

Joe crossed to her and squatted at her feet. His dark green
shirt and sweater made his eyes the color of the forest. He
grasped her hands in his. "It may mean a lot, and it may
mean nothing," he said.

Hope flickered in her mother's heart. "How?"

"Max came in while Luke was looking at the yearbook.
He said Webster had circled Josh's picture. Max shrugged it
off as another of Webster's idiocyncrasies."

Her gaze snapped to Luke. "Do you believe Max?"

Luke leaned against the edge of the desk and shrugged
flannel-clad shoulders. "He's got no reason to lie to me. And
after he told me that, he trusted me with something else, so I
think he's tellin' the truth."

She took in a deep breath. "All right. What do we do
now?"

"Well, a couple of things." Joe still squatted in front of
her. "But let me tell you what else we found."

"There's more?" Her voice trembled.

"Max got Luke into his and Webster's web site." He
glanced at the computer on her desk. "I'd like you to see it.
Luke can access it again."

"Go ahead."

Circling the desk, Luke sank onto her chair and booted up the computer.

"Are you all right?" Joe whispered, holding onto her hands, which had turned frigid.

"Josh?" She shook her head. "Oh, Joe. I can't believe it."

"This might not be as bad as we think. In some ways, it's no different from finding the hit list. It also tells us we're on the right track with Duchamp and Webster."

Stone-cold inside, Suzanna bit her lip to keep from crying. Joe pulled her head to his shoulder. "I'm here, Suzanna." His lips moved in her hair. "So's Luke. We'll get to the bottom of this. I promise."

She just held onto him; tonight he was her lifeline.

A cough came from the desk. "I'm in."

Joe rose and, still holding Suzanna's hand, drew her up and over to the computer. They stood behind Luke.

The site's home page came up first. It was done in stark black-and-white, simply advertised as *D&W—The Worst of the Worst*. There were four places for visitors to click, indicated by gun icons. The first was *Mad Meanderings*. When Luke got into that section, Suzanna saw it contained diary-type entries from D and from W. D's were concerned mostly with guns: why they should be available, how to fight against gun control. Suzanna knew Max and his father were gun fanatics. But she winced at language foul enough to make a sailor blush.

Then she got to Webster's entries. She almost couldn't read his obscenities. Hell, she didn't even understand some of the phrases. The second part of the site, *Fantasies for Fanatics*, invited readers to share their violent fantasies by e-mailing them to an address that incorporated an obscenity. Most were sexual. "This is sick," she told them.

"Suzanna," Joe said sternly, "you don't have to read this trash."

"I've never heard of skull-fucking."

But there it was: In some cultlike settings, a dead body was deliberately desecrated—an eye was cut out—and . . . she could barely take in the rest. But she did, just as she forced herself to scan the other two sections of the site:

Shoot Off to Other Places—web rings that sent people to gun sites, snuff movie sites, some pornography sites.

"Oh, no," Suzanna said at the last section, *Best Buddies*.

Sliding his arm around her, Joe pulled her close. "This is the worst part."

It was a personals-type board where people with similar *interests* could make contact. A kind of perversion clearing-house.

The room got quiet.

"These two are young boys," Suzanna said angrily. "How can they be into this stuff?"

"It's a complicated world, Suzanna." Joe cleared his throat, his voice sandpapery. "Horrible things happen to young boys."

After a long pause, Luke said, "That's it."

Sighing heavily, Joe eased Suzanna away from him. "Let's go sit down and I'll tell you our plan. We've had only a few hours to discuss this, but Luke and I have some ideas."

Suzanna allowed herself to be led to the couch. Shakily, she sank down and Joe took the cushion next to her. Luke dropped onto a chair across from them, spread his legs, and, hunching over, linked his hands between them.

"Obviously, the web site shows they're into violence, though Luke thinks, again, Max is on the periphery."

"Why?"

"Because he seemed a little green around the gills when I commented on some of the content." Luke was somber. "Like the snuff films. And there are no recent diary entries from him; it's as if he's lost interest."

"Well, that's something."

"It's Webster we have to zero in on," Joe told her, "though we should keep close tabs on Duchamp." The men exchanged meaningful looks. "We'll tell Josh that I found this yearbook in the library—defaced. We'll stress that it's only an indicator that someone might want to do him harm. That he has to be careful, for a while, until the police pick Webster up."

"Pick him up?"

"Yes, the school, or Kelsey, has to file assault charges. We talked about doing this last week."

"I want the school to do it." Though he wore his teenage uniform, tonight Luke was every inch the competent, savvy agent.

Joe scowled at him.

"If Kelsey does it, Webster will be even more furious with her. He might go after her." Luke's gaze sharpened. "Look, we've done enough to her. Let's not add to it."

"Webster could come after Suzanna if she files it," Joe said.

The two men faced each other down.

Suzanna ignored the territorial vibes between them. "It doesn't matter what you think. It's my responsibility. I wouldn't let Kelsey file even if you wanted her to. She's been through enough, and we're not being fair to her as it is."

Luke's expression was grateful.

Finally, Joe said, "We've got to arrange some protection for you and Josh."

"Protection? As in cops? And bodyguards?"

Joe shrugged. "We've come up with a good compromise." He threw Luke a self-effacing smile. They'd obviously come to terms with lying to Kelsey.

Luke said, "Yeah, tough job, boss. I feel bad for you."

"What's going on?"

Joe turned to Suzanna. His dark hair was mussed and there were deep grooves bracketing his mouth tonight, but his eyes shone with some kind of devilment. "Well, Suzanna, you and I are about to become an item."

"An item?"

He cleared his throat. "Yes, we're going to date. We're, um, attracted to each other. We want to spend time together." Again he coughed. "A lot."

"I can't date a member of my staff."

"Well, the superintendent is my boss. Technically, I don't work for you. I work for the administration."

"Still, it won't look good. At school."

"I'm sorry. I want people there to think we're dating, too, so my being with you so much won't seem strange. They'd suspect something anyway. Everybody found out about the tire slashing, even though we tried to keep that quiet. The school's grapevine is alive and well."

"I suppose."

"Kelsey'll get the same story, Suzanna."

She didn't like that at all. Any of it, really. "I hate the image of me this will create."

"You'll have to deal with it."

"Like everything else," she said, exasperated. When he didn't respond, she saw by his expression that she had no choice. "So, I take it we'll tell Josh directly about our relationship . . . to explain your being around the house."

"Yes."

"I won't let you spend the night here."

Luke stood. "I think this is my cue to leave. I brought my own car so you two could hash out the particulars." He gave Suzanna a sympathetic look. "I'm sorry we keep invadin' your privacy, Suzanna." He frowned. "And Kelsey's, too."

Nodding weakly at Luke, she watched him go. Then she faced Joe. "This keeps getting worse, doesn't it?"

Joe couldn't help himself. Feeling like a teenager asking for his first date, he said, "I know you're mad about this thing with Kelsey. But is the thought of spending time with me, pretending you're interested in me, so abhorrent to you?"

Brandy-colored eyes full of heat drew him in. "You know it's not."

He reached out, grasped a lock of her hair, and slid it between his fingers. It was as soft as corn silk. "Me, neither." He stared at her lips. "It's . . . it could be a problem, though. *Because* we don't find it offensive."

"How?" Her voice was a come-to-bed whisper.

He wanted to kiss her so badly, he felt turned inside out. But he had to remember who he was and what he was doing. Once, when he was a young agent like Luke, he'd been pursuing a would-be assassin down an alley. He'd been petrified, sidling in and out of doorways, trying not to be seen, knowing he could get shot and killed at any moment. He felt that kind of vulnerability now.

Dropping her hair, he stepped back and crossed the room. Nervously he stuck his hands in his pockets. "Suzanna, nothing can happen between us."

She didn't deny there was a possibility.

"It's important we both keep our heads in this. I have to stay sharp. I can't get distracted by you."

Still no answer.

"And you don't want to invest in me." *Any more than you already have.* "I won't be here much longer. I'll go back to my job in D.C., find another school, and. . . ."

Her eyes searched his. "And start all over again?"

He didn't like her tone. "What do you mean by that?"

"Has this ever happened to you before?"

He didn't ask what she meant. "No, not on the job." A woman's pleasure lit her face, made him add, "Never."

Silently, she wrapped her arms around her waist.

"How about you, Suzanna? Have there been any serious relationships with men since Lawrence died?"

She looked away. "No, there haven't been."

A swell of pure male pride jolted him. He tried to quell it. Still, a word slipped out. "Good." He cursed himself, then straightened. "As for the other, staying overnight here, it wouldn't happen so soon, anyway. I'll just be around a lot. Late. Eat dinner here. Work out with you. Relax with you."

She stared at him.

"We have no choice, Suzanna," he said tightly.

"Fine." The word was clipped. "What about Josh starting to talk to you? How will our involvement, phony though it is, affect his confiding in you?"

"I'll address it openly. If he still doesn't feel comfortable with me, it's a loss we'll have to absorb."

Her eyes flared with temper. "I feel like I'm doing all the sacrificing. My beliefs. My ethics. This newest thing with Kelsey. My relationship with my students and staff. And now that Josh is finally opening up to you, I may lose that, too."

Joe stiffened. He didn't want to face the reality of all that she said. This was part of the problem in caring about her, about coming to care for her son. It was why agents had to stay detached. "I'm sorry, but to insure the physical safety of Josh, your staff, and the rest of the kids, you'll just have to take it on the chin." When she remained silent, he said, "Go get Josh."

"Now?"

"Yes, I want him to know about the yearbook thing right

away. We can tell him the rest tomorrow night." He gave her a boyish grin. "You're inviting me to dinner."

She headed for the door.

"Suzanna?"

She pivoted when she got there. "What?"

"I'll try to make this as easy on you as possible."

Her eyes told him not to bother. Without answering, she turned to go get Josh.

And Joe wondered, deep in his heart, where the agent was not allowed to tread, how he was going to keep his hands off her and do his job right.

EIGHTEEN

———

KELSEY watched him from the bed, where she lounged back against the pillows. She wished she'd worn a sexy nightgown, instead of the cotton pj bottoms and thermal top. But he didn't seem to care. He stood before her and slowly dragged the green hand-knit sweater over his head. He dispensed with the black T-shirt he wore under it and stood before her, exposing that glorious bare chest; it was sprinkled with just the right amount of dark blond hair to make her mouth water. Her hands fisted in the bedspread, she wanted to touch him so badly.

He grinned, that half-kid, half-man grin that had tortured her for months. "You like what you see, Ms. Cunningham?"

"Call me Kelsey. You did when Webster overturned my desk."

His face darkened. This was no harmless teenage boy before her. "I could kill him for hurting you."

She didn't want to talk about that. "Come over here."

The grin reappeared.

He swaggered toward her, undoing the snap on faded blue jeans. "What do you want, honey?" He towered over her, then braced a knee on the mattress.

She reached for his hand and brought it to her breast. "Luke. . . ."

Kelsey awoke in a sweat; when awareness dawned, when reality set in, she was embarrassed and ashamed. The dream had come again. She lay back into the pillows and closed her eyes.

Dear God, what's wrong with me? I'm having sexual dreams about a student.

Okay, she shouldn't panic. First, Suzanna had told her having feelings for a student was only human. Not acting on those feelings was what was important. And the woman would never do or say anything that wasn't in her best interests. Also, Kelsey's psychology courses had taught her that you couldn't control your dreams; they were like unedited movies, and all parts of your life combined into sometimes bizarre situations. Maybe she was dreaming about Mike Wolfe touching her.

The thing was, she thought, settling back, something about the dream was familiar. As if it had actually happened. Oh, hell, maybe she just *wanted* it to happen. She moaned aloud, and glanced over at the clock. Five A.M. Well, she'd get up and dress. She was going back to school today. How would she face Luke? Not only after the dream, but after the fuss her father had made.

While Luke was there: *Don't you have any sense, young man? It's totally inappropriate to be prowling around a teacher's house like this.*

Luke had been contrite, agreeable. Kelsey had wanted to defend him to her father.

And later: *Kelsey Lynne, I do hope this was innocent.*

What do you mean, Dad?

The kid obviously has a crush on you. He seemed to think he had to defend you to me, for Christ's sake. He was overly solicitous.

Though she felt guilty about her feelings, she would never let her father know that. *It's not uncommon for kids to get crushes on teachers.*

That sounds like the liberal garbage Suzanna Quinn spouts. You shouldn't be teaching these punks. No telling what they'll do. Look what that one hoodlum already . . . and then Reynolds Cunningham was off on a tirade about her whole teaching career.

She'd been too weak from her injury, and feeling too guilty and too confused from her feelings about Luke, to stand up for herself, though she vowed that the next time she would. All in all, she'd just been relieved when her father left for Washington.

The only bad thing was that his absence had given her time alone to rehash the events of this weekend. Why had Luke really come here Saturday night? How long had he stayed? Could it be possible that . . . no, he'd have told her if he spent the night. If his touch had been real, and not a dream. . . .

Oh, God, please don't let him have spent the night.

Throwing off the covers, she sat up and flung her feet over the side of the bed. As she reached for the crutches, she was *not* looking forward to today.

Two hours later, she was hobbling to the door of her classroom when she heard, from behind her, "Hi."

She didn't have to turn. She knew it was Luke. Over her shoulder, she tossed him an innocent glance. "Hi." Leaning against a locker, he was freshly shaven and dressed a little more maturely in khaki slacks and a thin navy sweater. He crossed to her. "Let me do that." He took the key and inserted it in the lock. He smelled so good that her head started to spin, and she grasped the crutches.

Flinging open the door, he turned. "You okay? Maybe it's too soon to be back."

She dragged herself inside. "No, I was going crazy at home." Already exhausted, she dropped her backpack on the desk, took off her coat, and sank down on the chair. Stretching out her leg, she sighed heavily. She hadn't had much energy to dress, so she'd picked out baggy navy slacks and a striped cotton sweater. Luke followed her across the room, picked up her coat, and took it to the closet, where he hung it up as if he had a right to take care of her. Or was she just imagining things because of her dreams? Because of her feelings?

He turned and folded his arms over his chest, outlined by the thin sweater. He was muscular, just as she'd imagined. "Your father leave?" he asked pointedly.

She nodded. "I'm sorry he gave you a rough time."

Luke's hazel eyes danced. "I've had fathers say worse to me."

"I'll bet."

His brow furrowed, once again making him seem older. "I'm sorry I caused you trouble, though. Did he take it out on you?"

"A bit."

"You should call him on that. You know, like we talked about that day in the weight room. How you wanted to be honest with him."

"I didn't feel good enough to do that." Deciding to bite the bullet, she focused in on him. "Luke, I need to ask you something."

"Shoot."

"Did you . . . did you leave my house Saturday night?"

Jamming restless hands in his pockets, he said, "What do you mean?"

"I have a feeling that, I don't know, something happened. Like you *stayed*. After I fell asleep."

"At your house?"

"Yes. Did you?"

"Kel—"

"Oh, you're here." Suzanna spoke from the doorway, then entered the room, followed by good old Uncle Joe. Even though he'd catch hell from Stonehouse about being with Kelsey, Luke was grateful for the reprieve. Kelsey wasn't quite as unaware of what had happened Saturday night as he'd thought. Did that mean she remembered . . . ? His hand flexed again.

"What are you doing here, son?" Joe's tone was strained.

Like the kid he was supposed to be, he rolled his eyes in disgust. "What's it to ya, Unc?"

Suzanna addressed Kelsey. "We just came down to see if you were all right."

"I'm fine," Kelsey said. "Luke and I were just catching up." She smiled at him, and his heart did a funny flip-flop in his chest.

Ever so slightly, Suzanna and Joe stiffened. Luke shrugged, threw his "uncle" a long-suffering look, and sat on the edge of a desk.

Crossing to her, Suzanna lifted Kelsey's chin and examined her face. "You look tired."

"I, um, didn't sleep well." For some reason, Kelsey blushed like she'd been caught in flagrante delicto.

"You've had quite a week." Suzanna's voice was sympathetic.

Joe added, "You sure you should be back?"

"Yes. It would drive me crazy to sit home and think about things." Her gaze slid to Luke. He knew now that he was one of those things. He couldn't help but like that.

"If you're sure." Suzanna backed away, close to Joe. Kelsey's eyes narrowed at the gesture. Luke knew it was part of their act, that they wanted people to think they were a couple. "If you get too exhausted, let me know, and I'll call in a substitute."

Joe said, "Come on, Luke, I'll walk you to your first class."

Under his breath Luke mumbled, "Like a freakin' prisoner."

Indulgently, Suzanna smiled. Stealing a glance at Kelsey, Luke could see she'd hoped to continue the conversation.

Thank you, Uncle Joe. Luke wasn't sure he could keep lying to her about everything.

As it happened, he had a chance to find out. After the last class of the day, Psychology, where—ironically—they were studying pathological liars, she asked him to stay afterward. Had Luke been thinking straight, he would have found an excuse not to. But he'd been worried about Ben Franzi, who looked like Dracula's cousin today; he'd dressed all in black, had bleached his hair a funny orange-blond, and wore black nail polish. The boy seemed morose. Luke had asked him to jam tonight, and Ben had mumbled, "Maybe. . . ."

Max had been preoccupied, too. Though they did set a date to visit the gun club, Luke was worried about him. It was all swirling like an emotional tornado in his brain when Kelsey asked him to stay after the bell.

She was clearly exhausted. Her face was pale, and there were smudges under her eyes. Luke had been on crutches several times and knew the effort to get around was draining.

"You look tired," he said softly. "You should go home."

"I will, in a few minutes."

I could drive you. I'd take you home, carry you inside, and put you to sleep. His mind—twenty-six, not nineteen—conjured up images of removing the sweater that clung to her, undoing her bra, and clasping those breasts, bare this time. . . .

"Luke? I asked you to close the door."

Distracted by the hardening of his body, he coughed to clear his head. "How are you gettin' to and from school, anyway?"

"Um, Mr. Wolfe picked me up."

"I got the impression he was majorly pissed off Saturday night."

Her eyes widened almost imperceptibly at his tone. "He was. He got over it."

What the hell, he'd go for broke. "It wouldn't have been a big loss. I think he's—"

"Did you spend the night Saturday?"

Teenager. You're just a cocky teenager. And remember what she confessed about her feelings. Remember that she's hurt by them. Do what you have to do to fix this, Ludzecky. "What makes you say that?"

"Just answer the question. You avoided it this morning. It's almost like you're trained to deflect information."

I am. He kept himself rigid.

"Luke, what's going on with you? I have a feeling you're not, I don't know, what you say you are."

Give the lady a cigar. Oh, God, he had to thwart this. Quick.

Try to alienate her, Joe had said. "Maybe you don't want me to be what I say I am."

She looked away. "I don't know what you mean."

"Dontcha, Teach?"

A beautiful flush crept up from her neck.

"Kelsey—" He didn't say it like a lover. He said it like a kid on the make.

"Don't call me by my first name. I don't allow it."

He smirked.

"Luke, I like you. But you're out of line here."

He rolled his eyes. "Fine. I'm bouncin'."

Her pretty face paled, and those gorgeous eyes got so bleak he almost couldn't stand it.

Good job, Ludzecky. She probably hated him now. No matter what she felt, she'd stay far away if she thought he was putting the moves on her.

He got to the door and was about to exit, when he heard behind him, "You didn't answer my question. Did you stay at my house all Saturday night?"

Yes, and you were dreaming about me. You wanted me to touch you. And I wanted to touch you more than I've ever wanted anything in my life.

Because of that, he said, "Nope. I got better things to do with my time." Without looking at her—surely she'd see the truth in his eyes—he left the room.

FAIRHOLM High School was nearly empty at 6 A.M. on a Thursday. Suzanna's heels clattered on the vinyl floor and echoed in the halls as she made her way to her office down the deserted corridor.

"Morning, Suzanna." The small, dark-haired Italian custodian, who reminded her of Joe Pesci, smiled warmly at her.

She returned his smile. "Hi, Tom. How's it going today?"

"Good." He indicated the vinyl. "Careful, we've got slippery floors again, 'cuz of the rain."

Nodding to the twenty-five-year veteran, she said, "Have a nice day," and continued down the hall. Her eyes were gritty and her shoulders ached. Unbuttoning her raincoat, she sighed wearily. She hadn't slept well for the past few days— just a couple of hours each night. She was worried about Josh.

First, his reaction to the Webster thing. He'd been shocked when they'd called him down Tuesday night to tell him about finding the yearbook and what it might mean. "Really? You think, like, somebody might pull a Columbine?"

Suzanna's legs had started to buckle. Joe grabbed for her. Upset, Josh hadn't noticed Joe's solicitousness.

"No, not a Columbine." Joe's voice was calm, steadying her as much as his firm grasp on her arm. "We just thought you should be aware that this could be considered a threat to you."

"Jesus." He'd looked keenly at Joe. "How come you're in on this?"

"For one thing, I found the yearbook." Casually, like a liar of the first order, Joe eased away from Suzanna and slid his hands into his pockets. "Also, I worked as a psychologist with the Department of Education and the government in Washington on some security issues. Right before I came here, as a matter of fact. Your mom and I are thinking about doing some safety training for students and staff. Can't be too careful these days."

Struggling to conceal her concern, Suzanna had crossed to Josh. She brushed back his thick blond hair. "I want *you* to be careful, honey. Try not to be alone anywhere until Webster is apprehended."

"How do you know it's Webster?"

Joe had answered. "We don't. But we brought the yearbook to the police. He seems the most likely candidate." Joe smiled. "And he has reason to dislike both you and your mother. So in any case, you need to. . . ." Thorough yet concise, Joe had given Josh a litany of safety practices that had made Suzanna's palms sweat.

Then yesterday, she'd had to explain to Josh that she and Joe were *dating*. Joe had provided the perfect opportunity when red carnations had arrived at her house at five in the evening.

"Hey, Mom," Josh had said, wiggling his brows as she ripped off the green paper. "Got a secret admirer?"

She was stunned by Joe's gesture. "No, not exactly secret. Come and sit down, honey, I want to tell you something."

Without much fuss, Josh had accepted that she and Joe were interested in each other. "It's mad-cool, Mom. You need somebody in your life. I'm leaving for college in a few months."

She'd smiled and tried to broach the subject of Josh continuing to talk to Joe, but her son sidestepped it. She'd need to deal with that today. Damn, this was getting so complicated.

When she reached her office, she unlocked the first door and entered the large secretarial area. Neither Pat nor Nancy, her secretary and the school financial secretary, was in yet. The room was dim, and furniture shapes lurked eerily before her like surreal objects in a Dali painting.

Reaching for the light switch, Suzanna started a bit when it didn't turn on. After a moment, she picked her way through the area. When she bumped into Pat's desk, she swore. It took her a while to find her keys in the faint light filtering in from the hallway. Finally she had her own office door open.

She fumbled for the wall switch. Her hands were shaky. Damn, she was spooked by this whole thing. She breathed a sigh of relief when her office lights flickered on.

Everything looked familiar. But today, the stark reality of what was happening in her building hit her with sledgehammer force. And, as she removed her coat, she wondered, for the very first time, if she really wanted to be a principal, really wanted to work in one of today's high schools. She remembered the first highs of teaching, of helping kids reach their potential. She recalled being a novice principal and thinking she could change the world. Now, she wondered if it was worth risking her son's safety. Her own.

And the safety of two agents who'd put their lives on the line for her. What if something happened to Joe while he was protecting her? She'd tried to broach that, too, last night when he'd come over for dinner, as planned.

They'd been in the den, seated close and comfortable on the tapestry couch with the door wide open. Joe had brought her there after dinner, and sank onto the sofa with her. "I'm trained, Suzanna. I can take care of myself."

She'd scowled. "You've gotten shot before, damn it."

"I'll be fine."

He draped his arm around her. His eyes had sparkled with mischief when she'd looked at him questioningly. He'd leaned over and whispered, "We're playing a part, Suzie Q. Josh has got to see some affection."

She thought about the nickname this morning. Suzie Q? So unlike the conservative, staid widow she'd become. How would she be in bed with Joe?

Groaning, she put her head down on the desk. She was losing it. She was so tired, she couldn't control her fantasies. How would she ever survive *pretending* to be his girlfriend? Just being in his presence unnerved her. If he began touching her for show, spending more time with her, exactly how would she handle his proximity?

You're dead meat, Kelsey would say.

Kelsey, whom Suzanna had told yesterday that she was seeing Joe socially. The girl had been okay with that, but had been out of sorts, still, about her feelings for Luke. Suzanna was worried about her—beyond the betrayal of trust issue. She was so sensitive, so caring. Her feelings for Luke—more understandable than she would ever know—were chipping away all her self-confidence. Damn it to hell!

Stop worrying and do some work. First, she called the custodian to come fix the lights, but no one answered. She pulled out a folder on the school musical and was perusing it when she heard the outer office door open. She glanced at the clock. Six-thirty. Still too early for her secretaries, though sometimes Nancy came in before work to walk around the building as her daily exercise. The door squeaked, then closed. Had she relocked it? Suzanna couldn't remember.

She rose and circled the desk. Trying the lights again—no luck—she waited till her eyes adjusted. She didn't see anybody. Carefully she listened. A locker slammed in the hall. Her heartbeat escalating, she made her way through the semidarkness. Had someone seen her light and come in? Or had someone entered *because* the office was dark, *then* seen her light and taken off? Swallowing hard as she eased open the door, she stepped into the corridor.

And ran smack into Max Duchamp.

"Oh."

Automatically, Max reached out to steady her. Kids often

did that without thinking when they bumped into a teacher, but for some reason, the gesture calmed her.

"Max?"

"Sorry I bumped you." His voice was gravelly. His eyes bloodshot. And he reeked of cigarette smoke.

"Did you just come into my office?"

His light complexion blushed. "No." A belligerent chin jutted out, and he straightened. For the first time, Suzanna realized how much bigger he was than she. He was so tall, she had to look up at him. She remembered something from her reading . . . *Kids who bring guns to school often go after the people who meted out the discipline.*

"Why'd you think I was in your office?" he asked.

Smiling, she shrugged. "I thought I heard the door open."

He glanced over her head. "Looks like nobody's home."

She thought about his and Webster's web site. It made her afraid, but she said, "Max, you know, if you ever did want to talk to me, about anything, I'm here."

Briefly—but it was there, she was sure—need flashed in his eyes. Then he snuffed it. Kids like him didn't talk to teachers.

Suzanna remembered Joe's point about the young shooter in Alaska. *When we asked him what he would have done if a principal or counselor had called him in and asked him about what kids had been hearing about him, he said he would have told them the truth.*

She leaned against the wall of lockers in a show of her willingness to prolong the discussion. Nervous, she jammed her hands in the pockets of her brown silk skirt. "I have a son. I know boys are private. But I thought maybe—" She smiled soothingly at him. "I know your mom is dead. I think sometimes a teenage boy might need to talk to a woman."

This time, his whole face revealed naked longing. "I got my dad."

"I know. And I know how important that is." She indicated the office. "Would you like to come inside? Classes don't start for another hour. We could just chat."

His eyes were bleak. "Maybe—" he began, then looked

past her. Suzanna tracked his gaze. A teacher was coming down the hall. Mike Wolfe.

Max stepped back.

"Hey, Duchamp," Mike yelled. "Where were you during Phys Ed yesterday?"

A sneer came to Max's face. The aggressive stance returned.

"I was sick." He pivoted and, without a word to Suzanna, took off the other way.

Mike came even with her. "Nice way to start your morning."

With a heavy heart, Suzanna watched an opportunity disappear down the hall like snowflakes in spring. She remembered one of her favorite quotes: *Teachers change the world one kid at a time.* She'd almost had Max convinced to talk to her.

"We gotta do something about kids like him, Suzanna. Look what happened to Kelsey."

Suzanna sighed. Schools *did* have to do something for kids like Max, only not the way Mike meant.

"Let me deal with the class-skipping issue," she said simply.

He held up a referral. "I was just going to hand this in to Lester."

"Give it to me."

She took the paper and turned to go back to her office.

THE high school cafeteria was a sea of faces, some angry, some bored, some laughing.

And some dangerous. Big gatherings in schools like this set off Joe's trouble radar; as he stood scanning the area for Josh, he pictured how this room could be divided. If they split it in half and walled it off in sections, lunch periods would be safer. But one side would end up without windows, and it would be like eating in a cave. Joe made a mental note to talk to the government's architect consultant. He hadn't told Suzanna this, but there was a special grant for schools to improve the safety of their buildings, and he'd applied for the money for Fairholm.

Meanwhile, Joe had problems closer to home. "Afternoon, Dr. Stonehouse. Looking for your nephew?" The supervisor, Tom Gannon, a sober man who seemed to belong in a previous century, stood guard at the door. Many schools employed trained security to monitor these difficult areas. But the Fairholm student council had thought that too jail-like, and Suzanna had gone along with their decision. He'd argued over that with her.

Now, things were different.

Way too different.

Last night, she'd fallen asleep nestled in his arm while they watched TV in the den. They'd been trying to do normal datelike things for show. Even today he remembered the feel of her weight against him, the smell of the shampoo she used. Deep inside, he'd longed for the right to pick her up and carry her off to bed. With her son in the house, it was impossible, of course.

Shit, it was impossible for more reasons than that.

"He's over there with Mr. Duchamp."

Joe came out of the fantasy. "Pardon me?"

"Your nephew. He's over there with the Duchamp boy." Tom's tone was critical.

Matching it, Joe nodded. "I see. Not really happy about him pairing up with that one." His statement couldn't be more false. Joe had strategized with Luke on how to get closer to Duchamp.

Now, Max and Luke sat alone at a table's end, looking . . . up to something. Maybe Joe should add some fuel to the fire. He sauntered over. Luke stiffened, and Joe admired how he stayed in character. "Hi, Luke. This isn't your lunch period, is it?"

The proverbial teenage sigh escaped his lips. "Old Man Jenkins kicked me out of chem lab."

"Why?"

"I dunno." He exchanged an arch look with Duchamp. "I was just askin' what would happen if I combined two of the elements we were using, and he got pissed off."

"Somehow I don't think that's the whole story."

"So ground me."

"Maybe I will. We'll talk at home tonight."

From the corner of his eye, Joe saw Josh get up and leave the cafe. Joe said good-bye and followed the boy out. He caught up to him in the hall. "Josh, wait."

Josh halted. Dressed like many of the other preppy kids in blue jeans and a brand-name sweatshirt, he turned. His face reddened the way his mother's did when she was embarrassed. "Hi."

"Didn't you have an appointment this period with me?"

"Yeah. I was . . . um . . . just headed down."

"Fine, I'll walk with you." *Even if you are lying through your teeth, buddy.* Joe would bet his Ph.D. the kid had no intention of coming down to see him. Josh had skipped yesterday's Boys' Concerns group, too.

They were seated in his office with the door closed before Joe addressed the issue. He removed his navy sport coat and loosened his tie to make the meeting seem more casual. "Something's wrong, isn't it? You weren't coming to see me today."

Josh looked him in the eye. "No."

"Because of what your mother and I told you the other night."

After hesitating, Josh nodded.

"Do you want to talk about that again?"

"What's to say? You like each other. You should see each other. I don't fit in the equation."

"You know," Joe said steepling his hands, "your mom didn't want to see me socially because she was afraid this would happen."

Hot emotion suffused Josh's face. "No, Dr. Stonehouse, don't let her do that. My mother needs company. She never complains, but I know she's lonely as hell." He shook his head. "She even reads those freakin' romance novels at night before she goes to bed."

The image of Suzanna cuddled up on fluffy pillows reading some steamy sex brought a smile to his lips.

But he needed to address what Josh was really saying. "It must be hard, being her son."

"Because of the principal stuff? Nah, that's okay."

"No, I mean because your dad is dead. You're more responsible to your mother than most kids with two parents."

Josh's ears turned red. "Um, it's okay."

Joe continued as if Josh hadn't spoken. "Responsible in the sense that you probably feel you have to be home more, do more things with her because she's alone. Not to mention living up to her standards and beliefs."

The kid's Adam's apple bobbed. Ordinarily Joe would have drawn this out, but he sensed he might not get another chance to work with Josh.

"I'm right, aren't I?"

A long and thoughtful pause. "I don't want her to know I feel this way. She'd be hurt. It's why I don't want to tell you these things."

Joe faced the boy squarely. "I don't know how to say this other than the way I explained it that night, and at our groups. Things haven't changed because I'm seeing your mother. I swear by every degree on that wall I won't reveal what you tell me in confidence."

Josh rolled his eyes. "It isn't even that bad."

"I don't expect that it is. I'd guess it's pretty normal stuff teenage boys go through. I was one once, you know."

"Did you have a girlfriend in high school?"

Joe dug back into a nightmarish past he preferred not to think about. "Yes. Sarah Summers." He shook his head. "She was gorgeous."

"What happened to her?"

"She went to Yale to become a doctor."

"Why'd you break up?"

Joe's throat felt tight. "I had issues as a kid. My upbringing was unorthodox. My views weren't like hers." In truth, Sarah was a partyer in the broadest sense of the word. She'd wanted to have sex and do drugs and Joe had shied away from both since. . . . "High school was a tough few years for me."

"That why you took in your nephew?"

"Yeah. Though I'm not helping him much. I don't like seeing him with Duchamp."

"Duchamp might be okay if he'd stay away from that creep Webster."

"So, back to you, Josh. What can I do to convince you that I'll keep everything from your mother except if I think you're dangerously depressed or that you're going to hurt yourself?"

"Hurt myself physically or emotionally?"

"Are you planning to hurt yourself emotionally?"

Josh stood, crossed the room and stared at the degrees. When he turned around, he said in a very adult voice, "No, I'm planning to sleep with Heather in Italy when we go there for spring break."

NINETEEN

Super Freak screams
Sitting there alone.
But no one hears
No one knows.
So sick of these people
So tired of this place . . .

BEN Franzi stopped singing when he heard the gentle tapping on his window. Glancing over at Luke, he smiled, despite where the song had taken him. He set his guitar on his pillow bed that occupied the center of the room, crossed to the window, and yanked it up. "Hey, if it isn't Joey Potter."

Morgan, climbing through the window, smiled at the reference to *Dawson's Creek*. Luke couldn't get into the show at all, but he tried to catch it occasionally to keep up with the teenagers he was trying to fit in with.

"Can I come in, Dawson, honey?" she asked, but she was already clambering inside. When she pivoted, she said, "Oh, I didn't know you had company."

"Hey, Morgan." Luke gave her a warm smile from where

he sat on the floor by the "altar." The thing should have given him the creeps, but he found it interesting. Draped in an Asian print shawl, a low table held different shaped candles; stone, iron, and wax pentacles; a goblet; a cauldron; and some bumper stickers that read *Blessed Be* and *Something Wiccan this way comes.*

Ben returned to the bed and picked up his guitar. Absently he strummed.

"How's it goin'?" Luke asked.

Shaking back her shoulder-length blond hair, Morgan sat on the Chinese chest Ben said his father had bought for him before he died. "Good. I came to do a spread with Ben."

"A spread?"

Her eyes sparkled. "Ever had your tarot cards read, Rebel?"

Luke smiled. The kids had nicknamed him Rebel or Reb when, in Government class, he'd staunchly defended draft dodgers and protesters at the time of the Vietnam War.

"Can't say I have. I'm game, though."

Fishing in her purse, she pulled out a joint instead of the cards. "Can I?" she asked Ben.

Hmm. Must be they trusted him.

"We said we weren't gonna do that anymore." Ben nodded to the shrine. From his reading, Luke knew the Wiccan religion didn't approve of polluting the body.

Crossing back to the window, Morgan opened it again. "I need it tonight."

"All right. Save me some. Burn incense, too. My mother'll kill us if she smells pot." He looked at Luke. "Want some?"

"No, my uncle would kill *me* if he got a whiff of the stuff. He's got the nose of a bloodhound." Luke continued to strum on his Gibson. He'd been in situations like this before, where kids did drugs in front of him. It took all his willpower not to stop them.

He wished he didn't care so much about these two. It was harder to watch them make stupid decisions. Damn it to hell, he was really getting sucked in by these Fairholm people.

Like Kelsey.

Don't think about her.

He concentrated on Morgan and Ben. "You guys do any-thing else?" he asked, nodding to the weed. He wanted to know how deep they were into stuff.

They said simultaneously, "No."

"Is Lucy *home*?" Morgan asked.

"Nope, Mom's out tonight, doing charity work for her church."

"You're so lucky." Morgan's tone was wistful. "She's a great mother."

Luke glanced over at the girl with her natural blond hair, stacked body—encased in tight jeans and a thermal shirt—and an intelligent face. Her childlike tone was at odds with her savvy looks. She caught Luke staring at her. "What's your mom like?"

Luke pretended annoyance. "A drag. Always on me about something."

Lukasz, it's time you got married, gave me some grand-children to carry on your father's name. God, he missed her. He'd be able to talk to her about Kelsey, tell her his quandary, and she'd give him good advice.

"What about your dad?"

"He's dead," Ben said loudly. "Just like mine."

Morgan's face fell. She stared worriedly at Ben.

"What?" Luke said after a pause. "I knew Ben lost his dad."

Ben said, "The anniversary's coming up over spring break."

Ah, dangerous times. "Sorry, man."

"One year."

Even more worrisome. No wonder Ben was looking more and more like the witches of Eastwick every day.

Ben stood and crossed to the window. Silently, watching the stars, he finished the joint with Morgan. The sweet smell of pot and incense encompassed the room in its own special cocoon. Morgan laid her hand on Ben's arm. It warmed Luke to know they had each other, even though he suspected pretty little Morgan had a crush on Luke himself.

When they were done with the joint, she turned to Luke. "Wanna do your cards?"

"Yeah. Sure."

They sat on the carpeted floor, cross-legged. Together, Ben and his soul mate chanted a few pagan prayers to bless the spread. Luke watched them, fascinated. Even though he'd researched Wicca on the Net, he'd never seen it practiced firsthand. He found the soft monotone comforting, and their sincerity put him at ease.

Morgan dealt ten cards, spaced over two rows. She stared hard at the first one. It showed five youths dressed in medieval tunics, holding long sticks that they batted up against each other. "They aren't really fighting," Morgan said. "Their card means imitation. Like, you're pretending to be something you're not."

Luke shrugged, but felt weird inside. "What you see is what you get, guys."

As she went on to the next card, her brow furrowed.

"What is it?" Luke asked.

Scowling, Morgan stared up at him, deadly serious. "This is the Tower card. It means trouble's brewing below the surface."

Ben pointed to the next one. "Look at that, Morgy."

It was a body with ten swords in it. Luke said, "Jesus, you guys. I'm not gonna die, am I?"

Morgan shook her head. "It's the Ten of Swords. It means that if you don't find out what you need to know, trouble will surface with dire consequences."

Holy shit, this was getting downright eerie.

The fourth card told Luke he suspected the wrong people were creating trouble. The fifth revealed he needed to be looking for a dull, isolated man.

He almost swallowed his tongue when the seventh card, the Queen of Pentacles, was interpreted by Ben as "a woman who's been affected by your falsehood."

Morgan picked up on that theme. "The eighth card shows you've wronged her by not being honest. See how she's blindfolded?"

That's enough, Luke wanted to yell, forcing himself not to make the sign of the cross.

"In the ninth card the man and woman are fleeing, but it's upside down, so it means you have to confess. The tenth card"—a heart with three swords through it—"says otherwise the relationship will be permanently damaged." Morgan's voice was grave.

The room was still. Luke couldn't have come up with a funny quip if Jerry Seinfeld had written it for him.

"So," Ben asked, "who you deceiving, Ludzecky?"

Sidling closer to Ben, Morgan followed up with "And what are you hiding?"

Luke looked down at the cards. *Jesus!*

THE .22 caliber shotgun was as familiar to Luke as his own Beretta. Lifting it, he aimed at the target, got the sight where he wanted it, and pulled the trigger. No one at the Fairholm Gun Club knew he did this regularly.

However, he pretended to buck a bit with the recoil. At the station next to him, Max Duchamp Senior—the colonel—shot off his twelve gauge with the ease of a lion hunter in Africa. He even looked a little like Ernest Hemingway at fifty—gray hair and beard, but he didn't have the writer's paunch.

He had old Papa Hemingway's way with women, though, the younger Max had told Luke. Max laughed, saying he came from good stock. Even Vietnam couldn't beat down his father, who'd been decorated as a colonel and earned several medals. Luke had known all this, of course, and suspected that was why Max wore army clothes and took a somewhat rabid interest in guns.

Nodding to Luke, then to his son, who was on his left, the colonel indicated they should leave. Amid the acrid smell of discharged firearms—Max said he'd been weaned on the scent—they exited the firing range, removed their earplugs, and signed out. The gun club was strict in its policies; the colonel, who was the current president, made sure of that.

"Let's go get something to drink," the older man said, clapping Max on the back.

They wended their way down the corridor. The walls were white and freshly painted. NRA advertisements lined the hall, as did diagrams of various weapons. They reached the bar and took stools.

"Like the new sign over the bar, guys?" the colonel asked.

Luke scanned the display. The heading read, *Myths vs. Facts. Guns are not the problem!* Typed in big letters so they could be read from the stools were several supposed myths people held about guns, and then the facts were there in boldface. Luke read a couple: *Myth: Assault weapons are a serious problem in the U.S. Fact: In 1994, a person was eleven times more likely to be beaten to death than to be killed by an assault weapon. This was before the Federal assault weapons ban. Myth: Thirteen children are killed each day by guns. Fact: The stats cited here include children up to age 19 or 24, depending on the source. Myth: Schoolyard shootings are an epidemic. Fact: In states without the "right to carry" laws, there have been fifteen school shootings. In states that allow citizens to carry guns, there has been only one.*

Luke wanted to puke. This was bullshit.

"It's mad-cool, Dad. Your idea?" Max asked.

"Yeah, I went on the Internet and got the figures. They make a point." The colonel scowled and sipped the beer that he'd ordered with the boys' sodas. "Goddamn liberals want to take everything away from us."

Luke wondered if Max agreed with his father philosophically, or if he was simply after parental approval. The kid had dropped a few hints that being with his dad was important to him. Kelsey had talked to Max about the issue when he'd written an essay on gun control. Luke knew what it was like to want to please the man who gave you life.

And Kelsey, whom Luke was trying like hell not to think about—especially the look of disappointment in her eyes when he'd played the adolescent Lothario the other day.

"Colonel. Good to see you. Where you been keeping yourself?"

Luke came out of his fantasies to see a huge, completely bald man behind them.

The colonel said, "Just got back from Hong Kong. God, it was hot there." Max's father was a software salesman for a local company. "How are you, Jackson?"

"Fine. Big bucks keepin' ya on the road?" Jackson asked.

"Yeah." The colonel reached out and squeezed Max's

shoulder. Luke remembered wishing his father would show that kind of affection. "You know my son, right?"

"Yeah. Hi, Max, Jr." Jackson smiled.

They introduced Luke. "You two go to Fairholm High?"

"Uh-huh."

"I'll be over there Monday."

"Really?" the colonel said. "Why?"

"We're trying to get a Young Guns Club started in the high school. It's a nationwide movement." Jackson zeroed in on Max. "What do you think, Max? We got a chance at getting it in?"

"The principal's pretty liberal; my guess is she'll be as excited about a gun club in the school as she'd be about an epidemic of herpes."

Max's father laughed at his joke.

"What do you think, Luke?" the colonel asked.

"I think it's a great idea. But I agree with Max—Mrs. Q. won't like it."

"Female principals. What's this world coming to?" Jackson shook his head, and Luke wanted to tell him to join the twenty-first century. The man continued, "NRA lawyers say the school can't deny meetings of any groups—religious based, cooking clubs, et cetera. As long as we don't advertise as a school club, and have a teacher supervisor, we can meet." He rolled his eyes. "In my son's school, they got a Christian group that gets together every Thursday and the bigwigs can't do anything about it."

Max shrugged. Luke followed suit.

"You know any teachers who might supervise?" Jackson asked.

"I dunno." Max's gaze darted from his father's friend. "I'd have to think about it."

"Good." He smiled at the colonel. "Great kid you got here."

"I know that," the colonel said.

Jackson started to turn away. "Well, I'm off." Then he hit his head, as if he'd committed a first-class faux pas. "Jesus H. Christ, here I am going on about the club, and I haven't even congratulated you on your upcoming wedding. You sure you want to tie the knot after all these years?"

"Uh, yeah, I'm sure." The colonel glanced worriedly at his son.

Jackson must have picked up on the vibes. "Yes, well, as I said, congratulations. See you around, Colonel." He left.

Max's face had flushed. "You could have told me."

Oh, hell. The kid didn't know!

Drawing in a deep breath, the colonel said, "Son, it's been a long time since your mother died."

Though he was dying to hear this play out, Luke felt bad for Max. "Look, I'm outta here. You two—"

Max slid off the stool. "I'm coming with you."

"Max. . . ." his father said. "I've been lonely. For a long time."

Max's face said, *You got me, Dad.*

Shit, what was wrong with parents today?

The older Duchamp said nothing.

"Come on, Luke. I'm riding home with you." With that Max stomped off.

"Talk to him," the colonel said to Luke.

No, asshole, you talk to him. Instead of saying it, Luke followed Max out.

TWENTY

———

THE screech of the plane overhead made Suzanna's teeth hurt. Returning from the rest room, she winced as yet another flight took off. In a half-hour, one of Alitalia's finest would fly her son across the ocean.

She was happy for him. Josh would be safe, far away from the Websters and Duchamps of Fairholm. Suzanna had hoped she was making progress with Max until this past week. As she headed to the gate, she shuddered, thinking of Max's proposal and his belligerent insistence that they allow a Young Guns group into the high school. She was meeting with him and his father over spring break to discuss her objections.

As she neared the Fairholm group, she saw Heather talking with her mother. Suzanna liked the Haywoods, knew they adored Josh, and hoped the two kids were being sensible. But they were eighteen and in love; if things already hadn't progressed to what she knew was their natural conclusion, she was sure they would soon. She just hoped Joe had been able to discuss this with Josh. Joe wouldn't tell her, of course.

I met with him, Suzanna. And he's talking. But don't ask me what he says.

I won't. I'm just worried about him.

Trust me. I'm helping him.

She found Josh and Joe by one of the huge windows, both leaning against the glass. Josh nodded and shrugged. Joe spoke earnestly.

Things had gone well between Joe and her son, despite the ruse of Joe and Suzanna dating. They'd spent some good time together this past week before Josh left for Italy.

She quickly made her way to them.

"Uh-huh. I remember." Josh smiled at Joe.

"You remember what?" she said, coming up to her son.

"Nothing. Just guy stuff." Josh hugged her close.

She laid her head on his shoulder. "I'm going to miss you, honey."

"I know, Mom. I'll miss you, too." He kissed her hair. He had to bend down to reach her. When had he gotten so tall? She recalled vividly when he started to walk, when he learned to ride a bike, when he didn't come up to her shoulder.

Static from the PA system. "Attention all passengers on flight 861, Alitalia. This is the first call. . . ."

"That's me," Josh said cheerfully, and gave her a bear hug.

Suzanna groaned. She didn't want to let go.

"Mom, don't."

Joe reached over and drew her away from her son, and next to his own big frame. "Go on, kid."

With an assessing look, Josh picked up his backpack. "Watch out for her, will you?" he said to Joe.

Joe slid his arm around Suzanna. "I will. I promise. Be careful. And have fun."

Before he left, Josh kissed Suzanna's cheek again. With one last look over his shoulder, he headed toward the boarding area.

Suzanna's eyes blurred. These days, she was uncharacteristically weepy.

"He'll be all right, Mom." Joe's arm tightened around her.

She leaned into him. "I know."

Thinking, he waited a moment. "Let's go do some self-defense training. It'll work off some of your anxiety."

"All right."

After they saw the plane take off, the drive home was made in companionable silence. That had happened a lot since Connecticut. They were comfortable with each other, especially when they were alone.

When he steered toward Jordace Avenue, she asked, "We're going to my house?"

"I've got workout clothes in my car. You have to change anyway, so I thought we'd practice here." He swerved into the driveway. "Besides, Luke's got buddies over today."

"Who?"

"Smurf. I think Franzi's coming later."

"I'm worried about Ben."

"I'm worried about all of them."

Suzanna sighed.

"Let's forget it for today," Joe suggested.

Inside, they went in opposite directions to change. Suzanna trekked upstairs. Joe watched her go with resignation, feeling like he was walking an emotional tightrope. Already he was in deep with her, and now he had another attachment to shake.

Her son.

He could still hear Josh talking frankly about his plans with Heather. Joe had forced himself to remember the boy was eighteen and almost a man. He'd given his opinions, some warnings about safe sex, but refrained from preaching.

Crossing to the downstairs bathroom, he worried about the kid as a father would. *Don't go there, Stonehouse. You'll never be his father.* But as he passed the den where they'd watched a ball game, he thought about the other things they'd done together, as a family might.

One night, he, Suzanna, and Josh had seen a movie; on a cold afternoon, they'd gone cross-country skiing with Heather. When the women begged off after an hour, he and Josh had stayed out, trading sports talk, college plans, girl concerns. The boy was a deep thinker, had ambition, and really cared about the world. Joe had talked to him the way he used to talk to Josie. Today, that realization stunned him. He couldn't allow himself to care about Josh that much.

Or Josh's mother.

Staring in the bathroom mirror, he gave himself a stern

lecture. *You are a government agent. You cannot get involved with this woman and her son. You will leave Fairholm, alone, and never see them again. Got it?*

He got it.

He was in a black mood, moving den furniture, when Suzanna came down. She was dressed in clingy Spandex leggings and a peach T-shirt. Her hair was tied up on her head, with little tendrils escaping. Suddenly, he wished they had Luke to chaperone.

Sternly, he told himself he was strong enough to handle this. He was disciplined. He'd had to be, from the time he was ten years old. In his head, he knew he could resist this woman, but he had to be more sensible about the time he spent with her.

Gruffly, he said, "Ready?"

"Is something wrong?" she asked innocently.

"No. Let's get started."

Twenty minutes later, he wasn't so sure of his resolve. She felt soft, yet supple, under his hands. She smelled like black-market French perfume. And he wanted her so badly, he ached.

So he took it out on her. "You're not concentrating, Suzanna. I've taken you down several times."

She drew in a deep breath. "I'm sorry. I have a lot on my mind."

"Your *safety* should be on your mind," he said tightly. "Let's try again."

"Fine." He moved back. "I'm coming up from behind you. I get you in a neck clasp like this. What do you do?"

Swinging her hips out of the way, she brought her fist back but stopped short of smashing his crown jewels to kingdom come. He jumped back instantaneously. "That good enough for you?" she asked over her shoulder. "You'd be doubled over, Stonehouse."

Without responding, he grabbed her from behind again. She didn't react quickly enough, and he had her locked to him. He felt the heaviness of her breasts against his forearms. "Damn it, you have to react faster, Suzanna."

"I was surprised."

"Well, an attacker isn't going to announce himself."

Still in his arms, she circled around. "Why are you so grumpy all of a sudden? You're like Jekyll and Hyde since Josh left."

"I'd rather not be analyzed. Turn around."

"Yes, sir."

This time, she was ready when he went for her. She swiveled her hips. He parried her groin attack. Surprising him, she hooked her foot around his leg, and his arms flew out to balance himself. Her elbow dug sharply into his chest and he fell to the floor.

"That ready enough for you, Agent Stonehouse?" she asked sweetly, plopping her hands on her hips and peering down at him with the haughtiness of a queen.

Glaring up at her, he snaked his hand around her ankle, toppling her down next to him.

Quickly, he rolled over her. "Major lesson in self-defense, sweetheart. Never get too caught up in your successes."

She didn't respond. Instead, she watched him with something dangerous in her eyes. Suddenly he realized the folly of his maneuver. His body pressed into hers, and he could feel every curve and indentation. Her face was rosy from exertion, but she was breathing hard from his nearness.

He swallowed convulsively. Reaching up, he brushed a tendril of hair from her eyes.

"Joe," she whispered, lifting her hands to his shoulders. Her voice was after-sex hoarse, and it zinged through him.

Bracing his arms on the floor, he drew in a deep breath; he knew he was about to make the most momentous decision of his life. He'd never kissed her. If he did, it would be all over.

Honor warred with desire.

She felt so good beneath him. And she was looking at him like a woman who wanted . . . only him. His heart thrummed in his chest.

But he'd trained too long in the art of discipline. Not just in the Secret Service but before, when he was trying to support both himself and Ruthie. And those long weeks, months, years of forcing himself to be strong came to his aid.

Swiftly, he rolled off her and stood. Reaching out, he said, "Come on, get up."

Suzanna's hand shook as she put it in his. On her feet, she turned away from Joe. It had been building for weeks, layering over itself feverishly. A flush crept up her neck just thinking about the hot brush of his hands on her when they worked out, the clean scent of his soap and shampoo, which now mingled with the smell of sweat. But mostly, it was that smoldering look in his eyes that said eloquently, *I want you.*

"You're trembling." He was behind her, close. Too close. God, she craved that nearness, like an emotional junkie needing him for a fix.

"Yes."

"We went too far," he said meaningfully.

She didn't look at him. "Did we?"

When he said no more, she pivoted. Anger, just as potent as desire, swelled inside her. He'd turned his back, bent over now, and got a towel from his bag. Casually, he wiped his face. She could see he'd just gotten a haircut. His black ragged-sleeved T-shirt with the Stanford logo clung to his wet back.

"How do you do it?" she asked, struggling to calm her voice and the rush of hunger in her blood.

"Do what?" He didn't face her.

"How do you turn it off?"

"Turn what off?"

Without allowing rational thought to stop her, Suzanna grabbed his arm and dragged him around. His eyes were a cold, flat green. The agent was back.

"You know *what*. We talked about *what*."

A muscle twitched in his jaw. "Don't say anything more, Suzanna."

"Joe. . . ." His name came out soft, full of the craving she felt for him.

The twitch became a throb in his neck, telling her it wasn't so easy for him to resist her. "This would compromise my job, damn it."

She bit her lip to keep from begging. Her stomach clenched and her head spun, she wanted this man so much. "Then don't."

"Suzanna, I—" His hands fisted at his sides. He looked as

though he was keeping himself from grabbing for her. She broke the eye contact first and turned around.

A long hesitation. Moments passed. She heard him gather his things.

"I'm going to leave for a while. Either Luke or I will be back. Follow me out. Put on the alarm."

"I will. After you're gone."

"Now, Suzanna."

She drew in a deep breath. "All right." He always won. She wondered if his victories were always this empty.

AN hour had gone by, and Joe still couldn't contain it. As soon as he'd left Suzanna's and driven home, he'd gone out for a brutal run. The Devil was at his heels.

Goddamn fucking son of a bitch!

Sex had never been easy for him, given his upbringing. Usually he could control the images. Almost never did he allow them into his consciousness. But tonight, on this cold and lonely street, in grim solitude, the memories came to him, and he was too weak with desire for Suzanna to stop them. . . .

He'd not even begun to shave the first time a woman had touched him. His father had brought her to his stark room in the shack where they lived in the commune. "Joey, someone wants to see you." She might have been beautiful, but it was dark, and Joe was frightened.

Even at almost eleven, he'd known the way she fondled him was different, wasn't right somehow. "I don't want to, Dad."

His father had snapped on a light. "Go on, son, I'll be here."

Joe had thrown up after that first encounter. And he'd been so *confused.*

The next time was even worse, because he'd known what would happen. . . .

"Come on, baby," his mother had said, "We're going down to the pond to swim. We'll have fun." He'd been asleep, and remembered the clock had read midnight.

He moaned. "I'm tired. Please, Mom."

She'd let out a sultry laugh. "Everybody's waiting for us. You can sleep all day tomorrow."

"Please, no."

"Do as your mother says," she'd commanded.

But the worst had been the first time they'd gotten his little sister. He'd hidden her in a copse of trees, and was holding her close to him. "Don't worry, Ruthie," he'd said, terrified himself, knowing somewhere inside he wasn't going to be able to stop them. "I won't let them get you."

Her slim child's body trembled in his arms. "Joey. . . ." was all she said.

He hadn't protected her then, wasn't able to for a few years after that, but when he turned fourteen, he'd found a way to escape.

It was a miracle that he'd ever learned to enjoy women and be comfortable with his own body. But he'd had some luck along the way. The foster care people who took them in when they were finally found on the streets of L.A. were wholesome, happy people who had solid values. They soothed the glass-cut edges of his and Ruthie's souls. They'd gotten trained professionals in child abuse to work with both him and his sister, and it became clear that these people, at least, knew that what had happened to two innocent young children was wrong, was criminal, really.

After more counseling in college, Ruthie was able to open up to Al; Joe married a sweet and giving woman with whom he'd had a somewhat normal physical relationship. It had been the stress of the Secret Service job—and Joe's inability to truly lay himself open to her, to anybody—that had caused the divorce.

How do you do it? Suzanna had asked. *How do you turn it off?*

He shook his head. He'd had no choice, really, if he wanted to survive.

But tonight, he couldn't turn it off. He was open to Suzanna. Open, and very raw. His feelings wouldn't stay down. He felt a clawing need, a terrible thirst that he'd never known before, never wanted to know before. Calling on every one of his skills to stay detached, to do his job, he pounded the pavement. Still, a tapestry of muscles inside of him knotted with raw desire.

For her.

His mind wouldn't blank. He kept seeing her today, for the past three months, confronting him. He'd never respected anyone more.

Never wanted a woman more.

Images kept bombarding him: of her smiling at Kelsey; of her amber eyes misting when her son left today; of the anger lighting her face when she viewed Max's web site.

They just wouldn't go away. Which was why he found himself at her front door once again. He rang the bell.

Nothing.

Again.

Still no answer. He leaned on the button.

His heart, already drumming in his chest from the exercise, escalated to arrhythmic proportions. Raising his fist, he pounded the door. "Su-zan-na."

He started to remove his sweatshirt to cover his hand—he intended to put it through the tall, slender window of the foyer—when the door swung open.

She was dressed in a long, satiny robe the color of ripe peaches. From the vee in it, and the way it gloved her, he guessed she wore nothing under it.

Suddenly it was all too much. The wanting and not having. The danger she was in, and his urgent need to protect her. He grasped her shoulders roughly. His fingers bit into her. "Never open the door without checking to see who's there."

"I saw you through the window."

"Oh." His arms dropped. "What the hell took you so long to answer?"

"I was running a bath. I just heard you." She crossed her arms over her chest. "What do you want?"

You.

Without answering, he brushed past her and strode inside.

She stepped out of the way and he slammed the door. *Snicked* the lock. Her eyes widened at his peremptory actions. Clamping her arms around her waist, she shivered, as if afraid.

"You *should* be afraid," he said silkily.

"I should?"

Instead of his breath easing, he became more winded. Her eyes dropped to the rapid rise and fall of his chest.

He took a step toward her. A side of him had surfaced that he didn't know existed. "Of what you bring out in me."

Though he got close, towered over her, she stared up at him unflinchingly. "I'm not afraid of that."

He fisted his hand in her hair. It was heavy and thick and curled around his fingers like a lover's caress. He pulled— God, somehow gently—and her face tilted. "You won't necessarily like what you've unleashed in me."

"Of course I will."

"*I* don't like it."

She smiled then, Circe's smile, and it shot right to his gut. Lower.

Her reaction totally disarmed him. "You're playing hardball now, Suzanna."

Again, the feminine amusement. "Yes, I am."

"*Suzanna*. . . ." He said it wrenchingly, closed his eyes to get some control. He couldn't, so he buried his face in her neck.

It was a mistake. She hadn't showered yet. The thought that they were both sweaty, earthy, inflamed him. He kissed her bare skin, and she moaned. He bit her neck gently, and she whimpered.

Then he yanked her to him. He'd lost the battle. It didn't matter that this wasn't right. That he'd struggled for years not to let this kind of passion overwhelm him. That he was supposed to be protecting her, and to do it right, he had to have a clear head. All that mattered was that she was here, and for now, she was his.

His.

His grip on her tightened. He must be hurting her, but she didn't protest. Instead, her hands wound around his neck. "Joe." The word was filled with acceptance, with affection, with need.

He drew away, slid an arm under her knees, the other to her back, and lifted her. She gasped, then laughed that sultry sound again as he dragged her close. She should protest. She should pound on his chest for him to let go; instead, she clutched at him, buried her face in his sweatshirt as if she belonged there.

He took the curved staircase two steps at a time. Her weight was nothing with the adrenaline pumping double time through his veins. At the top of the stairs, a long hall stretched out. To the left, light spilled out of a door. "There?" he asked thickly.

"Uh-huh. Hurry, please." Her words were muffled by his shirt as she fisted her hands in it.

He tripped over himself trying to get to her room. Once there, he strode to the bed, set her down, then stretched out on top of her. And, for the very first time, he took her mouth. His mind exploded with sexual fireworks as he devoured her. He would have tried to gentle the onslaught, if he could, but she returned the kiss with equal fervor, gripped his neck, pulled him closer. His hands threaded through her hair; his body sank into hers. The mattress was hard, and her womanly softness poleaxed him with its contrasts.

When he let her mouth go, he kissed his way down her jaw to her chest and nudged open the vee of her robe. He saw the swell of her breast and groaned. "Suzanna."

She urged him down. He kissed the underside of her breast, tongued it. His hands came to her shoulders and eased off the robe, exposing her. Simultaneously, his knee came up; the bottom of the robe parted, and he wedged his thigh between hers.

"Ohhh. . . ." Her primitive response ignited more sparks in him that flared into painful desire.

"Ah, love." His mouth closed over her nipple, and he was lost. The sensation of suckling her overcame him.

Dimly he was aware of her movements against him. But it was as if he were in a black cloud of craving that blocked out everything else. Finally, her actions got to him. She was tugging at his shirt. "Off," she said. "*Off.*"

Her need gave him the necessary sanity to draw back. "Okay, shh, okay."

Her breath was coming in gulps. Her hands were clumsy on his shirt.

"Let me do it," he said. It took forever—his own hands were none too steady—but finally he removed his clothes.

Then he reached down and untied her robe. It fell apart, and he drew in a breath. "You are so lovely." Bracing a knee on the bed, he ran his palm over her. She started, so sensitized had his mouth made her. He let his hand wander over her stomach; she moaned again, and when he cupped her, she arced off the bed.

He took the opportunity to remove the robe completely.

When she reached for him, clasped him solidly in her hand, his body ricocheted.

"Now," she said almost incoherently. "*Now*."

He couldn't speak, only took the time to find his discarded sweatpants and fish a condom from the wallet in his zippered pocket. As he rolled it on, then parted her thighs and felt her wetness, insanity returned. With swiftness, and little finesse, with need and almost no tenderness, he entered her.

After the first thrust, he was lost.

LIGHT filtered in through the windows, but it was dim and private with the blinds drawn. "Hmm." Suzanna purred like a kitten at the soft trail of his fingers down her spine. She buried her face in the pillow.

"Want to sleep?" he asked, his breath fanning her ear.

"No, just touch me." *Never stop.*

A very male chuckle. "My pleasure." His hand went to her waist, began to knead there.

"Ahh."

"Hurt?"

"Um, no."

"I was pretty rough the first time."

"Were you?" A female giggle. "It was wonderful."

A long chuckle. "Better than the second?"

She studied the blond armoire, the matching dresser, the blinds on the window. They looked so different now. The last hour had changed everything.

"I remember the second more. It was longer."

And so, so special. He'd kissed her everywhere.

His hands moved to her buttocks. He massaged there. Another moan. "Mmm. J-o-e. . . ." The word strung out.

"You pack quite a punch, Suzie Q. You know that?"

No, she hadn't known that. She'd had a satisfying sex life with Lawrence, but this had been a blast of dynamite instead of small explosions.

"Suzanna?"

She turned over. It was a mistake. The agent was completely gone, and in his place was a sensual, skilled man. His dark hair was mussed from their lovemaking, and a beard was beginning to show. She reached up. "Scratchy."

His hand slid to her thigh. "I think you've got a brush burn there, sweetheart."

A slow, female smile.

"Don't do that, unless you want to get another one."

"I want to get another one," she said sleepily.

He whispered in her ear. "All right. After a nap."

"Promise?"

"I promise."

Eyes closed, she felt the weight of him on the mattress, on her pillow. He drew her close, into his chest, and pulled up the raspberry duvet. She nestled on his bare skin, inhaled him, and felt his hand come up to her hair. "Sleep now, sweetheart."

"You too," she said.

He tugged her even closer, and they settled in.

TWENTY-ONE

———

THINKING she'd go crazy if she spent one more minute in her house, Kelsey got in her car Monday morning and headed downtown to the pharmacy. She needed more muscle relaxants and would pick them up today.

How's the knee, Teach? Luke had asked her after the debacle in her room the day she'd returned to school.

Better. And I wish you'd address me as Ms. Cunningham.

Though in the dreams, which continued like X-rated movies, he'd called her Kel, honey, and even *baby*, for God's sake, a sexist term of endearment she hated. Her nocturnal fantasies were getting out of control. Everything was.

Even Suzanna. The principal was dating a staff member, something Kelsey thought she'd never see. But Suzanna had had myriad explanations: that they were attracted to each other, that she was tired of living her life by the book, that since Lawrence died, she'd been lonely and Joe was the first man she'd really been interested in. Still, something hadn't quite rung true about the whole thing.

Maybe it was just because Kelsey was feeling so confused about Luke that she hadn't understood what was going on with Suzanna. Luke. Ordering herself not to think about him, she found a parking space in the lot next to the drugstore and exited her sporty Camaro. Carefully, she picked her way across the pavement. The weather had warmed up, causing the snow to turn to a drizzly rain. Wearing thick-soled hiking boots, she was off crutches, and didn't need to fall.

Should you be off those crutches already? Luke had asked the day school ended for spring break. Sometimes, he reverted to his old solicitous self. It was almost as if he forgot to be surly.

The doctor says so.

He just watched her.

Have a nice break, Luke.

His eyes had darkened. *You goin' anywhere?*

That's none of your concern.

Mr. Wolfe is headin' for the Bahamas.

Is he? In truth, Mike had asked her to go with him, but she'd refused.

Forget it, Luke had said, and left.

As he walked out the door, Kelsey's heart sank at the thought of not seeing him for a week. And she was horrified at the intensity of what she felt for him. She'd gone to the doorway and watched him stalk down the hall. He'd punched a locker as he passed it, swearing ripely.

Steeling herself against the memories, she entered the drugstore; she tried to suppress her guilt, but she couldn't. The notion that she was warped, or at the very least unprofessional, wouldn't let her alone. First the dreams, then the longing to be with him. Even Suzanna's assurance that feelings like this were normal didn't help. This wasn't normal, and Suzanna would be ashamed of her. Oh, God, what if she lost Suzanna's respect? It would kill her. She. . . .

"Watch it." Not looking where she was going, she'd bumped into a customer and glanced up. Oh, for God's sake, this was ridiculous. "Luke?"

"Hi." He searched her face before the adolescent sneer claimed his lips. Again, she had a feeling he donned the expression on purpose, almost as if he had another persona. "Should you be out in this weather?" he asked.

"Really, Luke, I'm a grown woman." She stepped back. "I can decide when I'm well enough to go out."

He took in her jeans and short leather jacket with a lecherous grin. "I know you're a grown woman," he said silkily. "Out shopping today?"

She nodded.

He held up a bag from an exclusive women's shop in Fairholm. "Me, too. I had to buy a birthday present for my honey."

Jealousy, thick and potent, snaked inside her. And once again, she was horrified at her reaction to this *boy*.

"Oh, good. Well, I'll see you around."

"Sure, Teach." He threw her an innocent look. "I mean *Ms.* Cunningham."

Shakily, Kelsey walked away. She turned her head to the left, though, so she could see him saunter to the back of the store. His well-worn jeans gloved his butt and legs. With them he wore a lightweight leather jacket she'd never seen before; it accented the breadth of his shoulders. Waiting by the hair spray until he was out of sight, she stared blindly at the products for a long time. Finally, she headed toward the prescription counter, handed in her order, and sank down on a chair. Her knee hurt.

And her heart. She had no idea she could. . . .

He came into her line of vision. Frowning, he stared at a counter in front of of him. Her gaze strayed to the display. Boxes and boxes sat before him. There was a sign advertising the product.

They were condoms.

She watched him reach for a box, and her heart constricted. He was having sex, of course. He was so good-looking, so mature, so sexy. High school girls routinely fell at his feet. The present. The condoms. For a moment, she was frozen in her seat—staring at him, at his hand closed around a box. Looked like Luke Ludzecky had a hot date tonight. She put her head down, thinking she might be ill.

"Ms. Cunningham." The clerk called out her name.

She couldn't respond.

"Kelsey Cunningham," the clerk called out again.

She was forced to look up when Luke crossed to her and squatted down before her, the way a parent might to a sick child. "Give me that."

"Huh?"

"Your prescription card." He nodded to her hand, where she clutched her card and money. "I'll cash you out."

She handed him both. Standing, he headed to the counter. He turned everything over to the clerk, who said, "You want those?" The guy pointed to the condoms.

"Oh, yeah." He seemed flustered as he dug in his pocket for more money and paid the bill.

He returned to her and gave her the package. Taking it, she stood and, wordlessly, strode down the aisle. She was so confused, so afraid of her feelings, she had to get out of there.

Just as she stepped outside, he grabbed her. "Kelsey, wait."

Her voice rose. "I told you not to call me that." Her hands trembled as she shook him off. "Don't," she said frantically, tears misting her eyes. "Just don't."

"All right. All right. Calm down. I won't call you that."

The package slipped from her hands and toppled onto the wet sidewalk. Out fell the condoms. French ticklers.

"Fuck." The obscenity came from Luke's mouth as he bent down to scoop up the contents.

And suddenly it was too much. She couldn't breathe. She had to get away from him. Grabbing back the bag, she turned away and took off down the street.

"Kelsey. Wait."

She quickened her pace. Just as she got to the end of the sidewalk, she slipped. Her feet went out from under her and she went down right on her fanny. "Oh. . . ." She grabbed for her knee, but it twisted anyway. "Oh, shit."

He came up behind her; putting her head down, she battled back the tears.

Squatting again, he tipped her chin. "Are you hurt?"

She nodded.

"Come on, honey, I'll take you home."

"Oh, God, no."

Calm as a doctor in surgery, he stood and reached out his hand. "You're overwrought. You can't drive. I'll take you home."

Again, she shook her head. She'd sunk so low, sitting

there as the wet drizzle seeped into her jeans, lusting after a *student*.

Luke sighed and bent over; then she felt herself being lifted, just like that night in her house. She tried not to cuddle into him, but he felt so good, and she was so upset, and she was chilled, and her knee hurt. . . .

Soon, she was on the front seat of his car. "What. . . . Oh, no, Luke, I can't."

In a grown man's voice, he said, "You *can't* drive. I'll take you home."

"What about my car?"

"We'll worry about that later. I'll take you home. I promise, that's all."

He knew, of course. Felt it, too. Somewhere in her heart, she'd sensed that he reciprocated her feelings for a long time.

The silence in the car on the way to her house was deafening, broken only by occasional nervous coughs and sniffles. Okay, she'd deal with this, she thought as they hit a bump and she jolted against the door. She'd tell Suzanna tomorrow that Luke had to be taken out of her classes. No matter what Suzanna thought of her after that, she had to protect Luke from herself. And if she didn't have to see him, maybe she could face herself in the mirror in the morning.

At her house, Luke exited the car and helped her up the sidewalk; she was limping again. He took the key when her hands shook too much to fit it in the lock. Without looking at him, she entered the foyer and turned to close the door.

He blocked it.

"Please, Luke. Just go."

"In a minute." Luke stepped inside and shut the door. He couldn't leave her like this, no matter what he'd promised. Momentarily, the man inside him eclipsed the agent. He cared for this woman and refused to leave her when she was so upset—about him and her feelings for him.

Mechanically, she removed her coat and dropped it on the floor along with her purse. Limping, she went into the living room. She stopped at the couch. Stared at it. Seemed mesmerized by it.

So did he. He could remember the feel of her, heavy in his hand, and his fingers flexed with the memory. He could still summon her scent. He closed his eyes to recall it more acutely. When he opened them, she was staring at him. She looked from him to the couch. Then back at him again.

"You spent the night here that Saturday, didn't you?"

"Yes."

"I thought I was dreaming you touched me."

"You *were* dreaming." And though God would damn him, he added, "But I touched you." He ran frustrated fingers through his hair. "You surprised me. Pulled my hand to your. . . ." His eyes dropped to her breasts. "I wanted to. . . ."

She whipped around. Her face was ravaged, her eyes haunted. She'd come face-to-face with what she saw as a complete breach of ethics in herself. Still, she lifted her chin. "You need to leave here now. You have to be taken out of my classes. Maybe I'll quit Fairholm. Quit high school teaching. Go to Yale like my—"

"No." He couldn't allow this. "No, you won't. You don't understand."

"I understand only too well." And then she started to cry. She buried her face in her hands and wept for the woman she thought she was.

Without conscious thought, he crossed to her. "Kelsey, it isn't what you think."

She looked up at him. "Please just leave."

"Not like this. You don't understand."

She shook her head.

And he couldn't take it anymore. He pulled her close. She resisted. With force, he held her next to his heart. She tried to pull away again. Finally, when she couldn't, she let go, clutched his shirt, and sobbed into his chest. "I'm so awful," she said. "So awful."

He kissed her hair.

"Nooo. . . ." She cried harder.

She stayed in his arms until she calmed. Then, she pulled away. "Please, just go."

Sanity returned for him. He stepped back.

She swallowed hard. "Luke, if you have any feelings for me at all, you'll leave here right now."

He watched her.

"*Please.*"

"All right. I'll leave. For now."

But he'd be back. And soon. Something had to be done. He wasn't going to let this go any further. At the door, he glanced over his shoulder. She'd dropped down on the couch and was crying again into her hands.

"No further." He mumbled the promise to her and to himself, then strode out of her home.

HE was the epitome of sexiness, lazing back in the six-foot-long Jacuzzi that Suzanna had installed when she remodeled her bedroom suite. The scent of the tropics was in the air and steam rose off the water. As the jets swirled around them, her blood began to heat.

Again.

What had happened to her in the last few days? She was like another woman—another creature. Sensuous. Sexual. Very sexual. And it was because of Joe.

He was as he'd been in Connecticut. Relaxed. Happy. And now, of course, well-satisfied. Her leg bumped his, and she felt his corded muscles slide against her.

"What's that Cheshire Cat grin for?" he asked huskily.

That voice: *Turn a little to the right, sweetheart. That's it. Now ease up so I can get my hand under. . . .*

"I was just thinking how satisfied you look."

"Ah." Reaching out, he grasped her foot. His thumb kneaded the instep.

"Mmm."

A foot massage is better than sex, she'd told him in bed last night.

I'll have to do something about that, he'd retorted, turning her over. Taking his sweet old time, he showed her that nothing on earth was better than sex with him.

"That's because I *am* satisfied." He kissed her toes. "Because of you, *cara.*"

She laughed at his use of Italian, which he spoke fluently. For three days he'd been thanking the mother country for taking Josh away so they could have this stolen time together.

"Can you stay again tonight?"

The agent's scowl came back. "Luke's already suspicious."

"Didn't believe you needed to sleep on the couch in the den to protect me since Josh is gone, did he?"

"Not a word."

"Do you care?"

Joe's brow formed a vee. "If it wasn't for all that stuff about Kelsey—about their feelings for each other—I wouldn't."

The snake in the garden of Eden.

"I don't want to think about that now." She closed her eyes, lay back against the tub. "I don't want to think at all."

His hand slid down and cupped her. "That I can take care of."

"J-o-e." His name was one long moan.

After he took her, swiftly and without gentleness—she loved it—she offered to go get them some wine. The vision of him in the blue fiberglass tub kept her smiling all the way down the stairs.

The doorbell was chiming. They must not have heard it with the jets on in the tub. Then she realized Joe's phone, which he'd left on the foyer table, was also ringing. Before she could react, there was hammering on the door.

She peeked out the side window.

Luke paced the front porch, a phone at his ear and punching the bell. She tightened the sash on her white terry robe and opened the door. At the murderous look in his eye, her heart began to pound.

"Where the fuck is he? He's not supposed to be incommunicado."

Suzanna's eyes widened at Luke's language. Not once in the months she'd known him had he been anything but a courtly knight around her.

He ran a hand through his hair, much as Joe often did out of frustration. "I'm sorry. I'm upset."

She drew him inside. "Is something wrong?" Again the panicky tattoo of her heart. "Is someone hurt?"

"Not like you mean. Everybody's physically safe." He glanced to the back of the house. "Is Joe in the den? I have to talk to him."

"Um . . . let me take your coat."

"I don't want you to take my coat. I want to talk to Joe. Now." Brushing past her, he strode down the corridor to the den where Joe had told Luke he was bunking. Not sure of what to do, Suzanna followed. "He's not back there," she finally said.

Inside the empty room, Luke looked around. "He's here, isn't he?"

"Yes."

Luke faced her. Seemed, for the first time, to take in how she was dressed in the middle of the day. "Suzanna, what's going on?"

"I . . . let me go get Joe."

It wasn't necessary. Whistling preceded him down the hall, then, "Hey, woman, don't you know enough not to keep your man—" He appeared in the doorway, wearing only sweat pants and a mischievous expression on his face.

Simultaneously, he and Luke froze. Suzanna stilled, off to the side, waiting to take her cue from Joe.

After a moment, Luke's gaze whipped from Joe to her and back again to his boss. Then he rolled his eyes. "Oh, great, this is just great."

Suzanna was pretty sure that up until now, Luke, too, had thought hers and Joe's relationship was only a ruse.

Joe eased away from the doorway and over to Suzanna. He placed himself between her and Luke. "Has something happened?"

Luke was all adult now. "Yes." His face darkened. "We have to tell Kelsey right away that I'm not really one of her students."

Shoulders relaxing, Joe sighed. "We've already been through this, Luke. I'm sorry, she can never know."

"Yeah, well, that was before she started to think she was a pervert." His voice was full of outrage.

Suzanna stepped out from behind Joe. "What happened?"

His hazel eyes were full of remorse. "I did something stupid."

"What?"

Luke looked to Joe, and once again Suzanna was reminded of a son seeking approval from his father. She was stunned by the intensity of Luke's expression. "I . . . something personal happened between us."

Joe's face went blank. *"What?"*

"I can't go into it."

"We talked about this. Suzanna told you how Kelsey felt about you. You promised to stay away from her."

"I did stay away from her. This was the before that conversation—the night I stayed over. She remembered it and. . . ." He reddened. "Look, it's too private to go into." Stepping closer to Suzanna, he swallowed hard. "We've got to go over there. I've never seen her so upset. She's calling herself all sorts of names. I'm afraid she'd going to leave Fairholm, Suzanna."

Turning to Joe, Suzanna said, "We have to tell her."

"No." Again the cold stoniness. "I made this decision once, and nothing's changed." Gone was the tender lover of a few moments ago. In his place was the agent, stiff, formal, and uncompromising.

Suzanna crossed her arms over her chest. "That was before she thought she was some kind a deviant. I know Kelsey. She won't be able to live with herself if she thinks she's done something unethical. She'll quit teaching altogether."

"Oh, God." Luke groaned.

"She'll get over it." Joe's tone was implacable.

"Not Kelsey. She's a perfectionist. An overachiever. She'll berate herself in the worst way. Just being attracted to Luke brought her down. Knowing she did something with him she thinks is unethical will destroy her self-confidence and self-esteem."

"She'll get over it," he repeated.

"No, Joe, she won't. It'll alter her decisions for the rest of her life." Suzanna's voice quavered. "I should have pushed harder for this before. I shouldn't have betrayed her trust and let it get this far."

Still, Joe didn't budge.

Luke stepped forward. "You can have my badge. I'll

leave town right away, and you won't have to worry about how she treats me in school. And I'll never see her again. But you can't allow her to think of herself like this. I won't let you." In a gesture more reminiscent of affection than pique, he grasped Joe's arm. "I can guess what's happened between you and Suzanna. What if she was in Kelsey's place? What would you do?"

Joe stared at Luke, then transferred his gaze to Suzanna. There was deep conflict in his eyes, and Suzanna's heart ached for him.

To help Kelsey, yes, but to help him, too, she said softly, "I know the man you really are, Joe. I know you won't let her suffer. Not a girl who's like my daughter."

Filled with angst, Joe closed his eyes, and the man battled with the agent. *Please, God, don't let the agent win.* Suzanna knew in her heart this was the right thing to do. Joe didn't realize it, but they could trust Kelsey.

What would she do if Joe refused, like the last time? Whose side would she choose?

He opened his eyes. "All right. Let's get dressed. We'll go tell her."

KELSEY drew the paper out of her printer. As her father had taught her, she scanned it for errors. The simply stated words cut like glass slivers into the skin.

Dear Dr. Maloney,

It is with great regret that I must resign from my teaching position at Fairholm High School, effective immediately. Given the events of the recent weeks, I no longer feel capable of performing my duties as a teacher.

Sincerely,
Kelsey L. Cunningham

Picking up a pen, she signed two copies—one for the district and one for Suzanna.

Suzanna, who'd done nothing but be there for Kelsey her

whole life, always with her best interest at heart. Suzanna, who would be so disappointed in her.

It's okay to have those feelings, sweetie. Just so you don't act on them. He's a virile young man . . . you can't control your reactions . . . you can control what you do about them . . . my money's on you.

Yeah, well, Suzanna, you lost your bet. Big-time. "I blew it right out of the water," she said aloud. Sinking back into the desk chair, she scanned the room. It was a mistake. The wall facing her was full of accolades. Hours before, she'd been proud of the Teacher of the Year Award given by the Honor Society, the Social Studies Teacher of Excellence recognition she'd received from the state. There were pictures of her track teams. Her gaze fell on the bookshelf. She stood. Her leg ached, but she limped over, scooped up the scrapbook full of memories, and sat down on the floor.

Methodically she opened it, turned the pages, and came face-to-face with all she'd lost. Her first year of teaching she'd taken pictures of her classes so she'd remember them. She'd saved letters from kids she'd helped, reviews from the administrators she'd worked under, a certificate from the first track meet her team had won.

Tears streamed down her cheeks, and she swiped impatiently at them. She'd broken the implicit promise every teacher makes to her students—to behave ethically, to put their welfare above her own. So much had been lost. So much tainted.

You deserve to feel bad. You let a student touch you intimately.

She went through the entire scrapbook, the emotional self-flagellation well deserved, necessary to drive home what she'd given up by letting herself care for one of her students as a man.

Her mind wandered to him; he'd been stricken by what had happened between them. What psychological damage might she have done to him? Had she scarred him permanently? What did it do to know your teacher wanted to fuck you?

Oh, God.

Needing to talk to Suzanna about this, she crossed to

the desk and reached for the phone. But stopped herself. She couldn't face Suzanna's disappointment right now. She couldn't tell the woman she loved like a mother that she hadn't been honest with herself or with Suzanna. Tomorrow morning, Kelsey would find her and confess what happened. Then she'd clean out her desk at school over vacation, so she'd have no contact with kids ever again. She picked up the resignation and stared at it.

Clutching the paper in shaky hands, she put her head down on the desk.

Eventually, she became aware of a ringing. And pounding. Oh, God, no, please don't let Luke have come back. He'd been muttering something like *No more* or *No further* as he stalked out. She didn't know what he meant, what he was going to do.

He was a kid, for God's sake. Hot-tempered. Volatile. He could do anything.

No, in her heart, she knew Luke wouldn't hurt her intentionally. That was something, at least.

The pounding got louder. She remembered the cops coming here that night Luke had watched her through the window. Shakily she stood and limped to the door. Through the peephole she could see Suzanna and Joe on the porch.

Joe.

Luke's uncle.

Had he told his uncle? No, he wouldn't.

Oh, my God, Luke was upset. He'd torn out of the driveway like a maniac. What if something happened to him? No, no, please. . . .

She whipped open the door. "Suzanna, what's—"

Then she saw him, standing there behind Joe. Oh, God, he *must* have told Joe. And Joe told Suzanna. Kelsey's hand clapped over her mouth. She thought she might be ill. Her vision blurred.

Joe reached out to grasp her arms. "Steady, there. It's all right."

All right? Nothing would ever be all right again. Not when she was the kind of person, the kind of woman, she despised.

They were all inside now, and Luke shut the door. When he turned around, she caught his gaze. He looked sad, but not . . . but something. . . .

Suzanna said, "Come in here, Kel. We need to talk to you."

Well, nothing she didn't deserve. But why wasn't Suzanna angry, or at least disappointed? She looked . . . guilty.

Confused, Kelsey allowed herself to be led to the couch. Suzanna pulled off her coat, Joe shed his, but Luke kept his jacket on. Like Jesse James, ready for a fast getaway.

Kelsey dropped onto the couch. Suzanna sat next to her. Pointing to her hand, Suzanna asked, "What are you holding, sweetie?"

Kelsey looked down. She still held the resignation. Wordlessly she handed it to Suzanna.

Suzanna scanned it, said, "Oh, Kel," and gave it to Joe. He read it. Passed it to Luke.

After glancing at it, Luke said, "Son of a bitch."

Automatically, Kelsey opened her mouth to tell him not to swear. Then shook her head. What was she thinking?

Joe said, "Kelsey, we have to tell you something."

Kelsey shook her head. What could they say to her that she hadn't already said to herself? She began to tremble. Suzanna's arm slid around her. And Kelsey began to cry again.

"Oh, sweetie." Suzanna pulled her into a deep embrace. Kelsey burrowed into her, thinking this might be the last time Suzanna would hold her like this, remembering the other times this woman had given her solace: when her father disapproved of her choices, when he wanted to move to New Haven, when he refused to pay her college tuition, and a thousand other times when she needed an adult to depend on. After more than fifteen years of having Suzanna as a surrogate mother, she was going to lose her. The knowledge made Kelsey cry harder.

A hand smoothed her hair. "Shh, Kelsey, stop crying," Suzanna crooned. "You need to know some things."

Finally she drew back. Joe had come closer and was holding out a handkerchief to her. As she took it and mopped her face, she saw Luke had turned away, staring out the window with his hands jammed in his jeans back pockets. It was as if he couldn't stand looking at her.

"Sorry. Say what you have to say. You deserve to."

Seeming upset, Joe shook his head. "Kelsey, Luke isn't eighteen."

Oh my God, he was under eighteen? Could she get arrested for. . . . "He . . . he said he was nineteen."

"No, he's not. He's twenty-six."

"Twenty-six? You can't be a high school student when you're twenty-six."

"He's not a high school student."

Puzzled, Kelsey glanced at Suzanna.

"He's not Joe's nephew." Suzanna's voice was raw.

Kelsey sat up straighter. "I . . . I don't understand."

"That's because we've kept things from you." She could tell Suzanna was trying to be all business. "Luke and Joe are Secret Service Agents assigned to Fairholm High School to prevent some potential violence they think might be brewing."

She must be dreaming. This sounded like a late-night TV show. "I don't understand," she repeated.

Joe squatted down before her. "Your school's been targeted as at risk for eruptions of violence. Luke and I are part of a team that comes to secondary schools to stop that from happening."

"You're not a psychologist?"

"No, I *am* a psychologist. I just work for the government."

Her heartbeat speeded up. She glanced at Luke, who'd circled back around and was facing her now. His posture was erect, his arms crossed his chest, and his face was blank. Suddenly things fell into place . . . his intelligence . . . his mature attitude . . . his befriending Ben, Smurf, Max . . . all the troubled kids.

Ludicrously she said, "No wonder he knew so much about the Secret Service."

Joe smiled. So did Suzanna. Luke did not.

Still stunned, she looked to the woman she loved more

than anyone in the world. "How did they do this without your knowing?"

Suzanna shot Joe a surprised look. A worried look. Then she focused back in on Kelsey. "I knew about it, sweetie."

"You knew?" Kelsey tried to wade through the muddle of her mind. "No, no, you couldn't have known. At least not all this time. Not when I told you last week. . . ." She broke off.

"Yes, I knew then."

"You knew *then*?"

"Yes."

"No, Suzanna, you misunderstand. You couldn't have known when I told you . . . you know . . . about Luke."

Misery claimed Suzanna's delicate features. "I did know then, Kel."

Kelsey swallowed back the emotion in her throat, the significance of Suzanna's statement crowding out the surprise. "And you didn't tell me? Suzanna, I confessed my deepest secret, my worst fault. And you didn't tell me that Luke . . . ?"

"It was unconscionable, I know, given how you feel about trust. I'm sorry."

"No. You can't take the blame." This from Joe, who stood abruptly. "I wouldn't let her tell you, Kelsey. She begged me to bring you in on this, especially after we realized what was happening with you and Luke. I refused, more than once."

Kelsey's head snapped up at Joe's comment. "She *told* you about me, about my . . . feelings?"

"Yes, and I still wouldn't allow her to tell you what was going on."

A horrible thought came to Kelsey. Her gaze whipped back to Suzanna. "Tell me, Suzanna. Please tell me you didn't let Luke know how I felt."

"Yes, Kel, I did. I'm sorry."

"Sorry? You're sorry?" It was too much to take in. She drew away from Suzanna, stood, and crossed the room to the fireplace, far away from all of them. Sightlessly, she stared into the ashes, trying to make sense of what she'd been told, of what Suzanna had done to her.

"Kelsey, you're limping again," Suzanna said. "You should be off that leg." It was a mother's comment.

For a long moment, Kelsey didn't speak, trying to internalize what she'd been told. When the implications set in, it was like frostbite warming up. Now that she could feel again, the pain was bone-deep. She turned. "Let me get this straight. You two have been infiltrating our school since February, tricking me, the staff, our students, everybody, for what, three months?"

Joe moved in front of the others, every inch the leader. "Yes."

Again she looked to Suzanna. "And you allowed this?"

"She had no choice," Joe answered for her. "Neither did Luke."

Oh, God. For the first time, her gaze snapped to Luke. His posture was stiff; his lips, thinned. And he was staring at her. "Did you get a kick out of that, Agent Ludzecky? Did your male ego get stroked when she told you a teacher was attracted to you?"

"It wasn't like that, Kelsey." Luke spoke for the first time, his voice hoarse. "You know it wasn't."

"I know *nothing*," she said. She faced Suzanna. "Especially about you. I thought I could trust you."

Suzanna's eyes widened. "I know what a disappointment that is to you, sweetie. Maybe if we could talk about it—" She took a step closer.

"Don't come *near* me."

Halting midstep, Suzanna paled.

"Do you remember when I was eighteen and my father took the job at Yale without telling me?"

"Yes."

"Do you remember what you promised me that night when I said I'd never be able to trust an adult again?"

"Yes. I said I'd never lie to you, no matter what."

Kelsey shook her head. "You lied."

"No, *I* lied." Joe was agitated, something Kelsey had never seen before. "Haven't you been listening? I *forbade* her to reveal this operation to anyone."

"Nobody else knows about this?"

"The superintendent knows," Joe said hurriedly.

Suzanna opened her mouth to say something, and Joe cut her off. "Kelsey, people get hurt in undercover situations. It can't be helped."

Luke blew out a breath and jammed his hands in his jacket pockets. "He doesn't mean that the way it sounded, Kel. This isn't coming out right."

She whirled on him. "Why? Didn't you have time to plan what spin you'd put on it?"

Luke stepped toward her.

She backed up. "Don't you *dare* come near me."

He stopped, too.

The three of them exchanged glances. *Surprised* glances. *Oh, for Christ's sake.* "What? Did you all think I was going to be happy about this?"

Joe said, "Maybe if you saw the reports. You have to let us explain our rationale here. . . ."

She raised her chin. "No, Agent Stonehouse, I don't have to do that." She walked to the table and picked up her resignation, which Suzanna had dropped there, and thrust it out. "Here, Mrs. Quinn. Take this. I'm officially resigning from your high school. As of now, I don't *have* to do anything for you. For any of you." She turned her back on the hurt in Suzanna's eyes. "Now, get out of my house. And take your spies with you."

LUKE had seen Suzanna face down tough punks and take on Joe better than the Secretary of State had been able to do. But now, she was close to tears. Her pretty complexion was mottled, and she was holding her stomach as if trying to contain the emotion swirling there. Despite all her warnings about Kelsey's need for trust, neither he nor Joe had really understood what the ramifications of their secret would be. Luke tried to imagine how he'd feel if his *Matka* had betrayed him the way Kelsey thought Suzanna had betrayed her. He couldn't fathom it.

"Let's go." Joe's voice was gruff. "Kelsey can use some time to digest this."

Biting her lip, Suzanna looked torn. Kelsey had faced away from her, from all of them.

"All right." Straightening, Suzanna crossed to her. "Sweetie, I'm sorry. Please think this through."

Kelsey didn't answer. Luke would have given up state secrets to know where her head was.

Because of that, he said, "I'm not leaving just yet. Kelsey and I have some things to say to each other."

"I think you should come with us, Luke." This from Suzanna.

"No, let him stay." Joe straightened. "Come on, Suzanna." He grabbed their coats and escorted her out of the room.

In moments, the front door snapped shut.

As soon as it did, Kelsey whirled on him. Temper sizzled in her eyes. "So, what does the hotshot secret agent have to say to me in private?"

"Just one thing."

"Shoot. Or is that too much of a pun among you guys?"

"Getting shot is nothing to joke about." He rubbed his shoulder.

Her face paled. "You've been shot?"

"Yes."

She didn't say anything.

"My one point is, how much is a kid's life worth, Kelsey?"

"A kid's life?"

"Uh-huh." He jammed his hands into his jacket pockets. "That's why we're here. To save lives. Your students' lives."

"Pretty melodramatic, isn't it?"

"The parents at Columbine wouldn't think so."

Again her face went ashen.

He was sorry to slap her down so brutally when she was already raw, but she had to know why he'd deceived her. "Isn't that worth a few hurt feelings?"

"Hurt feelings? *Hurt feelings?*" When she began to pace, her knee buckled. "Shit."

He started toward her.

"Don't come near me!"

"All right. Sit down."

"Son of a bitch!" She limped to the couch. Reclining on the cushions, much like that night he slept here, she stared up at him with a lethal glare. "I've got more than hurt feelings, Agent Ludzecky. For weeks, I've questioned my integrity. The kind of person I am. I felt like a pervert having . . . caring . . . wanting. . . ." She didn't finish.

"The operative word here is *felt*, isn't it? You didn't do anything."

"Damn it, I won't let you twist this around to suit your purposes."

He went on as if she hadn't spoken. "And you didn't even have feelings for a *kid*. You had feelings, *sexual* feelings," he couldn't help adding, "for a hot, twenty-six-year-old man."

"A modest one, too," she shot back.

"Look, it was hurtful to trick you. To trick all the teachers and kids at Fairholm. Suzanna has had a hell of a time with this."

"I don't want to talk about Suzanna." Her voice had lost its heated tone and gone deadly cold.

"She's hurting."

"I don't want to talk about her." Kelsey's voice rose a notch. "I won't."

"All right, then listen to this. The government is trying to stem the wave of school shootings. Maybe if you knew more about our operation. . . ."

"I don't want to know more. I just want to be out of this situation. Away from you."

"Why? We can be together now."

"Not in your wildest fantasies."

He arched a brow. "Hmm. They *have* been wild."

"Don't flirt with me, you bastard." She thought for a minute. Steam came to her eyes again. "Damn you, I believed all that shit about your mother, your father . . . your troubled soul."

"Actually, most of that was true. I do miss my mother. And my sisters. It's hard not seeing them."

"Yeah, well, if it's true what you said about your father, I can understand now why you disappointed him."

Zing, zing, right through his heart. He didn't have to fake the pain. "That was cruel. Purposely cruel." He swallowed hard. "Especially since it's true." He crossed his arms over his chest. "You know, I never did one thing to intentionally hurt you the way you just hurt me. Not one thing that wasn't necessary for the operation."

"No? How about playing the lecherous teenager and insulting me? You did that intentionally, didn't you?"

"I did that to push you away." He began to pace. God, he hated explaining himself. "I knew how you felt, that you were having feelings for me. Sexual feelings."

"Jesus Christ." She stood again, and despite her limp, crossed to the other side of the room. "Suzanna told you everything I confided in her. I'm so embarrassed."

"I felt . . . feel . . . the same way about you, honey."

"Don't call me that." She turned around. "And don't think for a minute I'm going to be your playmate while you're here impersonating James Bond, and then have you move on when you're done. What? Do you find a young teacher to seduce in every district you infiltrate?"

"No," he said quietly. "It's never happened to me before."

"I don't believe that."

"I'm sorry that you don't."

She said, "All right, I've listened. I've heard your explanations, paltry though they are. Now get out of my house."

"God, you're stubborn."

"Why, because I'm not falling at your feet?"

Well, yes. Usually women were all over him when they found out he was an agent.

She knew what he was thinking. "An ego to match your gall, I see. Let me tell you something, Ludzecky. I happen to prefer mature men who are honest and forthright."

"Oh, like Mike I-Wanna-Blow-Your-House-Down Wolfe?"

"At least Mike's honest about what he wants from me."

That did it. Luke stalked to her. Grabbed her arms like the man he was. "And you've been giving it to him?"

He saw it in her eyes. The primal response to his proximity. To his jealousy. So he took advantage of it. Yanking her close, he crushed her against his chest. Not gently, his arms banded around her. Before she could protest, his mouth took hers. Devoured it. She tasted the way he knew she would— hot, sweet, and as tempting as Eve. His tongue mastered hers as he explored her.

And she allowed it. Participated. Encouraged.

The kiss was merciless and went on for a long time.

Finally he drew back. "Now you have to deal with me as a man. Think about that." Turning, he strode to the door, dragged it open, and slammed it as he left.

TWENTY-TWO

SUZANNA barely made it home before she collapsed into a storm of weeping. As Joe held her, he cursed himself, the Secret Service, and teenagers in general for forcing adults to deceive each other in order to protect them.

"Shh," he whispered against her hair, holding on to her tightly. "It'll be all right." He'd seen Suzanna cry so few times, her breakdown unnerved him. "It's my fault."

She shook her head, her face against his chest. She burrowed into the sweater he'd thrown on with jeans.

"Yes, it is. I should have listened to you and Luke last week, told Kelsey then."

Struggling for composure, she drew back. Her lashes were spiky, her eyes filled with remorse. "It's nobody's fault. Especially not yours. You did what you thought was best."

"No. I miscalculated." It was time for some honesty, no matter how painful. "I knew about her relationship with her father. How she trusted *you*. I should have listened to you." Though he hadn't understood, really, because he never had a mother, or any adult in his life, he could trust the way Kelsey trusted Suzanna. Still it didn't excuse the damage he'd done. He'd destroyed something beautiful, and more fragile than he could ever have imagined.

"You're not responsible, Joe."

When she started to cry again, he pulled her back in his arms. Seeing her overwrought was his punishment, he guessed, for being so pigheaded. And now, three people he'd come to care about had been hurt by his decisions.

Eventually, Suzanna calmed. He held her until he realized she'd fallen asleep. Gently, he eased away and stretched her out on the couch. Covering her with a lap blanket, then kissing her forehead, he left the den and had just pulled out his cell phone when the doorbell rang. Outside he found Luke.

A sharp pang shot through Joe at the sight of the young man's face. It was then that Joe realized Luke felt about Kelsey the way Joe felt about Suzanna. He also became aware that he'd come to care about the kid, too. How had years of avoiding relationships been overturned in such a short time?

Luke said hoarsely, "I didn't know where else to go."

"Come on in." When he closed the door, Joe went over to Luke and put his arm around his slumped shoulders. "Suzanna's asleep in the den. Come in here."

Silently Luke accompanied Joe into the living room. Sinking down onto the couch, the young agent bowed his head and linked his hands between spread knees. Joe sat across from him.

"My father was right." Luke's voice was flat. "I fuck everything up."

The friend, the part of Joe that would have been a good dad, surfaced. "If your father said that, he was a fool."

Luke's head snapped up. "I thought you'd agree."

"Why? Because you came to care about Kelsey?" He glanced in the direction of the den. "I'd have to be a major hypocrite to get on you about that, wouldn't I?"

Luke gave a self-effacing smile. "I guess." His eyes narrowed. "You serious about Suzanna? 'Cause I think she's a lot more fragile than she lets on."

Always playing Sir Galahad. "Yeah, she is. I'm serious, Luke. But this won't be going further. With me and Suzanna. Or you and Kelsey. STAT has to continue, and we've compromised it already." The thought of leaving here and never seeing Suzanna again gutted him. Still, he said, "It's non-negotiable."

Leaning back against the couch, Luke seemed to accept that. "I can't believe how upset Kelsey was. First at me. Then Suzanna. Her world's been shifted."

"Tell me what she said."

As he listened to Luke's stark recitation, an idea came to him. Maybe, just maybe, he could help the kid and Suzanna. After Luke was finished, Joe stood. "I want to talk to Kelsey."

"I don't think that's such a hot idea."

"It is." He jammed a hand through his hair. "I was the one who insisted on the silence. I should take the blame. But I have a plan, too." He headed for the foyer.

Luke followed him. "Joe, are you sure?"

Shrugging into his jacket, he said, "Yes. Stay with Suzanna. And call headquarters. See if they've got anything new, especially on Smurf's instant message. They're having a hell of a time finding out what PBB stands for. They've got to crack it soon."

At the desperate look on Luke's face, Joe reached out again and squeezed the younger man's arm. "I won't make it worse, I promise."

"It couldn't be worse," Luke said bleakly.

Unfortunately, Joe saw what Luke meant when Kelsey opened her front door ten minutes later. Her face was ravaged, and for the first time since he'd known the young woman, she did not look good. He was astounded by all the lives he'd affected by one simple decision.

"I don't want to talk to you." She gripped the doorknob as if it were holding her upright.

"I'm a member of a law enforcement agency. I can have you hauled to the police station for questioning, if you'd rather."

Her jaw gaped. "Are you always such a bastard?"

"When lives are at stake, I am."

She paled even more.

"I don't relish upsetting you further, Kelsey, but if you could see what Luke and Suzanna are going through, you'd—"

"I won't discuss Suzanna."

Hmm. Just Suzanna. Though he was in over his head here,

he'd be damned if he wouldn't give fixing her relationship with Suzanna his best shot. Barging his way inside, Joe shed his coat. Kelsey took it, hung it on the coat tree, and limped before him into the living room. They sat at opposite ends of the couch.

He met her gaze squarely. "All of the secrecy is my fault. I'm in charge of this operation. I insisted Suzanna keep it from you. I threatened Luke with loss of his job if he let you in on the undercover. Even last week, when you told Suzanna how you felt about Luke, I bullied them into silence."

She bit her lip. "I feel so violated."

He knew the meaning of that word. And the scars that could result from violation. "I'm sure you do. But do you realize what's at stake?"

"Lives, you said. It seems convenient to fall back on that."

"It isn't. You're upset and not thinking clearly, or you'd see the danger schools are in these days."

"I see the danger," she said, fire lighting her eyes.

"Do you understand how at risk your school is?"

She rubbed her leg. "Because of kids like Webster?"

"Not just them. Let me tell you all of it. Then, if you still can't understand that we needed secrecy, I'll leave and not bother you again."

Her inner integrity surfaced. He was counting on that. "All right."

It took an hour to fill her in . . . Zach's suicide, the hit list, the risk factors, Ben Franzi and his depression, the bullying Smurf suffered, Max and guns, Rush's angry outbursts.

She got paler, but paradoxically, she seemed stronger as he cataloged the reasons the Secret Service had targeted Fairholm.

"Given her beliefs, you can imagine how Suzanna felt, having this forced on her."

"I can't talk about Suzanna now." Kelsey held his gaze. "But I understand why you're here. It . . . frightens me."

"It should."

"How did you get involved in all this?"

The slow twist in his gut came, as usual, when he thought

about Josie. He knew if he told Kelsey about his niece, she'd be more sympathetic, more willing to forgive the other two. Could he do that for Suzanna? for Luke?

"My niece was killed in a school shooting three years ago."

Her big brown eyes clouded. "Oh, Joe, I'm so sorry."

"Don't be sorry, Kelsey. Help us to stop this senseless violence. You're in an ideal position to assist us."

"Assist you? How?"

"You have all these at-risk kids in class. We can work with you now to throw them together with Luke. And you can ferret out information on your own."

She glanced at the table where Suzanna had dropped her resignation. "I'm quitting."

"I'm asking you not to."

"Surely you can't think I'd . . . that I could have Luke in my classes . . . that I. . . ."

The doorbell rang. She rolled her eyes.

"Are you expecting someone?"

"I'm *expecting* the sky to fall next."

He grinned. She returned it weakly. Then they heard pounding on the door. Joe tensed. "Let me see who it is."

Hurrying out to the foyer, he was surprised to find Luke and Suzanna on the other side of the door. He'd told Luke to stay put, to watch her. She'd been sleeping.

He yanked open the door. "What happened?"

Luke stormed in, and Joe pulled a shaky Suzanna inside after him. Closing the door, sliding his arm around Suzanna, Joe said, "Tell me."

Gone was the battered young man Joe had left earlier. Now, Luke was every inch the agent. "I talked to Mack." Mack the Hack was the web site expert who'd been tracing online information for them. "PBB stands for Pipe Bomb Builders. He finally got into the Colosseum. It doesn't look good, Joe."

KELSEY'S head was spinning and her knee hurt. It didn't help that she felt like she'd been thrust into the middle of an Ian Fleming novel. Her eyes were glued to Luke, and she was shocked to see the changes in him. Even his body language was different. It brought home how much he'd deceived her. But something important was going on here, and she kept quiet.

"Let's go into the living room." Joe glanced past Luke's shoulder. "All of us."

Luke whipped around. His gaze focused on her. She held it, still amazed at the transformation. "Are you all right?" he asked tenderly.

"I'm fine."

In charge, Joe shepherded them into the living room. They sat. He turned to Kelsey. "You can stay for this if you're willing to help us."

"Help us?" Luke's parroting made Kelsey smirk. "I thought you were quitting."

She raised her chin. "Joe had some convincing arguments. I might stay the rest of the year. Maybe work with you."

"Think fast, Kelsey," Joe prodded. "We have to move on this."

Suzanna said nothing. Just stared at her.

"I'll help," Kelsey finally said.

"Good girl." Joe's voice was firm, fatherly. She felt good about pleasing him.

"I mentioned Smurf is one of the kids we're afraid could be on a pathway to violence. Luke was playing on his computer last week and Smurf got an instant message. Seems he's part of a group called PBBs. The home office had a hell of a time tracing it." He faced Luke. "What kind of group is it?"

"A support group for building bombs. They give instructions on how to make all kinds of explosives, sites to order material, even offer phone assistance."

"A regular Weapons R Us network." Joe's tone was disgusted. "Well, this changes things. It's an imminent risk factor."

"What will we do?" Luke asked.

"Not *we*, kid. You. You've got to get to Smurf. See how serious he is about building bombs."

"That shouldn't be too hard." Suzanna spoke for the first time. "Smurf's got a bad case of hero worship."

"He could do worse." Joe looked at Luke. Something passed between the two men. Out of the corner of her eye, Kelsey saw Suzanna smile at it. Kelsey felt out of the loop.

Joe finished, "You should get in touch with him right away."

"I can't. His parents took him to Hilton Head for spring break. He's gone until Sunday night."

Kelsey remembered something. "Smurf wasn't doing well the day school got out. Some of Webster's buddies stuffed him in a gym locker. I found him crying just outside the boys' locker room."

"Damn it. That's the last thing he needs." Joe faced her. "See, Kelsey, no one else on our team knew about that bullying—which, incidentally, was the cause of the only school shooting perpetrated by a girl." He smiled at her. "You're going to be a big help to us."

BEFORE Kelsey could comment, two cell phones rang. One was Luke's; the other, Suzanna's. Luke shot off the chair and strode to the foyer. Suzanna knew he wouldn't want any kid who might be calling him to hear them all in the background.

"Answer yours." Joe's voice was grave.

She flicked it open. "Suzanna Quinn."

"This is Lieutenant Latham at the police station. We have a line on Raymond Webster. Kids apparently call him Rush."

"Webster's in town?" She could hear her own voice quaver.

Joe tensed.

"Yes. Two patrol officers spotted him near Pickles, then followed him to Max Duchamp's house."

"Did you arrest him?" They'd filed formal charges.

"No, he dodged us. Long story how. The Duchamp boy won't talk. I thought you and that young teacher should be warned."

"Well, thanks for the heads up."

She ended the conversation just as Luke returned. He waited for her to go first.

"Webster's back in town. They didn't get him. He's loose." She turned to Kelsey. "You're in danger, sweetie."

Luke ran a hand through his hair. "Jesus Christ! What next?"

"You're in danger, too, Suzanna," Joe said. He faced Luke. "Was your call important?"

Luke sighed. "It was from Ben Franzi. He was really jonesing, like he was on something. This week is the anniversary of his father's death. I'm afraid he's coping with drugs."

Suzanna saw Kelsey's gaze fly back and forth between the two men. She wasn't used to this intrigue. Hell, it still amazed Suzanna that she was living through it.

Once again, Joe assumed control. "All right, we have to do a couple of things. First, Luke, you go see Ben."

"I'm meetin' him at Pickles in fifteen."

"Then get over to Duchamp's. See what you can find out about Webster's plans."

"I'll call him on the way to Pickles. Set something up."

Kelsey frowned. "Isn't that dangerous, going to Max's? What if Webster's still around? He hates you."

"Worried about me, babe?" Luke asked hopefully.

With fear crowding her heart, she couldn't think of a retort.

Suzanna said, "Kelsey shouldn't be left alone here with Webster back in town."

"She won't be." Joe faced her. "Kelsey, go pack some things. You're staying at Suzanna's."

"I—"

"Don't protest. It's a fait accompli. You need protection."

"Suzanna's going to protect me?"

"No, Luke and I are. We're all moving in together."

LINES of grief etched themselves out in every pore of Ben Franzi's face. In a dim corner of Pickles, at eight o'clock at night—near where the hit list had been found, Luke thought ironically—Ben toyed with a french fry and stared off into space. He was on a downer now, instead of seeming high, as he had on the phone. His hair was in tiny little braids—and dyed an inky black. His clothes were like the night.

"Hey, Benjy boy, talk to me." Luke lounged in the booth, scrambling for an answer for Ben, though he knew there weren't any. Still, he had to help the kid somehow.

For a half-hour, they'd been shootin' the shit. Ben had mumbled one-syllable responses to all of Luke's overtures. His eyes were glassy.

Finally, Ben said, "I'm losing it."

"Losin' it?"

"Yeah, like I can't control my feelings. What I do."

Luke's agent instincts kicked in. He forced himself not to stiffen. "You aren't thinkin' about doin' anything, are ya?"

Ben nibbled on a french fry. "Like?"

"Like Zach Riley?"

Hopeless eyes stared back at him.

"Jesus, Ben."

"There were pills. I took a few." His expression got even more desolate. "I wanted to take them all."

"Hey, man, that is *so* not okay."

He shifted his gaze. "Who cares?"

"Morgan. Your mamma, and your sister."

Wearily Ben leaned against the vinyl and closed his eyes. "Yeah, but they're not enough since. . . ."

"Since your daddy died?"

Eyes still shut, Ben nodded.

"I know how it is, buddy."

His head still back against the booth, Ben opened his eyes and spoke haltingly. "I can't stand this stuff inside of me. Sometimes I feel like it's gonna explode right out of me. I don't want it to take anybody else down."

Shit. Luke was in way over his head. "You need to talk to somebody, man."

"I'm talking to you."

"I don't know what to do with this stuff. You need somebody trained."

Ben's eyes narrowed. "Like?"

"My uncle."

"Hey, man, I told you if you shared this with him, I'd. . . ."

Kill me.

"I haven't shared nothin'. But you should. He's a dick-head as an uncle, but the kids at school say he's a good counselor." No response. "You were in one of his groups, weren't you?"

"Yeah. But he hasn't done anything for you."

"Well, I'm a lost cause." He smiled weakly. "It's like, you know, doctors can't treat their families." Luke had to push. *Please God, let me find a way to get help for Ben.* "What you got to lose?"

"Nothing," Ben finally whispered.

Ben's tortured acquiescence broke Luke's heart. Quickly he pulled out his cell phone and punched in Joe's number.

Joe answered after the first ring. "Stonehouse."

"Uncle Joe. This is your long-lost nephew. My buddy Ben would like to talk to you."

"He's not all right, is he?" Joe's voice was concerned.

"Give the man a cigar," Luke said in his best teenage voice. "We're at Pickles. Can you come down?"

"I don't want to leave the women alone. Is it that urgent?"

"Clock's tickin'." It was their code for urgency, and taking pills—thinking about taking more—was definitely urgent.

Joe thought for a minute. "Skip going to Max's. Hustle back over to Kelsey's after I get to Pickles."

"You betcha."

"I'll leave now."

"Thanks, Unc."

Luke made small talk with Ben, mostly about music, until Joe burst through the door ten minutes later. "The cavalry to the rescue," Luke joked.

Ben gave him a weak smile. "I'm embarrassed."

Luke squeezed Ben's arm. "You should talk to him alone. You don't wanna spill your guts in front of me. I might cry."

"Fuck you." But it was said with affection.

Joe crossed to their table. "Hi, guys."

Ben looked down at his soda. Luke slid out of the booth. "I'm goin'. I hear enough of your advice, Unc."

As Luke stood up, Joe sat down. "Get out of here, boy. Go do your homework."

Luke mumbled good-bye to Ben and headed out the back door of Pickles. He needed to hurry to Kelsey's. It was already getting dark, and if Webster was in town, the punk could do anything. Reaching his battered truck, worrying about the bleakness in Ben's eyes, Luke fished for his keys in his pocket.

An arm went around his neck and pressed against his windpipe. Luke bucked; other arms grabbed his, and yanked them behind his back. A hand slapped across his mouth. Somebody said, "Gotcha, city boy."

Somebody else laughed.

Luke tried to throw them off. The arm at his neck tightened and cut off more of his air. His face was smashed into the glass, sending sparks of pain through his skull. Somebody yanked his head back by the hair, and in that instant, he caught a glimpse of Rush Webster's sneering face in the window. Then his head was whacked again on the glass, which cracked. Something steel, with force behind it, hit him in the ribs—twice, three times. As he slid to the ground, another blow landed on his head.

The world went black.

SUZANNA stared at the clock. Something was wrong. Joe had been gone two hours, and Luke had not returned to Kelsey's. She shivered, despite the fleece sweatsuit she wore. It was aquamarine, and Joe liked the color on her. *Stop thinking about that. Think about safety.*

When Joe left, she'd gone around Kelsey's house and locked the doors, checked the windows, drawn the blinds; but she was still edgy. Joe had said he'd call his police contact on his way to Pickles to have a black-and-white cruise by; she'd seen the headlights intermittently. It made her feel better. Still, she wished Joe or Luke was here.

At Kelsey's stove, where Suzanna had stood a hundred times, she fixed hot chocolate. Kelsey had gone to her room to pack. Was the girl worried, too? She'd said almost nothing to Suzanna since the revelation this afternoon.

Suzanna tried again to reach out to her when Kelsey entered the kitchen, carrying a duffel bag. . . .

"Can we talk, sweetie?"

Kelsey had looked at her, at least, for the first time. "It's too much to take in. I don't want to discuss it now."

"I've always been able to help you sort things out."

Swallowing hard, Kelsey pushed back her hair. She'd changed into a sweatsuit, too—baby pink, making her look young and innocent. "I don't want to hurt you, Suzanna, and I understand how this went down, but I can't trust you with my feelings."

"Ever, or just now?"

She shrugged. "I don't know. I forgot something in my room." And she left. . . .

Finished at the stove, Suzanna poured the hot chocolate into a mug, brought it to the table, and sat down. Everything was wrong—except for the most elemental thing. She remembered the intensity of Joe's lovemaking, and had to smile. Sipping the cocoa, she was back in that bed with him . . . when she heard it. A thump against the house. Startled, she sloshed hot liquid over her hand. She heard it again, then again.

Webster's in town. I thought you and that young teacher should be warned.

Suzanna drew in a breath. Kelsey's kitchen faced the backyard; one wall had big sliding doors without blinds so she could enjoy the trees with no obstruction. Rising slowly, Suzanna crossed the room and flicked off the lights. The kitchen plunged into darkness. She was concealed now, but she could see out. Was it Webster? Would he break the glass? Was he alone, or was Max or somebody from the city with him?

She was heading for the phone in the dinette area when she heard, "Suzanna, why are the lights—"

"Somebody's out there," Suzanna whispered.

Kelsey stilled.

Nothing, then, "What can I do?"

"Call 911 and stay back. I'm going to turn the outside light on. Maybe it will scare him away."

She thought about going for a knife, but she'd just read somewhere that knives were the worst self-defense for women because the wielder needed strength. Women victims usually ended up having the knives used on them, instead. So Suzanna grabbed hold of a big cast-iron frying pan Kelsey had left in the sink.

As she heard Kelsey make the call, she crept down the counter. Crouching when she got to the end, she managed to reach up and turn on the outside light. She heard another thump. This time closer, against the door.

"Oh, my God," she said as she saw Luke slump against the glass and slide to the ground.

SOMEBODY was sticking a hot poker in his back, and his head was on fire. Luke surfaced from unconsciousness, only to feel acute pain jetting through him.

"Son of a bitch." His words were muffled in the pillow, where his face was buried.

"Thank God he's awake." Luke recognized Joe's voice. When he tried to raise up, the world spun around him, and he gagged.

Burying his head in the pillows, he tried to stem the nausea. Darkness and immobility helped. He felt a hand on his bare shoulder, soothing him.

"Luke, are you going to be sick?"

Opening one eye, he shook his head, then closed it again when the movement plunged him into a miasma of agony. "Oh, God."

Joe's fingers squeezed him, didn't let go. It felt good. Fatherly. "You'll feel better soon. The paramedics gave you a shot."

"'Medics?"

"The ambulance was here."

It came back to him. The alley behind Pickles. He'd been jumped. Hit with something in the back, over the head.

Gotcha, city boy.

He opened an eye again. Joe had pulled a chair to the side of the bed; his face was white with strain. A muscle throbbed in his jaw.

"Webster . . . jumped me." It hurt to say the words, and he moaned with the effort. "Saw his face . . . in the window . . . from behind," he got out.

"Joe, you shouldn't be questioning him now." Suzanna's voice came from across the room.

"It's 'kay." He gripped the pillow. "At Pickles."

"You were at *Pickles* when this happened?"

He heard a gasp. A feminine gasp. Then caught the scent of the sheets. Familiar. Nice and familiar. "Where am I?"

Joe said dryly, "In Kelsey's bed."

Despite the pain clawing its way through his whole system, Luke grinned. "Wanted to get here. Not like this." He heard a female groan. "Kel? Come 'ere."

Movement. Joe stood, Kelsey took his chair. Luke raised his hand off the mattress. She clasped it in hers. Her fingers were ice-cold. Even from this angle, with his vision growing fuzzy, he could see she was pale. She bit her lip and watched him.

"I'm okay." He tried to squeeze her hand, but had no strength.

Her grip tightened. "You're in pain."

Joe stood behind her. "Luke, you need to sleep."

Shaking his head again, he tried to talk, but couldn't remember the words.

"Sleep, Luke."

He looked at Kelsey. Her face blurred. "Stay with me."

Holding his hand, she said, "I won't leave."

When he awoke, he felt a little better. His back was only a dull throb, painful but tolerable. "Kel?"

"I'm here." She came to the bed and sat down in the chair. Took his hand automatically this time.

He nosed the pillow. "It smells like you."

"Is he awake?" Joe's voice.

"Yeah," Kelsey called out over her shoulder, "just now."

He heard Joe come to the bed. "Joe, help me turn over," Luke said.

Kelsey stood and let go of his hand.

Joe took her place on the chair. "Not right now, cowboy. The paramedics said you should stay on your stomach for a few hours. You've got a couple of bruised ribs. They're painful but the medics said hospitalization was optional."

"I feel better."

"Modern drugs at their best." Joe scowled. "Can you tell me what happened?"

"Two guys. I saw Webster. Somebody punched me with a chain wrapped around his fist."

"Oh, my God" was Kelsey's stifled outcry.

He let himself sink into the pillows. Talked with his eyes closed. "I was on my way over here, and they jumped me."

"At Pickles?" He could picture Joe shaking his head. "How the hell did you get here?"

"They took off. I came to, crawled in the car, and drove over."

"Jesus Christ. Why didn't you call me for help?"

"Ben needed you . . . those pills."

Joe swore under his breath.

"I'm tough, Unc. How's Ben doin'?"

"Okay. We talked for a few hours, then I followed him home. I spent a while with him and his mother, discussing his depression. She confiscated the pills in their house."

Luke said, "Good. I'm glad she knows."

"He's okay for now. We're going to meet again in a day or two at school. I made him promise he'd call my cell phone if he felt despondent in the meantime."

"You do good work."

Joe's tone softened. "How'd you drive over here, kid?"

"I have no idea. I puked first, then again when I got here."

Joe didn't say anything. Suzanna came up behind him and placed her hands on Joe's shoulders. "What were you doing in the back of the house?"

"The cops kept cruisin' by. I didn't want to get picked up for bein' at Kelsey's again. Especially in the shape I was in. They already think I'm Danny Delinquent."

Suzanna shook her head.

"Sorry if I scared you."

"Oh, Luke, that doesn't matter. I just want you to be well."

"I'm tired," he said, suddenly weary.

"I'll bet." Joe sounded tired, too. "Go back to sleep. When you wake up, we'll assess the damage and see if you can be moved to Suzanna's. It's more secure there."

"I can go now." But his heart wasn't in the protest.

"Sleep, hero. We'll let you rest."

"I want Kelsey to stay." Again his words were slurred.

Joe mumbled something.

"I'll stay." Kelsey's voice was thready. Or was it the drugs?

Luke closed his eyes. He heard Suzanna and Joe leave. Kelsey sat down on the chair. He lay still. In a minute, he felt a hand on his hair, stroking it.

"Mmm. Feels good."

She stilled. "I thought you were asleep."

The drugs made his tongue loose. "Why don't you climb in here with me?"

"Not on your life."

"Now, don't go sayin' words you'll have to eat, darlin'." He moved, and pain rocketed through him, making him moan again.

Leaning close, she whispered, "Please, Luke, let's not get into this now. Go back to sleep."

"Promise me you won't leave."

"I promise."

He lifted his hand again. After a moment, she took it.

Comforted, he went to sleep.

TWENTY-THREE

———

THREE days later, Kelsey strode into Suzanna's kitchen in a huff. They'd managed to get Luke moved, and were all residing at her house temporarily. "He's driving me crazy."

"He's been *trying* to drive you crazy."

"Sick men are such wimps."

Sipping her coffee, Suzanna said, "I don't have to go in to work. I can help."

"No, you're meeting with Max and his father today." Kelsey rolled her eyes. "Anyway, he won't let anybody else help. 'Kel, get me some water . . . rub my shoulders . . . I think I need another blanket. . . .'"

"He's not that sick."

Kelsey's face paled. She tugged at the yellow sweater she'd donned with jeans. "His ribs are bruised. And that goose egg on his head . . . the other black-and-blue marks." She shivered. "He got hurt, Suzanna."

"I know, sweetie." Suzanna nodded to the tray. Scents of bacon and eggs filled the kitchen. "His food is ready. Joe and I should be back by noon."

Joe and I. Kelsey was very aware of the sleeping arrangements for the last three nights, though no one mentioned them. She and Luke slept in the guest wing, in separate rooms connected by a bathroom. Joe slept in the family wing. Not in Josh's room, Kelsey was sure. Apparently the dating story, which might have started out as a ruse, had turned into something serious.

Adjusting the coffee carafe, Kelsey went to pick up the tray from the counter.

Suzanna grasped her arm. "How about you? Feeling any better?"

Kelsey stared at Suzanna—dressed for work in a navy blue suit and the opal earrings Kelsey had helped her choose on one of their shopping trips. Since she was sixteen, they'd shopped together, and Kelsey had always remembered those excursions fondly. Sleeping in the same room where she'd stayed when she lived with the Quinns brought back a lot of memories. She'd trusted this woman so much then. And now . . . .

"I'm okay." She was trying to be, anyway. "Look, I don't want to keep hurting you with my anger . . . my confusion, but I can't talk about this yet."

"I understand." When had she ever heard Suzanna's voice so raw?

"I'm sorry." Impulsively, she leaned over, hugged her friend, and whispered, "We'll work this out, Suzanna." Then she drew back, scooped up the tray, and made her way upstairs.

As she reached the doorway of Luke's room, she heard Luke's voice. "Is it loaded?"

"Yes, but the safety's on."

"Let's hope I don't need it."

"Chances are you won't. I'll set the alarm when we leave."

They noticed her when she stepped inside. Luke slipped the gun under the sheet. She stared at the hump for a moment, then walked in. "Here's your breakfast."

"I—" The house phone rang.

Dressed in a gray suit for work, Joe chuckled as he checked the caller ID. "You have to take it this time. I can't stall her any longer."

Luke rolled his eyes.

Kelsey tensed. A woman. Of course, he had a woman. Sitting there battered and bare-chested above his taped ribs, his hair mussed, Luke would make any woman in the world want him. Even with his temple swollen, he was . . . enticing. She took note again of the bullet-size scar on his upper arm and shuddered at what had happened to him, what could happen to him at any time in the job he did. There were many, many reasons not to let herself care about this man.

Joe turned, gave Kelsey a squeeze on her shoulder, and left. She set the tray down. The phone kept ringing.

"I'll leave so you can answer that."

Luke grabbed her hand. "Stay." He picked up the phone. Into the mouthpiece, he said, "Hey, gorgeous."

Kelsey stiffened, and he winked at her. *The shit.* Still, mesmerized by this side of him, she stayed by the bed, her hand in his, as he listened to the caller.

"*Dobrze,*" he finally said. "*Tak.* Yes, I am good. I'm not lying to you. I'm laid up, but it's not serious. I had a scuffle a couple of days ago. But I'm all right." He listened, frowned. "Your dreams again? *Matka,* I swear, I'm fine. As a matter of fact, I got this cute little . . . nurse waiting on me hand and foot."

Kelsey tried to leave. He tugged her down to the mattress. His grip was a vise she couldn't escape, even if she wanted to.

"All right, put them on. *Matka? Kocham Ciebie.*" A pause. His brow furrowed. "Yes, Cat, I am . . . no, I wouldn't lie to you. A bump on my head . . . ha-ha, that's funny, sis. My back, too. Now *that* hurts."

Kelsey sat open-mouthed, listening to his affectionate tone. He was obviously talking to his family.

"*Kocham Ciebie.*" He smiled into the phone. "Yes, Toni," he began again. And a while later, again, "I promise, Paulie." A frown, not faked. "Is that her in the background? Oh, for Christ's sake, put her on . . . Lizzie, I'm all right. *Nie,* stop crying and I'll tell you." His gaze caught Kelsey's. He shook his head. "Baby, honest, I'm okay. I know *Matka* had a dream. Yes, I was hurt, but I'm okay. Elizabeita, I mean it, get control." A few more comments in Polish. Another "*Kocham Ciebie.*" He clicked off and sank against the propped-up pillows. "They're exhausting."

"*Matka* . . . as in mother?"

He nodded.

"What does *Kocham Ciebie* mean?"

He shrugged boyishly. "I love you."

"They know what you do, Luke?"

"Only that I work undercover. No details about what or where. I check in once a week to let them know I'm all right. They knew something was wrong when Joe called this time."

"They?"

He let out a frustrated breath. "My beautiful but meddlesome seven younger sisters." His eyes flashed with affection. This was a man who would care deeply.

Kelsey fingered the sheets. "*Seven* sisters?"

He smiled engagingly. "Big Polish family."

"I'll say."

He cocked his head, accenting the bruise on his temple. It was less swollen now, but turning yellowish. "There's a lot about me you don't know, Kel."

She stiffened. "I gather that."

"Are we ever going to talk about this?"

"No."

With his trademark arrogance, he arched a wheat-colored brow. "You are a difficult woman."

"Used to them falling at your feet like your sisters?"

He laughed, then moaned and grabbed his ribs. "Ohh. . . ."

"Be careful." Automatically, she reached out to his chest. Snagging her hand when she tried to pull it away, he held it flat against him. His skin was taut over a road map of muscles above the bandages. "My sisters would die if they heard you say they fall at my feet. They're staunch feminists, every last one of them. I've never known what they'll do—still don't."

She wanted to hear all about his family, about his life. It was such a strong desire, she snatched her hand back and stood to shake it off. Standing, she picked up the tray and placed it on his lap. "Here's your breakfast. I'm going downstairs."

"Fix my coffee for me first, will you, honey? I can't get the top of the carafe off without jarring my ribs."

With a disgusted glare, she poured coffee and added cream and sugar.

"I have a master's degree from Columbia University," he said, as if confessing state secrets.

Jesus. "Bully for you."

"I graduated summa cum laude."

"So you're a smart asshole. Big deal."

"I have a photographic memory, and I'm a computer whiz. Butter my toast."

Without thinking, she obeyed him. Joe had helped him clean up, and she could smell the soap on him. The scent, combined with a chest sprinkled with dark blond hair, made him the epitome of maleness.

"I was going to be a lawyer, then changed my mind. Want to know how I got into the Secret Service?"

"No."

"I've been thinking, I might teach now."

She rolled her eyes as she fussed with his food, but she admitted to herself the kids would love him.

"I'm great in bed."

Her actions stilled. She swallowed hard. "I don't care."

Again, he grabbed her wrist when she started to walk away. "The hell you don't. Why can't you just admit that you're glad I'm not a high school student?"

"Stop it!" she yelled, appalled by how close to tears she was. "This is just a game to you. Well, it wasn't to me. It isn't." She yanked on her hand. He let go, and she drew back. "Don't flirt with me. Don't call me honey. Don't try to charm me into your bed. You hurt me, and I'm still reeling from it."

"I'm sorry."

"If you are, then stop all this." She made a motion with her arm to encompass the room.

He watched her assessingly; suddenly she realized this was no boy she could control. No ordinary male she could snap her fingers at and make him do what she wanted. The sheet slipped, and she saw the glint of steel in the morning sunlight. This was a dark and dangerous man who could, maybe had, killed.

His voice was deadly calm when he said, "I don't know

exactly where this thing between us is headed, given my job, my lifestyle. But if you think for one second I'm letting you go without finding out, you're crazy."

She stared at him, then turned and hurried out the door.

She had never been more scared in her life.

And it wasn't because of Rush Webster.

LATER that morning, Suzanna and Joe walked down a deserted hallway at Fairholm High School. Vacations at school were always a breath of fresh air; though she went in to work almost every day, she was glad for time without the kids to catch up on a thousand things to be done. "You don't have to escort me to my office, Joe. Both Pat and Nancy are coming in."

"Are they here yet?" he asked casually.

"No, it's still early."

"Hmm." At the door, he asked for her keys, unlocked her office, and scoped it out. She stood back, acknowledging that her life was never going to be the same. Danger and intrigue were a part of it. So was this man. Her feelings for him had deepened in the last few days. From making love, of course. But also from his tenderness with her, his concern for Ben, and the way he treated Kelsey and Luke.

She sighed.

"What was that for?" he asked, opening the inner office door.

"I was just wondering how Kelsey and Luke are doing."

"Think they'll be in one piece when we get back?"

"I hope so. She's really upset." He flicked on the lights. "I—" She stopped in the doorway. "Oh!"

On the credenza were the most delicate peach roses she'd ever seen. At least two dozen of them were arranged in a vase, standing upright as the sun from the window glinted off them. Their sweet scent filled the office. She turned to Joe. He'd closed the door and, leaning against it, stared at her with a fiery green gaze that melted her insides like candle wax. "That first time, you wore a robe this color."

Her eyes clouded. Her heart hurt.

"Sweetheart, what's the matter? Flowers aren't supposed to make you cry."

"Thank you; they're lovely."

Frowning, he pushed away from the door, drew her to him, and kissed her hair. "Why the tears?" he asked after a moment.

"We . . . this is almost over . . . isn't it, the undercover work?"

He nodded.

"I. . . ." She swiped at the tears. "I'm going to miss you."

A look of profound sadness swept across his features. He brushed back her hair. "I'm going to miss you, too."

Which meant he was leaving. She knew it, of course. But sometimes, when she lay in his arms, when her skin still burned from his touch and his male scent filled her head, she hoped he'd find a way for them to be together. "This is foolish. I knew the score when I. . . ."

"Seduced me?"

She gave him a sideways glance. "Did I seduce you, Dr. Stonehouse?"

"Hmm. And it was magnificent." He pulled back. "I'd better go. I'll be right across the hall if you need me." He ran a finger down her cheek. "Bring me coffee when you're done with the Duchamps."

She rolled her eyes. "You and Luke are cut from the same cloth," she said, thinking of Kelsey's complaints this morning.

He kissed her nose. "Flattery will get you everywhere."

After he left, she wandered over to the roses. She wondered how he got them into her locked office. Stupid question—he was Secret Service. She fingered one, brought it to her nose. She remembered the robe she'd worn that afternoon, and how he'd taken it off her. . . . *Arrgh. Think of something else.* She went to her desk, picked up the phone, and dialed Brenda at work, only to be told her friend was home ill. When she tried the condo, she got the machine and left a message.

Suzanna worried about Brenda as she hung up. Lately, her friend seemed unusually interested in Kelsey and Luke, and in Suzanna's state of mind. Brenda was normally solicitous, but there was something about her latest inquiries that didn't . . . .

Hearing the outer door open, Suzanna glanced at the clock. It was early for the Duchamps. "Pat?" she called from her office. No answer. "Nancy?" Still none.

Spooked, she was just getting up when Max appeared in the doorway. He looked like a Skid Row bum again today. His face was gaunt, his hair greasy. His army fatigues were wrinkled enough to have been slept in. "Max, are you all right? Come on in and. . . ."

"I'm not staying."

"We have an appointment at nine with your dad."

"My dad ain't coming."

"Why?" Though she'd called and asked both Max and his father for an appointment to discuss the Young Guns issue, she planned to get at more about Max if she could pin down *the colonel*.

The boy's shoulders sagged. He sank against the wall. She rose and came around her desk. Again she could smell the cigarettes. With motherly authority, she drew him to the furniture grouping and pulled him into a chair next to her. "What's wrong, Max?"

"Nothing," he said wearily. "My dad got called out of town. I think his all-important fiancée went with him."

Suzanna knew about the surprise engagement from Luke. One of the risk factors in Joe's studies cited big changes in a kid's life. "He's getting married?" she asked carefully.

Max nodded.

"Are you upset about it?"

"I don't care what the fu—hell he does."

"I think you do."

Max leaned back and closed his eyes. Suddenly he seemed like a little boy. "It doesn't matter. I decided to sign on with the army. I'll be leaving in a few months. She can have him." The boy opened his eyes and scanned the room; his gaze landed on the roses. "Those are phat." He thought for a minute. "Your husband died, didn't he?"

"Five years ago."

"You never found nobody else?"

She thought of Joe. "No." She waited. "How long has your mother been dead?"

"Ten years."

"It's hard with one parent. Harder still when someone else enters the equation."

"He needs more, he says."

The stupid jerk. How could you tell a kid that? "He didn't mean you weren't enough."

"Yeah, sure." The boy sank further into the chair.

"You eaten anything lately, Max?"

He studied her with hollow eyes. "Yesterday sometime, I think."

She rose. Before he could object, she circled the desk and removed her purse from the drawer. "Come on, Maxwell. I'm taking you out to breakfast."

She'd never seen such shock on a kid's face. "Why?"

"I don't know, because I'm hungry, maybe."

"Don't bullsh . . . give me any bull, lady."

She cocked her head. "I'd like to get to know you better. And the mother in me *doesn't* like how you look."

Scowling, he watched her. "They say you're like this."

"Who says?"

"The other kids. They say you . . . take an interest in everybody."

At one time she'd wondered if being an educator these days was worth it. She smiled. "Why, Max, that's one of the nicest things ever said about me."

He stood. "Can we, um, go someplace nobody'd see us?"

She laughed. "Yeah, there's a little diner just outside of town. Your reputation will be intact."

"HI, Ruthie. This is a nice surprise." Waiting in his office for Ben, Joe was having trouble concentrating on work when his cell phone rang.

"Can you talk?" his sister asked. She was used to catching him when he couldn't.

"I'm expecting somebody in about ten minutes. Until then."

"How are you?"

Satisfied. Happy. More content than I've ever been in my life. "Good."

"Hmm."

"What does that mean?" He tapped his pen on the desk.

His sister hesitated. "Suzanna still in the picture?"

"Ruthie, don't go there."

"You were different with her, is all."

Oh, Christ, you don't know the half of it.

"Joey, is there any chance a relationship with her could work out for you?"

Pushing back his chair, he lifted his feet to the desk, lounged back. "No. When I leave here, I'm required to cut off all contact." He sighed. "Even if I wasn't, you know the stats on Secret Service agents. Most relationships don't last two years. My marriage only lasted four."

"Would you, if you could?"

"Be with her, you mean?" He pictured Suzanna under him, on top of him, between his legs, loving him. "In a second. But there's not a snowball's chance in hell of that happening." The words broke his heart. He tried to harden it. "Tell me what's going on with you."

She chatted about her church activities, about Mark's web site, Shelly's new interest in field hockey. He laughed, picturing his vibrant, alive niece and nephew. Then Ruthie said, "Something odd happened, though."

Joe stiffened. Because of Josie's death, he was acutely sensitive about his family. "Odd?"

"Yeah, I met Al for lunch last week at the diner where Suzanna took us; the waitress there had found a picture of Josie in a booth."

Swallowing hard, Joe remembered the pixie face and eyes full of life. Juxtaposed was the memory of her, waxen and lifeless, in the coffin.

"Joe?"

"I wonder what the picture was doing there," he managed to say.

"I'm sorry," Ruthie said. "It upsets you to talk about her."

"No."

"You told Suzanna about her."

"I did." He forced himself to relax. "Was it Josie's senior

picture? Maybe a kid had it in his wallet and it fell out when he went to pay."

"No, it came from the Internet, downloaded off of a *New York Times* site. It was from when she was killed."

This did not sound good. Joe felt the slippery edges of worry crowd him.

"I don't know what to make of it." Ruthie's tone was casual, but inflected with concern.

"Let me think about it."

Ben came to the door.

Joe dropped his feet to the floor and sat up straight. "My appointment's here. I gotta go. I'll call you tonight."

"You don't have to call me. I'm fine, big brother."

"Talk to you soon." He clicked off his phone.

"I can wait," Ben said hopefully. Joe recognized that he didn't want to talk. Still, he'd come.

"Why would you do that?"

He nodded to the phone. "You were busy."

"My sister."

Ben's brooding eyes lightened. "Yeah? You got a sister?"

"Uh-huh. We're close." He nodded to a chair. "Sit down, Ben."

The boy dropped into a seat.

Joe asked, "You get along well with . . . what's your sister's name?"

"Ashley. Yeah, she's okay. She's at college."

"You miss her?"

He nodded. Didn't say anything more, just stared bleakly at his black sneakers with red dragons on them. He wore shiny black pants and a black long-sleeved shirt with matching red dragons. With his hair still dyed the color of midnight, the kid did a good imitation of a vampire.

Joe stood to close the door, then sat down. "You've had a lot of loss in the last few years. Your dad. Ashley going to college." He waited a bit. "Zach Riley."

Again the silent nod, indicative of a thousand sighs.

"It's hard to cope with loss, isn't it, Ben?"

"Yeah."

A word. Good. "Want to tell me what you feel inside?"

Studying the floor, he shook his head.

"Why?"

"I'm afraid if it comes out, it'll eat me alive."

Joe had felt the same way about Josie. He'd kept it in for too long. "That's not good. It'll eat you from the inside out."

"I want to be in control."

"We all want that. But we can't control death." *Or kids' obscene actions that bring it about. Josie had been so full of life.* "You need to talk about it."

"I know. I can't stand it anymore."

"Then tell me as much as you can."

An hour later, Ben leaned back in his chair, exhausted. "I'm whipped. I can't do more right now."

"That's okay, you've done enough for today."

"I don't feel any better."

"Talking about it can make it worse, initially. I'll bet you'll feel better tonight."

"I hope so. Mom's pretty freaked."

"She had to be told about this depression. It's my job as a counselor—"

"I know." He nodded to the outer office. "She drove me here. She's outside, waiting."

Joe smiled. That kind of support for a kid was vital. "I'm glad you have her."

"Me, too." He stood. Scowled. "I been trying to call Luke, but nobody answers."

"Oh, he went to see *his* mom for a few days." That was the story they'd decided on. When the kids saw his battered face, Luke would say he'd been in a fight at home. "I'll have him call you when he gets back."

After Joe spoke with Mrs. Franzi, an outgoing, concerned mother, he was feeling hopeful . . . and young. He glanced at the clock. Ten-thirty. He decided to go find his girl. He made his way to Suzanna's office. Inside, he found Nancy and Pat hard at work. "The boss in?" he asked lightly.

Pat scowled. Her matronly shape and graying hair made her look like everybody's mother. "No, she isn't. Her calendar says she has a meeting with the Duchamps, but she didn't show for it. Neither did they."

His insides went cold. "I saw her early this morning."

"Her purse is gone." Pat shrugged. "I checked. I'm sort of a mother hen."

"Well, tell her to give me a buzz when she gets in." His tone was nonchalant, but concern clawed inside of him. He strode back to his office and called Luke. Kelsey answered, said Luke was asleep, and no, Suzanna hadn't come home or called.

By eleven, Joe was pacing his office. He checked with her secretary twice more, and still she hadn't shown up. He didn't know what to do. Had someone visited this morning after he left her? Had she gone out and. . . .

He paced. By eleven-thirty he was ready to spit nails. . . .

She came strolling into his office ten minutes later, when he'd just begun to pray.

"Hi." She was smiling. Excitement danced in her amber eyes.

His hands were shaking, so he stuffed them in his pockets. "Close the door."

"Why? None of the counselors are working today."

"Suzanna, *close the door.*" He emphasized each word. His tone, deadly calm, was one he'd used on drug dealers and porno kings. She must have caught its seriousness.

Wide-eyed, she closed the door, then leaned against it.

"Where were you?"

"Max came in this morning. His dad copped out on the meeting, so I took him to breakfast."

Joe tried counting to ten. Twenty. "Breakfast. You had *breakfast* with one of America's Most Wanted?"

"That's an exaggeration." She grinned. "Joe, it was such a breakthrough. I got him to talk. He even told me. . . ."

Joe missed the rest of the sentence. He was trying desperately to get control of the fear that had gripped him as he pictured her alone on the road with a dangerous boy in her car.

"Joe, is something wrong?"

"Wrong?" His temper spiked; he tamped it down. "*Wrong?*" His hands fisted in his pockets so he wouldn't grab her. "Have you no common sense? Going out alone with Duchamp?"

She frowned. "I have common sense. I did what I thought was right for a student today."

"And what about your safety? How can you be so idiotic as not to consider that he could have hurt you?" he asked tightly.

"Look, Joe, I can see you're upset, but you don't have the right to talk to me this way."

He swallowed hard. "Oh, I have the right. I was *worried* about you." His voice rose a notch. "I love you, damn it." As soon as the words left his mouth, he regretted them. He swung around, unable to face her.

At that moment, Suzanna's entire world shifted. Everything changed, everything was altered forever. For a long time she just stared at Joe's back, their labored breathing loud in the small space. Then she crossed the office and sidled around to face him. "Joe," she whispered.

His shoulders sagged. His hands came up to cradle her cheeks; he leaned over, and his forehead met hers. She grasped his wrists and held onto them while he calmed. His body eclipsed the light, his presence dwarfed her. But she had never felt more powerful.

"I shouldn't have said that," he whispered raggedly.

Words like that couldn't be taken back. "Did you mean it?"

"Yes, I just didn't plan to tell you."

"Ever?"

"Ever."

Tenderly, she slid her arms around his neck. His hands came around her back, and he drew her to him. Burying his face in her hair, he held on to her.

Understanding, she waited, let him regain some composure. Then she inched back, wanting to see his face. His green eyes were like live fire. But he wasn't smiling, and brackets creased his mouth.

She raised her hands to his face and cradled it. She said simply, "I love you, Joe Stonehouse. I love you, too."

TWENTY-FOUR

WELL, Brenda thought wearily, at least her hands had stopped shaking. The early afternoon sun shone through her window, creating a disgustingly cheery atmosphere. She'd been up only an hour, having not slept well through the night. She'd called in sick at work.

It was the dreams. They'd come again.

As she glanced up from the computer screen, her gaze caught the bottle of liquor on her desk. So what if she'd had to doctor the coffee with vodka? It was the fucking dreams that had caused it. No big deal. She was still in control.

She didn't want to think about the dreams, but she couldn't stop her mind from going there. Conrad had kept popping out of the shadows all night. At first, his face was normal—the big shit-eating grin, the ears that stuck out, his receding hair. Just the way a father should look. But throughout the dream, he metamorphosed.

First he became the porno counterfeiter the Secret Service had arrested in New York. Where Brenda had met Joe.

"Don't think about this," she said aloud. "Conrad would want you to follow through on your plan."

She forced herself back to the present. Staring at her notes, she reminded herself that she had an appointment with an editor in New York City in two weeks. Just enough time to get this outline done. To soothe her nerves, she lit a cigarette, took a long drag, then typed, *Section 1: The Stark Statistics: school shootings in America.* She listed Columbine of course; Austin, Texas; DeKalb, Missouri; Orange County, California. Forty-three altogether. So far.

Her fingers stopped as she typed *Elmira, New York.* A pipe bombing, targeted for the high school, was averted because the bomber told a girl he knew, who then reported it to a resource officer.

Kids don't snap. These incidents are well planned. The shooters tell other kids.

In the Elmira case, because the school had openly discussed with teachers and students what they should do if they got wind of a threat, a kid had told an adult, and a tragedy had been averted.

"Don't think about it, Brenda." Her voice was hoarse from all the Marlboros. Determinedly, she finished section one, outlining the findings of the FBI, the Department of Education, the American Psychological Association, and finally . . . ta da . . . the Secret Service.

Did they go too far? she wrote with flair. Where was her research on the First Amendment? She fumbled with her folders. Her hands were shaking, and she noticed the pasty color of her skin. "Shit." Again her eyes strayed to the bottle. Maybe just one more dollop in the coffee. What was a dollop? She poured out the booze and sipped the drink, savored it. Then she went back to the computer. *Section 2: The Precipitating Event: Josie Callahan was an honor student, beloved by all, including her family—one of whom just happened to be. . . .*

Images from the dream came again. This time Conrad emerged from the shadows as Al Callahan. His face was ravaged as he stood before a coffin. Then he turned to his wife, and his whole demeanor changed. *Whore*, he spat out, and walked away from her. Stonehouse appeared by her side, brought his sister close, and told her not to worry, he'd take care of her like he always had.

Then Conrad became Stonehouse. Against her will, Brenda remembered something else. Something real. . . .

Stonehouse with *her*. She'd waited after that counterfeit/porno press conference to see where the agents would go. Apparently it was time to celebrate, because she followed them to a quiet bar in the Village. Joe drank a lot of champagne, and she'd seduced him back to her apartment. Though she was pretty drunk herself, she remembered that he was good in the sack.

"Type," she told herself. *Section 3: The Plan of Action: Modern high school. Has the typical problems of any secondary institution—vandalism, kid attacks teacher (remember Rush Webster). . . . High school principal Suzanna Quinn is the epitome of honesty.*

Brenda grabbed for another folder on her desk and smiled at her cleverness. It was red for Joe McCarthy and the Communist scare. Again, Conrad's face in the dream came to her, but this time, he'd changed into Nathan Carson. Late last night Brenda found information on Suzanna's father by tracing military records. Wasn't the Net grand? There in black and white, had been Carson's entire history. His victimization. His disgrace. His suicide. That personal story would add a dimension to the book. Could she get Suzanna to talk about it from a daughter's view?

In the last dream, Conrad had come as himself again. *Hey, kiddo, what the hell are you doing? Suzanna loves you like a sister.*

Her head began to pound, and she rose from the computer. She could do this. She *could*. With all these side stories, there'd be no way the book wouldn't sell, wouldn't hit the *Times* list.

"Concentrate," she said to herself. She needed more information on the younger set. More insight into Kelsey Cunningham. What was going on with her and the handsome young agent?

Brenda paced. She was betraying everybody.

"Freedom of the press," she said aloud, and went back to the computer. *Section 4: Enter Starsky and Hutch.* No, scratch that, it was too dated a reference. She picked up the green file labeled *Agent L.* Luke Ludzecky. This was easier to stomach. She might even get some laughs out of it. Seven sisters who idolized their brother. His high school transcript had been absurdly simple to obtain. Even his disciplinary folder. He'd been a rebel all right. Somebody had even put notes in the file from Stash Ludzecky to the school about his son. Didn't take Einstein to theorize how he'd let the old man down.

Idly, Brenda sighed and leaned back against the chair. She saw her phone message light on. She pressed the button.

The third caller gave her pause. "Hey, Brend, it's me, Suzanna. I wondered how you were. School's out this week, but I'm . . . a little tied up. Maybe we can get together, though. I miss you. Call me. Um, not at home. Call at school. Or on my cell."

Not at home. That was odd. Why not call her at home? What was going on at home? Absently, she picked up the bottle and drank. Was Stonehouse staying there? Maybe Brenda would just drive over and scope out the situation. Do a little of her own spying. At least she'd forget the dreams.

Buzzed by the liquor, she typed in *Section 5: The Juicy Details.*

KELSEY'S eyes were gritty and her shoulders ached. She'd come downstairs to do the dishes and straighten the house, and had ended up on the couch in the living room; she was trying to figure out where her head was at, but she was so tired she could barely think straight. Lying down, she closed her eyes. Luke was asleep upstairs. Suzanna had called to say she and Joe would be home soon.

Luke.

Suzanna.

Deceiving her.

Get it together, Kel. This isn't the end of the world. No, of course it wasn't, but trust had never come easily to her after her father's total disregard of her needs. Suzanna was the one person she'd been able to count on.

She had no choice. Don't be an idiot about this.

Sinking farther down into the pillows, she stretched out— and admitted she was overreacting. For one thing, she was exhausted, and she never had a handle on things when she was this tired. She'd found it almost impossible to sleep with Luke so close by. Mostly she was worried about him. Every few hours, she got up and crept through the connecting bathroom to see if he was all right. The last time she'd checked, he'd been sleeping on his stomach, and the crisscross pattern from the outside light they kept on all night cast him in harsh planes and angles. She was hard pressed not to touch him, had stood over him, watching him breathe deeply and clutch the pillows.

Climb in, baby. . . .

I'm great in bed. . . .

If you think for one second I'm letting you go. . . .

She wanted to scream. The doorbell rang, and it startled her already frayed nerves.

Webster? No, he wouldn't announce his arrival. The chimes sounded twice more, then she snuck out to the foyer. The noise could wake Luke, and he needed his sleep. Through the side window, she saw Brenda Way on the porch. Kelsey smiled. She liked Suzanna's irreverent college roommate. They had become friends.

But oh, dear, Luke was upstairs. The bell again. Shit. She had no choice but to pull open the door.

The alarm buzzed loudly. "Oh, hell," Kelsey said, and punched in the code.

From the porch, Brenda frowned. "Kelsey? What are you doing here? And why is the alarm on in the middle of the afternoon?"

Think fast. "Oh, well, I got hurt last week, and, um, I'm staying with Suzanna for a few days."

"Yeah, I heard about that." Brenda looked past her shoulder. "Can I come in?"

Panicky, Kelsey said, "I just took some painkillers and I'm. . . ."

"Jesus Christ, woman, why the *hell* are you openin' that door?" Luke's voice came from above.

Kelsey closed her eyes. Just what they needed. For someone else to know. Well, at least it was Brenda. Kelsey pivoted. Luke stood at the top of the steps. He wore only his navy blue boxers and the rib bandages.

In his hand, he held his gun.

He wavered a bit.

"Luke, what—"

He grabbed the railing.

Kelsey flew up the stairs. "What are you doing out of bed?"

"I heard the alarm go off." Sweat had beaded on his forehead. She slid her arm around him, and he hissed with pain. "Sorry."

"No, it's okay." He glanced down, saw Brenda, and seemed to relax. "Help me back to bed, honey."

Dimly aware of Brenda coming inside, Kelsey held onto Luke and assisted him back to the room. God, he was big. And muscular. His weight was heavy on her. His legs were corded with sinew, too. His stomach was flat. . . .

She got him to his room and eased him into bed. He set the gun down on the table. He was sheet-white, and sweating.

"You want something?" she asked. "Some water?"

His breath came hard. "Yeah. I was asleep, and bounded out of bed when I heard the alarm." He swore ripely. "I'm better, damn it. I guess I just can't move that fast."

"Oh, Luke, I'm sorry. I should have answered the door sooner."

His eyes cleared. He grabbed her and tugged her down to the bed, where she fell half on top of him. "Sorry enough to kiss and make it better?"

She was inches from his face. "Luke. . . ."

"Well, isn't this cozy?"

Startled, Kelsey looked up to find Brenda standing in the doorway. The older woman was smiling. And something else. There was a gleam in her eye. Oh, God, she thought Luke was a student. Kelsey's head spun as she tried to figure out what to do.

Brenda stumbled into the room. It was then that Kelsey noticed how shaky the other woman was. Unsteady on her feet. Jittery. She reached the bed and picked up Luke's gun.

"Hey, careful, Brenda, it's loaded."

Careful, Brenda? Did Luke know her? How could he?

Brenda set the weapon back down. She weaved a bit, and Luke and Kelsey exchanged puzzled looks.

Abruptly turning to Kelsey, Brenda said, "So, is the

young agent as good in bed as his partner? I can vouch for Stonehouse's performance. . . ."

Kelsey's world tilted. *The young agent.* She stared at the newspaper reporter, then at Luke. "I thought . . . I thought . . . you told me only Ross Maloney knew about the undercover."

"Honey, listen—"

From downstairs came a shout. "Luke! Kelsey!" It was Joe's voice.

Luke said, "Shit!" and yelled, "Up here."

There was pounding on the stairs. Joe raced in first. Gun out. Raised. He halted, and blew out a breath. "Jesus Christ, Brenda what are you doing here?" His gaze went to Luke, who shrugged.

Suzanna rushed in behind Joe. "Oh, God, we were so scared. The front door was ajar. We thought Webster might have gotten in." Her gaze rested on Brenda. "Brend, what are you doing here?"

Everyone stared at Brenda.

Kelsey stood and moved away from the bed; she wrapped her arms around her middle. "Brenda knew about this whole thing, didn't she?"

Suzanna and Joe exchanged a guilty look.

"You said only the superintendent knew."

"I—"

"You lied again." And Kelsey was just beginning to reconcile the whole deception in her mind.

"It wasn't exactly like that. . . ."

Infuriated, Kelsey wanted to strike out. She glanced from Suzanna to Joe. "So, Agent Stonehouse, does Suzanna know you're sleeping with Brenda?"

"*What*?" Suzanna's voice was hoarse.

Joe stiffened, then ran a hand through his hair. "Son of a bitch."

"Guess not." Kelsey had gone cold. She shook her head, disgustedly. "You two are a pair. A pair of goddamned liars." With that, she ran out of the room.

She'd reached the bottom of the stairs when Stonehouse caught up with her. "Where are you going?" he demanded, grabbing her arm in front of the door.

"I'm leaving here."

"No, you're not."

"You can't make me stay."

"I can try." Suddenly he seemed to tower over her. Her eyes widened. But then his whole demeanor softened. "Kelsey, Webster attacked Luke. He's in town." Joe glanced to her knee. "He already hurt you once."

From the corner of her eye, she saw Brenda on the landing.

"Think this out. Don't be foolish."

Kelsey was pissed, but she wasn't stupid. "All right. Let go of me. I won't run off."

Joe sighed and stepped back, catching sight of Brenda. His look was homicidal. "What the hell *are* you doing here?" he said angrily. "Taking notes?"

SUZANNA stood in her den and stared out the bay window. The weather was warming up. The grass was green. Spring would be nice.

"Suz." Brenda's voice came from behind her.

Suzanna turned around. Her friend was in the doorway, looking . . . odd. Though dressed in tailored beige slacks and a white shirt, she seemed unkempt. Even her hair didn't look normal. "Brenda, are you all right?"

"Sure. I'm fine."

Suzanna studied her. "Have you been drinking?"

"No, of course not. Why?"

"You're acting strangely."

Shakily, Brenda ran a hand over her face. "I am a little out of it. I took cough medicine and an antihistamine. I'm not feeling well."

"I know. I called you at work and then at your house."

Brenda moved farther into the room. Up close, her face was drawn. But it was more than that. Suzanna couldn't put her finger on it. "I know, Suz. That's why I came over here."

Suzanna fiddled with her turquoise earring, toyed with the matching bracelet. "You knew I wasn't home. I told you to call me at school. What's more, you upset everybody up there. Surely you see that."

"*I* did? It seems to me Miss America's the one who was out to get you."

So, Agent Stonehouse, does Suzanna know you're sleeping with Brenda?

"Kelsey's upset."

"She knows that Luke and Joe are agents, doesn't she?"

"Yes."

"How did she find out?" It was a reporter's query.

Suzanna felt chilled and stepped back. "Brenda, I don't want to keep talking to you about this operation. Joe has asked me not to discuss it a thousand times."

Brenda regarded her carefully. "Why did Kelsey think it was necessary that Joe tell you he and I—"

"I don't want to talk about that, either." She could barely think about it, had blocked it after she walked out of Luke's bedroom.

"You're sleeping with him."

"That's none of your business, Brenda." This from the doorway. Joe.

Closing her eyes, Suzanna wished for a little time alone to collect her thoughts. Kelsey was holed up in her room, and Suzanna had come down here to calm herself and think.

Brenda stared at her, then faced Joe. "Oh, hell," she finally said. "I'm going home." She crossed the room and squeezed Suzanna's arm. "We'll talk later."

"All right. Be careful driving if you're on that medicine."

Brenda brushed past Joe, and Suzanna turned back to the window. She sensed Joe come up behind her. Only hours ago she'd been ecstatic at his declaration of love. Now, she felt . . . she didn't know what she felt.

"What are you thinking?" He didn't touch her.

She waited a moment. "That you told me this had never happened to you before."

"This?"

"That you'd never gotten involved with someone during an assignment." She hesitated. "That you'd never felt this way about anybody. Or did I misinterpret the last part?"

"No, you didn't misinterpret anything. Both are true." Gently, he placed his hands on her shoulders. "I met Brenda after an assignment had just ended, and my team and I were celebrating. We were together once, Suzanna." His voice was hoarse. "I'm not into one-night stands, but I'd had too much to drink and it just happened, I guess."

"How did Kelsey find out about you and Brenda?" she asked.

"I don't know. Luke's fit to be tied. He's ranting about God knows what, and I can't calm him down."

"So many lies."

He rubbed up and down her arms. His hands felt good on her. How would she live without this, now that she'd had him?

"I'm sorry," he said. "I've hurt you again. Maybe we should stop this thing between us now. If you're feeling like this *already* . . . when I leave. . . ."

Ah, the agent was back, slowly taking over the man.

Suzanna thought about his hoarsely uttered words as he loved her. *Oh, God, sweetheart, I want this so much. I want you so much.* And later, *I like what I become with you. It's how I am with Ruthie, my family.* And once, when he woke up in the night, *You make the loneliness evaporate, lady. . . .*

She struggled to put this right. Still facing away from him, she said, "When Lawrence died, I was angry at how he'd been taken away so suddenly. That I had no control over it." Turning, she stared up him. "If I have any say in this, I want what time is left with you."

His eyes closed, he sighed with relief. The man was back. "You don't know how much I wanted to hear that."

She raised her hand and brushed his jaw. It was bristly. "I love you, Joe."

He swallowed hard. His fingers clenched on her.

She slid her hands up his chest and around his neck. Her heart swelled with feelings for him.

His arms banded around her, and he buried his face in her hair. "Suzanna."

And she just held on. For a minute. For tonight. For however long he was here. She'd just hold on.

TWENTY-FIVE

———

WHEN the red light on the clock flipped to 3:55, Kelsey gave up trying to sleep. She'd stayed in her room after the fiasco with Brenda and tried to deal with this newest discovery. Her rational, adult mind kept telling her to handle the revelation that Brenda knew about the undercover better. But the little girl inside of her, the frustrated, angry teenager she'd once been, kept surfacing. She'd counted so much on Suzanna's honesty; the foundation of her life was shaken by an emotional earthquake, and tonight, the aftershocks rocked her. Yet again, Suzanna, Joe, and Luke had lied to her.

You can trust me, sweetie. I promise I'll always tell you the truth.

Exhausted, Kelsey had fallen asleep in the the early evening and awakened at three. Rested now, she slid out of bed, threw on a sweatsuit, and left her room. Creeping down the steps, she found her way to the kitchen. She hadn't eaten earlier, so she fixed herself hot chocolate and toast, then wandered around the room where she'd spent so many wonderful hours with the Quinns. She'd loved sharing their life and had been grateful to be a part of it. Again, she pushed the good memories out of her mind. It was all too hard to think about. What could she do at four in the morning to distract herself?

Heading for the den, she decided to use the computer. All staff and teachers could access the district network from their homes. She'd check her E-mail and maybe surf the Net a while.

The ping to boot up the system was loud in the quiet den. She'd only turned on a small desk lamp, and the glow from the computer spun eerily through the room. It was cold in here, too. She ran her hands up and down her arms to warm herself. Going through the commands, calling up Netscape, she was into her E-mail in no time. Several messages had accumulated in a file for students to contact her. There were a few queries from kids about assignments. Some funny forwards they'd copied her into. One from *bastardinc*. She didn't recognize the odd name.

She called it up. No salutation. No punctuation. It just read *WATCH OUT CUNT* in boldface letters. She swallowed hard. Was someone threatening her? Oh, God, what next?

Saving the message to show Luke, she exited her school folder. In her personal file were three notes from her father. She hadn't called or e-mailed him since he'd stormed out of her house because she wouldn't agree to leave Fairholm. Had it only been two weeks ago?

She read the first.

Dear Kelsey Lynne,

I've been trying to reach you. I hope you didn't go away for spring break without telling me. I know you're angry about my comments before I left, but I simply can't believe you're so involved with those . . . boys. First Webster. Now this Ludzecky character. You know I only want what's best for you. I always have. . . .

Kelsey closed her eyes. "Have you, Dad?" she whispered aloud, remembering that night he'd told her they were moving to Fairholm. . . . *You're thirteen years old. A good age to move so I can take this job* . . . his decision to go New Haven her senior year. . . . *Think of the opportunities to develop your mind in a college town of such caliber* . . . his refusal to pay college tuition if she didn't toe the line . . . *I can't be a party to your poor decision making, young lady. I only have your best interests at heart.*

Other thoughts intruded. . . .

So, is the young agent as good in bed as. . . .

WATCH OUT CUNT

It was all too much. She was just beginning to see things from Suzanna's point of view, intellectually at least, when she'd found out about Brenda. Damn it! Couldn't she count on anybody, trust anybody, believe in anything? She simply didn't know what to do.

So she cried. Pillowing her head on her arms, she let go.

She didn't know how much later she heard "Kel?" Luke's voice penetrated the haze of misery she'd fallen into. Firm, gentle hands rested on her shoulders. "Honey, I'm so sorry. About this newest thing. About *everything.*"

She sat up, still facing the computer. "You know, before you came here, I can't remember the last time I cried. Now. . . ." She shrugged, hating herself for the comfort she took from his touch.

His fingers kneaded her neck. "You don't always have to be strong, you know."

"Now I do. Now I. . . ."

Her comment was cut off by the familiar chime of an instant message. It drew her gaze to the screen.

"Who the hell would be IM-ing you at four in the morning?"

She wiped her eyes and stared at the sender's name. "I don't recognize the sender. The kids have this E-mail address but, geez, it's early."

"Accept the message."

As she clicked on the Accept icon, she heard a chair scrape across the floor. Luke drew up beside her. He wore dark green sweatpants and no shirt; though bandages bisected his rib cage, she could see his muscles ripple with tension as he leaned in close, his arm braced along the back of her chair. His black-and-blue marks had turned yellowish green.

Together, they stared at the screen.

"Hey, Ms. C.? What you doing up at this hour?"

Luke said, "Answer. Ask who it is."

She followed his direction.

"It's me, Smurf."

"Smurf? He's in Hilton Head." Kelsey was surprised, but not so worried now. She had a good relationship with the boy.

"Ask him how his vacation is."

Quickly, she typed the query.

"Bor-ing!" came the reply. "The place is mad-cool, though. I'm thinking about staying here."

Luke said, "Let me do this."

Glancing over at him, she saw his face was full of intense concentration. Tonight, he seemed at least twenty-six.

They switched chairs. He typed in, "How can you stay there? You have school next week."

A long interval. Finally, "I might not go back. That place gives me nothing but grief. And right before vacation . . . never mind. I just might not wanna go back."

Luke wrote, "Not going back? You have two months left of your senior year, Smurf." Before he sent it, he said to Kelsey, "What's an upcoming event he'd be excited about?"

"Not the prom. He'd never go. But everybody attends the after-prom Senior Bash."

"You have to be here for the Senior Bash, Smurf. I'm counting on you."

"Are you, Ms. C.?" Smurf shot back. "Seems like nobody cares."

"Smurf, you sound depressed."

"Went off the Lummox."

Kelsey said, "Lummox is an antidepressant, right?"

"Uh-huh." Luke typed, "That's not such a hot idea, Smurfy boy."

"Luke, I wouldn't call him Smurfy boy."

"Damn." He corrected his message.

"Who cares?" came the existential reply.

"I care, Smurf. And you have friends. Morgan. Ben. Luke."

"Yeah, sure. They're the only ones. The rest of them I'd like to. . . ." He cut off.

Under his breath, Luke said, "Shit," and waited a decent amount of time.

"You'd like to what?"

After an interminable pause, two simple words came across the screen. "Erase them."

Kelsey gasped.

Luke's hands fisted. "Get Joe. I don't know where to go with this."

She stood just as another message came over the screen. "Signing off, amigo. See you in school. Maybe." A pause, then he typed, "POW!"

Luke shot a plea to Smurf to stay online, but there was no response. Both he and Kelsey wilted like flowers in need of water. Then they looked at each other.

Kelsey's mind whirled. Suddenly, she was very glad Joe and Luke were Secret Service agents.

JOE wandered into the kitchen at 6 A.M. and found Kelsey and Luke drinking coffee. From the expressions on their faces, he guessed they were still at odds. Pouring a cup of the hot brew, he said, "You two are up early," and crossed to the table. "Long night?"

They exchanged weary looks.

He decided to try to help clear the air. "Kelsey, you need to know some things about Brenda. What she knew and why."

Luke said, "I already told her all that. We've been up for hours." He drew in a breath. "We got a bigger problem right now. Kelsey and I had an interesting conversation early this morning with Smurf."

Joe scowled. "Smurf? As in Jimmy Smurfella?"

"Yep."

"I thought he was out of town."

"He is. He instant messaged Kelsey at 4 A.M. when she was on the Net." Luke relayed the rest of the details, then reached down for a paper, which he handed to Joe. "This is a transcript of the conversation."

"You can't copy IM's." His eyes narrowed on Luke. The kid was a computer whiz. "Or can you?"

"Not even I can do that. I typed it out afterward so you could see it."

"That photographic memory again." He scanned the copy. "Son of a bitch."

"There's more." His mouth tight, he gave Joe another sheet. It was an E-mail to Kelsey.

Joe read the three words. He looked up. "Kelsey, I'm sorry."

She smiled tremulously. "I'm just glad you're here."

He smiled back. "Well, that's music to my ears." He focused on the E-mail. "We need to report this to headquarters so they can try to run down who sent it."

"It's from Webster. That E-mail address was his link on their web site."

Joe hadn't noticed that, but Luke's quick brain must have picked it up.

Kelsey stood and, taking Luke's empty cup and hers, crossed to the coffeepot. "I can't believe all this. Danger keeps leaping out of every corner."

"It's tough when you're not used to dealing with this kind of thing." Joe stood. "I'll call Captain Caruso. He—"

The shrill of the phone cut him off. Everybody tensed. Six A.M. phone calls spelled trouble.

Joe answered it. "Quinn residence."

"This is Lieutenant Latham," said a deep voice from the other end. "I'd like to speak to Mrs. Quinn."

Joe covered the phone. "Kel, go wake Suzanna."

In minutes, Suzanna appeared in the doorway. She was sleepy-eyed and wearing the peach robe again. Despite the gravity of the situation, Joe took pleasure in the picture she made. Crossing to the phone, she said to him, "Kelsey told me who it was," then into the mouthpiece, "Lieutenant Latham. What's going on?" As he spoke, her pretty brown eyes widened. She looked to Joe and covered the phone. "They picked up Webster. He was at a buddy's house." Suzanna listened again. "Really? When did that come in?" More silence. "Yes, all right. Yes, of course, I feel better. Thank you for calling."

Hanging up, Suzanna sagged against the counter. "This is unbelievable."

"They got Webster," Joe said matter-of-factly. "Where?"

"At Robert Morton's house."

"'He's the guy who was bullying Smurf the day before vacation," Kelsey put in.

Joe had drawn Suzanna coffee. He gave it to her and brushed a hand down her hair. "What else did Latham say?"

"Two things." Her voice was shaky. "They got an anonymous tip late last night that they traced to Pickles. The kid told them where Webster was."

"Any lead on who called?"

"They have reason to believe it was Max Duchamp."

Joe remembered her comment about having breakfast with Max. *Joe, it was such a breakthrough. I got him to talk. . . .* "Seems like a little attention might be just what the kid needed to keep him on the straight and narrow."

Suzanna's eyes sparkled like aged brandy catching the sun. "That's not all. Webster and Morton had guns in their possession. And they were high; Webster threw a tantrum when the cops burst in and let it slip he was responsible for a couple of things. The slashed tires." She smiled. "And the hit list we found."

"Jesus." This from Luke.

"They were arrested. Vandalism. No license for the guns. The earlier assault on Kelsey. Intent to do harm with the list. The lieutenant says they won't be bothering anybody for a while." Suzanna blew out a breath and faced Kelsey. "Looks like you'll be safe now, sweetie."

"I can go home then, right?" she asked.

Luke put in quickly, "What about Smurf?"

"He's in Hilton Head." Joe glanced briefly at Luke, then back to Kelsey. "Yes, Kelsey, you can go home."

LUKE didn't want Kelsey to leave, but he knew that none of them could stay at Suzanna's. Josh was coming back from Italy tomorrow, and they wouldn't involve him in this. Besides, Kelsey *wanted* to leave. And in his head, he knew she needed time to sort things out, to think things through. She was a fair, basically kind person, and when she had time to wade through the emotional baggage, he had faith that she'd come to terms with this breach of trust by all of them. Now, she was bombarded by too much, too fast, to think clearly. But in his heart, he wanted her with him. Still, when she'd scooted upstairs to pack fifteen minutes ago, he let her go without argument. He was sitting in the kitchen with Suzanna and Joe when the doorbell rang.

Joe said, "Hell, this place is a goddamned circus. Who do you think that is?"

"Your guess is as good as mine." Suzanna stood. "I'll get it."

"I'll come with you." Joe stood, too.

Luke watched them leave the kitchen, leaning into each other, shoulders touching. Then he rose, crossed to the doors, and stared outside. As the sun beat down brightly, warming the glass, he admitted he'd give his eye teeth to have Kelsey treat him the way Suzanna treated Joe. He wanted that closeness with her, damn it.

"Luke, you have company."

He turned from the the doors. And almost dropped his coffee cup. "Lizzie? What the hell are you doing here?"

Her blond hair disheveled, a backpack thrown over her red jacket, his sister angled that damned Ludzecky chin. Luke had seen the gesture a thousand times from every single one of his stubborn siblings. "I came to see if you were all right."

"How did you find him?" Joe was all business.

Lizzie arched a disdainful brow. "Who are you?"

"I'm his boss."

"Oh." She faced Luke. "We were all worried about you. So I"—she fidgeted with the backpack strap—"I got this guy at school who has the hots for me to trace the call to this house. It took two days."

"Can you get just anybody to do that?" Suzanna asked.

Lizzie gave Suzanna what Luke called her princess look. "Of course, if you're good enough. I don't associate with jerks."

Suzanna stifled a laugh.

"Everybody said you were okay, Lukasz, but *Matka* had another dream about you, and I wanted to see for myself."

Luke's temper simmered. "And how did you get here, young lady? You don't have your license yet."

"I have my permit," she said.

"Tell me you didn't drive."

The familiar teenage roll of the eyes and cluck of the mouth. "*Prosze*, don't insult me."

"Elizabeita, I want to know how you got here."

She angled that damn chin again. It always spelled trouble. "A train came out to Fairholm from Grand Central this morning. Then I took a cab here."

"You went into the city by yourself and took a train out here? I've told you a million times not to do something like that alone." Luke's voice had risen several decibel levels and he felt his face flush; he was going to kill her.

"Kids my age do that. I'm not a baby."

Setting his coffee down on the counter with a snap, he crossed the room and grasped her shoulders. "Then don't behave like one. I should spank the daylights—"

Her eyes filled.

"Aw, shit, Lizzie."

She raised a slender hand to his cheek. "Your face. It's black-and-blue." She touched the bump on his forehead. "Oh, Lukasz."

He drew her to him, too roughly, and he groaned.

The tears fell. "See, you aren't all right." She fussed with the shirt he'd retrieved from his room. "Let me see."

Quickly, he stayed her hand. "*Nie*." She'd just cry more at the bruises. He turned to Joe and Suzanna, who were watching the scene with open-mouthed interest. "I need to talk to her alone. Then we have to get her back to Queens."

Joe bit back a grin. "Good luck."

Luke put his hand on Lizzie's neck and guided her down the hall. She leaned into him, sniffling. When they reached the living room, they sat down on the couch. Holding her close, he studied the flowers on the sideboard facing them, near the pictures Suzanna had displayed there. He was struggling for calm; his baby sister taking chances was not acceptable. "Lizzie, you can't do things like this. You could compromise our operation by coming out here." He brushed a hand down her hair. "Worse, baby, you could have walked into a dangerous situation."

She buried her head in his shoulder. "I know. I'm sorry. I just worry about you so much. I'd die if something happened to you."

"Honey, nothing's going to happen to me."

"Bullshit. You're hurt."

"Watch your mouth."

"I'm not stupid. I know you could get killed on any assignment. We all know it. We live in fear of it happening."

That shut Luke up. And forced him to admit to himself what his sisters and mother went through because of his profession. Could his work possibly be worth that torment? His family was the most important thing in the world to him. He pulled Lizzie closer. "Honey, you can't seek me out on jobs."

"I know. I was wrong." Lizzie sighed and settled into him. After a while, her pluckiness returned, and she sat up and scanned the room. "This is a nice place. Who owns it?"

"Nobody you need to concern yourself with."

She stood, wandered to the window, then to the sideboard. Luke let her go because he knew the squirt wouldn't rest until she satisfied her curiosity. She bent over to smell the flowers. "These are pretty. I like—" Her gaze dropped to the photos. She frowned. Picked one up. "Um, Luke, I've seen this lady before."

"What are you talking about?"

She looked up from the picture and turned it around to face him. The photo was of Suzanna and Brenda, arms linked, smiling at the camera.

"I've seen her before."

"Yeah, baby, you have. Just now, in the kitchen."

"No, Lukasz, not the blonde. The other one."

STILL stunned, Suzanna sat in the front seat of Joe's sedan as they drove to Brenda's. Luke sprawled in the back, staring pensively out the window. A heavy fog of tension filled the air.

I don't believe it, Suzanna had told Joe and Luke when

she'd listened to Elizabeita's story about seeing Brenda in the restaurant.

I have a bad feeling about this, Joe had said. *Somebody downloaded Josie's picture off the Internet and it was found in a Connecticut diner this past week. Then Luke's sister recognizes Brenda from a diner in Queens. Are you sure you haven't suspected anything, Suzanna?*

No, of course not. I know Brenda wouldn't . . . what do you expect her to do, anyway?

She's a newspaper reporter, Luke had said. *She could use this in a number of ways. And who's Josie?*

I'll explain in the car. We're going to Brenda's now. Kelsey can stay with your sister. . . .

Listening to Josie's tragic story on the trip over, Suzanna's heart broke at Joe's roughly uttered words. It was worse than hearing the details the first time, because now she loved this man, heard the nuances of his sorrow, and felt his pain deeply. All she could think to do was grasp his arm gently in silent support.

When Joe finished, Luke settled his hand on Joe's shoulder. *I'm sorry. Now I can see why all this is so . . . vital to you.*

They swerved into the driveway of Brenda's condo. Luke and Joe bolted out of the car in seconds. Suzanna hurried up the walkway behind them.

Joe was already ringing the bell when she caught up. He and Luke flanked the door. Both were dressed in jeans and nylon fleece jackets. Both wore somber expressions.

No one answered the bell.

Luke nodded to the left. "That's her car, right?"

"Yes." Suzanna's mouth was dry with worry. She stuffed her hands into the green blazer she wore with jeans and a yellow blouse.

"Does she date? Would she be out with someone?"

"I don't know. Kelsey and I are her close friends. Other than some people in New York."

Luke scowled. "New York?" He punched the bell this time.

"She worked for the *Times.* She quit four years ago."

"She was fired for drinking, Suzanna." Joe's voice was grave. "And screwing up a story."

"*What?*"

Joe stared at her. "I had her investigated after she recognized me."

"The *Times*?" Luke said. "She could sell them an exposé on us."

"No, I don't believe it."

Running a hand through his hair, Joe scowled. "She's not answering."

"I'm worried." Suzanna thought for a second. "I have a key."

"Use it." This from Luke.

"We can't just walk in."

Joe grasped her arms. "Sweetheart, if she is here and not answering, something could be wrong. And if she's innocent, she's got nothing to hide. Open the door."

After a moment, Suzanna inserted the key in the lock. Joe and Luke led the way in. "Where would she be?"

"She likes the view from the den in the back."

They found Brenda there.

Sprawled on the couch.

Passed out.

"Oh, no, she's ill."

Joe and Luke stood back as Suzanna rushed to her friend. As she squatted down, her knee knocked something. She picked it up. It was a bottle of vodka. An empty bottle.

Luke followed her and knelt down. He lifted Brenda's wrist, then let it fall back limply. "She's drunk. You can't smell it on her because it's vodka, but I've seen my share of people passed out."

"I . . . I didn't know she had a drinking problem," Suzanna said.

Gently placing his hand on Suzanna's arm, Luke drew her up. "I'm sorry, Suzanna."

When she turned around, Suzanna saw Joe approach the desk. He stared at the notes spread across the surface, then at the computer screen. The machine was on. "Son of a bitch," he whispered, and dropped onto the chair, as if he needed support.

Suzanna and Luke crossed to him.

Joe clicked to the beginning of the document.

It said, *Notes for Under Cover/Above the Law.*

Suzanna read it and gasped.

"It's about our operation," Luke said tightly.

Joe scrolled down. They read over his shoulder: *Section 1: The Stark Statistics: school shootings in America.* Brenda's notes summarized the past shootings and the findings of the various agencies.

The room was deathly quiet, except for the hum of the computer and a soft snore from Brenda. Farther down. *Section 2: The Precipitating Event: Josie Callahan was an honor student. . . .*

"Oh, God," Joe said simply. "Ruthie, the kids, Al. . . ." He looked up at Suzanna. "She knows it all."

Suzanna's hand gripped his shoulder and she leaned into him. "Joe, I'm so sorry."

He turned back to the computer. They read on.

Section 3: The Plan of Action: Modern . . . school . . . typical problems . . . High school principal Suzanna Quinn. . . .

Joe said, "Goddamned son of a bitch." He reached up and covered Suzanna's hand with his.

She froze as she read on.

Carson's victimization. His disgrace. His suicide.

It couldn't be. Suzanna didn't believe what was before her in black and white.

"Sweetheart, are you all right?" Joe had risen and circled his arm around her.

"I . . . I never told her any of this. How does she know?" She grabbed onto Joe. "What is she going to do with this?"

He drew her close. "Use it for an article."

Luke had taken Joe's place at the computer. "More like a book," he said scrolling though. "We're in here, Joe."

They turned back to the screen. *Section 4: Enter Starsky and Hutch.* "Who the hell are they?" Luke asked, and on the heels of that, "Jesus Christ! She got my transcript and file from high school? And. . . ." This time Luke stilled, his hands hovering above the keyboard.

Joe bent over for a closer look. "What the hell . . . your father. . . ."

Suzanna read, too.

"I let him down," Luke said, clearing his throat. "How does she *know* about it? What I felt about him?"

Placing his hand on Luke's shoulder this time, Joe squeezed tightly, then moved away and began to pace. Suzanna turned and watched him. His agent mask was in place, but his body vibrated with anger. She was just about to speak when Luke said, "Holy Mother of God."

"What now?" Joe whirled around.

"You'd better come and read this." Luke's voice was strangely gentle.

"I don't want to read any more."

"You have to see this, Joe."

Joe crossed to him. Luke got up. "Sit down."

At the ominous tone, Joe sat. Luke stood behind him with Suzanna, and they all focused on the screen.

It read, *Section 5: The Juicy Details: All four adults—paired up. "Sex and the Secret Service" . . . the pièce de résistance: the commune where little Joe and Ruthie were brought up.*

The letters began to squirm as Suzanna read further. Commune . . . parents . . . sex at an early age . . . rites of passage . . . escaped when fourteen . . . does Al Callahan know? She remembered Joe's words when she saw Webster's web site.

Horrible things happen to young boys.

Suzanna's stomach turned sour. She couldn't begin to fathom what the story before her meant in real terms, the horror the man she loved had gone through. "Joe," she said simply, and her hand joined Luke's on his shoulder. They flanked him, as if to protect him somehow from this obscenity.

He was deathly still, staring at the screen. Then he threw back his chair, stood, and, in one violent motion, swept the monitor and computer off Brenda's desk. The equipment crashed to the floor. The sound of glass shattering was deafening. Electrical sparks sizzled out.

From the couch, Suzanna heard a slurred, "What the hell?"

Brenda had roused at the noise.

Joe whirled around and stalked to her. "Do you have any idea what revealing this information would do to my sister? To her kids and husband?"

Sitting now, Brenda just stared up at him, bleary-eyed.

He bent over and grabbed her shoulders. "And to Suzanna? Nobody knows about her father. She doesn't *want* anybody to know about him." He shook her hard. "And what gives you the right to toy with Luke's psyche?"

Luke flew across the room and grabbed Joe's arm. "Joe, don't. She's not worth it."

Joe's fingers bit into Brenda so that she cried out. "What kind of a fucking monster are you?"

"Joe," Luke said harshly, "this isn't you. Let her go."

Finally Joe stepped back. Suzanna saw that his face was pale and he was shaking. He stared at Luke as if he didn't recognize him. Luke didn't release his arm. After a moment, Joe shrugged him off, turned, and strode out of the room.

Suzanna said, "Go after him, Luke. I have some business to take care of here."

When Luke left, too, Suzanna crossed her arms over her chest and stared hard at the woman who had been her best friend for more than twenty years. "You'll have to explain this to me, Brenda. You'll have to tell me how you could even consider using that man's horrific suffering, Luke's insecurities, and my father's godforsaken life to promote your career." She gave her a scathing look. "Have you really turned into Benedict Arnold?"

BRENDA stared at the carnage before her—the computer in a broken heap on the floor, the desk chair upended, the empty vodka bottle. The stench of stale tobacco stung her nostrils; worse was the look of disappointment on Suzanna's face. Brenda remembered a statement one of the counselors in rehab had made: You'll know when you've hit bottom.

Brenda knew.

Not letting her shrink from it, Suzanna crossed the room to stand in front of her. "I asked you a question, Brenda. I'd like an answer." The anger and confusion in Suzanna's tone,

Brenda could deal with. The hurt and betrayal on her face were harder to take. *Was* Brenda being a Benedict Arnold?

"I have reasons." Though right now, the liquor's haze made her thoughts fuzzy. She could see the rationale, like the snowy picture on a TV screen, but it wouldn't come into focus. "I need some coffee. And a cigarette."

Bending over, Suzanna scooped up the bottle and held it out. "You're an alcoholic."

She thought of a thousand excuses—the ones she'd been giving herself since she came back to Fairholm and started drinking again. "I am."

"Why didn't you tell me? I could have helped you. I would have stood by you when you *got* help from professionals."

"I went to rehab. After I lost the *Times* job."

Suzanna cocked her head. "You said you were on a cross-country trip. I thought it was odd. You were gone for what . . . two months?"

"Sixty-five days." Brenda stood, and the world wavered. Suzanna became a blur of green and yellow. "I need some coffee."

Her friend didn't offer to fix it for her. Mother hen was mad at her little chick.

"Fuck it," Brenda said, and headed to the kitchen.

Suzanna followed her. At least she let Brenda get the coffee on, though it took several tries; grounds spilled from the tablespoon every time she transferred them to the pot.

Then Suzanna asked, "Do you have any idea how many lives you'll endanger, how many teenagers will die, if you stop the Secret Service's operation?"

Turning around, Brenda anchored her hands on the edge of the counter. Her slacks and sweater were wrinkled, and her mouth felt like day-old fuzz. She studied Suzanna; even overwrought, the woman was fresh as a spring flower. "Joe Stonehouse has gotten to you, Suzanna. What you're saying is pretty melodramatic."

"Is it? Do you know what they've accomplished already, not just in my school, but in the others they've targeted?"

"No, they wouldn't share that with me," she said bitterly.

"Couldn't find it in your research? Along with what happened to Josie, and how Joe and Ruth were raised? With Luke's problems with his father? Weren't there any *juicy details* like the two agents sleeping with the women of Fairholm—which, by the way, isn't true about Kelsey and Luke." Suzanna's color heightened. "In addition to the danger you'll put schoolchildren in, do you have any idea how many other lives you'll ruin by this tawdry exposé?"

Brenda turned back to the coffee, mostly to avoid Suzanna's blistering gaze. "Stop overdramatizing this." Jittery, she poured coffee; it sloshed over her hand, and she winced. Then she turned around. She took several sips of the hot brew, and it began to clear the fog in her brain.

Suzanna said, "I don't believe you can do this."

"You don't know me, Suzanna."

"How can you say that? I've been your best friend since we were twenty years old."

Feeling even more shaky, Brenda crossed to the table and sat down. "But you don't know the real me. Who I am now, at least."

Suzanna poured coffee for herself; when she faced Brenda, her expression was anguished. "I know you well enough to believe you can't live with the knowledge that you prevented Joe and his agency from stopping kids who bring guns to school." Her voice cracked. "Brend, Josh could have been a victim if Joe and Luke weren't here. You love him like a son."

"I don't believe they're doing that much good."

"You don't want to believe it. But, in any case, think about the other lives you'll ruin. The story of Joe and Ruth's upbringing made public could destroy his sister and her two kids. And Kelsey will never teach again if it becomes public knowledge in a national best-selling book that she was involved with a boy she thought was a student. Luke's career and Joe's could be over if their undercover operation is exposed. That job is Joe's life."

"What about *my* life? This story is my way back to the top of journalism. With a book like this published, I could work at any newspaper in the country."

"At what cost?"

"Conrad always said that freedom of the press often hurts people," Brenda tossed back angrily.

"Would Conrad agree with your plans?"

"Of course."

"That's a lie. If you do this obscene thing, at least admit that you're sacrificing your integrity. Conrad was for freedom of speech, not destroying people. He loved you like a daughter and taught you better than this. If he was alive, he'd be ashamed of you."

"That's cruel."

"No. It's what you need to hear." Suzanna strode to her, sat down at the table, and took her hand. "I'm not going to stand by and let you make this mistake, hurt all these people, without fighting to stop you." She squeezed Brenda's hand. "I know you, Brend. I know the real you. Inside, you'll never be able to handle this. It will eat at you. You'll spend your life drinking and smoking and partying to forget."

"You're just saying that to convince me not to hurt Joe."

"I love Joe. But I love you, too. I'd do anything to protect both of you." Her eyes brimmed with unshed tears. "Please don't do this to yourself. To Joe and his family. To Luke and Kelsey. To all those kids the Secret Service can help."

"What about you? What about the stuff on your father?"

Suzanna swallowed hard. "I don't care if you use that. I'll give you all the details—an insider's story. Maybe you can write an article or something without including the Secret Service project. But please don't shut down STAT. . . ." Her voice broke off. "You're better than this, Brenda. I know you are."

Brenda just shook her head.

Suzanna stood then. "I'm leaving. For what it's worth, I have faith in you. I don't think you'll go through with this."

Brenda heard Suzanna in the foyer, heard the door open and close. Tapping out a cigarette from the pack on the table, she brought it to her lips. It took three tries to get the lighter to work, two more to get the cigarette lit. As she inhaled the smoke, her nerves began to soothe. Several streams curled in the air like a lazy fog.

Suzanna was wrong about her.

But for one brief minute, she wished like hell she was the woman Suzanna thought she was.

JOE'S house on Milburn Avenue was dark when Suzanna pulled up to it; she'd driven over in her own car after she'd called Luke from outside of Brenda's to come and get her.

Luke had been like a panther ready to spring when he'd picked her up; Kelsey said he'd been prowling the house, not talking to her or Elizabeita, who was waiting for one of her sisters come out and take her back to Queens. Joe had called in, said he was at home, and asked not to be disturbed unless they needed him.

Afraid Joe might refuse to answer the door, she'd gotten Luke's keys and let herself into their house. The formerly cozy rooms were cold and lifeless. She made her way back to Joe's den. She'd just approached the doorway, and was able to make out his silhouette, when he leaped off the chair and crouched before her. He held his gun trained on her.

"Joe, it's me, Suzanna."

His body sagged. He sank back into the chair and said, "Don't you know it's dangerous to creep up on a government agent?"

Determined, she stepped farther into the room and switched on a small light. "I'll take my chances."

"You shouldn't be here."

"You wouldn't hurt me."

His laugh was brittle. "I've done nothing *but* hurt you, Suzanna, since I came to Fairholm."

Edging toward him, taking in the manhattan next to the gun he'd laid on the table, she reached the chair and dropped onto the floor at his feet. He stared past her shoulder. She picked up his hand. "Joe."

He swallowed hard. Cast in shadows, his face was blank. A bristly growth of beard covered his jaw, and his blue striped shirt and jeans were rumpled. But she could tell by the stiffness in his body that the agent was back. "It's my fault," he told her in a gravelly voice.

"What is?"

"That Brenda Way got as far as she did with her deception. If I hadn't been so caught up in you, I might have seen this coming. I knew I couldn't trust Brenda. But she was your friend. You trusted her. And I didn't *want* to believe she'd do anything harmful." After a moment, he added, "But there were signs."

"What signs?"

"Her asking to sit in on meetings. Her constant questions." He looked at Suzanna for the first time. His green eyes were like ice. "She pumped you, didn't she?"

"I guess." Suzanna ran a hand through her hair, sat back on her legs, and peered up at him. "I thought she was concerned for my welfare." Suzanna hesitated. "If anything, it's my fault, Joe. I let it slip about your niece. She must have found out you took me to Connecticut; then she went to find Ruth . . . I don't know how she got the rest."

"A private investigator. I saw his name in the information on her desk." He drew in a deep breath. "When she first recognized who I was, I should have aborted the operation at Fairholm."

"Why didn't you?"

"Pride. Ego, maybe. Fairholm High School had been targeted and needed us. Oh, I told myself I could control her. But I didn't. She got the *juicy details* on all of us." He shook his head. "Poor Luke. And Kelsey. They're just kids, really. This will hurt both their careers."

"I'm so sorry."

"And you, sweetheart." Against his will—she could tell—he lifted his hand to caress her cheek. "She'll use the information on your father. I know how you hate that being out in the open."

Taking advantage of his action, she grasped his hand. Kissed his palm. "I can survive that. I'm mostly worried about Ruth and you, and the details she uncovered about your background."

Joe's jaw hardened like granite. Through gritted teeth, he said, "You know, Ruthie and I never talk about it."

Suzanna remembered Ruth's words, *We never talk about how we grew up.*

"Does Al know, Joe?"

He nodded.

"Thank God."

"But the kids don't. Honestly, I'm not sure they can survive this blow. After losing Josie, anything could push them all off the deep end." His hand gripped hers—unconsciously, she guessed. "I don't know what to do."

"I tried to talk Brenda out of writing the book."

"What did she say?"

"Not much. I still can't believe it. . . ." Her voice cracked. She put her head down on his knees. "I'm so sorry."

His hand smoothed her hair. "Shh, it's not your fault."

"Yes, it is. Like you said, if I hadn't fallen in love with you, maybe I could have seen the signs, too." She sniffled; she wanted to offer him comfort, not take it. But she felt so bad.

"Come here." He drew her onto his lap, hugging her close to his chest. The man peeked out of the agent. "It's not your fault." He kissed her forehead. "Someone you love tricked you. Like I did, initially."

She grasped his shirt and burrowed into him. He held on to her. Occasionally he sipped his drink, brushed a hand down her arm, down her back.

After a long time, she asked, "Do you want to tell me about it?"

His chest heaved with emotion. "Not much to say. I've tried to block out those times, suppress them. The details, at least."

"How old were you?"

"I was ten and Ruthie was six when we went to live there. The . . . sex stuff started soon after."

Tears seeped from her eyes. "Oh, Joe."

"It was scary, mostly, foreign and unpleasant." He cleared his throat. "I vividly remember begging my mother and father to stop the whole thing, at least to leave Ruthie out of it. Other than that, I can't recall the details. The counselors said that was probably for the best."

"Counselors?"

"Ruthie and I got away—far away—after four years. When the authorities found us, we were put in foster care. They were good people and got us therapy. When I turned eighteen, I took Ruthie and supported us both. I got us more counseling; I think it helped."

"How did you go to college? How did you live?"

"We worked jobs, got scholarships. At least we had each other." He smiled. "I remember when she met Al at college in California. He fell hard for her, and followed her around like a puppy. She rejected him, of course, like she did all men for a long time. But he eventually coaxed her to tell him why, then they got some counseling together on campus; she married him before they graduated."

"What about you?"

"I was one of the few who went into the Secret Service right out of college. I liked the discipline of it. Especially the undercover work, being somebody I wasn't."

"What about women?"

"It was tough at first, but I compartmentalized a lot. I also got more counseling in the agency. The commune thing came up. They helped me." He smiled against her hair. "Not till you did I realize how much I held back, though."

"You held back with me?" The thought hurt. She'd had no inhibitions with him.

"No, love, you're the first woman I *didn't* hold back with."

"Then don't start now, Joe."

"What do you mean?"

"Don't cut me out."

"We're almost done here."

"I know. I don't care. Let me have what time is left."

"Ah, Suzie Q."

She sat up and took his face in her hands. "Please, don't end it now. Wait till you leave. Let us be together for a little while longer."

He brushed back her hair. "I can't deny you. I can't deny myself."

Sliding off his lap, she stood and reached out her hand. "Come to bed, Joe. Let me erase the bad memories tonight."

"All right." He climbed out of the chair, slid his hand into hers, and let her lead him upstairs.

Where she worshipped him. There was no other word to describe her ministrations. Tenderly, she eased off his shirt, jeans, shoes, and socks. When he tried to undress her, she whispered, "No, just let me."

He lay down on the bed. She shed her clothes, never unlocking her gaze from his, then joined him on the mattress. Her mouth found him then—his chest, his stomach. When she nuzzled lower, he arched off the bed. "I want you," she said as she caressed him boldly. "I need you," she repeated as she loved him with her mouth. "I love you, Joe," she said as she took him inside her. "I love you."

Tears clogged her throat and sprang from her eyes as she brought him to a shattering climax. It was only when she sat up and raised her hands to his face, that she realized his cheeks were wet, too.

TWENTY-SIX

Monday, April 23
5 A.M.

LUKE rolled over in his bed and buried his head in the pillows, trying to block out the noise that had awakened him. He'd been up late, thinking about his relationship with Kelsey, wondering if they could get over her hot button about trust, thinking about the fact that even if they could, there was the whole thing about his work undercover, his lifestyle, and the danger he routinely faced. Consequently, he'd gotten nowhere in his ruminations and lost a lot of sleep.

The noise continued, then he realized his phone was ringing. Blindly, he groped along the nightstand, where he had dropped his cell phone. "'ello."

"Luke?"

"Yeah."

"It's Ben."

Alert, Luke flipped over, checked the clock through gritty eyes, and struggled to sit up. "Jesus, buddy, it's five in the morning." No answer. "You okay?"

"Yeah. No."

"Well, that's definite."

"I'm cool. It's not me."

"What's got you up with the birds, then?"

"Smurf just called me." Ben's voice quavered. "His parents stayed in Hilton Head, and sent him and his sister on home yesterday, alone."

"What the fuck. . . ." Luke shook his head. "Parents."

A long pause. "His sister said she didn't want to be with her dumb brother, so she'd be bunking at a friend's house. Smurf stayed there alone last night."

"And?" Luke slid out of bed and crossed to the dresser. He pulled out a cigarette and lit one. It helped jump-start his brain.

"Smurf sounded like he was, I dunno, depressed. You know the way I sounded, before. Even edgy, maybe. He said something about going back to school today, and how the kids weren't going to bully him anymore. He told me he was one of Cassius's soldiers now, and could do something about how they mocked him."

Cassius's soldiers. A reference to the Pipe Bomb Builders instant message Luke had intercepted.

"He, um, Jesus, Luke, I probably shouldn't be telling you this, but it's not right."

"What's not right? Tell me, Ben." There was authority in Luke's tone. He knew kids responded to that unconsciously.

"Oh, hell. He told me not to go to school today. That I. . . ." Again Ben stopped.

Luke gripped the phone. "Ben, this isn't a little thing. Smurf might need help."

"I know. That's what I thought. Smurf said I could get hurt if I went to school today."

"Holy shit!"

"Maybe your uncle can do something. Like he did for me."

"He can. Don't go to school today."

"Okay, I'll call Morgan and tell her, too."

"I gotta go."

"Luke?"

"Yeah?" He was out the door and on his way to Joe's bedroom.

"What if it's nothing? What if he's just blowing smoke up my ass?"

"Then we jumped the gun. But it's better to be safe than sorry."

"You sound like a cop."

"You tryin' to insult me, buddy?"

Ben laughed.

"Now stay put. I'll be in touch."

5:10 A.M.

THERE was pounding on his door.

Joe reached for Suzanna, then remembered she'd slept at home last night because Josh was back from Italy. She'd also said something about an early start to her day.

"Joe, wake up."

Rolling over, he came awake immediately. He bounded out of bed and crossed to the door. When he pulled it open, he found Luke in the hall, dressed only in boxers, like Joe himself.

"What's going on?"

Luke held up his cell phone. "Ben Franzi just phoned me. He said Smurf called him this morning and told him not to go to school today. That he could get hurt if he went."

"Oh, fuck."

"Joe—"

"Get dressed. This is serious. We'll head to Smurf's. You can fill me in on the way." Then he added, "Bring your gun, Luke."

In five minutes, they sped toward the outskirts of town, both wearing jeans with oversize shirts that concealed their weapons. Joe listened attentively to Luke's story for a few minutes, then said, "Suzanna always goes in early. Get her on the phone. Tell her not to go to school." He was good at tamping down his feelings, but the fear was struggling to get out now like an emotional jack-in-the-box.

Luke punched in Suzanna's number. Joe waited. The phone must have rung several times.

"No answer."

Joe glanced at the dashboard clock. "It's only 5:30. Where the hell is she? Try her cell phone."

While Luke followed his instruction, Joe gripped the wheel. Maybe she was in the shower. He wouldn't panic. He needed to keep sane and think about how to handle Smurf. Jesus Christ, what was the kid up to?

"No answer on her cell." He thought for a minute. "I'm gonna call Kelsey. Just in case *she* decides to go in early, too."

When there was no answer at Kelsey's either, both men quieted. They didn't discuss what this meant.

Luke glanced out the window. "We're almost at Smurf's. Should I go in by myself? We could keep our cover that way."

"We'll try to maintain our cover as best we can, Luke, but I have a gut feeling about this, and I'm not taking any chances. We'll both go in." Joe swerved into Smurf's drive-way. The house sprawled, eerily isolated, on the outskirts of town. The just-beginning dawn bathed the area in an amber glow. It looked as peaceful as a church. Joe grabbed Luke's arm before they left the car. "Promise me, Luke. No heroics."

Staring at Joe, Luke said, "I promise. I learned a lot from you this time around, Unc. I'll go by the book."

They exited the car and took the porch stairs two at a time; Joe's spine prickled and his heart was a steady thump in his chest. He just had a hunch about this one. As he rang the bell, he prayed, *Please, let us be on time.*

No answer. He rang again. Still no sign of life. After four tries, he said, "Okay, use that photographic memory of yours, kid. Tell me the floor plan."

"Smurf's bedroom is in the back left-hand corner of the house. First floor. Off it, there's a hallway with a bathroom; there was a locked door to the left of the john. At the end of the hall was a private entrance."

"Let's go." They headed around back, down a slate pathway rimmed with spring flowers. When they reached the side of the house, Luke said, "Shit."

"What?"

"There's a light on in that locked room."

Joe opted for the back door first. It was ajar, as if some-one had left in a hurry; he knocked on it anyway.

Luke called out, "Smurf." No answer. "Hey, Smurfy boy, it's me, Luke." Again, no answer.

They inched their way inside and caught sight of a door open down the hall. "Keep your gun accessible, but out of sight," Joe said as they crept down the corridor.

The room was empty.

Joe scanned the area. There were tables along one wall, and shelves above them. On the corkboard next to the shelves were diagrams. Below was a desk. Luke followed Joe across the room. Soberly, they studied the contents of the shelves. Bleach. A large Pyrex container. Potassium chloride. The diagrams next to the stuff were complex enough for the U.S. Defense Department. On one of the tables sat a hot plate, a hydrometer, and some containers. Joe picked up a sheaf of papers. The heading read, "Making Plastic Explosives from Bleach." There were two pages of directions. Joe flipped the page. A third sheet was titled "Igniters" and listed CO^2 bombs, paint bombs, dynamite, firebombs, and two dozen or so other kinds of homemade explosives. "Let's go," Joe said, turning and sprinting out of the room.

6 A.M.

LUKE tapped his fingers on the steering wheel as they sped to the high school. He was driving carefully but at an illegal speed; Joe was on the phone.

After trying both Suzanna and Kelsey again—still no an-swer—Joe called the police. "Cordon off the entire perime-ter of the high school and administration building," Joe told Caruso. "Don't let any students, buses, or teachers on the school grounds." He waited. "Yes, I have reason to believe there are bombs on the premises. We'll need the bomb squad, too, but I'll call down there myself." After he gave the squad instructions and called Ross Maloney, the superintendent, Joe tried Suzanna's cell again, and swore like a sailor when there was no answer. Then he punched in Kelsey's number.

Taking in a deep breath, he waited, and said finally, "Neither is answering."

"Fuck."

"Maybe they went out to breakfast together."

"I think—" Luke's cell phone rang. They were almost to school. He whipped the phone out. *Please, let it be Kelsey or Suzanna.* Adrenaline pumped wildly through him, and his heart clamored with fear. "Ludzecky."

"Luke, it's Ben again. Morgan . . . I called her to tell her not to go to school. There was no answer on her private line. So at six, I went over there. Woke her mother up. Luke, Morgan had a Student Court breakfast meeting with Mrs. Quinn, Ms. Cunningham, Josh, and the rest of the gang."

"*What*?"

"You sound worried."

"I am. I'm with my uncle now. We're headin' over to school. Ben, don't go there."

"I won't go." The boy drew in a breath. "But find Morgy, please."

"I will. I promise."

Joe's face was stony when Luke clicked off. "They're at school, aren't they?"

"Yes. For a freakin' breakfast meeting of the Student Court. Kelsey. Suzanna. Josh. Morgan."

Joe swore again, even more ripely.

Luke stepped on the gas. As he whizzed by the student parking lot, he said, "There's Smurf's car. Should I drive by it?"

"No. Time is of. . . ."

They'd gotten about a hundred yards past the parking lot when Smurf's little Toyota exploded in flames.

Luke felt the vibration as their own vehicle shook. "Holy Mother of God."

"Suzanna and Josh. . . ." Joe's voice cracked, and he white-knuckled the panic strap. "They have to get out."

"Custodians and other teachers come in early, too." He thought for a minute. "Will they have heard the explosion?"

"Not likely. The student parking lot is on the other side of the campus. Suzanna's conference room is buried in the center of the building."

"Damn."

Luke pulled into the first parking lot, and the car screeched to a halt in front of the gym entrance. Some of the lights were on in the building. The gym blazed menacingly. Bolting out of the car, they raced like marathon runners to the entrance and found it unlocked. Once inside, Joe said, "I'll find Suzanna. See if you can locate Smurf. Keep your phone on."

"All right." Luke headed for the gym.

Over his shoulder, Joe called out, "No heroics."

Luke tried every door to the gym. They were locked. He circled around to the Phys Ed offices. The door to the men's office was open. Luke strode inside and accessed the main gym through the teachers' entrance. The huge arena was empty and smelled faintly of disinfectant and sweat. The boys' locker room door was ajar. He hurried through it.

The locker room felt different. There was something about it that pricked Luke's instincts. A chill ran through him, and he checked his gun. Carefully, he crept down the aisles. It was dim and eerie in here at this hour. When he reached the last aisle, he remembered that this was where Smurf's gym locker was, and where, once after class, Webster had stolen all Smurf's clothes. Luke had gotten them back for him.

"Whatcha doin' here, Luke?"

Luke squinted in the semidarkness.

Smurf sat on the floor, dressed in jeans and a *Have a Nice Day* T-shirt.

Surrounding him were several pipe bombs.

In his hands he held a sawed-off shotgun.

6:15 A.M.

JOE burst into Suzanna's office and whipped open the conference room door. Around the table filled with food were Suzanna, Kelsey, Josh, Morgan, another girl, and two other boys.

Calmly, Joe said, "Don't panic, but do exactly as I tell you." He faced Kelsey. "Kelsey, get these students out of the building. Get to your car as fast as you can, and drive off the school grounds. The police are on the perimeter, keeping everybody out."

"What's going—" one of the kids started to ask.

Kelsey grabbed him by the arm. "Don't ask any questions. Let's go." She herded the students out of the office.

Josh stayed behind. "Mom, what about you?"

Suzanna touched his arm. "I'll be along, honey. Now go."

"No, I—"

"Go son," Joe said. "I'll take care of your mother. I promise." Joe pushed the boy out with Kelsey.

Once Josh was gone, Joe turned to Suzanna. "Get on the PA system. Use the code we came up with for an emergency to get everybody out of the building immediately."

Her eyes wide and worried, she glanced after Josh.

"He'll be all right."

Taking a deep breath, she hurried to her office and picked up the PA phone. "I want everyone's attention. This is Mrs. Quinn." Her voice was as steady as a trained government agent's. Joe had never been more proud of her. "There's a gas leak in the building. All students and staff are to exit the premises immediately and to remove themselves from the school campus."

Joe asked, "That'll get everybody out?"

"The teachers and custodians know that's the code for an evacuation emergency. The students will take it at face value, though I don't think there are any kids in the building yet but the Student Court." She came around her desk. "We need to check, anyway." As they reached the corridor, she said, "What happened?"

"I think Jimmy Smurfella has bombs in the building. Bomb experts should be here any minute." He grasped Suzanna by the arm as he led her down the corridor toward the closest exit. "You need to leave now. We'll comb the building."

She clutched at him. "You come, too."

"No."

"I'm not leaving without you."

He expected this. Over her head, he saw Ross Maloney burst through the door with Caruso. "Ross, the police need to sweep the entire building. Meanwhile, get Suzanna and yourself out of here."

"Joe!" She gripped his arm.

Joe faced her. "Trust me, Suzanna." He said to Ross, "Do it." Whipping out his cell phone, he punched in a number. "I have to find Luke."

6:30 A.M.

LUKE sat on the floor across from Smurf, as if they were two kids hiding out for a smoke. He took a pack of cigarettes from his pockets and lit one. His hand had nudged his gun, but he knew that particular weapon wouldn't solve anything now. He had to rely on his wits.

"Those'll kill ya, Luke buddy."

Snorting, Luke pointed to Smurf's shotgun. "Yeah, it seems real important now." After he took a drag, he said, "They know."

Red eyebrows raised. "Whatda they know?"

"That you're in here. With those stupid-ass bombs." That sat silently, lethally close to Luke.

"How did you know I was here?" He nodded to the bombs. "And about them?"

"Somebody called Uncle Joe. I came with him; he thinks I'm safe in the car, but I snuck in to find you." It didn't make a lot of sense, but Smurf didn't catch on. "He's lookin' for you right now, Smurfy boy." Luke took a long drag. "Shit, what are you *doin'* here?"

"Showing them."

"Who?"

"Those dickheads."

"What dickheads?"

"All those dickheads that pick on me." His eyes lighted with something not quite sane. Freckles stood out on his pale complexion. "I'm good at this." He indicated the bombs. "They said I'm not good at nothing." With narrowed eyes, he scanned the locker room. "Especially the jocks. Well, pretty soon there won't be no more gym. And no more lockers to stuff me into." Smurf's tone was that of a little boy who'd decided to take his toys and go home. Except that this game was deadly.

Luke tried to stay calm and nodded to the bombs. "These in the hall lockers, too?"

"Yep. Theirs."

"How'd you get the combinations?"

Smurf looked askance at Luke. "Gimme some credit, Luke. I hacked into the school's computer system."

"How powerful are the bombs, Smurf?"

"I set 'em off in the woods behind the house. One of them brought down a tree," he said proudly. "And one shoulda taken out my car, already."

"You're gonna do some major damage to the school, buddy."

"That's the plan." He seemed to go off somewhere. "What does it matter anyway. The world sucks—terrorists' bombs kill tons of people. Nobody's safe."

"Look, why don't you—"

Luke's cell phone rang, and Smurf jumped, lifting the gun. His eyes widened, and in them Luke saw something wild and irrational.

"It's probably my uncle. Checkin' up on me."

Smurf said, "Go ahead. They can't do nothing anyway. It's all set to go off." He patted the gun. "And I got *this* to keep 'em away from me until it happens."

Luke asked, "The bombs are all set?"

"Yep. Timed to go off. You see the one in the parking lot?"

Luke nodded.

"That was just for demonstration. To show 'em I mean business. Besides, I don't need my car anymore."

The message was clear. Smurf planned to go down with his bombs. Which meant Luke would, too. He thought briefly of Kelsey and all they never got to do together. He pictured his sisters and *Matka*. Like hell! He wasn't going to let this happen without a fight. Luke flicked on the cell phone. He'd have to play this right, use all his smarts and his glib tongue to *end* it. "Hi, Unc."

"Did you find Smurf?"

"Yeah, clock's tickin'."

"Where?"

"Where I was headin'."

"He has bombs, doesn't he?"

"Right on."

"With him?"

"And elsewhere."

"In the school?"

"Uh-huh."

"Get out of there now."

"Can't."

"Fuck, Luke, get out of there!"

Smurf said, "You can go, Luke. I don't wanna hurt *you*."

"You find Ms. C. and Mrs. Q.?"

"Yes. They're safe. We got everybody out."

"What?" Luke pretended alarm. "Who can't you find? Well, you better, Unc. They could get hurt."

"What the hell are you talking about?" Joe sounded confused. "I told you we got Kelsey, Suzanna, and the kids out."

Luke said, "What? Look I'm breakin' up here. I can't hear you no more." And he clicked off the phone.

Smurf said, "What's goin' on? I said you could go."

"Seems like Josh and Morgan left the meeting, Smurf. They're off somewhere in the school lookin' for some old records of the court. Mrs. Quinn and Ms. C. can't find them."

Smurf scowled and whined, "They're not supposed to be here."

Ever the little boy. "Come on, Smurfy. You don't want anything to happen to them."

"Everybody else out?"

Luke shrugged. "Not the people you like."

Glancing up at the PA, Smurf said, "The gas leak."

"Hey, you know Mrs. Quinn and Ms. Cunningham. . . ." She *better* be out of the building. "They're some stubborn broads."

"Your uncle will get them out."

"Maybe. . . ."

"Damn it, why don't you just leave, Luke? I said I don't wanna hurt you."

Luke shook his head. "No can do, buddy. Not with you in this mess."

Smurf looked worried. *Please, God, let him be worried.* There was noise outside.

"See, Smurfy you aren't only gonna take yourself out. You'll take out my uncle, who's done a lotta good at this school. Maybe Morgy and Josh. And two teachers who never did anything but try to help you. You want that?"

"I want to show them."

"You did. You showed them with the parking lot bomb that you're not somebody to be messed with." When Smurf didn't relent, Luke said, "You know, the dickheads who picked on you? They aren't here. The rest of us are. Josh never once teased you. Morgan helped you with your Social Studies. All those bomb guys probably got families." He gave him his best buddy grin. "And me. Didn't I pick you on my team every chance I got, Smurfy boy?"

Slowly, Smurf nodded.

"Come on, buddy. Tell me what to do to stop this." He glanced at the clock. "There's still time, isn't there?"

Smurf was silent for interminable seconds. Finally he said, "Yeah, there's still time."

6:55 A.M.

POLICE lights flashed and blazed in the morning sun. It was a crystal-clear April day when the rest of the scene unfolded. Dr. Joe Stonehouse came out the front of the building first, his arm around a handcuffed Jimmy Smurfella. Next to Stonehouse was his nephew, Luke Ludzecky; no one was sure if the boy had been in on the plan with Smurfella. He wasn't handcuffed, though. Several police officers exited, and then some bomb experts, carrying disarmed weapons. Another Columbine had been averted. From the perimeter, the police officials breathed a sigh of relief and raised their eyes to the sky to thank God.

•   •   •

11 A.M.

KELSEY watched Suzanna rush to the door when she heard the car pull into the driveway. Luke and Joe had been at the police station for four hours, and though Luke had called to say they were fine, both women had worried.

It had been a horrendous morning, one Kelsey never wanted to live through again. She'd never really thought about what a Secret Service agent's life must be like, living on the cusp of danger, courting death with every assignment. It was too much to take in, and she'd just blocked it, prayed for long, soul-searing minutes that Luke and Joe were all right.

After Smurf's surrender, no one was allowed back on school property, not even the high school principal or the superintendent. Searches by bomb-sniffing dogs and police sweeps had been instituted, and there would be no admittance to school today. She and Suzanna had returned to the Quinn home to wait for their men after Joe and Luke had accompanied Smurf to the police station.

Joe came through the door first, and Suzanna threw herself at him. "Are you all right?"

"Yeah, I am." He hugged her close, kissed her hair. His eyes were tired—and sad.

Suzanna held on to him. "Thank God."

Luke followed Joe in. His jaw was scruffy with a beard, his jeans and T-shirt wrinkled; his face, still somewhat battered, was lined with fatigue. He looked like a man who had faced down death, which of course he had. Word had filtered out about the gun and the bombs.

Without hesitation, Luke came directly to her, but his gait was uneven, as if his ribs were bothering him. "Heroes usually get welcomed on their return from battle, woman."

She had to smile. In so many ways, he was a little boy. Clasping his hand around her neck, he pulled her close. Despite all that was between them, she hugged him tightly.

He kissed the top of her head. "There. That's better."

"I. . . ." She almost couldn't speak. "I was so worried." She shuddered when she felt the outline of the gun beneath his shirt.

"I'm fine, honey."

When he drew back, he looked over at Joe and Suzanna.

"How did this happen, Joe?" Suzanna asked as they crossed to the couch and dropped down on it; all the while she clung to him.

Taking a chair, Luke drew Kelsey down on the arm. His hand clamped around her waist. She didn't let go of him, either.

"Little Jimmy Smurfella was making bombs in his spare room," Joe said.

Suzanna sighed. "Was this because of that PBB group?"

"He told the police that's how he got the idea. He stumbled across them on one of the bomb web pages." Joe scrubbed his hands over his face. "All you have to do is go on the Internet and type in *bomb building*, and you get set up with a bunch of sites."

Kelsey shook her head. "Did he say why he did it?"

"To get back at the bullies," Luke answered.

Suzanna moaned. "We didn't do enough for him."

"Sweetheart, he's a troubled young boy. Psychologically, we were dealing with a loose cannon."

"I suppose. I just feel so bad."

Joe pulled her close and kissed her hair. "I feel bad, too."

"What happened when you went in?" Suzanna wanted to know.

Joe deferred to Luke with a glance. Luke told them he'd found Smurf in the locker room. When he described how he'd gotten the boy to surrender, Kelsey stood abruptly.

"Where you goin'?" Luke asked.

She shook her head. "I can't listen to this." The thought of him in so much danger was intolerable. She turned to leave.

Grabbing her shirt, he didn't let her go. "Stay put."

Joe said, "He was a hero, Kelsey. He could have saved his own hide, but instead defused the entire situation." He smiled. "Pardon the pun."

Hands on her hips, she asked incredulously, "Aren't you mad at him for risking his life?"

With the authority of a high-ranking government official, Joe said quietly, "He did his job, Kelsey."

"Besides," Luke added, tugging on Kelsey's arm so she sat back down, "Joe would have done the same thing."

Joe nodded.

Suzanna paled. She asked, "What's going to happen to Smurf now?"

"He's at the police station, waiting for his parents to fly home from Hilton Head. He'll be charged with a laundry list of crimes. I'm not sure after that."

"So your cover's blown," Kelsey said.

"Actually, it's not. At least until Brenda Way does something to expose us." That threat had yet to be *defused*. "Luke thought fast on his feet. He played it smoothly right to the end. The kids, and everybody else, will just think Ben called us, and I worked with the police. Nobody knows Luke talked Smurf down. They just think he snuck into school out of some misguided sense of being a friend."

Kelsey frowned. "The kids will suspect more."

"Maybe." Joe and Luke exchanged a meaningful look. "But it doesn't matter now."

Suzanna stilled. "You're leaving, aren't you?"

Again Joe pulled her close. "Yes, we are. We think we've ferreted out most of the problems. Before we go, we'll do some in-service with the staff, and I'll leave you with directives to implement in the next year or so. But essentially, we've done about all we can at Fairholm."

Suzanna said, "You've done a lot. Webster. Ben. And of course Smurf."

He brushed his knuckles down her cheek. "And Max is better, thanks to you."

"So," Suzanna said bravely, "when will you go?"

"We ought to be able to wrap this up in a week or two."

Kelsey's heart shuddered in her chest. So soon? Her gaze whipped to Luke. He was lying back against the chair, eyes closed.

Joe stood. "Come with me a minute." He drew Suzanna up and out to the kitchen.

"What's that all about?" Kelsey asked.

Luke had opened his eyes. They were muddy with fatigue. "He's leavin', Kel. We're done here. She's tryin' to be brave about it, but she's lost her heart."

Kelsey sighed.

He stood, jammed his hands in his disreputable jeans, and looked down at her. "So, how about you?"

"Me?"

"Yeah, you feel bad that I'm goin'?"

"Even if I did, what difference does it make? There's no future for us."

"There's no future for them, either, but they're not bitin' each other's heads off."

Because she was frustrated and confused, because she was still feeling hollowed out at the danger he'd placed himself in, she snapped at him. "What do you want me to do, Luke? Jump into bed with the hero of the day as a final farewell?"

"Sounds good to me."

"This isn't funny. You could have died in there today." Her voice cracked, and she had to force back the tears.

His shoulders sagged. "Look, I didn't mean it that way. Nothing comes out right around you."

"Unless you have time to plan out a strategy with Joe." She could hear the ice in her voice. But damn it, what did he expect? She asked him.

Wearily, he stared at her. "Nothin', Teach. I don't expect nothin' at all." With that he turned and left Suzanna's house.

TWENTY-SEVEN

WITH a self-effacing smile, Joe stood in front of the high school faculty, custodians, secretaries, cafeteria workers, and bus drivers. "Well, thanks for meeting me here like this."

Several people chuckled. They were a captive audience, and they knew it. But even if they hadn't been required by the district to take these Friday afternoon workshops, most of them would have. The incident with Smurf had spooked them but good—especially after the events of 9/11—and brought home just how dangerous today's schools could be.

Word of Smurf's activities, and Joe's role in stopping the bombing of their building, had spread like wildfire in a drought. The papers had most of the story—except that Joe and Luke were Secret Service agents and that Luke had saved the day. Actually, Joe was given credit for ending the scene without violence.

Over the past week, the district administration had been frenetic, trying to deal with the fallout of Smurf's actions. Suzanna had called an emergency faculty meeting Tuesday morning, sent letters home to parents, and had Q & A sessions with the student body and the community. She'd even gone to see Smurf. He was in juvenile detention until psychiatrists gave their recommendations when his court date came up.

This in-servicing was the last thing for Joe to implement, and then he'd be leaving.

"I'd like to start out with some background on myself and why I was specifically involved with this incident, and with the training you're about to embark on. Though I know most of you, and hopefully my work with our kids speaks for itself, I have some areas of expertise from my previous jobs that can benefit you now. Primarily, my association with the Department of Education in Washington."

Together with the school officials, Joe had decided to stick with this story until they found out what Brenda Way intended to do with her information. She hadn't called or talked to any of them all week; Suzanna had tried to reach her several times, with no luck. They lived in a tense limbo about it, but had to proceed with a plan. There was so much to do.

"During my stint with the DOE, we worked with the government—the Secret Service, mainly—on the Safe School Initiative." *Not really a lie,* he thought ruefully. He held up a copy of the document he'd been partly responsible for creating. "If you'd like to read this, I'll have copies available on Monday. In any case, let me tell you about that study."

He filled them in on the information he'd given Suzanna a few months ago: how they'd interviewed shooters . . . found that profiling was ineffective . . . how they came up with recommendations for effecting safe schools.

Carefully, he omitted the one thing no one was ever to know—their undercover work. Because of Brenda Way, the whole world might find out, but for now, he kept it under wraps, where it belonged, so their good work could continue.

His gaze landed briefly on Suzanna, who sat in the back of the room, her shoulders stiff in her dark pink suit, her mouth grim. She'd suffered over the incident with Smurf, over the subject at hand—her school being at risk—and over the fact that after this weekend, she'd never see Joe again. *Don't think about that.* But deep in his hardened heart, he knew that memories of Suzanna would linger in his mind like a dream you couldn't forget or a scent you couldn't escape.

"Out of all this research," he continued, "and other studies we reviewed, and after meeting with the Board of Education and superintendent, we've come up with a three-pronged approach to make Fairholm High School as safe as it can be. After the incident with Jimmy Smurfella, I know you all realize the importance of having the proper plans in place." Mumbling among the crowd. "Before I introduce all that, are there any questions so far?"

There were a few queries about Smurf, which Joe fielded obliquely; Suzanna had answered most of them earlier in the week.

A young science teacher raised his hand. "We heard you're leaving, Joe. Is that true?"

"Yes, Jeff. I was hired to be an interim crisis counselor until the end of the year, but I've been offered a permanent position in the Department of Ed beginning June one. I'll be leaving a month early. This is my last day."

More mumbling. It was obvious the staff was not happy.

"How about a last question or comment?"

Tom Gannon, the AP Social Studies teacher, stood. "I'd like to say you've done a good job here, Dr. Stonehouse, getting us over the hump of Mr. Riley's suicide and working with our pupils. We also know you were instrumental in solving the Smurf incident without anyone being hurt. Thank you for all that."

The entire staff clapped rousingly.

Stunned, Joe felt an unfamiliar warmth spread through him. Despite its problems, being an educator today carried with it a deep sense of satisfaction. The thought that he'd like to be a part of this faculty permanently snuck up on him like the most cunning of assassins. "Thank you, Mr. Gannon. I'll miss you all."

He saw Suzanna smile at him. He smiled back.

"Now, I'd like to explain our three-pronged approach." He turned to his computer and brought up the first diagram on an overhead screen. In vivid color, using graphics that Luke had constructed, *the Physical Building, Student Orientation*, and *Staff In-service* came up. "These are the areas that need to be addressed. First I'll talk about what we already do right here at Fairholm. Then I'll suggest the things we need to do better." He called up a smiley face—Luke's idea—with a list underneath. "The research shows that small classes, monitoring school grounds access, and an adequate security force are all done well at Fairholm, and coincide with the New York State requirements. Also, our no-back-pack policy, wide, well-lighted hallways, and the clean, kept-up physical building contribute to pride in our school, which in turn makes it a safer school."

He smiled. "Good job. However, we can do more." Quickly Joe outlined the major changes: adjusting the class schedule to have minimum hall traffic; reworking the layout of the cafeteria—for which he'd gotten the grant money; closing off dangerous areas, like a few back hallways and some isolated places around the gym and music suites that were hard to supervise.

These were accepted with murmurs of assent. Grumbles—not many—came when Joe recommended staggering end-of-day dismissal times, closing the campus at lunch, and hiring a security force to monitor the cafeteria. He let them complain a moment, then said, "And last, all teachers and administrators need to supervise the halls between classes and before and after school."

Suzanna watched the man she loved work the crowd and give her staff recommendations that he and the administration had hammered out. She cringed every time she thought of what Smurf had done, and what he'd *almost* done, but for Joe's and Luke's intervention. On top of that, they still didn't know what Brenda was going to do with her information. Brenda's lack of communication was nerve-racking. The threat of exposure hung over their heads like the legendary sword of Damocles, and it was getting harder and harder to wait. In addition to those very practical concerns, it hurt like hell that Brenda had betrayed her.

To avoid thinking about it, she listened as Joe fielded questions, pride swelling her heart as he handled the group well. The staff didn't agree with everything, of course, but they were scared and they were willing to consider what he suggested.

As she watched him, she wondered how she was going to let him go. He would leave Sunday. Never again would he sleep with her, hold her during the night, laugh with her. The knowledge brought tears to her eyes.

I'll be going soon, he'd said.

Do you know when?

Luke and I think another week will do it. It'll take that long to set up a plan we'll leave with you.

She'd smiled because she didn't want to cry. *You'll leave us with a better school, Joe. A safer one. Thank you.*

I appreciate your telling me that, Suzie Q, since you were so against my being here.

She'd leaned over and kissed him on the cheek. *Which is exactly why I'm telling you,* she said lightly, though the nickname almost did her in; she was losing that part of herself when Joe left. She was *Suzie Q* with no one else.

With a heavy heart, she tuned back in to Joe's words. "Let's go over the second part, which is what we already do well with kids. First, despite what happened with Smurf, we *do* listen to them. We have good communication with them and with each other. We've also got a fair discipline policy and consequences spelled out in our handbook according to the state's new Code of Conduct. In place is a solid referral system for troubled kids. And—some researchers think this is the single most important factor in keeping violence out of your school—there are numerous opportunities for kids to spend time with adults during, before, and after school. Again, the incident with Smurf doesn't negate these things. We just need to do more of all that. Even better than we do now." He flipped the screen. "And, incorporate these things."

The list on the screen, Suzanna knew, consisted of recommendations that would have been a hard sell if it hadn't been for last week's incident. She listened to the low, masculine cadence of his voice as he outlined the psychological factors the school had to yet to address. The first was thoroughly investigating *all* complaints of kids, especially bullying.

"We'll also have in place an outline of what teachers can do when they become aware of bullying, and how to preclude it. In our handbook for September will be suggestions for what actions students can and should take if they're being bullied."

Suzanna thought of poor Smurf getting stuffed in lockers and picked on by bigger, macho boys in gym class. The school—Suzanna herself—should have done more. What had happened *could* have been precluded.

Joe continued, "Then there are the risk factors that you need to be aware of."

Lester Wells, the assistant principal, raised his hand. "I read the Secret Service report when it came out. It discourages profiling."

"I'm talking warning signs here, not creating profiles. The DOE compiled general risk factors and imminent ones. All staff needs to be made aware of what to watch for in kids, what to notice and evaluate, then report it so our psychologists can do a threat assessment."

"How is that different from profiling?" Lester asked.

"A threat assessment is after the fact: a teacher sees a number of risk factors in a kid and suggests he be evaluated. In a profile, you're given traits and asked to fit your students into them. The first is an observation. The second is a stereotype."

Finally, Joe got to the last part. "We also need a way for students to report both the problems they're having in school—like bullying—and the suspicions they have about others' violent tendencies and even threats. We have to help kids see they need to tell an adult about these things."

"Sounds like a Nazi state," Mike Wolfe grumbled. He'd been uncooperative and surly since Kelsey had stopped seeing him. It didn't help that the Phys Ed staff had been specifically targeted for training in how to stop the age-old practice of picking on weaker kids in gym class.

Joe looked back to Suzanna. They'd agreed to let her handle this kind of negativity. She stood. "It isn't a Nazi state, Mike. We have to teach kids the difference between being tattletales and taking responsibility for the safety of their school. We'll give them a way to report what's happening to them personally, and an anonymous, safe way to report what they hear about others. As Joe said, out of forty-one cases of school shootings that the Secret Service studied, forty young shooters told other students they were going to do it."

"We aren't psychologists," Wolfe continued, like a dog with a bone.

Joe put in smoothly, "Which is why you'll be in-serviced in these three areas."

Kelsey listened to Mike Wolfe complain about Joe's plan and shook her head. Though the staff knew, of course, that Smurf had built bombs and could have blown up the school, they had no idea their school had been under watch and had been studied for potential violence. They also didn't know that Luke and Joe had very possibly saved lives by their work with kids like Max and Ben. Now they were completing the circle with plans for the future.

Her heart ached as she watched Suzanna and Joe react as a team. Wasn't it obvious to everybody how close they were, how they belonged together? But Joe was leaving this weekend, just as Luke was. Again that empty feeling inside her surfaced. In a few short hours, Luke would be gone.

At least they'd made a truce.

To finish the charade, he'd attended classes all week. In addition, he'd been busy helping Joe develop this plan, but had stayed after school a couple of times to talk to her.

How's the knee? he'd asked.

Better. The bruises?

He touched his brow. *Fit right into my disguise. I told the kids I was goin' back to live with my mother. Uncle Joe finally had enough after this newest fight.*

So it's over?

Yeah, I guess.

It was. Not only had Joe told Kelsey that after a job was finished, the agents were required to leave town and have no contact with anybody in the school, but she'd heard Suzanna and Joe talking about the lifestyle of Secret Service agents. They were always on the move, and were constantly in danger. She didn't think she could live knowing Luke faced down bombers and shooters every day of his life. Add that to his deception, and the hurt feelings her lack of trust had caused, and any kind of future with Luke looked impossible. Neither of them was in any position to make promises.

Deliberately dragging her mind away from Luke, she tried to concentrate on the in-service courses everyone in the building would take. "These will be held every other Friday afternoon, and the kids will be dismissed." Another ripple of murmurs. When Joe had asked her opinion, Kelsey had suggested giving release time for the staff so they'd know the district valued the training. She also suggested they continue the in-service with voluntary courses, and he'd asked her to be on the committee to plan them.

Joe began to wind down. "The three areas of in-servicing are Early Warning Signs and Imminent Risk Factors, Responding to Troublesome Behavior in Students, and a Crisis Response Plan: what students and staff will do if a crisis occurs."

Having heard it all before, Kelsey half-listened. The Secret Service had accomplished what they'd set out to do at Fairholm High School. Too bad she felt like a casualty of their operation. And it could get worse. If Brenda went ahead and published what she'd found out, it could mean more emotional wreckage—and professional consequences—for them all. Kelsey couldn't bear to think about it.

Finally, the meeting ended. She wanted to talk with Suzanna. Though she was still raw, she'd come to truly believe she'd been wrong to blame her friend for her part in their deception; Suzanna had been as much of a victim as she was. And they needed each other now. Turning, she saw Suzanna heading toward the back of the room.

Where Brenda Way leaned against the wall.

AS Suzanna approached her, Brenda felt a sense of loss she'd experienced only once before—when Conrad Schenk had died. That feeling was why she'd come to the high school today, and partly why she'd made the decision she had. As her best friend in the world came closer, Brenda was assaulted by the evidence of Suzanna's suffering—her mouth was a grim slash in her face, and mauve smudges marred the skin beneath her bloodshot eyes.

Defensively, Suzanna crossed her arms over her chest. "Hello, Brenda."

"Hi, Suz." The affectionate term made Suzanna's eyes widen.

Behind her, Kelsey approached them; in the background, teachers milled around. Brenda saw Joe was surrounded by the staff; some also stood back, waiting to speak with Suzanna. Myriad questions had been raised by this meeting. Brenda thought Joe had done a good job with his explanations.

When she reached them, Kelsey touched Suzanna's arm lightly. "What do you want?" Kelsey asked Brenda.

"I'd like to speak with you, Joe, Luke, and Suzanna. Now, if possible."

Suzanna glanced over her shoulder. "I have to be here for a while longer. And Luke's out of the building."

"What's this about?" Kelsey was cool, and obviously angry.

"I'll tell you all at once."

Kelsey agreed to call Luke while Suzanna and Joe met informally with the faculty. It took almost an hour for them all to assemble in Suzanna's office, where Brenda had gone to wait.

When they finally arrived, one after the other, Joe's eyes burned with angry intensity; Luke stood guard behind Kelsey, both looking frustrated; and Suzanna just seemed tired.

"I'll make this quick." Brenda nodded to a box on the floor that she'd dragged in earlier. "That's all the information I gathered on your operation. Files. Reports. Research. Disks. And the hard drive on my computer is ruined," she said—a reference to Joe's smashing her computer—"so there's nothing on there either."

Joe placed a protective hand on Suzanna's shoulder. Luke did the same with Kelsey. "What does this mean?" Joe asked.

"I'm not going to use it." Brenda lifted her chin. "I'm not blowing you in."

Tears came to Suzanna's eyes. "I knew you wouldn't," she said, choking back the emotion.

"You give me too much credit, Suzanna. You always did."

"I don't think so."

Luke asked, "What made you change your mind?"

Wishing like hell for a cigarette, Brenda sank back into her chair. How much could she tell them about Conrad's things—his effects that she'd gotten when he'd died? For some reason, over the past soul-searching week, she'd gone through the boxes. Among them, she'd found copies of his work—incisive, innovative articles and essays, one of which he'd thought might win him a Pulitzer. Right down to the very last, they were scrupulously ethical. But it was mostly perusing the lucrative stock portfolio and rereading the letter he'd left her, which explained that he was making it possible for her to live comfortably and never be forced to do something illegal or unethical for money.

"I gave this a lot of thought." Which was true. "Mostly my decision hinged on what you said about kids being hurt in other schools across the country if your undercover work was exposed." She shrugged, once again feeling the weight of that responsibility. "And from what I hear, Jimmy Smurfella could have blown up the school if our two James Bonds–in–the–flesh hadn't stopped him." She nodded to Joe. "You *are* saving lives. Basically, I couldn't live with the knowledge that I might have precluded that intervention."

"Of course you couldn't." Suzanna was a saint right to the end.

Brenda shook her head at her friend's generosity. "I'm going away," she said, abruptly standing up before she lost it in front of an audience.

"Where?" Suzanna asked.

"The rehab place where I went before." She picked up her purse. "I want to get straight before I decide what I'm going to do."

"What do you mean?"

"I've quit the *Fairholm Gazette*."

"Why?"

Because I sunk the lowest here. "I haven't been happy in this job. I need to try something else."

"Let me go down with you, Brenda. Get you settled in."

Brenda slipped on her shiny brown raincoat. "No, I need to do this alone." Though a major part of her decision to not follow through with the exposé was, indeed, Suzanna,

Brenda wouldn't depend on her now. "When I'm ready to face you, I'll get in touch."

"Brend. . . ." Suzanna stepped forward.

Coat on, Brenda held up her hand. "Don't, Suz." Turning, she headed for the door. Suzanna caught up with her just as she opened it. She tugged Brenda around and hugged her.

The rush of emotion came then, and Brenda couldn't backstop it. She felt like she'd just lost the biggest scoop of her life, and it had nothing to do with a story.

"I'll be here when you get back," Suzanna whispered.

Brenda didn't answer. She just held on to the woman who had stood by her during every single thing she'd ever fucked up. Finally she eased away and walked out the door.

She didn't look back. She couldn't.

KELSEY was in her classroom, gathering up her things, when Luke walked in. He shut the door and faced her. She almost couldn't look at him. Again, he seemed so much older, so professional in pressed designer jeans, a silk T-shirt, and a lightweight taupe blazer which showcased linebacker shoulders. He'd also gotten a haircut. "I came to say good-bye."

Good-bye. The word carved out a hole in her already wounded heart. She dug her hands in the pockets of her red skirt, which she wore with a lacy beige blouse. For good luck, she'd even put on the ruby earrings and bracelet her father had surprised her with when she finished her graduate degree. She'd dressed with care every day this week, knowing Luke would be in her classes.

He'd done well with that, giving her only one or two smoldering looks a day. It was her own reaction—an acute awareness, combined with a deep sense of loss—which had been the problem. Particularly yesterday, when the Psychology kids had given him a party once they heard he wouldn't finish the year at Fairholm and was going back home to live with his mother, maybe get his General Equivalency Diploma.

I have a Master's Degree from Columbia . . . I graduated summa cum laude. . . .

She leaned against the desk, not inviting him to sit. Knowing she had to get through this didn't make it any easier. "When do you leave?"

He yanked up his sleeve and checked a watch she'd never seen before. "My plane takes off in an hour."

For something to do, to stop the scalpel-sharp pain his words caused, she glanced at the clock. "Then you need to get to the airport."

He shrugged boyishly. "I like to live dangerously."

Smiling back, she said, "I know." She studied him and shook her head. "You look so different."

"I am different, Kelsey. I've been tryin' to tell you that." He still clipped his endings, though, and that little boy grin was genuine.

God, she wished she'd known him in another context. Because her yearning for that was so strong, she straightened and moved around the desk, started to clear it, anything to distract herself.

After a moment, he came in close enough for her to smell his spicy aftershave. "Tell me what you're feelin'."

She faced him then, and noticed a little nick from shaving just under his chin. "This whole thing hurts."

"I know, honey."

"Don't call me that, please."

"Why?"

"Like I said, this hurts." She threw back her head and stepped away from him. "Joe told Suzanna that after STAT is finished at a school, the agents can't have any contact with the people there."

He was quiet for a moment, then said, "Yeah, that's the plan."

"So, when you leave today, I'll never see you again."

"Is that what you want?"

"Does it matter?"

"Maybe."

"I don't see how." She had to distance him to get through this. "You work for the government. I was a temporary diversion. That's all."

"If you really think that of me, maybe we don't have anything more to say to each other."

"Luke, neither of us in a position to make promises now. There's so much between us."

"You mean the deception. I thought you understood why that was necessary."

"I do. It still hurts, but I'm working on that with Suzanna. And I'm thinking about seeing a counselor. I have to get some help dealing with my exaggerated need for trust. And I need to figure out how to deal with my father better."

"Well, that's all good." He jammed his hands in his pockets. "So what else is between us?"

"Are you playing dumb? You just acknowledged that when you leave a job, you can have no contact with anyone from a previous assignment. Besides, there's your lifestyle— you're away, undercover all the time."

He studied her, that quick mind, that bright intellect seeing through each obstacle. "That's not all of it, is it?"

She drew in a breath. She owed it to him to tell him the whole truth. "No. You jeopardize your life every single day, Agent Ludzecky. I don't see how I could ever deal with that." She glanced meaningfully at his shoulder. "You've been shot. I saw the scar. You routinely walk into situations where a bomb could explode—like with Smurf—and put your life on the line." She finished, in a raw and ragged voice, "I thought I'd die, waiting to see if you came out of the school alive."

Without warning, he kicked the wastebasket. Papers went flying. "Son of a bitch."

"You know it's all true." Her insides churned. "That's why you're angry."

He said nothing. What was there left to say?

Tears clouded her eyes. Damn, all they needed was a scene. "Please, Luke, just leave." She turned her back on him then, crossed to the open window, and stood staring out. End-of-April weather had transformed Fairholm into a spring paradise of green grass, maple trees, and a rainbow of flowers. Its beauty hurt, as did the pain in Luke's hazel eyes.

He came up behind her. "All right, I'll go. I'm sorry you're so convinced there's no other way."

"Joe and Suzanna can't find another way. He's leaving after this weekend."

"Yeah, well, it's not over till it's over." Tenderly, but with a man's strength, he grasped her shoulders and said, "Go ahead. Get your head on straight about everything. Just remember this." He kissed her hair. "I'll never forget you, Teach."

She felt cold when he stepped away.

Only when she heard the door close did she let the tears come.

HIDDEN Cove, the bed-and-breakfast an hour outside of Fairholm, was an idyllic retreat. The trees had bloomed, and Suzanna could see dogwood blossoms from the window where she stood late Sunday afternoon. A breeze wafted through and made her shiver.

"Cold?" Joe came up behind her. He circled her waist with his arms and nuzzled her neck. She was surrounded by him.

"No."

"This is how I want to remember you. All tousled from my lovemaking, wearing this flimsy, sexy-as-hell slip of a thing."

"This slip of a thing cost a week's pay."

He bit her shoulder. "Hmm. It was worth it."

Purposely, they'd kept the weekend light. They didn't hash out alternatives, didn't speculate on their imminent separation. Instead, they made love, slept, took long walks, and, overall, steeped themselves in each other.

"What time do you have to leave?" she asked.

"In an hour." He tensed. Kissed her hair. "I've got a car coming to take me to the airport."

"I thought I'd drive you."

"I can't do that, Suzanna. I need to say good-bye here."

She nodded.

"Will Josh be home when you get there?"

She snorted. "Yes, with more of a lawyer's interrogation, I'm sure."

Her son had been very adult when she'd told him she was going away for the weekend with Joe. *Hmmm, shouldn't I object to this?* he'd asked teasingly.

Oh, honey, I don't mean to set a bad example, but Joe's leaving Sunday, and I want some time alone with him.

Hey, Mom, I was kidding. Go for it. Then he'd frowned. *I don't know why he has to leave, though.*

The question of the day! And it was time to ask it. She pivoted around, still in his arms.

Joe was wearing only black boxer shorts, and his beard was scratchy. With his disheveled hair and sleepy smile, he looked more like a movie star *playing* a government agent than the real McCoy. She had no idea how she was going to cope when he walked out of her life.

"I need to know a few things."

He scowled.

"Don't worry, I won't fall apart on you." She wouldn't. "Where will you go today?"

"Back to Washington, to file the reports on our Fairholm operation. After the case is closed, I'm going to Ruthie's for a while."

At least he'd be safe. Briefly they'd discussed seeing each other until his next assignment, but how could they explain that to Josh, to her colleagues? His cover was that he had another job. Besides, it would be hell ticking off the days. They had to make a clean break. Better a slicing wound that would heal than reopening one over and over.

"Will you. . . ." She coughed to clear her throat. "Will you go undercover again soon?"

"Sweetheart, don't. You'll just worry."

"I'll worry anyway."

"For a while. If you knew what I was doing every day, you'd worry more." He gripped her shoulders. "I want you to get over me, Suzanna. Get over us."

She bit the inside of her mouth so she wouldn't scream at him, cry and wail like a crazy woman that his request was impossible. Obscene, even. "Will you get over me, Joe? That easily?"

Joe brushed his knuckles down her jaw, wondering how he'd ever survive the loss of her. He studied the way her hair fell around her shoulders and how full her lips were, how the diamond stud winked out from her delicate earlobe. "You know I won't."

"I'm sorry. Let me go a minute." Pulling away, she slipped into the bathroom—to compose herself, he guessed. She was the strongest woman he'd ever met in his life, but ending their relationship was tearing her apart.

It was bound to come, though he'd delayed it as long as he could by keeping her in bed and talking about nothing significant. Not even Josh.

Before Joe had left, he'd managed time alone with the boy. . . .

I won't ask how it went in Italy, Josh. That's private. But do you want to talk about anything with me?

Josh had faced him angrily. *Yeah, I want to know why you're leaving my mother.*

That's between me and her.

I'm not blind. I can tell you care about her. And she's crazy about you. How can you hurt her like this?

I have no choice. My job at Fairholm was only temporary. Your mother and I both knew that. Accepted that.

Things can change.

Some things. Not this.

I don't understand.

I'm sorry. He reached out and squeezed Josh's arm, then handed him a slip of paper. *Here's my cell phone number. If you ever need me, now or when you're at college, just call me.*

Josh's face had reddened, and he'd blurted out, *I want you to stay, too.*

Unable to stop himself, Joe had hugged the boy. It was awkward for them both, but Josh had held on to him, too. And Joe had felt a crushing sensation in his chest. One child had already slipped from his life, and now he was losing another.

He heard Suzanna come out of the bathroom. She smiled bravely at him. "I'm all right. But I have to say one last thing."

"Suzanna. . . ."

She held up her hand. "I have to. I could leave Fairholm, Joe. And come with you."

He was ambushed by the comment. He'd never allowed

his mind to go there, to let it spin out how they could be together. "It's not that simple."

"It is if you let it be."

"Your life is here."

She shook her head. "Not without you. I love you. I can work anywhere."

"But I can't. I don't stay in one place. I'm gone on a job, like now, for months at a time. It's no kind of life for you."

"It would be a better life than one without you in it."

"No. I'd never allow you to live that way. Do you know that the department unofficially recommends that female agents not change their names when they marry, because the union isn't predicted to last more than two years?"

Though she paled at the stark statistic, she said, "Shouldn't this be my choice?"

"No. I won't discuss it further." He touched her throat, fingering the gold chain that lay there. "Now, do you want to spend our final hour together fighting, or. . . ." He glanced to the bed. Prayed she wouldn't argue. Prayed harder that she wouldn't cry. He was strong enough to do this, but only if she cooperated.

Shaking back her hair, she faced him squarely. "Of course I don't want to fight." She took his hand. Led him to the bed and pushed on his shoulders so he sat on the edge. Then, in the pretty blue silk that cost her a week's salary, she knelt in front of him.

And suddenly, he wasn't so sure that he was going to be able to walk away after all.

TWENTY-EIGHT

Four weeks later

"SO," Suzanna said as she sprawled on the weight room floor, stretching, "how'd it go with your father last night?"

Kelsey increased the speed on the treadmill, and though her breathing was labored, she ran faster. She and Suzanna had taken to working out late after school, ever since Luke and Joe had left Fairholm. The physical outlet, combined with the biweekly therapy Kelsey had gotten for the past month, had really helped her, in more ways than one. "Surprisingly good."

"You can tell me, sweetie. I won't criticize him."

"All right." As she filled Suzanna in on the details, Kelsey pictured the scene at her father's condo yesterday when she'd gone down to New Haven to visit him. . . .

"Kelsey," he'd said as he opened the door. "This is unexpected."

Just wait. "I need to talk to you, Daddy."

He cocked his head at her use of the childlike term. "Well, that's good news. Considering you haven't wanted to see me or talk to me for a few months now." He stepped aside and allowed her in.

Removing her coat and taking a chair, she said, "A lot's happened to me lately."

He sat on his expensive couch, in a Polo shirt and tailored pants. His gray hair was a little shorter, and she noticed for the first time that it was beginning to recede. That small sign of age softened her. "Do you want to tell me about it?" he asked.

"Some of it." She lifted her chin. "I've been getting counseling, some professional therapy, really."

His gray eyebrows shot up. Concern darkened his eyes. "Is everything all right?"

"It's getting there. Dad, we need to talk about our relationship."

He stiffened. "Therapy always dredges up uncomfortable things, Kelsey. I'm not sure I want to work through this with you."

His reaction hadn't surprised her. "Well, you've got a choice. You can *work through* this with me and be part of my life, or you can refuse to acknowledge the changes in me and what that means for our relationship, and stay on the fringes of my life."

"I don't like ultimatums, Kelsey Lynne. This sounds remarkably like when you lived with the Quinns instead of coming with me to Yale. When you took their money to go to college because I objected to your choices."

There was something about his tone that made her ask, "Did that hurt you, Dad?"

He just stared at her.

"Did it?"

Slowly, he nodded.

"Well, we need to talk about that."

As he swallowed hard, his face suddenly seemed more lined, older. "I, um. . . ." She'd never once heard him stutter. "I don't want something like that to happen again. Your mother's gone . . . you're really all I have. . . ." He stopped to compose himself.

"You don't want to lose me again."

Again, he nodded.

"Then listen to me. Listen to where I am about things."

"All right."

They'd spent hours together. Some of the time was tearful. Much of it was painful. But before she left, he'd hugged her and told her he wanted—no, *needed*—her in his life, and would try to let her make her own choices. . . .

"Well," Suzanna said, staring up at her from the floor. "That's quite a story."

"I feel freer," Kelsey told her, slowing down on the treadmill. "I knew I carried baggage around about him, but I didn't know how it weighed me down, affected my decisions."

"It took a lot of courage to confront your father. To get to this point in your life."

"I appreciate your support, particularly after how I acted with you about the undercover." Even though she'd apologized to Suzanna about her behavior—the therapy had helped her there, too—she still felt bad about hurting this woman.

"Oh, sweetie, you had a right to be angry at me. I betrayed your trust."

"You had no choice. Besides, I need to keep that kind of thing in perspective. I went overboard about trusting you, anybody. I'm an adult now. Not a kid who needs unconditional trust."

"You've learned a lot in that therapy. I'm so proud of you."

Moved, Kelsey stepped off the treadmill, knelt down in front of Suzanna, and hugged her tightly. "I love you."

"I love you, too. Now let's forget all that; I'm just grateful to have you in my life."

Suzanna *was* grateful; she needed Kelsey now. Because, Kelsey knew, if anyone was suffering more than she was about the aftereffects of the undercover work, it was Suzanna. Her misery was apparent in the lines bracketing her mouth, the slump of her shoulders, and the pervading sense of sadness that surrounded her. Other teachers in the school had approached Kelsey to ask if they could do anything to cheer up the principal. It was one reason Kelsey got Suzanna into exercising more actively, as opposed to just going to yoga class.

They faced each other on the floor. Suzanna said, "Now

that you're on track with your father, what are you going to do about Luke?"

Kelsey sighed. "I haven't heard from him."

"Did you think you would?"

"No. Before he left, he seemed to want something from me that I couldn't give, or wasn't ready to give." She thought for a minute. "I had a feeling the same was true for him."

"What do you think he wanted?"

"A compromise, maybe. To agree to find some way for us to be together."

"Is there one?"

"Maybe."

"Oh, sweetie, if there is, pursue it. I wish Joe and I had a chance. But Joe closed the door completely. *I* couldn't convince *him* to give our relationship a shot. If there is one for you with Luke, go for it."

God, Kelsey wanted to. For weeks, she'd thought about him all the time. She missed his cocky smile, the way his hair caught the sunlight and turned wheat-colored. Lying in her bed, she remembered how he'd slept there when he was hurt, and she could almost smell him. She ached for him—physically, yes, but emotionally, too.

"I've been thinking about it. A lot."

Suzanna let it go then. This was something Kelsey had to do on her own. In companionable silence, they finished working out, left the gym, and started down the corridor to Suzanna's office. But Kelsey couldn't shake thoughts of Luke, and Suzanna's advice.

"Supper?" Suzanna asked. "I don't have any meetings tonight, and Josh is with Heather." She smiled. "Only a few more months until they part."

Josh had chosen Georgetown University for pre-law, and Heather was going to Cornell in pre-med. Graduation was two weeks away, then the summer. Kelsey knew that Josh's departure in August would threaten Suzanna's already fragile control.

Before Kelsey could respond to Suzanna's query about dinner, they heard behind them, "Hey, Ms. C., Mrs. Q." They turned to find Ben Franzi. His hair was dyed midnight blue, and he wore a tank top of the same color with a shiny silver shirt over it.

But his eyes were clear and his heart lighter these days. In class, he was more upbeat. Before Joe left, he'd set Ben up with an outside counselor who'd been a big a hit when Ben discovered the guy was into New Age philosophy.

"Some awesome blond chick was looking for you, Ms. C. I told her where your room was."

Kelsey frowned. "Who?" It was almost 5 P.M., and the last thing she wanted to do now was meet with a student. She wanted . . . she wanted to see Luke. Damn, why had it taken her this long to decide she was ready?

"Never saw her before. She was a hottie, though." He smiled. "Gotta bounce. I just came back to pick up Morgy from a review class." Ben and Morgan were closer than ever, and were off to Northwestern together in the fall, pursuing music and acting, respectively.

"So, what about dinner?" Suzanna asked after Ben left.

Kelsey straightened. "Would you mind if I didn't?"

"No, of course not. Do you have other plans?"

Smiling, she said, "Maybe. You don't happen to have Luke's home address, do you?" She scrunched her nose. "His phone number?"

"Yes, sweetie, I do." Suzanna hugged her. "I know it's the right thing to do, Kel."

After accompanying Suzanna to her office, and another hug for good luck, Kelsey jogged to her classroom. Wearing a red Fairholm High T-shirt and nylon shorts, and smelling like the inside of a gym bag, she wasn't presentable to anybody. Usually, it didn't matter. Since Luke left, she'd taken little interest in her appearance. But maybe she'd go home and change first. No, maybe she'd just call him from school.

She jogged faster. When she reached her room, the door was open; she froze at the sight of what greeted her. Seven blond women—and a baby—were all over her room. Two, sporting Rapunzel's hair, examined the pictures on her desk. Another two, wearing pixie cuts just as thick and blond as the others, read her posters in the back. One—a rope-thick braid dangled down her back—rifled through books, folders, and papers housed on bookshelves. One, with a sleek bob framing her face and cradling the blond baby to her chest, sat at a student desk. And the last—Kelsey thought she recognized that tousled mane—stared out the window.

They were the Ludzecky women. Luke's sisters.

Kelsey's heart began a nervous tattoo in her chest. "Hello," she said for lack of a clever opening.

Each turned, then, as a group, they started toward her. Though they were all of ordinary height and just a little bigger built than Kelsey, when they converged in front of her, she was reminded of statuesque Amazons.

They were, quite simply, gorgeous. All that hair. And with Luke's hazel eyes and thick lashes. When she noted the similarities to their brother, her own eyes clouded. The girls literally surrounded her.

"Geez, who would have thought he'd pick a brunette?" the braided one said.

"I told you." This from Elizabeita, who Kelsey looked to for friendliness, and instead got a frigid stare.

"Well, she doesn't *look* stupid," put in the oldest one as she crossed her arms over her chest. "She must be, though."

"I thought we were going to be nice," the one who looked most like Luke commented. Cat, he'd told her.

"I—" Kelsey began.

The Ludzecky sister with the baby cut her off. "Why should we be nice? After what she did to him."

Two stepped even closer. Kelsey didn't shrink from them, but she wanted to. One plopped her hands on her hips. "Do you have any idea how much you hurt him?"

"He came home drunk last night," the other one said. Kelsey shook her head. These two were identical. Beautifully identical.

"So drunk," the first twin picked up, "that we had to put him to bed; he was still sleeping when we left at noon."

"And he'd been smoking. We could tell!" Elizabeita was horrified.

Kelsey's heart twisted in her chest at how Luke was suffering. She remembered his smiling mouth and mischievous grin.

"He's been surly and snapping. Even to us."

"Or morose and brooding."

Finally, they allowed Kelsey to speak. "Why are you here?"

They exchanged wordless glances. Cat began. "We want you to know the real him. You can't know him if you dumped him."

"I didn't du—"

The comments came like rapid-fire bullets. . . .

"He's paying for my college."

"He came home just to see me in my junior prom dress."

"When Papa died, he was only a teenager, but he did everything."

"He threatened to beat up boys who made me cry."

"He's so nice to *Matka*. Calls her once a week so she won't worry."

"He's—"

"Um . . . in the doorway." This from Cat.

All of them gasped collectively.

Kelsey's head snapped to the side. Sure enough, there he stood, rumpled and worn in denim shorts and a ragged-at-the-sleeves shirt. This was a man with a hangover if she ever saw one. His scruffy beard framed an angry scowl.

Luke watched his sisters circling Kelsey like vultures going in for their prey, and felt his temper spike. His head pounded and his stomach churned from his foolishness last night. He wasn't in the mood for this!

He wouldn't let himself look directly at Kelsey. He'd finally gotten his act together about things, but that didn't mean she had. Instead, he concentrated on his sisters. Whom he was going to kill. Every last one of them. Christ, they even brought little Donuta with them. Stalking over, he said tightly, "I didn't believe *Matka* when she woke me to tell me you'd come here."

Seven chins lifted. "We had to do something," Ana said, holding tightly to the baby.

"We couldn't watch you suffer anymore, Lukasz." Paulie's voice wavered a bit. He took advantage of it.

"*Prosze*! You have no right to *descend* on Kelsey."

"She has no right to make you this unhappy," Elizabeita shot back. "We've never seen you so . . . despondent."

Geez, he had to get them out of here before they told her

everything. He'd been in a black hole of depression, and nothing could pull him out. Not even his long and frequent talks with Joe helped. He'd ended up doing some stupid things even his sisters didn't know about. And he certainly didn't want Kelsey to come to him out of pity. He pointed to the door. "Out, all of you."

"Luke." Cat grabbed his arm. She, of all people, should have known better.

"*Nie*. I'm angry, Cat." He shook her off. "Don't try to placate me."

Knowing him the best, Cat shrugged. "All right, let's go, ladies."

Each one gave Kelsey a last look that would wither Ma Barker, then paraded past Luke. They all touched him—kissed his cheek, patted his arm; he stooped over when Ana went by, and grazed his niece's head. But it was Lizzie who stopped before him and peered up at him with eyes that would bring any man to his knees. Luke felt sorry for all her future victims, all the male saps who would fall for her.

"We were just trying to help." Then the tears came, big, fat crocodile ones that he could never steel himself against.

"I know, baby." He hugged her. "It's all right," he whispered. "Go, now."

"You'll . . . you'll come home, won't you?"

"Yeah." He patted her back. "Now go." Still without looking directly at Kelsey, he ushered Lizzie to the exit, kissed the top of her head, and closed and locked the door.

Then he faced Kelsey. Sweat dampened her skin and her hair was sticking up at all angles, but she had never looked more beautiful. Exposed by the gym shorts, the long expanse of her legs made his breath hitch. "Hi."

The corners of her mouth turned up. "Hi." She nodded to the door. "That's quite a cheering section."

He ran a shaky hand through his hair. "I'm sorry. They—"

"Love you. You're lucky to have them."

"Please, you have no idea what's it's been like." He studied her. There were signs of stress—she was a little thinner, and the skin beneath her eyes was smudged. "You okay?"

"No. You look pretty much the worse for wear yourself."

"Rough night."

Leaning against the desk, she crossed her arms over the thin T-shirt that showed her breasts to perfection. "They've all been rough for me," she told him.

"Me, too. It'll get better," he lied.

She shook her head. "It won't."

He braced himself against a desk. The hell with it. He was tired of waiting. "I'm quitting the Secret Service."

"*What*?"

"The lifestyle sucks." He nodded toward the door. "It's hard on them." He jammed his hands in his pockets. "Anyway, I think I just joined to prove to myself, and my pa maybe, I could be straight." He grinned. "There's no straighter bunch than the U.S. Secret Service."

"You didn't fit in."

"No, so I can't figure out why they begged me to stay."

She smiled. "I can. What will you do, Lukasz?"

He grinned at the name. "I'm going to teach. Computers, maybe."

Her face lit from within. "You'll be a wonderful teacher."

"I hope I'm as good as you." He scanned the room. "You're almost done, right?"

"Two more weeks."

"Have a good end of the year?"

"No." She took a step toward him. "I'm miserable." Another step.

Geez. "Me, too."

"What are we going to do about it?"

He swallowed hard as she reached him. His throat closed up as she placed her hands on his chest, slowly slid them to his neck, and pressed against him, right there in her own classroom. His arms went around her like steel bands. "Kel," he whispered, his voice catching.

"I was wrong about us. It took me a while to get my head on straight, but I finally realized I'd made a big mistake. I've been trying to work up the courage to come and find you." She shook her head, drew away, and held up the paper she still gripped in her hand. "I just got your number from Suzanna. I was going to call you."

"Oh, honey." He sagged into her arms, unable to speak.

She smoothed his hair. "I'm sorry for making you miserable."

Still he could say nothing.

For a long time, she held on, then finally pulled back. "Oh. Luke." She raised her hands to his cheeks. They were wet. "Oh—" She kissed away the moisture. "I'm sorry it took me so long to realize how wrong I was about you. About us."

He met his forehead with hers. "Thank God you did." He took a minute to compose himself, then wiggled his brows. "You can spend the whole night making it up to me." He stepped back and clasped her hand. "I've got to have you. Right now."

Kelsey laughed aloud. "Think you can wait till we get to my house, big guy?"

He didn't let go of her. "Barely, if we hurry." He dragged her to the door.

Again, Kelsey laughed. It was the most beautiful sound in the world.

RIP.

Tear.

Buttons popped.

Shoes flew.

Luke's mouth found Kelsey's ear while her fingers dug into his butt. His hands groped for the hem of her T-shirt. "Put your arms up, baby."

Obeying, she raised her arms over her head. He whipped her shirt up and off. "Oh, God," he said, "Jesus Christ. You're gorgeous. And red lace." With a violent thrust, he melded his lower body to hers. "I'm never gonna last."

Her grin was Eve's, Delilah's.

He lowered his head, licked between her breasts, closed his teeth over a lace-clad nipple and bit gently. She moaned and shut her eyes. "Like it?" he asked roughly.

"Are you kidding? I'm going to explode, I want you so much."

His hands skimmed down her bare arms, seared the tender flesh of the inside of her biceps. Again, he reached for her breasts but she blocked his way.

Impatient, she tore off his shirt and zeroed in on the snap of his shorts. "I can't get it. I'm shaking . . . oh, God. . . . " She stopped as he cupped her through the nylon of her shorts. "There, right there."

"Oh, yeah. There."

"Ahh. . . . "

"Say my name. Say it. Like a lover's, like a man's." His words were slurred by the skin he was exploring, as if he were drunk. On her. "I've waited months to hear you say it like that."

"Luke, love. Luke . . . *Luke*. . . ."

His body jolted into hers. She took advantage of it and ground her hips to his, jammed her fingers inside the loose waistband of his shorts. He'd lost weight in a month. He startled as her hand came around front and she found him; he was full and erect and very adult in her palm. She massaged him, learned him. "Don't, Kel. I'll go off . . . I don't, Christ." In self-defense he dropped to his knees.

She felt the cold air against her bare skin as he slicked her shorts down past her hips.

"God*damn*, a thong." He shimmied her shorts off all the way and buried his face in her stomach. "Tell me you didn't wear these things to school."

"I did." She raked her hands through his hair, longer again. "I thought of you every time I put them on."

He traced the elastic of the thong, then slid a finger inside. "You're wet."

"Oh, God, yes." She let him touch her until she knew she was going to come. Then she dropped to her knees. Taking him by surprise, she pushed on his shoulders. He sprawled out on his back, laughed, and tumbled her down with him. She stretched out over his entire length. He cupped her fanny, hard.

Her head lowered, she tongued his chest, her nose wisping across the coarse hair there. "You smell so good." Her hands explored him, worked him, and her mouth went lower. As she kissed his abdomen, she tore open the snap on his shorts. Kneeling, she dragged them off, revealing skin-tight navy boxers that hit him mid-thigh. She buried her mouth in them.

"Oh, fu-u-ck. . . . Kel*sey*." He scissored off the floor when she grazed him with her teeth. "Don't! I won't. . . ."

She wouldn't stop, was mesmerized by the feel and scent of him, until strong arms yanked her up and flipped her to her back. His weight dwarfed her, sank into her. It felt like pure gold. After moments of agony and seconds of ecstasy, he said, "Here, baby, now."

"Oh, yes."

The pretty lacy bra came off first; the panties ripped in his haste. His underwear joined hers on the floor. He took a good look at her, then, and whispered, "Oh, Kel, you're . . ." he cleared his throat . . . "exquisite." Covering her, skin met skin from head to toe.

"Come inside me," she said throatily. "I want you inside me."

"Honey, I . . . shit!"

Her eyes flew open. "What?"

"Condoms. We need protection."

She moaned as if in pain.

"You got any? I don't."

She giggled then, her emotions on a roller coaster since his sisters walked into her classroom. "The French ticklers you bought that day at the drugstore. They're in my nightstand."

"Ah, good girl."

He rolled to his feet. Scooping her up like the courtliest of knights, he took the steps two at a time. He stumbled after a few steps because of her bold caresses. He stopped near the top of the staircase to kiss her deeply and tell her again how lovely she was. How it hurt just to look at her. They made it to her room, but barely.

In his haste to have her, he dumped her unceremoniously on the bed and wrenched open the nightstand drawer. It crashed to the floor. Almost blind with need, he rummaged around in the mess and found the box. She was reaching for him as he stood and tried to roll a condom on. He batted her hand away, suited up, and covered her with his body.

Their gazes locked. He smiled. So did she. He knelt between her spread thighs and drew her up so they were face-to-face. Her breasts crushed his chest and her legs wrapped around him. Then he plunged into her.

The pleasure of his filling made her eyes close. He felt so full, so male; he thrust again, whispered against her ear, "Kel," and thrust yet again.

Once more, and she exploded. The world turned silver and red; huge bursts of light obscured everything. She cried out his name as spurts of pleasure followed one on top of the other, became a steady stream. It encompassed her, took her under, and still the acute peaking did not stop. The only other things she was aware of were his long, low groans, then his bark—her name, an obscenity—and how he gripped her tightly as he came.

His possession was irrevocable.

Luke surfaced from sexual semiconsciousness brought on by an orgasm so intense it should go down in the *Guinness Book of Records*. He was buried deep inside Kelsey, his hands still vising her shoulders. They were prone now, and when he drew back, he couldn't take his eyes off her face. It was sweaty, and her hair was damp. Her eyes glowed like priceless jewels.

She smiled. He traced her mouth with his fingertips.

"Wow," she said.

He kissed her lightly. "Yeah, wow." His heart was bursting from his chest. "I need to tell you something."

She smiled again, and he imagined he'd still be moved by the sight of that smile when they were seventy.

"*Kocham Ciebie*," he whispered softly.

She remembered the words. Her eyes misted.

His eyes clouded.

"Oh, Luke." She swallowed back the emotion. "I love you, too."

Their foreheads met, neither able to move for the exquisite beauty of the moment. Luke knew he'd never in his life feel quite like this again.

After a while, he eased off her and cradled her to his chest. He was a man used to protecting women—everybody—but he'd yet to feel the surge of tenderness that swamped him now. "It's gonna be good, love."

"Yes, it is."

He smoothed his hand down her softer-than-silk hair, brushed knuckles over her cheek, grazed lips over her shoulder where the faint outline of reddish marks the size of his fingertips marred her skin. "Real good."

She cuddled close, entwining their legs, stroking his chest, inhaling him. "I'll teach somewhere else."

"You can stay at Fairholm until I finish my degree. I'll apply to the State University for courses. We can live somewhere in between."

She inched away and looked up at him. Her eyes filled again. "After so much, I can't believe we're together. That we'll be together forever."

"You can believe it, Kel," he said, settling back into the pillows, taking her with him. "That's a promise."

EPILOGUE

———

Two weeks later—Graduation Day

IRRITATED, Suzanna held the phone to her ear while she motioned Josh into her office. "Really, Ross, I can't possibly interview anyone today. I have graduation practice at one, and the ceremony tonight."

Dressed in baggy khaki shorts and a navy golf shirt, Josh rolled his eyes and sank into the chair in front of her desk. Did he just look older because he was graduating, or was he really a man? "And it's your birthday. . . ." he whispered.

Smiling, she winked at him. "Oh, all right. Just for an hour." She checked the clock. She could still have lunch with her son and make the practice if they ate somewhere close. "I'll be right over."

"No fair," Josh said as she hung up. "I wanted to spend time with you today."

She gave him a sideways glance, her heart stopping when she thought about this boy leaving her. "Gee, I guess you'll just have to hang out at Heather's for an hour. I'll meet you at Carney's at noon, okay?"

"You all right?" he asked, scrutinizing her. She knew the sleeplessness and the sadness showed on her face; others had commented on it. "Interviewing this candidate is going to remind you of Joe, isn't it?"

I don't need reminders. He's there every night—lounging against my pillows, in the bathtub, sitting on our couch. "A little, but I'm coping, honey."

"I miss him."

"I do, too."

"Are you glad the board approved a full-time crisis counselor?"

"Of course. He'll be able to help kids like Smurf."

Jimmy Smurfella had been sentenced to three years in a juvenile detention center, and was getting mandated counseling. Because no one had been hurt, the court would reevaluate his case after that.

"Everybody feels bad about him." Josh rolled his eyes. "But the kids miss Ludzecky more. Heather still talks about how cute he was."

Suzanna smiled. She'd been thrilled when Luke and Kelsey had come to her house two weeks ago and told her of their plans to be together. He'd quit the Secret Service and enrolled in a SUNY branch two hours away. Kelsey had put her house up for sale, and planned to move to an apartment halfway between the college and Fairholm; she'd work at the high school for the time it took Luke to get his degree. Then, they'd move far enough away where they wouldn't be known.

I'll still see you, Suzanna, I promise.

"Mom? You okay?"

"Of course. I—"

Her secretary appeared in the doorway carrying a huge spray of tiger lilies. "Happy Birthday, Suzanna."

Suzanna cocked her head and transferred her gaze questioningly to Josh. He held up his hands. "Don't look at me. The tickets to that musical were my present."

Maybe they were from Brenda. Suzanna talked to her friend weekly but hadn't seen her since she'd gone to rehab. From all appearances, Brenda was making progress and would be released soon.

She tried not to wish the flowers were from Joe. She'd heard nothing from him, though Luke saw him regularly and had told her he was at his sister's for a long break. He'd also spoken to Josh a few times on the phone. Slowly she eased the card out after Pat set the vase on her desk.

It read: Happy Birthday, Mrs. Q., and Happy Graduation. Sorry I can't be there in body, but I'm there in spirit. Love, Max.

Suzanna smiled at yet another success story. She and Max had gotten close in the last few months of school. She'd had that meeting with his father, who'd finally begun to understand his son's needs, but Max had decided on a career in the army, regardless. His SAT scores had been high, and though he'd never used his potential in school, with her recommendation, the army had taken him in an officer's training program. The drawback was that he had to leave before graduation.

She read the card to Pat and Josh, said good-bye to her son, made her way out of the office and down the hall, and exited the building. Spring in Fairholm was a riot of smells and sights: the rich loam of the earth, newly cut grass, and crocuses and daffodils sprouting everywhere. She tried to appreciate the flowers and the comforting sound of a lawn mower in the distance as she headed toward the Administration Building.

This was how she'd met Joe—whom she missed with every fiber of her being. At least the board had agreed to the safety measures he'd outlined, as well as a few of her own, one of which was filling the crisis counselor position permanently. Over the summer she planned to have in place groups and sessions for kids like Max, Rush Webster, Ben, and Smurf, as well as all the teacher in-service. She just wished Joe was here to implement it all with her.

She entered the Ad Building with a heavy heart. The receptionist told her to go to Ross's office and wait. The superintendent was across the hall with another administrator. Taking a deep breath, she opened the door.

The first thing she saw was a vase of pink roses on Ross's desk—odd for the superintendent. Then the air caught in her throat, and for a minute she thought she was imagining things. Joe stood behind the flowers, big and unbreakable, wearing a lightweight navy sport coat and khaki slacks.

Joe was dumbstruck by the sight of her; the first thing he noticed was how fragile she looked, the brown and gold of her dress accenting the color of her eyes, her hair drawn back in a clasp, gold hoops gracing her ears. He remembered his plan, though. It had something to do with starting over and keeping it light.

"I'm Dr. Joe Stonehouse. You must be Mrs. Quinn, the principal."

"What . . . why . . . what are you doing here?" she asked, her voice thick.

He managed to look surprised as he crossed to her. She'd suffered the last weeks—six, to be exact, and three days and a few hours. He could tell by the lines around her mouth and the shadows under her eyes.

"I'm applying for the crisis counselor's job at your school," he told her. At the stunned look on her face, he said, "Why don't you sit down, Mrs. Quinn?"

Never taking her eyes off him, she found a chair.

He sat across from her and lifted a folder. "All my credentials are in here. I thought you might have some questions for me."

"A thousand," she said.

"Well, let me tell you about my last position. I was a member of the United States Secret Service, where I worked in the school security division. My job was classified, so I can't tell you what I did."

"*Was* a member? What you *did*?"

"Yes, I resigned from the Service, to take effect July one." She gasped. "You did?"

"I decided I wanted to work directly with kids. I got more satisfaction from that than orchestrating plans for the government."

"Oh, Joe."

"But I have some special requirements if I'm to take a job at Fairholm."

She smiled, finally catching on.

"I'm a very desirable commodity, Mrs. Quinn. You should be trying to entice me to come to Fairholm."

Amber eyes narrowed on him then. "Oh, I'll entice you—"

"First, you need to hear my requirements."

Suzanna nodded.

"I'd like to reside at 33 Jordace Avenue." Her house. "You'll have to make the arrangements."

"I think that can be done."

"Let me make myself clear." He rose, then squatted down in front of her. And for the first time in forever he touched her; he picked up her hand. "Legally, I want to reside there."

"Legally?"

"Hmmm." He drew from his pocket a sapphire and diamond ring that outshone the stars. He slipped it on her finger, then kissed it. "Marry me, love."

Tears slid down her cheeks. "I . . . I don't understand."

He told her the stark, simple truth. "I couldn't live without you."

"Oh, Joe." She clutched at his hands, linked his fingers with hers. "I never expected this. How could you give up. . . ." She peered at him through spiky lashes. "The Secret Service was your life."

"For too long," he told her. "As Ruthie reminded me every day I was in Connecticut."

Suzanna gave him a watery smile, raised her hand to his face, outlined his cheekbones, his jaw, as if learning his features again. The tender caress touched his soul, as she had.

"I did a good job with STAT. With the whole Safe School thing. It's in place, and someone else can run it, go undercover."

He frowned. "Even though young Ludzecky beat me to the punch."

"The government must be unhappy about losing both of you."

"Not nearly as unhappy as I've been."

"Me, too," she said, still touching his face.

"I want a normal life, with you, with Josh, with my family."

She frowned. "What will we tell Josh?"

"For now, just that I changed my mind about the Education Department job because I wanted to marry you and be a counselor in your building. Maybe later on we can tell him more. Just like with Kelsey's father. I haven't gotten that far in my plan."

Laying her head on his shoulder, she whispered, "How far did you get?"

"Just here. Just back to you." He stood, drawing her up with him. Then he pulled her close and encircled her with his arms. "Happy birthday, Suzie Q," he said softly.

And before she could cry again, his mouth closed over hers.

If you enjoyed *Promises to Keep*, you won't want to miss Kathryn Shay's exciting new romance. . . .

TRUST IN ME

Here is a special excerpt from
the forthcoming novel from
The Berkley Publishing Group. . . .

"OH my God, look at that blouse."

"I haven't seen leather like that since Doc took me to my first . . . Never mind!"

"What the *hell* does she have on under that suede shirt?"

Like twelve-year-old boys discovering girls, Joe, Tucker, and Linc stared at the door where Annie, Beth, and Margo had just appeared; the girls hadn't noticed them and pranced by.

Linc started to stand but Joe restrained him. "Not a good move," Joe said. "They look like they're out for blood."

"They look like they're out to get laid."

Tucker moaned and turned aside, shifting his position.

Joe rubbed his eyes with this thumb and forefinger and moaned, too.

Feeling his own body harden at the sight of Margo dressed like . . . like the star of *Debbie Does Dallas*, Linc recognized the reaction of the other two males at his table. And since camaraderie had been established early on as they'd shared ribs, cornbread, and a few beers, Linc just smiled. "We're pathetic."

Joe grunted. He angled his head toward Tucker. "Hey, it's your sister he's ogling."

Tucker reddened.

"Yeah, well, she deserves to be ogled in that outfit." Linc stared at Tucker. "But I can't believe I missed the signs."

Still speechless, Tucker scrubbed a hand over his face. The Menace was a private man. Finally he was able to look Linc in the eye. "It's complicated."

"It's always complicated." Joe continued to stare at Annie.

Tucker checked him out. "Still got the hots for your ex, Murphy?"

"Not until about five minutes ago." He shrugged. "Or at least I wouldn't let myself admit it."

"Join the club." Tucker watched Linc. "What's with you and Margo?"

"Irreconcilable differences."

The women finally took a booth. It was then that they noticed the guys. Margo's brows arched in arrogant acknowledgment as she shimmied into the seat. Linc swallowed hard.

Beth's head snapped up, catching Tucker devouring her outfit. She gave him a soft smile full of promise.

Annie peeked around Beth and scowled.

"Maybe if we turn our backs, it won't be so bad." This from Tucker.

"Maybe." Joe said.

The three men continued to stare.

A half hour after they arrived, and after they'd blisteringly cursed the occupants of a certain table on the far side of the bar, a hulk of a guy asked Margo to dance. She got up with as much sass as she could muster. "All right, big guy."

On the floor they did a mean two-step. Hulk's gaze lingered on her shirt and she rolled her eyes. Damn, this wasn't turning out as she'd planned. She'd just wanted a fun night out with the girls. She never expected to see the good Reverend here, looking sexy as hell in plain jeans and a red shirt. When the song ended and the bruiser tugged her toward him for a dance to *Midnight Train to Georgia*, Margo drew back. "Ah, I. . . ."

She felt a hand on her shoulder. "Sorry, this dance is mine."

Hulk puffed out his pecs. "Yeah, who says?"

"I do."

"Who're you?"

"Her friend."

"Oh." He scanned Margo's top and skirt. "You let your friend come out lookin' like this? What are you, nuts?"

"Yeah, I'm nuts." He tugged Margo to him. They were equal height when she wore four-inch boots.

Margo didn't even think about resisting. It felt so good to be close to him, smell him, feel his hands on her. As the song began, she melted into him. His hand clenched hers, and his arm banded around her waist.

She remembered seeing him with Jane at the diner, then at the movies, then in the PK's car. She nestled in closer, and inhaled him. Two slow songs later, she whispered, "I'm sorry."

"Me, too."

"I should have told you I was coming home."

"Why didn't you?"

"Just because of this." Her body had been aligned too close to his for her not to notice. She bumped his middle with hers.

He laughed, low and sexy. "I'm in pain, baby."

"So am I." She grinned against his chest. "We could always go out and screw in the backseat of your car, like we used to."

Lifting his hand to her hair, he caressed it tenderly. "If only it were that easy."

She sighed. "It hurts, Linc. To be with you."

"It hurts me, too." He said, "Why'd you come home?"

"To be with Beth and Annie. To help out at the diner, and with Annie's kids." She found his ear, and admitted, "To see you."

"You were going to Cancún."

"It lost its appeal."

He drew lazy circles on her back. "What are we gonna do, honey?"

"Nothing. Let's just not fight."

"I've been miserable."

"Me, too. And jealous."

"I'm not sure we can keep going on like this."

"We've done it for years." She hated the pleading tone in her voice.

"It's getting too hard."

She rubbed against him.

"I'm serious."

"I know."

"I love you, Mary Margaret."

She drew back, looked into his face. "I love you, too, Rev."

BETH detoured to the jukebox when Tucker rose and headed to the men's room. He'd gotten up as she did, so she went to play some music instead of going to the ladies' room. In a few minutes, she felt him come up behind her.

"Hi," he said as he pressed *Black Magic Woman*.

Slowly lifting her eyes from the song listings, she smiled. "Hi."

She wanted to jump his bones. He looked so good in tight jeans and a long-sleeved green shirt with a racing logo on it.

The song began to play. He raked her outfit with a hundred-watt gaze. "Appropriate tune," he said.

She blushed.

Shaking his head, he took her hand. "It's beyond me how any woman can blush wearin' something like that." Without her consent he drew her to the dance floor. For a minute she stood a little away from him, but then stepped right into his arms.

It was just like in the dream. His touch was electric. The feel of his arms around her made her nerve endings tingle. Beth sank into him; her skin heated at his nearness. He smelled of the same cologne as at the diner—woodsy and very male.

She felt him smile against her hair. "Do you have any idea how good you feel?"

Inching closer, she shut her eyes. "As good as you do?"

He chuckled.

They swayed to the music. His hand came up and caressed a strand of her hair. He drew back. "What'd you do to it?"

"It's Margo's handiwork." She shrugged. "So's the outfit."

He let his hand wander lower. Caress the leather. Flirt with her hips. "It'll haunt my dreams, Mary Elizabeth, but I'm damned grateful to your friend." His green eyes sparkled with appreciation. His body hummed with arousal.

So did hers. "I thought you liked your women natural."

"I like *you*," he said honestly. "Much more than I should."

A lump formed in her throat. "Oh, Tucker, I . . . Ronny will. . . ."

He abandoned her hand and placed his fingers on her mouth. "Hush, I know."

She stared up at him.

"Don't say anything more. Especially about your son. For tonight, just let me hold you." He kissed her hair and brought her face back to his chest.

She burrowed into him. Shutting out the world, she let him hold her.

It wasn't because she was suddenly alone at her table that Annie stood and made her way to Joe's table. Several men had asked her to dance. It wasn't that Joe sat alone, sipping a coke, angling his body to the wall so he didn't look at her. It was because all week she'd been making some decisions. When she reached him, she said simply, "Joe?"

He whirled around. And the look of surprise on his face, combined with the pleasure there, gave her courage.

"Can I sit down?"

"Sure." He cleared his throat. "You want something to drink?"

"No, thanks. I've had my limit."

His eyes smiled. "About two glasses."

He'd always coaxed her not to drink much because she got sick if she had more than a couple of glasses of wine. In some ways, he'd taken good care of her. She tried to summon those memories.

"I wanted to talk to you." She scanned the bar. "I guess this isn't the best place." She tugged self-consciously on the front of her shirt.

He grinned. "Not your usual style."

She rolled her eyes. "It's Margo's. I'm bigger than she is and. . . ."

He gave her a wry grin. "Yes, I remember. You still look good, Mary Ann."

For a moment she startled. But she'd worn the damn shirt of her own free will. She couldn't condemn him for noticing. "I've been thinking, Joe."

His gray eyes lit up, matching the silvery sweater he wore. "About?"

She bit her lip. "I think you're right about Matt. I've decided you can coach his team. Be alone with him."

Swallowing hard, he closed his eyes. "Thank you."

Her heart turned over in her chest at his honest reaction. "Let's see how it goes for a while. Then maybe you can start coming over to the house to see the kids alone, too." She glanced out at the dance floor where Margo and Linc were locked in a deep embrace. No surprises there. But seeing Tucker and Beth wrapped up in each other was a shock. Beth was in for some explaining tonight. "Linc already has too much to do. He shouldn't have to take care of us."

Joe said, "I won't hurt them, Annie. I give you my word."

"I want to believe that."

"I won't hurt you, either."

She angled her chin. "No, you won't, Joe. I'm not the girl you left here six years ago. I wouldn't allow it, even if you wanted to."

"I'd cut off my right hand before I touched you in anger again." His voice was heated, passionate.

She noticed the phrasing. He didn't say *before I touched you again.*

Are you attracted to him, Annie? her therapist had asked.

Against her will, she studied his face. He had such sculpted features, perfect really; and his hair only made him handsomer, especially with his gray eyes. No wonder they'd chosen him for modeling. To lighten the atmosphere, she said, "You'd lose your second job if you cut off your . . . arm, *Joey, baby.*"

He actually blushed. "Please, don't remind me."

"I'm sorry for what I said about the modeling a few weeks ago. I've given it some thought. I want you to have changed. And if you have, you must've gone through hell to get where you are."

He started to say something; she held up her palm. "I'm not there yet. But I'll give you the space to prove it. For the kids' sake."

"I will, Annie. I promise."

Suddenly she felt drawn into the silver heat of his eyes, which shone like liquid mercury. And it scared her, because that feeling had once made her do whatever he asked, made her allow unspeakable things. She stood abruptly. "We can discuss this more tomorrow." Nodding, she started across the dance floor. As she passed by Linc and Margo holding each other, and Tucker and Beth cuddling like kids hiding out from the world, she felt a wave of loneliness and regret so great she was physically shaken by it.

She refused to wonder if Joe was feeling the same thing.

NEITHER Linc, Tucker, or Joe nor Annie, Margo, or Beth saw the two boys behind the pillar at the bar.

"Fuckin' A," the one with the spiked blond hair said. "That fox in the black leather is Ronny boy's mother."

The ponytailed guy with him chugged the last of his beer and focused hazy eyes on the dance floor. "The one draped all over the racing dude?"

Maze began to laugh. It was an evil sound. "The racing dude who killed his father, Loose, my man."

"Holy shit. I wonder if Ronny knows."

Maze laughed, looking like he was about to pull the wings off a fly. "He will, buddy. He will. As soon as he gets back from the pen." Maze shrugged into his jacket. "Man I wish I could be around for the fireworks."

"I dunno, Maze. Ron's in a shitload a trouble already."

"Hey, I'm just bein' a good buddy. Wouldn't you wanna know if your old lady was screwin' your worst enemy?"

Loose smiled. "You're such a good Samaritan, Maze. Sometimes you just make me wanna cry."